Exalted

A Last Heir of Re'Vall Novel

KAREN THROWER

This is a work of fiction. Names, characters, places, and incidents are products of the author's imagination or are used fictitiously and are not to be construed as real. Any resemblance to actual events, locations, organizations, or persons, living or dead, is entirely coincidental.

World Castle Publishing, LLC
Pensacola, Florida
Copyright © 2025 Karen Thrower
Hardback ISBN: 9798281762113
Paperback ISBN: 9798891263932
eBook ISBN: 9798891263949
First Edition World Castle Publishing, LLC, May 13, 2025
http://www.worldcastlepublishing.com
Licensing Notes
Cover: Cover Designs by Karen
Editor: Karen Fuller

CHAPTER 1
MEETING OF A LIFETIME

Foster Voltain approached Salthole and could smell the ocean in the air. The scent of salt and fish was soothing, and he could feel the hurt of the last few weeks ebbing away. Many of Otto's worshippers found the sea comforting. It was His domain, after all. Foster figured Salthole was as good a place as any to find a group. He could shoot a bow with great accuracy and fight with a sword. That should be enough for anyone looking to add to their numbers. Just outside of town, Foster picked an apple and decided to eat it before looking for work.

It was still early in the port town. The only people in the streets were the bakers and servants for the town's Lords, gathering things for breakfast. He found some benches outside of a shop and decided to sit down and enjoy his breakfast. The apple smelled so sweet his mouth was watering at the thought of eating it. He cut it into several slices, the juice dripped down his hands and he licked it off. But as he was about to take that first delicious bite, something hit him hard from behind. Whatever it was tumbled over him and the bench, knocking him to the ground.

He landed with a grunt, and Foster could only watch as the apple slices leapt from his hands and fell, meat first into the dirt. He pushed his hair out of his eyes and looked up. What hit him was a woman. She had long dark hair and colorful robes, which told Foster she was a mage. And she was clearly irritated at the shop owner behind them as she started yelling fast and angry in a language he didn't know. He turned and saw the owner was yelling at her through the window, and with one last rude gesture, the woman huffed and started dusting off her robes.

Foster stayed on the ground and crossed his arms. "Ahem!"

The woman stopped and looked over at him, her eyes filled with disdain. "What?" Her accent was so exotic. Common was clearly not her first language.

"You made me drop my apple." He was surprised at how calm he sounded.

She scoffed, "Oh, piss on your apples!" Her words were like acid, and she walked off, mumbling angrily to herself.

Foster looked at his dirty breakfast and sighed. "Great." He stood and mourned that sweet, juicy apple as he walked around town. A person was most likely able to find work as a sell sword from a public board. Thankfully, he found one by the Temple of Otto and saw exactly what he was looking for.

Men/women wanted to join adventuring group
Must know how to use a sword. Interested parties
see Lucius Silverblade at the Deadly Dwarf Tavern.

The 'Dwarf' was easy to find, and Foster confidently walked in. There were a few people sitting at the tables, mostly trying to get rid of the previous night's festivities. As his eyes wandered around the tavern, he noticed a half-elf sitting by the wall. He was dressed fine in a long dark duster, a fancy black hat with a colorful feather in it, and shiny boots that were up on the table. He was dressed much too ostentatiously to be from Salthole, so Foster decided to take the chance and walked up to him.

"Excuse me, are you Lucius Silverblade?" The man tipped his hat up with his finger and gave Foster a once over. He had a goatee, and his skin looked sun-kissed. Foster could see a rapier at the man's side.

"Indeed, I am. What can I do for you?" He motioned for Foster to join him, so he pulled out a chair and sat down.

"I saw the ad on the Temple's board. I'd like to offer my services."

Lucious nodded. "How old are you, twenty-three, twenty-four?" People often thought he was older than he was due to his height, but he figured the truth would be best here.

"Eighteen, sir."

Lucius' eyes widened. "Eighteen? You certainly had me fooled. I don't usually take on people under twenty. Can you fight?"

Foster put his arms on the table and laced his fingers together. "Yes, sir. I trained with the knights of Raventree."

"It's Lucius," he said with a wave of his hand. "Raventree, eh? What's your name?" Lucius crossed his hands over his stomach and settled in.

"Foster Voltain." He could feel the man's eyes roaming over him again, clearly looking for something holy on him. Foster had expected that, being who his mother was, the famous Mother Lily Voltain, Priestess of Otto and one of His most loved clerics. He had the usual seashell around his neck, but it was tucked under his shirt for now.

"Voltain?" His left eyebrow lifted, and a small smile curled on his lips.

"Yes."

"You related to Mother Lily?" Lucius rubbed his chin.

"She's my mother."

"Hmm," Lucius sucked through his teeth, "well, once again, I ignore my own rules. I bet we could use you. Welcome aboard."

He held out his hand, and Foster shook it heartily. "Thank you, sir, you won't regret it."

"Lucius. I'm sure I won't." He waved at the barmaid, who promptly set an ale in front of Foster.

"Thanks. Could I get something to eat? Doesn't matter what you have." The barmaid nodded and walked away. "So, how many of you are in the group?" Foster asked as he sipped his ale. He had to be careful with an empty stomach. The last thing he wanted to do was get drunk in the morning in front of his new boss.

"Seven with you," Lucius said. "We're a large group, but

I feel our mage and paladin will be leaving us soon. That's why I put the word out."

Smart of him, Foster thought. "Why are they leaving?"

Lucius took a big swig of ale and put his feet down. "They're in love and want to settle down."

Foster rolled his eyes. "Oh," he said and chugged his ale. "Good for them." The 'good' was a hearty burp that made Lucius laugh. The barmaid set down a plate of bread and cheese, and Foster dug in.

"Yeah, good for them. We leave tomorrow morning on the 'Blue Wind,' so you made it just in time. Feel free to stick around the tavern or wander the town. We all have dinner together. It's one of the few rules I have that I don't break. So, join us, and I'll introduce you to everyone."

Foster nodded. "Sounds great."

After he finished his little meal, Foster spent the rest of the day wandering around Salthole. He figured it would be a while before he could do what he pleased, so he took full advantage of his 'freedom.' He found 'The Blue Wind' at the docks. It looked like a seaworthy ship, so he decided to stock up on things he thought he might need on the sea. A few rations, a hat, and a new coat. He left home so fast that he didn't really pack everything he should have. One of many mistakes he made that day. But it seemed his mother snuck him a bag of fifty gold when she visited him the night he left. He'd have to thank her for that when he got home.

That night, he met up with Lucius for dinner so he could meet the rest of the group. The serving girl seemed to know them as she walked by and put seven plates of dinner on the table without being asked. It wasn't bad for tavern food, roasted chicken, mashed potatoes, and rolls. The chicken was a little dry, but the flavor was lemony and herby. One by one, the group came down, and the half-elf introduced them. The first to come down was a muscular man in his mid-twenties. He had shaggy, dirty blonde hair, brown eyes, and the symbol of Otto around his neck.

"Foster, this is Bereck Carvel, our paladin. Bereck, Foster

Voltain. He'll probably take your place when you leave."

Foster held out his hand, and Bereck shook it. "Nice to meet you, Bereck."

A little smile started spreading across the man's face. "Voltain? Not—"

"Lily's my mother." Foster didn't bother waiting for him to finish the sentence. He knew he was about to ask.

"How fortuitous. Pleasure." He gave Foster a big, friendly smile before tucking into his dinner.

"So, you're the one that's leaving with the mage?" Foster picked at his potatoes.

Bereck nodded. "Yes, when we're not sure, but eventually."

"Speaking of our mage," Lucius cleared his throat and straightened in his seat. "Is Sunette coming down?"

Bereck licked his lips and shook his head. "She's already on the boat," he said rather sheepishly. "She said, 'I can't wait to get out of this provincial town.'"

Lucius scoffed, "Sounds like a fight not worth picking. Guess you'll meet her tomorrow." A small, skinny man walked up and sat next to Bereck. He didn't look much older than Foster, and his red hair was a coordinated mess like he wanted it that way.

"Sunette still mad?" He was clearly amused by the situation from his mischievously sparkling gray eyes.

"You know her," Bereck said, taking a bite of bread.

The red-haired man laughed and looked up at Foster. "New recruit?"

"Yes, I'm Foster."

"Mason Fray, nice to meet you." Mason picked up a fork and began to gobble down his dinner. It reminded Foster of when his little sister Saphira was a baby and used to try to shove the food in her face instead of her mouth.

Lucius must have seen the look on Foster's face. "Mason's eating is something to get used to." The half-elf shook his head, clearly embarrassed at the display.

"I was raised in a barn," Mason said, his mouth completely

full of food. Foster laughed and turned back to his dinner. Nothing worse than cold mashed potatoes. A few minutes later, a priestess joined them, dressed in the blue robes of Alar. She was tall, and her long, dark red hair and gray eyes were lovely together. She sat and prayed over her food before she noticed Foster.

"New guy?" She put a napkin on her nap as she studied him.

"Yes, Lessa, meet Foster. Lessa is our priestess," Lucius said with a smile.

"I see that. Pleasure." She nodded her head in his direction and started eating. Something made Foster think she didn't smile much, which was a shame. She was lovely, and he thought her smile would light up a room.

"Don't mind, Lessa," Mason said, his mouth still full of food. "She's a sourpuss by nature."

Foster watched as Lessa calmly filled her spoon with potatoes. "You need to put more food in your mouth, Mason. You're speaking." And flung the potatoes at his face. They hit with a satisfying splat, and Bereck and Lucius laughed loudly as another joined the table.

"What's so funny?" The newcomer asked. He was a big, half-orc, the orc more prominent than the human side, with his green skin and dark hair that was tied behind his head. It looked like he also trimmed his tusks, so they didn't stick out much.

"Lessa was just teaching Mason some manners," Bereck said as he composed himself and wiped his eyes. "They're siblings if you didn't catch that," he said, leaning towards Foster.

He chuckled, "I think I see it now, yes."

"Twig, meet Foster, a new recruit." Lucius introduced the two.

"Twig?" Foster was surprised at the name. It didn't seem to fit him.

"Yep, smallest in my family." He smiled an orcish smile and started eating.

"So Foster," Lucius sipped his wine. "Tell us about

Raventree. I've never been, but I hear it's a wonderful place."

Foster nodded and put some potatoes on top of his roll. "It's peaceful for sure," he took a bite, and the buttery potatoes went perfectly with the sweet bread. "Lord Raventree never cuts corners when it comes to our safety. It's always growing, though."

"I always thought Raventree was too far for the Empire to really bother. Except that one battle, of course," Bereck said. "But I imagine with the orc god taking sanctuary there, it's needed." Sobrei Re'vall, a literal god to the orcs and heir to their throne, had been kidnapped many years ago. Foster's mother and Lord Raventree had freed him, and ever since, they had tried to put him back on his throne to no avail. After the failed battle, Sobrei decided to make Raventree his home. That was almost twenty years ago. That decision helped keep it safe, but every so often, someone would come and try to disrupt the peace. Their attempts had yet to be successful.

"True," Foster agreed. "And I think he wants to protect my mother to an extent. She and Raventree are old friends. They all made enemies wherever they went, especially my mother."

"Lucky her to have the backing of a Lord." Lessa sat back, crossing her arms. "Do you have any siblings?"

"I do, younger brother and sister." He did his best not to sound sad while speaking about them. He still felt horrible about what he had done to his brother. "Christopher wants to be a priest like our mother, and Saphira, well, she likes to hide and scare the shit out of me when I least expect it," he said with a chuckle.

"How old is she? Ow!" Mason leaned down and rubbed his leg.

"Clearly too young for you, little letch," Lessa chastised him.

"I was just asking Lessa, damn," he said while the rest of the table chuckled.

"Well, she is right. She's only fourteen, so too young for you, *ever*," he teased and cleared his throat. "What about you and your lady Bereck? How long have you been together?" Honestly, it was the last thing he wanted to talk about, love. Love made him sad, angry, and sorry for leaving home like he did. But he had to put on a brave face and get to know these strangers.

Bereck smiled as he spoke of her. "We've known each other for a few years, but we've been together for a year now. I asked her to marry me last month."

Twig shook his head. "I still don't get you two. She's so wild, and you're so...not." The group laughed.

"She helps me love life, Twig, not just the gods, and I will protect her the rest of my life." Music floated through the air, and Foster watched as Twig turned excitedly towards the stage. A human woman with short brown hair was taking the stage. People were clapping and cheering as she bowed and started singing. Her voice was incredible, soulful, and husky. Foster had never heard an equal. The rest of the music seemed to come from a spell as an incorporeal violin appeared next to her. He'd never seen a bard perform like that and wondered why she wasn't playing big cathedrals with her talent. He noticed glinting light coming from her ears and saw they were both pierced several times and had little jewels and dangling stars in them.

"Lucius, can I please ask her to join us?" Twig asked, not looking at the half-elf. "We could use a bard."

"A bard or a lover?" Lucius teased, and everyone chuckled.

"Hey, that's up to her," Twig smiled. "I don't know why you're so opposed to her joining us."

Lucius shrugged. "I'm not opposed. I just think she'd be a distraction, is all."

"Why?" Foster tore his eyes away from the woman and looked at Twig. He looked completely enamored. "Oh."

Twig stared at the bard as he spoke. "I am capable of doing my job with pretty women around me," Twig pointed at Mason. "Lessa and Sunette are just as pretty." Mason laughed and pretended to toss his short hair over his shoulders.

"Well, thank you, Twig," he said in a high voice. Twig grabbed his head and gave him a push, keeping his eyes on the singing woman.

Foster turned back to the bard. "What's her name?"

"Raven Bladespell." Twig practically sighed the name.

Foster could hear how entranced Twig was by the woman. "There's a stage name if I ever heard one," he teased.

"It's a good one," Lessa nodded. "She's nice, I've had a few conversations with her. She'd mesh well with us." Foster turned and watched Lucius. He was tapping his fingers on the table, his eyes staring at his dinner.

"Fine." Foster heard a quiet 'yes' from Twig at that. "But if she says no, we leave her alone."

"Deal." Foster enjoyed the music until she stepped down from the stage to take a break. She walked up to the bar, and the bartender gave her a drink, which she sipped while counting the coins people threw on the stage for her.

"Wish me luck." Twig took a big drink and walked over to her.

"Bet she says no." Mason laid a gold on the table, a smile on his face.

"I'll take that bet." Bereck laid a gold on the table, and they both turned to watch. Foster didn't think the bard minded the interruption to her break like some would. She was smiling and laid her hand on Twig's arm.

A few minutes later, he led her over to the table. The smile on his face was huge. "Everyone, this is Raven, Raven this is Lucius, our leader, Bereck, Lessa, Mason, and another newcomer, Foster. Raven would like to come with us."

"Ha!" Bereck slammed his hands over the two gold, "told you."

"That's a bet I'm happy to lose," Mason said, smiling up at her. "Welcome."

"Thank you. Honestly, I've been itching to travel for a while, I appreciate the ask." Foster had only heard one other person with that accent in his life, which meant Raven was from Dal En Val. Stolen seat of the Orc Empire and a haven for cultists who worshiped the most evil god there had ever been, The Shackled One. In the last twenty years or so, his followers had flooded the orc city since the human on the throne worshipped him. Foster knew if Sobrei were on his throne, it wouldn't be like that, but the cultists had their claws dug deep into that land. Foster hoped Raven had left for obvious reasons. He never thought of himself as the type of person who would instantly judge a book, but he didn't want to trust her just yet.

"Did Twig tell you we're leaving tomorrow?" Lucius asked.

"He did, I don't have much, so I'll be ready. Honestly, I'm surprised you didn't ask me sooner." She turned to Twig, a hand on her hip.

Twig looked over at Lucius. "See, I told you."

"Yes, you told me I'm a horrible leader," he put his hand over his heart. "Welcome Raven. Guess that makes eight now. Don't think I've ever had such a large group before." He looked at Bereck, who shook his head. Foster assumed the two men had been traveling together for a while.

Raven smiled up at Twig. "I have one more set, so I will see you in the morning." She gave Twig's arm a little squeeze and made her way back up to the stage.

"This is going to be a great thing, Lucius, you'll see." Twig gave him a wink and sat back at the table.

"I hope so." Lucius finished his wine. "I think I'll head up. Foster, do you have a room?"

"No, I can get one."

Mason waved his hand. "Don't bother. You can bunk with me."

"Oh, thanks, appreciate it." Lessa was the next to leave the table, followed by Bereck and Mason. Twig and Foster stayed down and listened to the end of Raven's set. She was incredibly talented, and he could see why Twig seemed to fancy her.

———

Mason snored like a bear. It was impressive from such a little guy, but Foster did manage to get some sleep. Early that morning, everyone who stayed at the inn walked to the 'Blue Wind.' Mason was talking excitedly to Foster while Twig and

Raven brought up the rear, Twig talking her ear off as well. When they reached the ship, the captain, a woman named 'Slick Stella,' welcomed them. She looked to be in her mid-thirties with long dark hair and dark eyes. Foster thought she was tall for a woman. When he shook her hand, her nose was even with his chin. He was over six feet himself, but his father always teased him that he had more growing to do.

"Hello all, welcome back to the 'Blue Wind.'" Stella waved her arms in a grand gesture of welcome, and Foster watched as Lucius quickly settled into them and spun her around.

"Thank you, Captain. It is most appreciated," he said before he surprised her with a deep kiss. Stella was a good five or so inches taller than Lucius, but neither seemed to care.

Foster leaned over to Mason and whispered, "He do that a lot?"

Masons snickered. "Lucius and Stella have known each other for years, but yeah, he does. 'Luscious Lucius,' some call him," Mason said as he walked past Foster down the stairs into the depths of the ship. Everyone followed the little rogue down below except Foster, who walked to the other side of the boat and stared out at the ocean. The sea looked calm, and the sky was full of happy, fluffy clouds. The perfect sailing weather.

"Ever been on a ship before?" He looked down at the voice and saw a little girl with a smudge of dirt on her cheek. She looked to be a few years younger than Saphira, and her eyes were slightly elven in appearance. Her brown hair was tied back in a messy ponytail, and her clothes seemed a bit too big for her.

He smiled. "I have. It's been a while, though."

"What's your name?"

"Foster, what's yours?" He held out his hand, and she shook it.

"Te'a, but everybody calls me Shadow, 'cept my mom and Lucius," she started rocking back and forth on her feet.

"Where is your mom?" Te'a turned and pointed at Stella, who was laughing a seemingly private kind of laugh as Lucius continued to nuzzle her neck. "Captain for a mom, huh? Must be exciting."

"Oh yeah! I travel all over." Her eyes got wide with excitement, "I can already speak three languages besides common, I mean."

Foster chuckled and put his pack on. "Well, that's one more than me. It was nice to meet you, Te'a."

"Nice to meet you, too." She ran off to the other side of the boat. Foster walked down the stairs and saw the paladin walking down the long hallway that lay before him.

"Bereck!"

He turned and motioned for him to follow. "This way, young man." Bereck waited until Foster caught up to him, then showed him where the group was sleeping. The room had enough hammocks for everyone, and a few were already taken. Foster looked around but didn't see anyone he didn't already know.

"Is your mage around?" He could admit to being curious about meeting Bereck's betrothed.

"Yes, she went up to tell Stella the weather for the next week." Bereck pointed up towards the deck.

Foster also noticed that Lucius wasn't there. "Let me guess, Lucius is staying with the captain."

Mason laughed, "Catches on quick." Foster shuffled to the back of the room and claimed a hammock by putting his bag in it. There was a jolt that made them sway a little, and Foster assumed the ship was underway.

"All right, gather around. Lucius gave me some impromptu instructions," Bereck said. Everyone took a seat around the Paladin and listened. "So, first stop is Fairwinds," he started before a woman walked in behind him and spoke.

"Okay, we're underway now." Foster looked up at the familiar voice and saw the woman who made him drop his apple standing next to Bereck with a big smile on her face.

"You!" He sat back and crossed his arms over his chest.

She looked over and smirked. "Apple Picker, what are you doing here?" She didn't look pleased to see him.

"You're Sunette?" He couldn't believe it was the same

woman and could suddenly understand how Twig didn't understand the couple.

"Yes. Do you have a problem?" Foster looked around at the group, Bereck looked confused, and Mason had his hands over his mouth, no doubt holding in massive giggles.

"No, no problem. I just won't eat apples around you."

"So, you've met?" Bereck looked up at the mage.

"Not formally," Sunette said as she sat next to her paladin.

"Well, this is Foster Voltain, Foster, I guess you already know Sunette, our mage." She gave him a quick smile filled with sarcasm. Bereck pointed over at Raven, who was biting her lower lip, looking extremely amused at their exchange. "This is Raven, she's joined up as well."

Sunette smiled warmly and took the woman's hand. "I've heard you at the tavern. You're talented. We need more women around here, welcome. You were saying, darling?" She said in that exotic accent.

"Yes, Fairwinds then east. He hinted at maybe dealing with dwarfs at some point." Foster watched as Sunette laid her head on Bereck's shoulder, and he kissed her head. Twig was right. *What an odd couple,* he thought.

CHAPTER 2
ACCIDENTS AND TEMPLES

The trip was smooth, the group hardly saw Lucius or Stella, but her crew was dependable, and little Te'a seemed to know what to do. Meals were fine, and Foster continued to learn about his new friends. Except Lessa and Sunette, the priestess was so seasick she could barely walk and spent most of her time by the rail at the back of the boat, just in case. And Sunette ignored him every chance she had by hiding behind her spell books.

On the third day, Foster walked up to Lessa. She was hanging her head over the railing, and her face was almost as green as Twig's. Foster wished he could help her. She must have been miserable.

"I can't believe there's no spell for sea sickness." He leaned on the rail next to her.

"I think Otto's priests know one? Bereck, unfortunately, is *not* a priest." She groaned, and he laid a hand on her back, rubbing in circles.

"Would you like me to get you some water? You must be dehydrated by now."

She took in a big, slow breath and nodded. "As much as I don't relish it coming back up immediately, I do need a drink. Thank you."

"I'll be right back." He rushed down to the galley and found Twig and Raven in an animated conversation and smiled at them. Clearly, he was wrong in his first assessment of her, and it was a good idea that she came along. She seemed like a great person, always happy and willing to help. Foster got some water and remembered he had some Nixyl in his bag. It was a last-minute purchase in Salthole. It could help calm a stomach, so he walked down the hall to their room. Foster turned the corner and froze as he saw Bereck and Sunette kissing passionately on the paladin's hammock. They didn't seem to notice him, and he really wanted to get to his bag. So, he tip-toed as softly as he could to the other end of the room. But halfway, he took a wrong step, and the wood creaked loudly under his feet.

He heard Sunette gasp. "What are you doing?" He could hear how mad she was at the interruption and probably thought he was spying on them.

He quickly ran to his bag and got the Nixyl. "I'm sorry, I'm sorry, I just wanted to get this for Lessa's stomach. I didn't see anything. I'm sorry!" He ran from the room and up the stairs, careful not to spill the water. *Oh man, that was embarrassing*, he thought as he walked to the back of the ship. Lessa hadn't moved an inch, so he put the encounter from his mind and laid his hand on her back.

"Here you go. I found some Nixyl, it might help." Slowly, she reached out for the little beans and popped them in her mouth, and took a drink of the water he brought her.

"Thank you. You know, I feel bad that Lucius doesn't get to see Stella that often. But again, I'm glad because I couldn't bear to feel this way more than once a year."

Foster smiled. "I understand. Feeling sick is never fun."

"Distract me, Foster," she stood straight for the first time in hours, "tell me of your siblings." Her hands gripped the railing as she focused on the horizon. Foster stepped close and rubbed the muscles on her back. They had to be sore by now from heaving and leaning for hours.

"We're pretty close, or at least we were." He took a big breath, hesitant to speak about the last time he saw them. But Lessa was a priestess. She had to be used to people unloading their feelings on her. "The day I left, I fought with just about everyone, Christopher, Saphira, my father. I feel so bad about leaving the way I did." She closed her eyes, and he felt her lean into his fingers, so he pressed harder on her muscles.

"What did you fight about?"

He paused for a bit. "Love, mostly."

"You and your brother love the same woman?" She turned and looked into his eyes.

"No, no, nothing like that," he chuckled. "But there was a girl, yes, and I…asked her to marry me. But she said no, and it really hurt." The memory of her rejection flashed in his mind, and another wave of grief hit him. *'No, Foster, I'm not for you.' She looked up and met his eyes, 'I can't marry you.'*

A look of pity flashed across Lessa's face. "Rejection on that scale can be devastating. Why wouldn't she marry you?"

He shrugged, trying not to meet her eyes, and concentrated on rubbing her back. "She said there was another for me. I assume it was one of her visions that she gets, so there was nothing I could say to sway her. Her visions are firm." Lessa turned her back on the rails for the first time in days, so Foster lowered his hands. "Saphira was trying to be nice, but I bit her head off, you know, little siblings." Lessa nodded as he thought back to his little sister. *"You don't look fine," Saphira said as she silently walked into the room. Usually, his little sister held the key to cheering him up, but today, he rounded angrily at her. "Well, I am!" She jumped at his harsh tone, and he saw her lip start quivering. "Fine! You don't have to be mean to me. I didn't do anything!"*

He sighed and shook his head. "Christopher…" his voice got softer as he spoke. "He spoke the truth, and it made me so mad I hit him." The memory of what he did to his little brother still crushed his heart. *Christopher got to his feet, his eye was puffy, and he had a nasty cut on his cheek. Suddenly, something else hurt Foster's heart. He had never hurt his little brother like that before, and guilt started to spread, but the anger was just too much, and he let it win.*

"I had never hit my brother before." He walked to the railing and laid his arms on them. "I feel guilty for leaving like that."

"Goodness, how dramatic." She reached out and laid a hand on his shoulder.

"Heartbreak is a part of life. I wish it weren't, it would

save us a lot of trouble. But if this woman had a vision of another for you, you should trust it."

Foster nodded. "I do, but I don't *want* to. That's the problem. I never imagined myself without Ada. It's hard."

Lessa nodded and took her hand back. "Time heals. One day, you won't hurt so much, and I bet your brother feels just as bad that it was left like that." She put her hand on her stomach. "I'm going to remember to get Nixyl next time we're on a boat. I haven't felt this good in days."

He gave her a little smile, even though it was the last thing he felt like doing. "Glad I could help, and thanks for listening to me moan."

Lessa chuckled. "It was a good distraction. Plus, that's part of my job, making sure our group is happy and unburdened."

He nodded. "Well, you're good at it." She really was. His mother pretty much said the same thing when she showed up at his camp outside of Raventree. *"I'm sorry you're in such pain, my son. But if Ada said there was another, I'd listen."* Deep down, he knew Ada was right, but it still didn't keep him from loving her. But hearing it from someone without a connection to him made it more believable somehow, easier to swallow.

———

The trip to Fairwinds took three weeks. Foster and Lessa talked every day, and every day, Sunette continued to ignore him. He felt he needed to apologize, or traveling with the mage was going to wear on him. So, on the last day of the voyage, he found her alone in her hammock. She was reading from one of her spell books, and he knocked on the wooden doorway.

"Sunette?"

She looked up and rolled her eyes. "I'm busy," she said shortly and returned to her book.

"I know, I just wanted to apologize." He walked in slowly and sat on the hammock across from her as she looked up from her book.

"Apologize?" She wasn't stomping away or hitting him with her heavy book, so he felt he had her attention.

"Yes. I'm sorry I walked in on you and Bereck. It was not my intention to spy. I just needed the Nixyl for Lessa. She was so nauseous, it couldn't wait." He had to concentrate and not talk too fast. He had the impression if he lost her attention, she'd storm away before he finished. But she didn't. He watched her face go from hard and accusatory to soft and confused.

"I know. She told me it really helped." She laid her book on her lap, "Do you mean your apology?"

He looked her in the eyes and nodded once. "Yes, I do."

Sunette closed her book and sighed. "Well, thank you, I accept." Her tone made him think she wasn't used to being apologized to or accepting them.

He smiled. "Good. I'm glad." He saw her staring at him, almost like she was studying him. "Something wrong?"

She stiffened. "Oh no, sorry. I'm not...you surprised me, that's all." She seemed flustered for some reason.

"Sunette, can I ask you something?" She nodded. "Where are you from? I've never heard an accent like yours before." Her words flowed from her mouth like they were stitched together without a space between them.

"Oh, well, my family is from the north."

"North?"

She nodded. "So far north, you've probably never heard of it." She smiled a little and cleared her throat. "It's called Emperia."

He smiled. "I've heard of it. My grandfather told me about it."

"He is from Emperia?"

"No," he shook his head, "he was a sailor. He said it was a lovely continent."

She smiled brightly. He could hardly believe she possessed such a smile. "Oh yes, it's lovely, from what I remember anyway. We left when I was young." Foster had never seen her smile like that. Even with Bereck, there seemed to be something sad in her eyes. As he listened to her talk of her homeland, he saw how it brightened everything about her, and he chuckled. "What?" she asked.

"I was just thinking how lovely your smile is." His eyes noticed her hands seemed to be running absentmindedly over her book.

Her eyes narrowed. "Hmm," she looked back down at her book and fiddled with the raised lettering on the front. "Thank you." Was she being shy? There was no way this woman who told him to piss on his apples was capable of being shy.

"Do you have a big family, Sunette?"

Her smile wilted a little around the edges as she looked back up at him. "I did, yes. I'm the only one left."

A pang of guilt hit Foster. "I'm sorry."

She chuckled. "That's all right, you didn't know, and it was a long time ago. You, Foster, do you have a big family?"

He nodded. "Some might say that. I have a younger brother and sister. Both my parents are alive. Even my grandfather, my mom's father, is still alive."

She nodded and fiddled with her book some more. "Is your grandfather a good man?"

"One of the best," he said proudly. That was another regret he had. He didn't say goodbye to his grandfather, Etienne. He had taught Foster how to shoot a bow before he took to learning with the Knights. He knew he'd miss his grandfather's stories while traveling, too. "Thank you for listening to me. I'll leave you to study." He gave her a little nod and walked away.

———

Sunette stared after him, stunned at his words. He said her smile was lovely, like that wasn't something only a lover should tell you. Perhaps it was the way he was raised? He certainly didn't seem shy about what he said. She sat back and tried to go back to studying her book, but she had no patience for it now. So, she closed it and headed up the stairs.

———

There was a lot of the usual on deck, Lessa and Mason arguing. She assumed whatever it was Foster gave the priestess really did the trick. She had never seen her friend speaking on a ship before. Bereck was honing his sword, and Twig and Raven were watching the horizon. She had a feeling Twig had a crush on the bard. She walked up the stairs to the back of the ship and was startled at what she saw. Foster was teaching Stella's daughter how to sword fight. They had broken broom handles and were clacking them together like swords.

She smiled and walked over to them. "Are you spoiling this little girl?" she teased.

"She wanted to learn, so I'm teaching," Foster said, not taking his eyes off the 'sword.'

"Little girls should be mages and princesses, not swordsmen." She chuckled, knowing Te'a would never be either of those things. Te'a started moving erratically around the big man, her arm flailing the 'sword' back and forth, which drew laughs from the nearby crew.

"I'm going to be a pirate when I grow up. I need to know how to fight."

"Oh, all right." Sunette smiled and started walking to the back of the ship.

"You want to try?" Foster called out after her.

She turned. "Pardon?"

He stopped fighting and held out his 'sword' to her. "Would you like to try?"

She held up her hands. "Oh no, I'm hopeless with a sword. You two keep having fun."

"Come on, live a little." Foster started moving over to her, holding out the 'sword' for her to take.

"No, really, I'm awful."

He stopped in front of her and put the stick in her hand. "Well, now's a good time to learn." He smiled and closed her hand around the stick.

Sunette looked at his face and couldn't help but smile back as she scoffed. "I'm more likely to treat this as a wand than a sword."

"In that case, we best get Te'a out of the way." He walked over to the wannabe pirate, and she handed him her stick with a smile and ran to the railing to watch. Foster turned back to Sunette and settled into a goofy, ready stance with his sword arm high above his head. "Do your worst," he said with a terrible 'evil guy' accent.

Sunette laughed. "Really, Foster, I'm terrible. Bereck's tried to teach, and I've learned nothing." She walked over and tried to hand him the stick, but he just taped it gently with his.

"Maybe he doesn't know how to teach you."

She saw a wicked smile spread across his face. "You brat." She whacked his stick with hers and laughed.

Foster chuckled and whacked back. "Maybe, but I got you to hit."

She scoffed and put her hands on her hips. "I refuse to play your little game." He stepped up and acted like he was going to whack her with his stick, but she quickly put hers in the way and blocked it with a loud clack.

"Seems like you're playing to me." He shifted and tried to hit her again, but she blocked.

"I most certainly am not," she said and quickly hit his arm.

"Ow!" Foster hopped up and down, wincing and holding his arm.

"Oh, I'm sorry!" She reached for him, but he quickly bent down and playfully whupped her backside with his stick and laughed.

He pointed the stick at her and began circling the deck. "Never have sympathy for those trying to kill you." She swore his eyes darkened as he said that. Sunette cleared her throat and rubbed her backside as she watched him, her eyes narrowed.

"I see." She raised the stick high above her head and formulated a plan. "Ow!" She gasped and dropped her stick, and brought her finger to her mouth.

"Got a splinter?" Foster walked over to her, "Let me see." She handed him her left hand, and while he was preoccupied looking for a splinter, she stole his stick and pointed it at his throat.

"I win." She smiled.

Foster looked at the stick and back at her and laughed. "Nice. You learn quick." He let her hand go.

"That I do." She was shocked at how fun it was to tease him. Foster chuckled as he bent over and picked up her old 'sword,' a smile on his face.

"Ready?" Sunette chuckled and pointed the stick at him.

———

She didn't know how long they were clacking sticks, but she had to admit it was fun. After a while, she looked over and saw Bereck walking up the stairs. He looked confused.

"What's this?" he asked with a little smile on his face.

Foster turned to him, breathless from the last 'charge.' "Messing around." Sunette walked over to Bereck, but not before smacking Foster in the butt with her stick. He let out a satisfying yelp, which made Te'a have a giggle fit.

She wrapped her arms around her strong paladin. "Foster was teaching me swordplay."

"Oh really? Did you learn anything?" One of his arms wrapped around her waist, and the other brushed some hair off her forehead before trailing along her cheek.

She turned and gave a thoughtful look at Foster. "He's not so bad," she said and walked down the stairs.

Bereck turned and watched her walk off. "That was quick. It took her six months before she'd call Mason by his name. What'd you do?" He asked, turning to the young man.

"I apologized to her about walking in on you two," he said sheepishly.

Bereck nodded. "Ah, Mason never did that."

"Not surprised," Foster said, rolling his eyes.

Bereck chuckled, "I'm glad you worked it out. She's much more pleasant to be around when she's not mad."

"Aren't most people?"

Bereck nodded. "Right you are, young man." He turned and walked down the stairs after Sunette.

———

The 'Blue Wind' reached Fairwinds the next morning,

and Bereck said a prayer to Otto, thanking him for a wonderful journey. The group gathered their things and started filing off the boat. Foster watched Lucius give Stella quite the goodbye kiss and Te'a a gold piece. He mussed her hair affectionately as she smiled widely at her new money.

Lucius walked them to 'The Mighty Lion Tavern and Inn.' It was loud and busy. There were servers running back and forth, trying to appease the many customers. Lucius walked up to the bar and got four keys and put them on the table they were sitting at.

"Split up as you like, enjoy the day, meet back here for supper." He turned and walked up the stairs, one of the keys in his hands. Bereck took one, and the couple walked up the stairs to put their things away. Foster picked up a key, it said eighteen, so he started up the stairs to find the room. It was in the middle of the second story, which made him groan a bit. Being in the middle meant the possibility of having noisy neighbors on both sides. He unlocked the door and saw the room was small, but it had two beds on either side of a window that looked onto an alley. He set his pack and his sword on one of them, and just as he sat down, he heard footsteps. His eyes went wide as Lessa and Raven walked into the room.

"Don't mind, do you?" Lessa asked. "I can't sleep with Mason or Twig. They have bulls in their noses."

"Same," Raven agreed and put her bag on the other bed. "Twig is a delight to talk to, but sleeping in the same room on that boat was not relaxing."

Foster smiled, "No, I don't mind. Help yourself."

"It'll be fun," Raven said. "Like a sleepover. I bet Foster needs a manicure."

Lessa laughed and sat on the bed. "You have a sister, right? I'm sure you're used to it."

He shrugged. "She's younger than me, so not really." And she wasn't into the typical things girls were into either. Hair, nails, dresses, but he suspected she liked dresses more than she let on.

"Then we shall have to show you how fun it is to have big sisters," Raven teased. "We share the bed or?" She pointed at Foster.

Lessa waved her hand at his bed. "He's too big to share with. We'll take this one."

"Yeah? Think so?" Foster flexed his arms, making sure his muscles popped, and the girls scoffed with smiles on their faces.

Lessa lay sideways on the bed. "Gods, I hate ships. I still feel sick even after I get back on land. I can still feel the swaying. I had hoped that wouldn't happen this time with the Nixyl." She covered her eyes and sighed.

"Land sickness, they call it, so annoying." Raven took off her boots and put on a pair of slippers, "Ah, much better." She started humming as she went through her bag.

"Sorry I don't have more Nixyl, but laying down won't help," Foster said. "You should get up and walk around."

"I should," she said without moving.

Foster shrugged his shoulders. "As you like," he started for the door.

"Wait, wait a second, I'll get up." Though she didn't sound happy about it. Foster waited by the door while Lessa slowly sat up. She swallowed hard and walked over to him. "Okay, where to?"

"Have you ever been to Fairwinds?" He opened the door, waiting to see if Raven wanted to join them.

"Once, for about five hours," she said. "You ever been Raven?"

"A long time ago, but I don't feel like sightseeing right now. I think I'll just loiter downstairs." She got up, and Foster locked the door behind them.

"Well, how about I show you around Lessa?" He held out his arm, and she took it as they walked down the stairs. In the tavern, they saw Lucius was already set up at a table with a pretty serving girl next to him. "He wastes no time," Foster chuckled.

Lessa turned and saw the sight. "No, he doesn't."

"You don't get a nickname like 'Luscious' by being chaste,"

Raven said. "Let's see how good he is with some company." Foster laughed as Raven quickly sat next to their boss and ordered a drink. The woman dutifully got off his lap to get it. They could see a smile on his face that said, 'Thanks a lot.'

Foster and Lessa walked out into the sun, down the road to nowhere in particular. A few people called out to Foster with greetings as they walked. It was nice being somewhere familiar. He felt less homesick.

One old man even yelled, "Pretty lady Foster, gonna worship Alar now?"

"Ha ha," he shot back.

"People seem to know you're here." Lessa looked around and smiled at whoever waved at them.

"My mother grew up in Fairwinds, so we visited often."

"Oh, that's right, Mother Lily is your mother.

He chuckled, "The one and only."

"That must have been an interesting upbringing."

"It seemed rather normal to me. But she does have the best stories. Are either of your parent's clergy?"

Lessa shook her head. "No, just me." She answered quickly, and he wondered if he was treading forbidden territory. Sure, he had given her Nixyl on the boat and spent a great deal of time talking after that. But he didn't think he was privileged enough to know everything about her.

"Are they proud of you?"

"What?" She turned her head so quickly, the land sickness grabbed hold, and she swayed.

Foster held her arm so she didn't fall over. "Mom said most parents are proud when their children join the church." He hoped continuing the conversation would get her mind off her stomach despite the sensitivity of the subject.

Lessa straightened. "Well, mine weren't." She pulled him down the road. Clearly, this was a sore topic.

"Sorry, didn't mean to pry."

"It's okay," she said quietly. He decided to wait until she felt a little better before he asked more questions about her past.

Foster snapped his fingers. "I know, I'll show you the most beautiful building in Fairwinds."

"You know beauty is in the eye of the beholder. I might think it's rather ugly," she poked him in the side.

He laughed and shook his head. "There's no way you'll find this building ugly. No one does."

"We'll see." They walked a few blocks as he led her to the Temple of Otto. It was a huge white building with stained-glass windows and black and white marble stairs. The top was domed, and huge marble columns went all around it. "Not a bad start. I've seen better. How about the inside?" she teased.

"Oh, it's much better," he gave her a wink. When they walked inside, he heard her gasp, and he couldn't stop the chuckle that came out.

"Foster, it's beautiful," her voice was barely above a whisper as she took it all in. Lessa let go of his arm and walked down the shiny, white marble aisle to the seashell-covered dais. Foster watched as her eyes took in the stained-glass windows that let in the colored light. It splashed over her skin, and she looked at her arms, amazed at the effect. She was covered in greens, blues, and reds. When she got to the dais, she gently touched the seashells. Foster watched as the head priest, Father Leif, walked over him. Father Leif had married his parents after the battle of Raventree and grew up with his mother. He was always a happy guy, clearly suited for the life.

"Foster, good to see you. Who have you brought us?"

He shook the priest's hand. "Hello, Father Leif. Her name is Lessa, she's a priestess in my group, but she seems unhappy. So, I thought I'd show her something beautiful."

"Well, you brought her to the right place," Leif said and walked up to the young woman. Foster stayed in the back and sat in one of the back pews and bowed his head in prayer. Christopher may have spent his life wanting to be a priest, but Foster found it comforting when he prayed to Otto as well. *'Blessed Otto, please look after my family as I travel. Let Saphira and Christopher find comfort in one another. And I know I've said it before, but I feel terrible about how I left it with my brother. Please forgive me for how I acted.'*

————————

Leif walked up behind Lessa and touched her shoulder. "Welcome, fellow priestess."

She looked at him and felt tears in her eyes. "Why do I feel this way?"

He led her to one of the front pews and sat down with her. "What way do you feel?"

She stared at the stained glass and felt a peace she had never known. "Stunted, unhappy. I know Alar is in my heart, but it brings me no comfort. Why?" She grabbed the priest's hand, and he patted hers.

"Why did you become a priestess of Alar?" She knew that tone he was using, it was more for her than it was for him. She used it countless times on people who knew the truth but weren't ready to accept it.

Lessa bowed her head, "My father was a priest of Alar. I thought it would be a good way to honor him."

"It would be if it was truly your destiny," Leif said in a wonderful, comforting voice.

"To be a priestess is my destiny. I know it," she looked into the priests' friendly eyes. "I love doing the god's work, but with Alar, it doesn't feel, I don't know, complete. He accepts me, I know that, but something's missing," she sighed, scared that someone knew her secret.

"Is your father alive?"

Lessa shook her head. "No, he died when I was eight. He was traveling with a group and was killed. My mother never forgave him."

"So, you following in his footsteps didn't make your mother happy, did it?" She shook her head, remembering the fight they had when she left to learn how to be a priestess.

"No. She follows Otto and cursed Alar's name as I left."

"But Otto's where your heart belongs, isn't it?" She felt tears roll down her cheeks and nodded, fearful of what Alar might do. "Child, it's nothing to be ashamed of," he took her hands and stood her up. "Why don't you go to the Temple of Alar here in town and do some soul-searching. We'll be here waiting if you decide anything."

He leaned in and kissed her forehead, and as she felt Otto's blessing, she cried, "Thank you, Father." After a few moments, she was able to compose herself. She stood straight and wiped her eyes and saw Foster in the back, praying. She slowly walked over to him and touched his shoulder. He looked up with a smile. "Want to escort me to another temple?"

Foster stood and held out his arm. "With pleasure."

CHAPTER 3
THE FIRST JOB

That night, all but Lessa had gathered in the common room for dinner. Food had been set out, and the drinks flowed. Mason was shoveling it in like usual, and Raven was wiggling in her seat as she ate like it was the best thing she'd ever eaten. It was cute.

"Where's Lessa? I told everybody to meet for dinner." Lucius was clearly annoyed as he turned back to the stairs for the fourth time in less than thirty seconds.

"She's coming, don't worry." Foster had left her in their room. She wanted to surprise everyone.

"Was she in your room when you came down?" Twig asked.

Foster nodded. "Yes, she was."

Twig leaned forward. "You two weren't up to anything, were you?" he teased.

"What?" He missed the potato he was aiming for, and his fork scraped noisily against the plate. "No!"

"Oh, I don't know," Raven started in on it, too, and Foster rolled his eyes. "Handsome young man sharing a room with a beautiful young woman, things happen." Raven and Twig chuckled as they bumped elbows.

Foster scoffed, "That's your room too, remember. Besides, I'm not interested in Lessa," he lifted his ale to his mouth. "Unfortunately, my heart belongs to another." He mumbled into his mug before he took a big drink. Sunette looked up from her plate at his words. She seemed to be the only one who heard him.

"Unfortunately?" She asked quietly, "She does not return your affection?"

"No, she does. It's complicated," he said before he took

another big gulp.

"I will not pry then." Foster put his mug down and noticed Twig and Raven were staring at the stairs. He looked shocked, and Raven was smiling. She had kept the secret, too. He turned and saw Lessa walking down, wearing the white robes of Otto. Lessa was smiling brightly as she made her way over and sat down.

"Hello," she said as she sat down between Mason and Lucius like she usually did.

Raven gasped. "You look divine!"

Foster chuckled at Mason's wide-open mouth. "Wow, what happened?" Mason reached out and touched her robe, "laundry accident?"

She gently slapped her brother's hand and straightened up. "I realized why I was so unhappy. I knew I had holy power inside of me, but I felt I had to worship Alar because of our father."

Mason sat up and became visibly subdued. "I didn't know that Lessa. You should have told me." He laid a hand on her shoulder, and she shrugged.

"I didn't really know myself."

He sighed and hugged his sister. "I hope you'll be happier now."

She hugged him back and smiled. "I will be." After one last squeeze, they sat back and noticed the group staring at them.

"What?" Mason looked quite confused.

"We just never thought you were capable of such affection, Mason," Sunette said with a smile.

He laughed. "Well, don't tell anyone." Lessa settled in and noticed Lucius gently running his fingers along the white fabric.

"You look lovely in white, Alessa," he was really turning on the charm.

"Thank you, Lucius." He picked up her hand and laid a gentle kiss on her skin. "Really, you needn't gush on me." Her cheeks turned bright red at the attention.

Foster watched the priestess during dinner. She seemed so

much happier, like a whole new person. She talked and smiled and laughed more than he'd ever seen her do.

When all was eaten and drunk, Lucius got the group's attention. "All right, everyone. We'll rest a few days, get our land legs back," he said, looking over at Lessa. "Then head east. I heard a rumor that the dwarfs are being troubled by something nasty below their city. Thought we'd give them some help."

"Do you know what the nastiness is?" Bereck asked, his hand running lightly over Sunette's arm.

"Not really. There are rumors of undead to dark elves. You know how rumors can get, especially when the underground is involved." He picked up his ale and took a long drink.

"Guess we'll find out when we get there!" Mason said as he raised his mug, "Here's to us! May we make it out alive!" Everyone clacked their mugs together. Foster watched Bereck give Sunette a loving kiss. Lucius kissed Lessa's cheek, and she once again blushed as red as her hair. Raven laughed at the display and turned to give Twig a kiss on his cheek.

"Can't have only women blushing now, can we?" She teased as Twig smiled at her. Foster swore there was a faint pink tinge on his cheeks.

————

Late that night, Foster and Lessa finally went up to their room. Raven told them to go up without her. She wanted to try and earn a few coin with some songs.

He sat down on his bed and started taking his boots off. "Alessa?"

She turned as she shrugged out of her new robes. "Hmm?"

"Your real name is Alessa?"

She nodded. "It is. Hardly anyone calls me that."

"They should. It's a pretty name for a pretty woman," he said as he pulled his shirt over his head.

"Is it?" She teased, but he thought she was blushing a little. Apparently, she was a blusher. After a few moments, she sighed and hung her new robe on the door. "I can't thank you enough," she said as she turned to him.

"Oh, I didn't do anything," he said as he got under the not thick enough covers.

"No, you did. I never would have gone into that temple without you. I believe Otto did send you."

Foster smiled. "He sends us where we're needed, according to my mother anyway."

Lessa chuckled and walked next to his bed. "Good night, Foster." She leaned down and laid a soft kiss on his lips before slipping into her bed. Foster felt heat creep up his face. Only Ada had ever kissed him like that. Then he cursed himself silently for thinking of her right before bed. He laid down and tried not to think of his beautiful half-elf, but the gods were not good to him that night as he dreamed a wonderful dream of her.

———

"Your skin is so soft," he said before he kissed her hand. When he looked up, Ada was blushing something fierce.

"Thank you." He held her hand in both of his and gently ran his thumb over her skin.

"Ada?"

When her beautiful half-elven eyes met his, he felt his heart stop. "Yes?"

"Forgive me if I'm too blunt, but I think you're the most beautiful woman I've ever seen."

She smiled and leaned closer to him. "You're the most handsome man I've ever known, inside and out," she whispered.

He leaned close and cupped her cheek. "I've wanted to kiss you since before I knew what kissing was."

She chuckled and put an arm around him. "Then kiss me, Foster," she whispered before he pressed his lips on hers.

———

After a few days' rest, the group bought a few pack horses and headed east. As they traveled, Foster noticed that Twig seemed completely enamored of the bard. They'd talk about everything and nothing. Every so often, she'd lean in and say something in a hushed tone. Whether it be something nice about Twig or teasing someone else, he always smiled.

Mason was chattering non-stop as well, always asking Foster questions about his family. He assumed growing up with Mother Lily meant Foster had some crazy divine-ness to him, but he really didn't. He was just a normal man. He didn't tell the young rogue about the crescent-shaped birthmark he shared with his father. While it marked them as favored, according to his father, he wasn't exactly sure what that meant.

A week before they reached their destination, the group was sitting around a roaring campfire. Lucius was trying to impress Lessa by balancing a dagger on his fingertip, and Raven was leaning against Twig. Foster noticed Bereck gently running his hand along Sunette's arm. Suddenly, memories of doing that to Ada flooded his mind, and he felt hot tears forming.

"Excuse me." He stood and quickly walked off. There was a big boulder about thirty feet away, and Foster sat behind it, trying hard not to cry, but tears fell anyway. He missed Ada so much, he still ached for her. It was like true grief. Sometimes, he was fine. Other times, the sadness threatened to overwhelm him, like now. Soft footsteps came around the boulder, and Foster quickly wiped his face and saw Sunette peering around the large rock.

"Foster, are you all right?" Her tone was gentle, and he could tell she was genuinely worried.

He cleared his throat, "Yeah."

She stepped around the rock and sat down beside him. "What's wrong?"

Foster sighed and looked at the ground. "I miss her," he whispered.

"The one who unfortunately returns your affections?" He nodded. "Hmm. Well, tell me about her." He turned and looked at Sunette. The moonlight was the only thing lighting the area around them. Her dark hair seemed to shine in it.

He cleared his throat. "She's a half-elf," he said quietly.

"Exotic," Sunette smiled.

He smiled a little. "Not as exotic as your voice."

Sunette chuckled. "Maybe, go on," she nudged him a little.

"Her name is Ada. I've known her my whole life."

"Childhood sweethearts, how sweet," she said wistfully.

"Something like that." He wasn't falling apart as he spoke, so he decided to keep going. He sighed heavily and told her the story of his failed proposal. How she told him he wasn't for her, how it hurt her too, but there was nothing to be done. "She's had visions her whole life, so I trust her, but…you must think I'm a fool for feeling like this." He crossed his arms and leaned back against the boulder.

Sunette reached up and gently touched his arm. "Not at all. You're young. I imagine you've never felt the sting of loss before."

Foster shook her head. "No, just this. Some days are better than others. Especially when Lessa and Raven try to cheer me up."

Sunette chuckled and squeezed his muscular arm. "They are good for you. But I think for now, you should focus on keeping us alive. Don't dwell on the past, and fill your heart with your new friends." Slowly, he looked over at the mage. She was smiling softly and resting her head on her knees. *She looks so sweet and friendly*, he thought, so different from his first impression of her.

"Thanks, I'll try," he whispered and patted her hand, which was still on his arm.

"Come back to the fire, Foster," she swiftly got to her feet and held her hand for him to take. "Come sit with your new family." He looked at her hand for a second before taking it and getting to his feet. It was surprisingly warm in his. "Time passes, soon you'll feel like your old self." He just nodded and followed her back to the fire.

"Back already?" Mason teased as they walked by. Sunette answered by smacking him on the back of his head. Twig and Lucius laughed as she sat down in her paladin's arms.

"Serves you right," Lessa said. Foster sat down and looked at the people surrounding him. He could learn more sword techniques from Bereck. Pray with Lessa and laugh with Mason.

Perhaps Lucius could teach him a thing or two about women when he felt up to it. He knew Twig was loyal and that he could count on him at his back and learn songs from Raven. He looked upon his new family and decided to cry no more over Ada. He'd mourn his love, but the time for crying was over.

A week later, they reached the peaks that were the beginnings of the Dwarven lands. They had sold their horses at the last small town since they wouldn't do well underground. Foster was sad to see his horse go but glad for more spending money. They walked about a half a mile into the twisted road of the towering peaks when Twig yelled.

"Look out!" Everyone looked up and saw boulders careening down the mountain on top of them. Sunette held her hands up and yelled words of magic, and the boulders landed hard on an invisible surface twenty feet above everyone's heads.

"Perfect Sunette, thank you." Lucius cautiously walked under the rocks out into the sunlight. They all emerged unscathed when they heard a voice.

"Oi! You all right?" They looked up and saw a dwarf repelling down towards them.

"Yes, we're fine!" Lucius yelled and waved at the dwarf. Soon, he was in talking range and turned to the group. He was large, as dwarfs go. His beard was bushy and brown, and his forearms were bursting out of his shirt. But Foster could see gray at his temples.

"Sorry about that, didn't know anybody was passing through. Teaching my boy how to excavate. Usually, people coming through the pass aren't an issue during the day."

"That's all right, no harm, no foul. But perhaps you could aid us, friend," Lucius said. He walked up to the wall, and the dwarf repelled to the ground and shook the half-elf's hand.

"Sure, happy to help. Call me Burgess."

"Lucius Silverblade, pleasure. We heard the dwarfs were having some problems with something nasty below. Is that true?"

Burgess nervously wiped his hands on a rag he pulled

out of his pocket. "Heard about that, didja?" he mumbled and cleared his throat. "Yeah, there's some…problem deep down. That's why we're out here. Started about six months ago. The men broke through a wall or a well? I don't know. They broke through something, then the miners started disappearing. One man came back, but his hair was bone white, and he'd only say one thing."

"What did he say?" Lucius asked.

Foster could hear a note of hesitation in the man's voice. "Don't know, some sentence in an odd language. No one knows what it means."

Sunette stepped up. "Is this man still afflicted so?"

"Aye, I believe he is."

She walked up to Lucius and touched his arm. "I might be able to decipher his words."

Burgess looked her up and down. "Maybe you could. We don't have many spell casters ourselves. Could be something you could do."

"Thank you for your help, Burgess. Are we going in the right direction?" He pointed down the chasm.

"Yes, yes, keep going that way. Should reach the city later today."

"Again, thank you for your help." Lucius shook his hand again, and the group walked off.

Foster swore he heard Burgess grumble. "Crazy humans."

————

Just as the sun set, the group reached the opening of the Dwarven City of Ral Hava. There were two guards posted outside, and when they walked up, their eyes turned to them.

Lucius raised his hand in greeting. "Hello! My name is Lucius Silverblade, and these are my men. We heard about your trouble deep in your mountain and wished to aid." The guards looked him over and motioned with their axes for them to enter. "Thank you." Lucius smiled as he walked inside. Everyone followed him down the narrow entryway, and when they emerged, the sight made Foster gasp. The cavernous city looked like it went for miles. It was built into the surrounding walls, and spiraling stone buildings came up in the middle. The walls glittered black, and the smells! Roasting meat and fire, it was breathtaking.

Torches lit everything, and it was warm inside. "Take it you've never been here," Bereck asked him.

"No, I'd not forget this in a thousand years," Foster said, still staring at the city.

Raven came up and pulled on his arm. "Come on, you giant of a man, don't get lost."

Looking at the city had made him fall behind the group. "Sorry," he whispered. The bard gave him a little wink as they caught up with the rest of the group. Lucius led them to a tavern about half a mile from the entrance called 'The Bearded Lady.' It had a picture of a female dwarf with a beard holding two steins of ale on the sign. They found a large, empty table and sat down. Foster's eyes wanted to take in everything about the place. It was made of stone, and he assumed it was carved out of the rock from the mountain. Big torches were high on the wall, lighting the place, and the wooden tables were so shiny they reflected the shine from the walls. They all ordered ale and food and waited patiently.

"So," Lucius tapped the table. "We eat, I'll get us rooms, and the rest of you try to learn as much as you can about what we're doing. The more we know, the better." When he finished, Foster took the opportunity to ask his boss something he'd been dying to ask.

"Hey, Lucius?"

The half-elf turned and put his hands behind his head as he settled in. "Yes, Foster?"

"Are you going to find a busty dwarven wench while we're here?" He smiled while Mason and Raven laughed.

Lucius just smiled. "As hearty as my appetites are, my friend, I'm afraid dwarven women don't mix well with me. Too short." He wiggled his eyebrows as the server sat down their mugs. As the woman left, Lucius quickly put a hand on top of

Foster's mug before he could take a drink. "Remember, dwarven ale is much stronger than ale on the surface. Careful how much you drink." He removed his hand and took a swig of his own mug. "Ahh, but it is so good." Foster took a sip, it *was* good, hearty, and he felt warmth spread along his body. Soon, their food arrived, some kind of meat and potatoes with a nice crusty bread. The meat melted in their mouths, and the potatoes were crispy on the outside and perfectly fluffy on the inside.

Everyone ate and drank and talked before a bard stepped up and started playing a bawdy song in the corner. What was surprising was the bard was an older human. True there weren't many dwarven bards, but the fact that an older man would be here was surprising to Foster. Mason laughed at his songs while Lessa and Sunette rolled their eyes and shook their heads. The songs were awful sexist, Foster thought, but he couldn't help but snicker to himself, glad that his mother wasn't here to admonish him.

"Gods, I thought he was dead," Raven said, staring at the man.

Everyone turned to her, shocked she knew him. "You know him?" Twig asked, finishing his ale.

"Aye, I do. I guess I shouldn't be surprised he's down here. Not many bounty hunters come looking this far down."

Lucius sat forward. "What did he do?"

"He didn't murder anyone if that's what you're asking, but there's a bounty on his head, not worth it," she said, looking at their boss. "He basically ratted out some people to even worse people. He said they were the ones they were looking for, they weren't, but they were killed anyway."

"Damn." Twig laid a hand on her shoulder. "Anyone you knew?"

She took a long drink of her ale and swallowed. "My parents. I was fourteen." Her eyes never moved from the singer. Foster could see hate and sadness in her eyes.

"If you want me to kill him, I will," Lucius said. Foster didn't bother being shocked at his words. He wanted the man dead for causing Raven such heartache as well.

Raven barked out a laugh and quickly finished her drink. "No, I think being stuck here is enough." She reached over and scratched at Lucius's goatee, "but thank you."

"If you're sure, I'm always up for some parental revenge." He sat back, his hands going back behind his head.

"I'm sure, but I appreciate the offer." She gave him a little wink, which he returned.

———

By the time they were finished eating, the tavern was full of loud, rowdy dwarfs. "All right, have a good night." Lucius tipped his hat low and set his feet on the stone table. Foster watched as everyone got up and started wandering around the tavern. Twig and Raven danced to the music while Mason simply listened. Lessa sat at the bar and ordered another ale. Foster looked around and saw a group of dwarfs by the door, all dressed in the same dark tunic. He decided to see if they knew anything about the darkness, so he walked up and introduced himself.

"Greetings! My name is Foster Voltain. May I join you?"

They looked him over, and one kicked out a chair. "Have a seat, lad."

"Thank you." He sat down with his mug. "So, what do you fine gentleman do here?"

They laughed. "Fine gentleman indeed. That's how you know someone's never been down here!" Foster shrugged with a smile. It wasn't untrue.

"We're guards to the deep," one said, ignoring the laughing of the others.

Foster leaned forward. He couldn't believe his luck. "Interesting."

"It's good and honest, can't complain," he said. "What about you, boy? What are you doing down here?"

Foster took a swig and let the warmth give him courage. "We're here because we heard about some trouble down deep. Thought we could help." The guards stopped what they were doing and looked at each other. Foster could tell whatever it was had to be bad enough to make them nervous.

"You don't want to go down there," one with a dark beard said before he chugged his ale.

"Maybe not, but we'd like to try and help." Several of them shook their heads like they couldn't believe he wasn't heeding their warning.

"Do you know what's down there, boy?" another asked.

Foster shook his head. "No, you know how rumors are. One day, it's undead the next, it's hellish unicorns."

The dwarfs laughed and drank some ale. "No, no hellish unicorns. We could only be so lucky. It's dark elves and something worse." Foster had never seen a dark elf, only heard of them. Their skin ranged from dark gray to obsidian and tended to strike first and ask questions later. He knew they were matriarchal and worshiped an evil god. He never wanted to meet one.

"Something worse than dark elves?"

One of the dwarfs nodded. "Yep, worse. Don't know what it is, though. Haven't seen it."

"Great." Foster chugged his ale and wiped his mouth, "I thank you for your information. It'll be most helpful." He stood and shoved the chair in. "Have a good night, gentleman." He raised the empty mug to them and headed towards the bar.

"Good luck, lad. Maybe the stone protect your crazy arses."

Foster took the empty seat next to Lessa at the bar and ordered another drink. "Did you learn anything?" she asked quietly.

"Yes, those guards said it was dark elves and something worse."

"Dark elves?" Her eyes went wide, and she laid her head in her hands, "Gods."

He thought she saw the color drain from her face. "Have you ever seen one?"

She shook her head. "No. Nor did I ever want to."

Foster took his new ale from the bartender. "Don't worry,

we'll be fine, Lessa."

"Yes, Otto will be with us." She took a drink of her ale and sniffed. "I believe Lucius plans on meeting with the Barrister tomorrow to get help and more information."

"Good idea." Foster studied Lessa's face. She looked unnerved. "You okay?"

She shook her head. "Hmm, I'm not sure anymore."

He reached out and laid a hand on her shoulder. "Do you want to talk about it?" Being a priestess, he was sure she was used to people talking about their problems. But he wondered how often she would get to speak to someone to unburden her own heart.

She looked over and furred her eyebrows. "Not really." She took a big swig of ale and wrinkled her nose. "Gods, that is some bitter ale."

Foster liked bitter ale, so it didn't bother him as much. "That it is." He watched as Lessa put her mug on the bar. His eyes drifted to her hands, which seemed to be shaking a little. "Lessa?" He reached out and took her right hand in his. She squeezed his hand tight and ordered another ale. Foster scooted the bar stool closer and leaned into Lessa. "What is it?" Obviously, something was more wrong than he first thought, and he didn't want to see her suffering like she was.

He waited a few moments until Lessa finally took a deep breath. "When Lucius said we were coming here, it made me nervous, but I thought I could handle it. Now I'm not so sure."

"Handle what?" She turned to Foster, still holding her hands, and he could tell how hard she was trying to be brave.

"Being here, underground." Lessa looked up and leaned close to his ear, and whispered. "My father was killed down here."

Foster sat back and took both her hands in his. "Lessa, I'm so sorry. Did Lucius know this when he decided to come here?"

She shook her head. "Mason doesn't even know."

"Why not?" Lessa took her hands from his and wrapped them around her new ale.

"We were so little when he died. I was only eight, and Mason was four. We knew he was with a group doing something, but Mom just told us he was killed during an ambush as they were traveling and nothing more. She never liked to talk about him after that. She was always so mad. She used to say that he 'selfishly died on us.' One day, when I was fifteen, a woman came to the house. She was tall and had long black hair. I remember her clothes were so colorful, and when I saw her, I knew she was a mage. She smiled and said, *'You're Aeson's daughter, aren't you? I'd recognize that hair anywhere. My name is Aine. I used to travel with your father. I have something for you.'* She started digging in her bag, but then my mom walked out and started screaming at her. That it was her fault my father was dead and that she wouldn't steal me away from her. She walked outside with Aine and slammed the door in my face. I could hear her yelling, and when I looked out the window, the mage just stood there and took it. Not once did she yell back or try to defend herself from my mother's onslaught. When the yelling died down, my mom walked back in, slammed the door, and told me to forget I had ever seen that woman." Foster was rubbing her back like his mother used to do to him, hoping it comforted her a little.

"What did you do?"

"After mom went to bed, I climbed out of my window and ran straight to the one tavern we had in town and hoped she was there."

"Was she?"

Lessa nodded and took a big swig of ale. "Ugh, she was. She said she was waiting for me, said that *'if you were anything like your father, I knew you'd show up.'* So, I sat at the table with her, and she told me what really happened to my father. He died when he took an arrow for her. It was poisoned. Aine said it normally wouldn't have been a fatal wound, but the poison acted so fast that no one could do anything. She handed me a handkerchief and told me my father asked her to give it to me when I was old enough. When I opened it, I saw this," She picked up her seashell and kissed it. "I remembered it from when I was little. My mom had given it to him as a gift, not to sway him to Otto but to always remind him that there were people at home who loved him and to stay safe." After Lessa was quiet for a moment, Foster reached up and lifted her chin so he could see her eyes.

"That's quite a story. Do you think your brother might like to hear it?"

She shrugged. "Like to? Doubt it," she turned into his hand, and he cupped her cheek, "but he deserves to, at least. I don't know if now's the right time, but thank you for listening, Foster." She reached up and put her hand over his. "I didn't mean to just lay all my family drama on the bar."

Foster smiled and shook his head. "Even a priestess needs someone to unload on, and what better place than a bar." She chuckled and gave his hand a kiss.

———

Later that night, Lucius watched his people around the bar. Sunette and Bereck were dancing and staring lovingly into each other's eyes. They looked so happy. Lucius had never really loved. The closest he thought would probably be Stella. He hoped the couple would have left by now, but he wouldn't complain. Her spells were powerful, and Bereck was an amazing fighter. They'd be fine.

Twig and Raven were talking in a corner. They really seemed like parts of a whole to him. He'd never seen Twig so personable before. Perhaps it was a bad idea to wait so long to ask Raven to join. Mason was listening to the bard, no doubt trying to learn the bawdiest song he could to piss off the women. Lucius had warned him several times his mouth would get him in trouble, but until it truly did, he doubted the young man would take the warning seriously.

It took him a while to find Lessa and Foster. He watched them earlier at the bar, talking quietly with their heads together, drinking copious amounts of the strong ale. Lucius finally found them tucked away in a dark corner. Lessa was on Foster's lap, petting his face and smiling. It looked like he was singing to her, but even with his sharp ears he couldn't hear Foster over the din.

"Boy works quick. I'll give him that," he said as he watched Lessa kiss the young man. *Hope she don't kill him in the morning*, he thought as he drank his ale.

———

The next morning, Foster woke as a hand touched his chest. He opened his eyes and saw Lessa lying curled around him. She was sound asleep and completely naked.

"Oh, Otto, forgive me," he whispered. When he looked down, he saw he was naked as well and tried to remember what had happened. Everything until his third mug of the ale was clear as a bell. After that, not so much. He slowly looked down again. Lessa was beautiful, curvy, and supple. Suddenly, flashes of the previous night appeared in his memory, the feel of her skin against his and her deep, deep kisses.

At the time, he wanted more, but now he felt guilty. He doubted she would have gone to bed with him if they hadn't drunk so much. Foster leaned over and kissed her cheek. "Lessa, wake up," he whispered.

She moaned and stretched across him. "What?" She sounded sleepy. He watched her open her eyes as they slowly widened in confusion. "Foster?" She sat up a little and noticed the lack of clothing and pressed closer to him, trying to hide. "Gods, what happened?"

"I think we didn't heed Lucius' warning about the ale." He noticed two large glasses of water on the nightstand. They were almost empty, and wondered who brought those in. They must have drunk them at some point, or they'd feel a lot worse.

"You could say that again." Lessa reached down and pulled a blanket against her torso. She slowly sat up and ran her fingers through her hair. "I don't remember much," she said. Her back was still bare, and Foster laid what he hoped would be a comforting hand on it.

"Me either, but I remember...snip-its."

She turned, and Foster sat up, sliding a hand to her waist. "What kind of snip-its?"

"The kind you remember after a night of, um, well, you

know. Drunken sex."

She turned and laid her head in her hands. "Great." Foster felt so bad. He knew something like this could happen, but with a priestess? He hoped she wouldn't hate him.

"I apologize, Lessa. I didn't mean to put either of us in this situation."

"Me either." She looked over to him and touched his face. "But I wish," she sighed and lowered her head.

"You wish what?" He braced himself, waiting to hear harsh words.

She looked up again. "I wish I could remember."

Foster chuckled, half relieved. "You want to remember?"

"I do." She turned and sighed, "I've never done anything like this before."

"Me either."

She scooted closer to him and laid a hand on his thigh. "I really wish I could remember last night." Lessa gently squeezed his leg and moved closer.

"Lessa?" He felt his heart speed up as she leaned forward and gently brushed his lips with hers. He reached up and gingerly held her face as she spoke.

"I know you don't love me, Foster. You don't have to." She kissed him again, and he felt his body react.

"What do you want of me, Lessa?" he whispered.

He watched as she dropped the blanket and straddled his hips. "Just you. You're kind and smart, funny, handsome, and I know you're special. I can feel it." She said as she touched his heart. Foster wrapped his arms around her hips and brought her closer, and kissed her deeply, giving her what she wanted.

———

Later that morning, Foster and Lessa walked down to the common room, hand in hand. Lucius watched them closely as they joined him and Raven at the food-covered table.

"Have a good night?" he asked slyly.

"I sure hope so," Raven snipped at them, the bags under her eyes told them how much sleep she didn't get. "I had to sleep with the snoring twins last night."

"Don't know, can't remember," Lessa said with a shrug. "Seems I drank a bit too much."

"Shame." Lucius smiled. "So, find anything out last night?"

Foster nodded. "Yes, the guards said it was dark elves and something else. They didn't know what but knew it wasn't hellish unicorns."

Lucius snickered, "Well, I should hope not. I'm going to the local Barrister to see what we can do to help. If you want to come, you're welcome."

"Sounds good," Foster said. He looked up and saw the rest of the group coming down. Twig sat next to Raven while Sunette and Bereck sat next to Lessa. Mason looked terrible, his hair was sticking up in odd angles, and he looked positively green.

"Mason, how much did you drink?" Lessa asked him, but all he did was slowly turn his head towards Foster.

His mouth was open, and it was clear he was still drunk. "Huh?"

"He drank so much he forgot how to speak," Twig teased. Everyone giggled quietly as Mason just stared at them, his mouth hanging open.

"Huh?" he said again.

"Lucius, you might want to tie his mouth shut," Foster suggested.

"Not a bad idea." He turned Mason around in his chair so he faced the other way, just in case. The young man did not protest.

Lucius told the rest of them about the dark elves and his plans to visit the big wig of the city. All but Bereck and Sunette said they would go. She wanted to check on the poor, afflicted dwarf. Well, all but Bereck, Sunette, and Mason would go as he passed out and fell to the floor. Twig picked him up and took him back upstairs. "Does he do that a lot?" Foster asked.

"He's never had dwarven ale before," Lessa said.

"Ah."

"A few of us haven't had it before, have you Foster?" Lucius asked. He knew their boss was teasing. He had to have seen them drinking too much the night before.

"No, never," he said as nonchalantly as he could. Lucius was about to stand up when a group of dwarves walked by, carrying a stretcher down from the second floor. Foster's eyes went wide. It seemed the old bard from last night had gotten his throat slit.

"Hmm, shame," Raven said as she took another bite of a sausage. Everyone but Lucius looked at her. "What? I didn't do it. Not that he didn't deserve it."

Lucius finally got to his feet. "Shall we?" As the group stood, Foster gently put his hand on Lessa's back and helped her up. He noticed Sunette was staring at him.

"What?"

She smiled. "Nothing," she said and took her paladin's hand, and walked out before everyone else.

———

It didn't take long for the group to get in to see the Barrister, apparently Lucius and the dwarf knew each other. They walked confidently into the office, where they shook hands and laughed.

"Lucius, you old hound, how are you?"

"Fine, Morac, just fine. May I introduce my traveling companions," he turned back to the group, and everyone shook hands with Barrister Morac.

"Sit, feel welcome. I can guess why you're here. You heard about our troubles."

Lucius nodded. "Yes, we've come to offer any aid we can."

"It is most appreciated. Currently, we're trying to 're-plug' the hole, but it's slow going. There are attacks every day, and we lose three to five workers in every raid. Our fighters can't keep up with the numbers that come through, and workers are starting to not volunteer."

"Did you dig too deep, Morac?" Lucius crossed his arms over his chest.

The dwarf sighed, "Perhaps we found a rich silver vein

and couldn't stop."

Lucius tapped the desk. "I know it's tempting."

"If you would take your group and help defend the wall, we would be forever grateful. I know if we could just plug it up, we'd be fine." Morac pulled out a paper and scribbled something on it. "Take this writ to the supply store by the road to the hole. They'll give you whatever you need." He handed the paper to Lucius, who folded it and put it in his pocket.

"Thank you, it's much appreciated." Lucius stood and shook hands with the Barrister again, "We'll get going as soon as possible. We'll do our best, count on that."

"I trust you will."

————

Bereck and Sunette were told the surviving dwarf was at a nearby temple, so they made their way there. From a distance, they saw the immense front doors of the temple, carved from the stone like everything else here, with intricate carvings and gems all over them. Dwarves tended to revere the stone and what the stone provided instead of the pantheon above. So, neither were surprised at the intricacy of the art around Ral Hava. It gave them shelter, warmth, and riches. Who wouldn't want to worship the stone?

"That's beautiful," Bereck said as they walked up the stairs. They heard running behind them and turned to see Raven coming up after them.

"Don't mind, do you? I'm allergic to bureaucracy."

Bereck chuckled. "No, not at all." The three of them walked inside, and the smell of incense hit their noses. It was different than what they would normally encounter in a temple above ground. It didn't have the same herb-y smell. It was rock and blood. A priest in brown robes walked up to them. His beard was decorated with lots of little braids and beads.

"Morning travelers, what can I do for you?"

They shook his hand, and Sunette spoke up. "I heard there was a survivor from an attack below who is speaking an odd language. If I may, I'd like to see if I can decipher his words."

The priest's eyes widened as he put his hands together. "Wonderful, we've had absolutely no luck in figuring out what he's saying. Please follow me and be warned, he's quite a sight." They nodded and followed him through the main sanctuary and down a few flights of stone steps. Finally, he turned into a corridor, and they could hear wailing at one end.

"Is that him?" Bereck pointed down the hall.

"Aye. Poor man, he sounds as if he's being tortured, but no one's there."

"Gods," Sunette breathed out. They reached the room, and the priest opened the door. The volume of the man's yells increased exponentially, and they fought hard not to cover their ears.

"Brother Jadol," their guide walked up to another priest in the room who was praying. "We've got some guests who want to help."

Jadol looked up, they could see the sweat on his brow, and he looked frazzled. "Well, good luck to them. Nothing I've done has helped." He moved, and Sunette sat next to the poor dwarf who was screaming as if he was afraid. She laid her hand on his forehead, and he quickly quieted and looked at her.

"My name's Sunette, I want to help." She closed her eyes and cast a spell. Bereck stood behind her, holding his seashell and praying to Otto that the dwarf would feel relief. He looked the dwarf over and could see he looked skinny, like he hadn't eaten in weeks. There were burn marks around his wrists and a wicked cut over his left eye. When Sunette opened her eyes, they flashed with light for a moment. "Can you tell me what happened?" The dwarf started mumbling quickly, the same thing repeatedly.

"That's the only thing he says now," Jadol sighed and wiped his brow.

"Whatever is down there is old and evil," Sunette said. "Bereck, can you heal some of these wounds?"

"With permission?" He looked at the other priests, who nodded.

"Again, good luck if you can. None of our magics work."

Bereck nodded and laid his hands on the dwarfs' wrists.

"Blessed Otto, this man is in need of comfort and restoration." He felt Otto's power flow through him but stopped. He watched as the wrists stayed raw and bleeding. "He can't be healed with magic." Raven walked up to the man. She had been standing in the corner, her arms crossed tight. She reached out and laid a hand on his forehead. His yells became louder, saying the same thing over and over again. *Odv vyizm Odv vyizm Odv vyizm.*

Raven took her hand back with a gasp. "Death has touched this man."

"No one raised him, that's illegal." The dwarven priest sounded offended at the notion.

"No, I don't mean he died, I mean something dead touched him, something…"

"Old." Sunette said, "Old death is what he's saying, in infernal."

"Infernal? He doesn't know that language. No one here does, clearly!" Jadol said.

Raven moved back to the corner, hugging herself tight. "Something old is down there, something we shouldn't mess with."

Bereck sighed. "Well, Lucius said we would help. I suppose it's better than going in completely blind."

"I don't think we should go," Raven said.

"I don't think you should either, lass," Jadol said.

———

The group entered the tavern and saw Sunette, Bereck, and Raven at a table. The mage was shaking her head and wringing her hands, and Raven was staring at the wall, not a hint of a smile on her face.

Lucius walked up and sat next to Sunette. "Looks like our dwarf had a lot to say."

She sighed, "He was saying 'old death' in infernal. What it means, I don't know." Lucius sat back and scratched his chin.

"I don't think we should go," Raven said. "Something evil

is down there."

Lucius ran his hands through his hair. "I promised we'd help. We don't have to face whatever it is. Just help the workers get that hole closed, and then they'll be safe. All right?" He looked around at the group and everyone, but Raven nodded. "We're no worse off than before, information wise. Maybe a little more horror than we anticipated, but we're going to supply up and head out. Get your things." He stood and walked up the stairs.

Foster sat next to Raven, but she didn't look at him. "Did you feel something?"

"Death." He put a finger under her chin and moved her to face him. She followed along, but as he touched her, he could feel something about her. Something he'd never felt in anyone. It was almost holy and familiar, like family.

"We'll be careful." He took his finger away, wondering what could make him feel that, and wondered if anyone else felt it.

"I hope so."

An hour later, the group assembled down in the tavern. Mason was no better but a little less green, for sure. Lucius led them to the supply store, and they loaded up on lanterns, flints, and food. The shopkeeper double-checked the group's directions and approved.

"You realize it'll take about three days to get there?" He asked them.

"That's what they tell me." Lucius nodded and closed his pack.

"That's a long time to be underground," Twig said as he shoved his rations into his pack.

"That it is, friend," was all Lucius said. They started the long walk with Twig in front. He wasn't much of a scout, but they weren't sneaking, and he was the only one who could see well in the semi-darkness. They rested when tired and ate while walking. Foster found he liked it when they rested. Lessa would curl up next to him, and they'd fall asleep in each other's arms. He knew he didn't love her, but the connection, the feeling of this wonderful woman, was too good to pass up. She seemed to feel the same way since she made a point of telling him she didn't love him, and that was fine with him. He didn't want anyone to love him right now. Raven never lost that worried look as they walked. The only time she seemed to relax was when she was asleep. Foster tried not to let that worry him.

————————

Late on the third day, they heard the unmistakable sound of picks breaking apart rocks. They turned one last corner and saw a large hole in the wall of the cave. Dozens of dwarfs were working furiously to try and close it.

"Ho there!" A voice called, and they turned. A stout dwarf wearing chainmail was walking towards them.

"Hello!" Lucius called out and walked over to the dwarf.

"What are you doing down this far?"

"Morac said that you needed help with some bothersome elves. We're here to help."

"Help huh? Well, dig in. They'll come soon enough." The dwarf walked away, his chainmail clinking as he moved.

"You heard him, dig in." The group set up some tents by the dwarfs and laid their belongings down. Twig started helping the workers by breaking up rocks, and Lucius talked with the head guard. Foster looked around for something to do when he noticed Sunette crawling into the hole the dwarfs were trying to close.

He ran up to the opening and crawled up next to her. "Sunette, what are you doing?"

Her hands were in the air, and her eyes were closed. "Sunette?"

"Shh," she whispered and walked down the tunnel.

"What are you doing?" He unsheathed his sword and walked with her about one hundred feet down the tunnel, where she knelt and touched the ground. Foster watched as a glowing glyph appeared on the ground and then disappeared.

"A warming. If anything wishes us harm crosses it, we'll hear an alarm." She stood and smiled at him. "Nice, right?"

Foster nodded. "Yeah, nice, now, can we get out of the tunnel?" Admittedly, he was nervous being in here, but Sunette seemed so calm. He was impressed.

"Of course," she said with a smile and walked calmly back to the opening. Foster walked behind her, ever vigilant in the darkness. Sunette reached out for the edge of the wall, and Foster noticed her boots starting to slip. He quickly put an arm around her waist to steady her but decided to just lift her up and set her on the other side of the hole.

"Thank you, Foster." She chuckled and squeezed his hand before walking to Lucius. As he watched her walk away, he noticed her dark hair shined, even in the darkness of the cave. He half expected stars to be shining in it. Not long after that, the workers stopped their construction and took cover by the chain-mailed dwarfs.

"Is it like clockwork when they attack?" Foster asked a nearby dwarf.

"Just about."

It only took five minutes before a shrill noise echoed in the cave. "They come!" Sunette yelled out. All eyes were on the opening as nearly twenty dark elves poured through the hole.

"Blessed Otto," Bereck said.

"Otto, be with us!" Lessa cried out and blessed all who would fight with them. Several dwarfs in the chainmail yelled out and ran for the group of dark elves. Twig joined them with a ferocious yell, and they watched him sink his ax into one of the dark elves. It shrieked with pain and fell to the ground.

"Let loose!" Lucius yelled and went invisible. Foster fired arrows at any dark elf in range while Lessa prayed. Raven started singing, and everyone felt braver while Sunette cast spell after spell.

"Something's not right." He heard Sunette say.

"What's not right?" he asked without turning.

Sunette shook her head. "Give me a moment." She closed her eyes and took a deep breath. When she opened her eyes, she yelled triumphantly. "Ha! There's only ten! It's an illusion!"

Everyone let their eyes adjust, and sure enough, there were only nine dark elves, well, ten, including the dead one that Twig got.

Raven moved faster than Foster thought she could as she faced their enemy. She blocked his blade and stabbed him almost in one move. It was impressive. Foster continued to fire arrows when suddenly he felt the air next to him move, and he quickly ducked to the side. He turned and watched as an arrow sank into Sunette's shoulder, and she fell backwards, her eyes wide in shock.

"Sunette!" Lessa screamed and knelt by her side. Foster saw the caster's eyes close and quickly turned back to the battle and searched for the archer.

He was by the opening and was staring straight at Lessa, readying an arrow. "No!" Foster yelled and quickly shot an arrow. "Please let it hit true, Otto!" he desperately prayed as he watched the arrow zoom through the battle at the archer. The dark elf didn't move, and the arrow sunk deep into his stomach. A second later, Raven was there, shoving her dagger into its neck and kicking its feet from under it so it fell hard to the ground.

Lessa started removing the arrow from her friends' shoulder while Foster protected them the best he could.

"How's she doing?" he yelled back. He heard nothing but the sound of his bow as arrows left it. Once the archer was dead, the battle went quickly in favor of the dwarfs and the group. Mason slit several throats, and Twig continued to cut them in half.

"Bereck!" Foster heard Lessa scream for the paladin and turned. The arrow was out now and covered in Sunette's blood, but there was also a thick residue coating the head of the arrow. Bereck ran to them and threw his sword on the ground as he knelt next to Sunette.

"Sunette honey?" He leaned over her and studied the wound, "Gods, it's poisoned," he whispered.

"Can you do anything?" Lessa asked.

Bereck shook his head. "I don't know." He laid his hands on the wound and prayed. "Blessed Otto, heal this woman. She will die without your aid." Foster saw the wound close a little, but it still looked bad. The skin around the wound was turning black, and he could see black streaks stretching from it. He was glad Sunette was unconscious. He'd hate for her to feel such pain.

Raven picked up the arrow and smelled the bloody tip. "Ugh, it's mind seed. It takes twenty-four hours for it to be lethal."

"Is there an antidote?" Bereck was frantic, his voice was strong, but Foster could see his eyes tearing up.

"There is, but I don't know how to make it."

Lucius walked up, dragging an unconscious dark elf by the hair. "Maybe we can get some answers out of this one." He let go of the white hair, and the elf fell limply to the ground.

Half an hour later, Sunette was in a tent while the unconscious dark elf was tied up nearby, with Twig guarding him. Bereck and Lessa worked to make their friend comfortable while Foster paced back and forth outside the tent, biting his thumbnail as he walked.

"You look nervous, young man." Lucius' voice startled him, and he looked up. Their boss was standing by a loose boulder, his arms crossed across his chest.

"I don't want her to die," he said as he resumed pacing. He'd never been around anyone so hurt before. And there was nothing he could do but pray while his heart pounded out of his chest.

"It's not your fault, boy."

"I know," he snapped at him.

"Do you?"

Foster just looked at him and sighed. "It should have been me."

"Who says?"

"I do!" He'd give anything to change places with her right now.

Lucius pushed away from the boulder and walked over to Foster. "Casters are often the target of archers. She knew that now you do." Foster continued pacing and stared at the dark elf, hate seething through every pore.

"Why are we keeping him alive?"

"To question. He may know something useful," Lucius said calmly.

They watched as Lessa came hurriedly out of the tent. "Wake him." She pointed at their prisoner. Twig bent down and gave the dark elf a few slaps as Foster turned to Lessa.

"How is she?"

He could tell the priestess was pale from effort, and she gave him a quick glance. "Not good." He could see the strain of watching her friend dying to the same thing her father did on Lessa's face and knew she'd stop at nothing to keep Sunette alive. The dark elf slowly woke and blinked his eyes. He looked around, his eyes wide like he was shocked to be there. A strange language spilled from his mouth to whoever would listen. To Foster's surprise, Twig started speaking with him, and after a few exchanges, he turned to the group.

"He says thank you for freeing him from the creature's grasp. He was not in his right mind when he attacked the camp."

"He's lying," Mason said as he walked up.

Foster looked up at Lucius. "What creature?" But he only had a shrug for a response.

The dark elf started chattering quickly to Twig. "He requests that if we are going to kill him, could we give him a sword."

"He doesn't get a sword." Mason ran at the prisoner, dagger in hand. Foster caught him and held fast to the struggling man.

"Wait, Mason, he could still be useful."

"That filthy beast should be slaughtered!" He was shaking with anger.

Lessa laid a hand on her brother's shoulder. "Calm yourself, Mason. Anger won't give us answers."

He rounded angrily at her. "This isn't anger, sister!" He roughly shoved her hand off and stalked away.

"I'll get him." Lucius followed the angry man away from them. Foster was glad Twig could talk to the dark elf and thought of something.

"Can you ask him about the poison on their arrows?"

Twig nodded and did so. "Raven was right. It's mind seed. There's an antidote, but he doesn't have any with him. He said he could get some if we figure out what's happening to his people."

"What's happening? Our friend is dying. That's what's happening!" Foster yelled at the dark elf, but he kept chattering to Twig, ignoring the furious man.

"He said there's a creature taking his people, have been for a while. Their magic can't find the missing ones. But he recognized one of the dead men as one who had disappeared about eight months ago."

"The real evil," Raven whispered.

"Helping dark elves. That's crazy," Foster said. The prisoner kept chattering. They could tell he was desperately trying to reason with them.

"He said if we're going to help, we need to act quickly for her sake," Twig translated.

"Damn," Foster cursed and ran to find Lucius. He found him talking with an enraged Mason behind a boulder. "Lucius, Raven was right. The poison will kill her in twenty-four hours, and the dark elf said he could get us the antidote if we helped him find what's taking his people."

"Gods, okay." Lucius turned back to Mason, his hand gripping the young man's shoulders. "You stay here with Sunette, okay? Keep her comfortable." He moved back to the rest of his group.

"Lucius, I want to go!"

He turned to the young thief who was running after him. "No, Mason, you're too upset. Stay with her, Raven, you too. You can heal a little, right?"

Her eyes went wide at the request. "Yeah, but…"

Lucius pointed at the dark elf. "Untie him. Tell him if he betrays us, we won't hesitate in killing him." Lucius gave the prisoner a look of such hatred that the dark elf leaned away from the sight. Twig delivered the message, and after the dark elf nodded, Twig untied him.

The dark elf stood slowly and said something. "He said he'll need his weapons."

"If we see trouble, he can have them," Lucius said. "Foster, get Bereck, we're leaving." The young man turned and rushed into the tent.

Bereck was holding Sunette's hand to his lips. His eyes were closed in prayer. "Please, Otto, don't let me lose her. Not now," he heard the paladin whisper.

"Bereck, we're going to get the antidote," he said gently.

"I can't leave her, Foster," his voice was quiet and calm.

"Mason and Raven will stay with her. We need you."

Bereck sighed and gave Sunette a gentle kiss on her lips. "We'll return soon, my love, I promise." With one last stroke of her hair, he stood. "This better work," he said as he strode from the tent.

Foster knelt by Sunette and took her hand. "Don't worry, Sunette. You'll be fine." She turned her head, and Foster watched her eyes open slightly.

"Apple picker?" She whispered so softly he could barely hear her.

Foster chuckled, "Yeah, it's me. You'll be fine." Sunette gave a weak smile and closed her eyes. "Otto, be with her, I beg you." Foster prayed before he ran out to join the group. Mason was shaking with rage as Lucius gave the plan. Raven was holding one of Mason's hands in both of hers, trying to calm him down.

"We'll follow the elf to his town and see what we can do. He said he'll be able to get some anti-toxin for Sunette."

One of the dwarfs walked up to the group. "Your help is much appreciated, but I can't believe you're gonna follow that thing in there."

"Me neither," said Mason. Raven hugged him tight against her. He was short enough for his head to fit perfectly under her chin. Foster could tell she was whispering something to him, but not what. It seemed to help a little as he stopped shaking.

"It's our only hope of saving our friend," Lucius said and turned to the rogue. "Raven, go in the tent and comfort our mage the best you can. Mason, stand guard." Mason nodded and slowly peeled himself off Raven before she walked into the tent. She looked angry to be left behind, but she wasn't voicing it like Mason. He pulled out a dagger and gave it a fancy flip in the air. "Let's go," Lucius said, motioning for the dark elf to start walking.

As they walked into the cavern, the dark elf started chattering with Twig. "He said his name is Zodrian if anyone cares."

"Not really," Bereck said. They heard Twig telling Zodrian their names, and he turned and nodded at them. Foster watched him chat with Twig. He seemed anxious but not threatening in the least. Maybe even a little relieved for some reason.

"How old is he Twig?" he asked.

After a few words, the half-orc said, "He's eighty."

Lucius scoffed. "Isn't that kind of young for guard duty down here?"

"He said since the usual guards are missing or dead, they're on their next to last leg."

"How about we stop making friends with the monster and just stay alert," Bereck said without turning.

"His information is useful, Bereck," Lucius said. "We should listen to him." The paladin scoffed and cursed under his breath.

"He's not really a monster," Bereck's angry face turned back to Foster, "he can't help how he was raised."

"Anyone who tries to take Sunette away from me is a monster," he growled, and Foster couldn't help but understand what he meant.

———

They walked for a few hours when they came to an opening in the stone wall. Zodrian turned and spoke to Twig. "He said we're to wait here, and he'll inform the guards of our arrival."

Bereck stiffened. "This better not be a trap," he said acidly.

Zodrian just sighed and walked through the doorway.

"Do you really think this is worth it?" Foster asked.

"I'd crawl through hell if it meant it could save Sunette's life," Bereck said. "This is about as close as it gets." Foster quickly realized he would, too. They waited quietly, ever alert, for twenty minutes before they heard excited chatter from the doorway. They all stood and faced the sound, and soon, five dark elves came through, including Zodrian. An older female walked through first. She was dressed in robes and walked up to Lucius.

"Thank you for bringing Zodrian back," she spoke perfect common.

"We only saved him because he said he could get some anti-toxin for our friend. She was shot with an arrow coated with mind seed," Lucius said as diplomatically as he could.

She waved a dismissive hand. "Of course, we haven't any at the moment, but it does not take long to make."

"How long?" Bereck asked.

"About four hours," she said with a smile. Zodrian bowed before the woman and started speaking in their language to her. "Ah, that is wonderful," she shooed the man off to the side. "Zodrian said that you would be willing to find out what has been taking our people."

Lucius stepped forward. "Actually, if we could get the anti-toxin first, we could be much more prepared for whatever it is."

"True, but like I said, we haven't any now." She clasped her hands in front of her. "You could perhaps look around while it is brewing?" Lessa sighed and shook her head. Foster could feel how stressed she was and leaned over and whispered in her ear.

"Don't worry, this'll work." He put his arm around her waist.

Bereck strode up and faced the woman. "We don't have time to play your little games, elf."

Lucius quickly stepped up and laid a hand on Bereck's shoulder. "Calm down, Paladin. You want to be alive when

Sunette's better, don't you?" Bereck sighed heavily and stalked off. Lucius put an arm around the robed woman, and they walked off towards the entryway. Foster could hear them talking quietly and prayed the half-elf could convince the old woman that they needed the anti-toxin.

He felt Lessa's hand in his and gave it a squeeze. "They're trying to blackmail us into helping them," she said. "I don't like it." She stepped up into his chest and laid her head on his shoulder.

"I know I don't like it either, but it may be our only option." He wrapped his arms around her and kissed her forehead. *Much better*, he thought to himself. "Raven was right. We shouldn't have come here."

"Bit late now."

"Okay all, gather around," Lucius said as he walked over to the group. "Babiena said she could speed up the process of making the anti-toxin if we try to figure out what is taking them. We don't have to nullify the threat. Just figure out what it is."

Bereck still looked highly agitated. "Fine. Let's go."

"Lessa, Foster, Twig? Sound good?"

"I really wish Mason were here. This is really more up his alley," Lessa said, running her hands through her hair.

"I know," Lucius put a hand on her shoulder. "But we're professionals. We should be able to figure it out."

"All right, let's go," Foster said. Twig nodded and started tightening his belt.

The group took a small chamber off the main one and started the long walk down the road that Zodrian had indicated. That was the route where most of the guards had gone missing.

"Did he say how far down the road they disappeared?" Foster asked.

"No. Try not to talk unless it's dire," Lucius whispered. Being underground was disorienting to Foster. It was easy to lose track of time. After walking for what seemed like hours, Lucius held up his hand, and the group stopped. He crept close to the stone wall, and Foster was amazed that he didn't hear the half-elf walking. He was as quiet as a mouse, and all he heard was the dripping of water somewhere. Lucius came back as stealthy as he left. "There are three dark elves around the corner acting as guards," he whispered.

"Well, what are we waiting for?" Bereck unsheathed his sword and walked around the corner. "All right, filth, come and get me!" He yelled as he walked out of sight.

"What is he doing?" Foster unsheathed his sword and started forward, but before he could raise his weapon, Bereck was pulling his sword out of one of the elf's necks. Blood poured from the wound as the paladin kicked the knee of another elf. He went down hard, and Bereck plunged his sword downward into their neck and twisted. A loud crack made Foster jump as Bereck simply punched the last elf, who crumpled to the ground.

Bereck picked the dazed elf by his hair. "See what he knows, Twig." Foster had seen Bereck fight before but had no idea he could be so ruthless. Twig kneeled by the live one who was bleeding from the punch to his cheek. Lessa walked next to Bereck and laid her hand on his arm. He had his own bad cut.

"I'm fine, Alessa," he said as he flinched away from her.

"No, you're not. You just can't feel it yet." She took his arm and healed the deep wound. Foster listened as Twig started speaking to the dark elf. But it didn't do much good. It said one word before a horrible gurgle escaped its lips, and it went limp.

"Well, that's just great," Bereck said as he unceremoniously dropped the dark elf to the ground.

"What did they say?" Lucius asked.

Twig shrugged. "I don't know, he didn't finish."

Bereck sighed in frustration. "Wonderful." He sheathed his sword and started walking down the now unguarded tunnel, his armor clinking loudly.

Lucius quickly caught up to him and stopped him. "Bereck, calm yourself. What good will it do if you get yourself killed?" He shook his head and continued down the tunnel less loudly. After a few more minutes of walking, Bereck suddenly stopped and raised his hands in front of him, like he was feeling for something.

"What is it?" Lucius whispered as he walked up next to him.

"Blessed Otto, protect us," he heard the paladin whisper.

Lessa joined him and gasped. "I've never felt anything, so much evil," Lessa turned to Lucius. "Whatever is down there is more than we can handle, I'm afraid." Foster could hear the fear in her voice. He stepped up next to her, and something made him shiver. The air itself felt heavy, and something primal in him told him to run. He had never felt evil before, but he imagined it felt like that. The birthmark on his left shoulder started tingling, and he rubbed at it.

Lucius sighed. "Unfortunately, we still have to see what it is." He turned to his group. "I'll sneak up and try to see what's going on. If I'm not back in five minutes, you leave and make something up about what it is so you can get that anti-toxin for Sunette. Understood?"

He looked at his group, and they nodded. "We understand Lucius," Bereck said. He nodded his head and started walking quietly down the tunnel.

When he was out of sight, Foster turned to Bereck. "We're not really going to leave him, are we?"

Bereck shook his head. "No, we won't leave him."

"He always says that," Twig leaned against the wall. "We haven't left him yet, so I don't know why he keeps thinking we will."

Lessa was hugging herself, and Foster thought she looked pale. "Are you okay?" She slowly shook her head, and he drew her close. "It will be all right," he whispered as he stroked her hair. Foster thought that Lessa was finally starting to relax when a scream pierced the air.

"Lucius!" Bereck yelled and started running after him, pulling out his sword. Foster, Twig, and Lessa followed suit, running towards their leaders' screams. Two more corners turned, and Foster fought hard not to scream as well, but Lessa couldn't hold back. There was a large dead tree about one hundred feet away. Dark elves and dwarfs were hanging from almost every branch in varying states of decay. Under the tree, they saw a figure, almost seven feet tall, readying a noose. It looked like its skin was stretched over its bones, and it wore a ceremonial skirt of bones and gold. As Foster's eyes roamed the macabre tree, he found Lucius pinned by a wicked-looking short sword through his left shoulder about six feet from the ground. He wasn't moving, and Foster hoped he had just passed out.

"Otto's might will destroy you, vile creature!" Bereck yelled and ran at the figure under the tree. It turned to them, and an evil, deep laugh echoed in the chamber that made Foster shiver. Running footsteps echoed around them, and Foster watched as elven warriors poured from holes dug into the walls. Their eyes were red, and their tattered clothes made Foster think they had been missing for a while.

"We have to kill that thing. Maybe then the elves will come to their senses," Twig said as he ran after Bereck, his axe raised high. Foster pulled out his bow and shot every elf he could see, but they kept coming. He heard Lessa praying furiously over the sounds of running warriors and screams. He dared to take a quick glance at Bereck and Twig. The paladin's holy symbol was glowing brightly, as well as his sword, but the creature hadn't backed down. His sword flashed at the creature, but there was some kind of barrier around it. Bereck screamed as the creature stabbed him in the chest with long, sharp fingers. Foster watched as blood poured from the wounds. Bereck fell to his knees, and the creature took a moment to relish its accomplishment, bringing his fingers to his lips and licking the blood away. That little distraction gave Twig the opportunity to attack, and he sunk his axe into its side, the barrier now gone. It screamed and grabbed Twig by his throat. His eyes went wide as the thing lifted him into the air.

"Twig!" Foster yelled and fired an arrow at it. It sunk into the creature's hand, and with a scream, he let Twig fall to the ground.

"Foster!" He turned just as Lessa ducked away from an

elven blade. She had a dagger and tried to stab it, but the elf was quick and dodged out of the way. Foster drew his sword and held it back from their priestess. She continued praying, and Foster could feel Otto's power fill him. After one slash, the dark elf went down. He turned to Lessa to make sure she was okay when everything seemed to go in slow motion. Lessa's eyes went from thankful to fearful. When he turned, he saw the horrible creature coming for them. It was hellishly tall. Its skin was stretched over a rotted and pitted face. A smell permeated the air, and Lessa gagged as she kept trying to pray. The creature smiled and laughed that awful, deep laugh while Foster lifted his sword and swung as hard as he could. But the creature blocked it with his own sword that materialized out of nowhere.

The resulting vibration made his entire arm go numb, and his grip loosened. Foster watched helplessly as his only defense fell to the ground. That one second of shock gave the creature time to grab Foster by the neck. Lessa screamed as Foster was lifted into the air.

"Pathetic human, your soul will be mine." Its voice was deep and gravelly. Foster felt if he lived through this, he'd have nightmares about that voice for the rest of his life.

It squeezed his throat, cutting off his air. "Otto!" Lessa cried desperately as the dark elves surrounded them. Foster felt his shoulder burning and thought someone had stabbed him. The pain intensified as his vision started getting spotty. He struggled as much as he could, but the last thing he remembered was hearing the creature scream before his vision failed.

————

"Foster, wake up," he heard Lessa's voice and felt hands on his face. "Foster." He opened his eyes and saw Lessa leaning over him, smiling.

"Lessa?" His throat hurt, and Lessa put her hands behind him and helped him sit up. He hissed in pain and looked at his shoulder. There was a hole burned into his shirt. He poked his fingers in it and could see his birthmark. The usually white crescent moon looked burned, and it stung like hell. "What the hell?"

"Do you need more healing?" She looked at the mark, "Did you get burned?"

"No," he shook his head. "That's my birthmark, but it hurts." He abandoned the burn and saw the dark elves walking calmly to and fro. Some were pulling dead bodies off the tree, and three of them were carrying Lucius, Twig, and Bereck back to their priestess. "What's going on?"

"I'm not entirely sure. The creature started screaming, and some light engulfed you both. When I could see again, it was ash on the ground, and you were unconscious." Lessa was so happy that she couldn't stop smiling. "All the elves, the ones that were actually alive anyway, stopped fighting us and started helping me." When the elves laid the three fighters next to Lessa, she immediately began healing them, and one by one, they woke.

An older elf who was directing the others sat next to Foster. "Thank you for freeing us."

"What was that thing?" Foster looked at the huge pile of ash and torn clothes on the ground at his feet and thanked Otto they were alive.

"A Litch. A powerful one. Must have been here a long time, dormant. It enslaved us group by group and sacrificed the ones who wouldn't succumb to his spell. I had hoped our people would have stopped sending scouts to find us. But clearly, they were as lost as we were when it came to dealing with this thing. It isn't gone for good but gone for now. We'll make sure no one comes here again."

Foster heard Bereck groan and saw him sit up. "What happened?" He looked around and gasped as he started going for his sword.

"Bereck no it's okay." Lessa grabbed his hands before he could fully pull it out.

"They're everywhere," he said groggily.

"Heal yourself, Bereck, you'll feel better." He didn't seem to believe her but healed himself anyway. Foster could see the paladin's eyes calm down.

"I guess we're no longer in danger?"

Lessa shook her head. "It's all over now."

Lucius sat up and saw the scene. "I thought I told you all to leave me." He moved his arm around, testing his shoulder.

"Like that'll ever happen," Lessa said while inspecting his wound. It was still bleeding a little, but despite the pain, he chuckled.

"Well, thank you for not listening to me."

"You're welcome." She moved over to Twig, and with a little spell, he opened his eyes.

"We made it?" He looked around cautiously and sat up.

"Seems that way."

He sighed, "Thank the gods."

————

A few hours later, Lucius' group, along with fifty missing dark elves, walked into view of the doorway to their home. The same group of elves were waiting for them.

Babiena clapped her hands together, a smile on her face. "You did it!"

Bereck stepped up to her. "Give us the anti-toxin." He held out his hand.

"Of course!" She dug into her pocket and produced a small vial. "Just pour it down her throat. She will be fine in twenty-four hours."

Bereck took the vial and tucked it safely into his pocket. "If she dies, I'm coming for you." He pointed angrily at her and walked towards the dwarven hole.

Lucius quickly walked up to her and played diplomat. "Please excuse him. The one poisoned is his love. I take it you won't be offended if we left to tend to her. Your people will explain what happened."

"Not at all, again, I thank you." She didn't look the least bit worried about the Paladin's threat.

————

Foster walked further and longer than he had his entire life and was exhausted when they got back to the hole. The dwarfs were still working furiously to close it, and the group knew they'd get it done now. When they finally came through, Lucius reported what happened to the head guard as the rest of the group raced to Sunette.

They found Mason sitting outside the tent, his head in his hands. As they got closer, they could hear him crying. Raven was sitting behind him, her arms wrapped around him as tight as she could. Her face was unreadable as her head rested on his.

Foster sped up and slid next to him. "Mason, what is it?" The young man lifted his head as Bereck and Lessa ran past into the tent.

"She's dying, I can't, she's bleeding, Foster!" was all he could make out.

"I'm not much of a healer," Raven said, her voice tired and scared. "There's only so much I can do, and I've done it. She needs the anti-toxin. Did you get it?"

"Yes, we got it."

Raven sighed in relief and squeezed the thief tighter. "She'll be fine, Mason, I promise." Foster ran into the tent. The sight made him fall to his knees. No wonder Mason was so upset. Sunette was bleeding from her eyes and ears. It seemed she had been that way for a while as her pillow was soaked with blood. Lessa gently lifted her head while Bereck poured the liquid into her mouth.

"Blessed Otto, please let this work," Lessa prayed.

Bereck threw the bottle down and held Sunette's hand. "You're going to be fine, love, I promise," he whispered as he wiped the blood from her face. The two didn't leave her side while Foster stood at the end of her cot and prayed.

———

No one knew what time it was or what day. No one really cared. Bereck lost his valiant fight against sleep hours into the vigil. He slept with his head next to Sunette's as he held her hand. Lessa slept on one side of the tent, trying to give them some alone time without going too far. After a well-deserved nap, Foster walked in and saw the sleeping trio. He knew he'd never get

Bereck to leave, so he sat across from him. Sunette still had little flecks of blood on her cheeks. So, he dipped a clean cloth into the water bucket nearby and wiped them away.

"Come on, Sunette, wake up," he whispered. He set the rag down and took hold of her other hand. She felt warmer than before. That had to be a good sign. "Bereck needs you, Sunette, we all do. Wake up, please." He sat quietly for a while before he realized her fingers were slowly moving. "Sunette?" She breathed in deeply and turned her head. "Bereck, wake up!" Foster reached over and nudged the sleeping paladin, who sat up with a start.

"What?"

"She's waking up."

Bereck opened his eyes fully and touched her face. "Sunette, honey, can you hear me?"

She sighed and licked her lips. "Bereck?" Her voice was soft and strained.

"I'll get some more water." Foster bolted from the tent. When he came back, Bereck was kissing her hand, and happy tears were falling freely down his cheeks. Foster felt like he was intruding on a special moment, but he handed Bereck the cup, who carefully helped Sunette take a drink. Foster walked over to Lessa and gently shook her shoulder. "Lessa, wake up."

She woke slowly as she always did. "Hmm?"

"Sunette's awake."

She gasped and dashed to her side. "Sunette, can you hear me?"

"Yes." Her voice was a little stronger. Lessa gave her a once over and determined the poison was still working its way out of her system, and she had another day or two of rest before she could walk out of here. Foster told everyone the good news, and one by one, they trickled in and said how happy they were that she was going to be okay. Lucius gave her a kiss on the cheek, and Mason just held her hand and smiled at her.

An hour later, Foster was sitting outside the tent, breathing much easier. "I'm glad the anti-toxin is working." He turned as

Raven walked over to him. "Mind seed is nothing to balk at."

He shook his head. "No, it is not."

She sat next to him, her knees pulled up to her chin. "Twig was telling me about the Litch. I knew there was something bad down there, but I didn't think it was that bad."

He turned to Raven. "How did you know there was evil down there?"

"I didn't know there was evil. I knew there was death. There's a difference." Her eyes squinted as she saw his sleeve. "You still hurt?" She reached out and poked a finger through the hole in his sleeve on his shoulder.

"Oh, you know I have no idea. It did hurt, but it's fine now."

Raven looked into the hole. "There's nothing there. What happened to your shirt?" He looked at the birthmark through the hole, and it was back to its usual snow-white color.

"No idea."

Lessa came out of the tent, and he turned, smiling at her. "She's really going to be okay, isn't she?" he asked.

Lessa smiled and nodded. "She'll be perfect." He sighed heavily and put his hands on his knees. The relief he felt made his shoulders relax.

"I was so scared we were going to lose her." Lessa walked next to him and reached down. He took her hand, and she gave it a squeeze.

"We all were."

Foster stood and gave her cheek a kiss. "Otto was really with us today or yesterday," he chuckled. "I don't even know how long we've been down here."

"Well, if you go by when we entered the city, almost two weeks," Raven said, looking like she was still trying to work it all out.

"Two weeks!" Foster huffed, "We're going to go blind when we get back to the surface."

Lessa laughed. "It won't be that bad." She wrapped an arm around his waist.

Foster looked down and gently ran his fingers along her cheek. "Thank you for helping her."

She gave the tips of his fingers a kiss. "It's my job, and I'm glad to do it."

He nodded and leaned close to her face. "You do your job well." Slowly, his lips pressed against hers, and he could feel her smile.

"I'm glad you think so," she whispered, her lips still touching his.

———

The next morning, Foster woke with Lessa sleeping on his chest. He smiled and ran his hand through her sleep-tousled hair.

"Morning, Lessa," he whispered.

She sighed and looked up. "Morning." She leaned up and kissed him. He took the opportunity to tickle her sides, and she squealed as he rolled her over until he was on top.

"Something the matter?" He teased.

"Not at all," she said, laughing. As Foster looked at Lessa, he realized how happy she made him, but something was missing. Maybe as they got to know each other, that missing thing would be revealed. But she was beautiful and funny, and making love to her felt so good. So, he settled into her arms and felt content.

"Foster, have you seen Lessa?" Mason's voice floated into the tent, and the lovers stiffened.

"Uh," Lessa quickly shook her head. "No," he called out.

"Well, when you do, will you tell her Sunette's asking for her."

"Absolutely." They heard him walk off, and Lessa chuckled quietly.

"Guess I should go see to Sunette."

"Good idea." He gave her a quick kiss and rolled off, letting her slip into her robes. "I'll come by to see her in a few minutes."

"All right." She smiled and cupped his cheek. "You are a really wonderful guy, Foster. Has anyone ever told you that?"

He snickered. "Just a few," he teased. She leaned over and

gave him a sweet kiss, and left him alone in the tent.

———————

Half an hour later, Foster walked into Sunette's tent. Bereck was still sitting next to her, telling her how they got the anti-toxin, while Lessa sat in the corner mixing some herbs. The priestess seemed to be smiling at nothing in particular. Sunette turned her head to him as he sat down. She seemed awake and alert but still a little tired.

"Hello, Apple Picker." The corner of her mouth tilted into a little smirk.

He chuckled and sat next to her. "I wondered if I'd ever hear you call me that again. How are you?"

"Better," she stretched a little. "Nothing hurts as much now."

"Okay, Bereck, someone else is here. Go get something to eat," Lessa said in a scolding manner.

"Okay, okay, I'll be back quick." He gave Sunette a kiss on the cheek and left the tent.

"All right, you two, fess up," Sunette teased.

"What?" Foster said.

Sunette chuckled. "I've never seen Lessa so rosy-cheeked and happy before, and you, my Apple Picker," she took his hand and held it. "Look much less sad."

Foster looked up at Lessa, his eyebrows raised. "Is she serious?"

Lessa bit her lip and tried not to smile. "I'm afraid so."

Sunette giggled. "So? Tell me." Lessa knelt by her ear and whispered. Sunette's face broke out in a smile, and she looked at Foster. "I knew you would find happiness again, Apple Picker."

Foster chuckled and tried not to blush. "Well, Lessa sure does make me happy."

"Does Mason know?" Sunette asked, turning back to the priestess.

"No. He almost walked into Foster's tent this morning," Lessa said as she poured hot water on the herbs.

Sunette chuckled. "Oh no! That would have been

awkward."

"Is Mason that protective of you?" Foster knew Mason did have a soft spot when it came to his sister, but he hoped he'd just want her to be happy.

"Well, there was one guy about six months ago," Lessa started. "Mason was a little drunk, but he knows you. Besides, I'm a big girl. I can be with whomever I want." She looked up at Foster and smiled. "And right now, I want to be with you."

He smiled back. "I want to be with you as well, Alessa."

Bereck stepped back in and saw Lessa and Foster smiling at each other. "Uh-oh. I know that look," he said, chuckling as he took his place next to Sunette. "I looked at Sunette that same way when I first saw her."

Both Foster and Lessa startled, "No, no, it's not like that," Lessa said.

"It's not?" He didn't sound convinced at all. He just smiled at Sunette and gave her a sweet, gentle kiss. Even Foster could see the love in it.

Lessa gave Bereck a shove. "Oh, Bereck, shut your mouth."

Sunette laughed while Bereck and Foster helped her sit up. "Yes, ma'am."

"I'm glad you're feeling better, Sunette." Foster gave her foot a little pinch, "I'll leave you to rest."

"Foster?" He turned to Bereck, "Be good to her."

Lessa shoved him again. "Bereck," she scolded him. The paladin laughed as Foster stepped out of the tent to get some breakfast.

———

That night, everyone except Bereck and Sunette were sitting around a fire waiting for dinner when Lessa walked up and sat next to Foster.

"How's dinner coming?" She asked.

"Maybe twenty or so minutes," Twig said, using his dagger to flip some long pieces of meat.

She sighed and laid her head on Foster's shoulder. "So hungry," she said.

He chuckled and put an arm around her. "Me too."

Foster saw Mason do a double take as he looked at them. "Hey, what are you doing?" he said, looking very confused as he pointed at the two of them.

"I'm resting my head on Foster's shoulder. What's it look like?"

He stared at them for a few moments, his eyes narrowing. "Why?"

"You see," Raven cleared her throat. "When a man and a woman really like each other, they kiss and have sex." Everyone laughed except Mason, who looked almost horrified at the notion.

Lessa sighed and sat up. "Mason, please don't make a big deal. I really like Foster."

Mason stared down the large man. "Do you like my sister?"

Foster nodded. "Yes, I do." He turned and kissed Lessa's forehead. "She's something special."

She smiled and kissed his cheek. "Fine, just keep it to a minimum in front of me, okay?" Mason said with a face that showed how much he hated seeing a man show his sister any kind of affection.

Lessa laughed. "We'll try." She kissed Foster full on the lips while everyone laughed.

"Lessa! Jeez!" Mason closed his eyes and shook his head while the others laughed.

———

Five days later, the group found themselves back in the dwarven city, and word had spread fast of what they had done. They got to stay at the inn for free and didn't drop a coin for food or drink. Two days later, the group saw daylight for the first time in almost three weeks. They all stood and basked in the sun for a few minutes. Foster had never felt anything so warm, then Lessa stood next to him and held his hand. He looked down at her and gave her a little kiss.

"What was that for?"

"For being sweet." He tucked some of her red hair behind

her ear. "For being here alive, all of us."

She sighed. "Otto was watching out for us."

"He certainly was," Foster said.

CHAPTER 4
INCUBO

The group traveled for a few months before settling in Blackridge. The first thing Foster and his priestess did was satisfy their bodily needs several times. It was late, and the streets were empty when they finally went to bed. Foster held Lessa close and listened to her fall asleep.

"You are so special to me, Lessa," he whispered. "I can't imagine what my life would be if you weren't in it." He kissed her forehead, closed his eyes, and let himself fall asleep wrapped around his beautiful priestess.

———

Foster woke and felt Lessa pressed against his back, her arms still around him. He smiled and looked down at her hands. "Good morning, Lessa." He turned and ran his hand through her sleep-tousled hair. But it felt odd, sort of sticky and wet, and when he brought his hand up from under the covers, he gasped. "Lessa!" Foster ripped the covers back and swallowed a scream. His beloved priestess was a bloody mess next to him. "Lessa, no!" He cradled her face, but it was hardly recognizable. "Oh, gods, what the hells happened!" Foster fell out of bed as he made his way out of the room. "Lucius, Mason! Help!" He screamed and wrenched open the door, but instead of the hallway, he saw the large tree outside of Raventree's castle, but it was dead. There were no ravens sitting on the branches like usual, but there were people hanging limply by their necks. Their stiff bodies swayed lightly in the breeze. "By the gods, what is going on?" he whispered to no one.

Slowly, he walked up to the nearest body. It was small and skinny, just a child. There was no noise save the creaking of the tree under its macabre weight. The little body had long brown hair and skinny legs, but the closer he got, the wider his eyes got. "Oh no, no, please, Otto, no." Foster stopped and ignored the pain he felt as he fell to his knees. It was Saphira. "Saphy?" He whimpered as he watched her blue, bloated body hang from the tree. "No, no, no." Tears streamed down his cheeks as he looked at the other bodies on the tree. Christopher was hanging by his own clerical robes, and his father, William, was hung upside down and looked like the birds had eaten at his stomach.

He frantically looked for his mother among the other dead bodies but couldn't find her. He slowly got up, thinking he would fall with every movement, when he heard loud sobbing. There was a woman under the tree. He hadn't noticed her earlier. She was wearing long, torn black robes, and Foster had never heard such a guttural sound of mourning before. "Miss?" He walked over and laid a hand on her back. "Miss, what happened?" He could barely speak, the images of his family dead wanted to paralyze him, but he couldn't stop, not yet. "Miss?" The woman sat up, and Foster gasped, "Mom?" She didn't acknowledge him and continued to wail at the bodies hanging above their heads. Her blonde hair was all white and in tangles, and her eyes were bloodshot from crying. "Mom!"

He shook her hard, and she finally looked up at him. "Foster?"

"Mom, what's going on?"

She wailed and wrapped her arms around him. "Foster, my boy! You're home!"

"Mom, what happened? I don't understand." His mother rocked side to side with him still in her arms as she began softly singing a song she used to sing to him when he was little. "Mom?" He managed to peel her away and hold her still, her eyes were closed, and she kept singing softly. "Mom, what happened!" Her eyes flew open, and Foster gasped as a deep, raspy voice spilled from his sweet mother's lips.

"Otto is dead, my son." He quickly got to his feet and backed away, but she crawled after him, "Foster, my only son, please don't leave me!"

"Who are you?" he screamed. His feet got tangled in something, and he fell backwards on his elbows. He wanted to keep moving, but fear held him still as a creature crawled up his torso and stopped above his face. It looked like a man with long, greasy hair, but his face was covered with a split-colored mask. The left side was white, the other black, and there was a horrible, cracked mouth that seemed to let out a raspy chuckle.

"Much better," it seemed to say without moving. Its hand laid on Foster's face, and he sighed, "So much fear." The voice sounded delighted as the creature lay along Foster's chest. "A lifetime's worth." Foster trembled as this creature got to his feet. He watched as chains slowly sprouted from its body and snaked their way around Foster. The longer they touched his skin, the more they burned, and he began screaming. The most awful laughing sound filled the air, and Foster wished he could cover his ears, but it just got louder and louder. "You and your children and your children's children shall be my nourishment. All who share your blood will be bound to me!"

"No!"

"Foster, wake up!" His eyes flew open, and he saw Lessa hovering over him. She looked terrified. "Foster!" She quickly hugged him as his arms flew around her.

"Lessa, my gods!" He hugged her tight, thankful she was okay. "I dreamed you were dead. Everyone was dead," he whispered, trying to hold back the tears as he kissed her head. She sat back, and Foster saw a familiar face sitting on the edge of the bed. "Xavier?" Ada's eldest brother leaned forward and seemed to be studying Foster. He looked extremely worried.

"Foster, are you okay? I could hear you screaming from my room."

He quickly sat up and composed himself. "Um, I just had a nightmare, I guess. What are you doing here?"

"I'm performing in the tavern downstairs," he sighed and visibly relaxed a bit. "I thought someone was being murdered."

Lessa took Foster's hand and kissed it. "I'm glad you two

seem to know each other. I was a little angry that some stranger just forced his way into our room."

Xavier chuckled, "I apologize, Miss, but I thought someone was in trouble. I am rather shocked to find Foster here, though."

Foster turned and put his feet on the floor as Lessa gasped. "Good gods, what is that?" The bed moved, and when Foster turned, he saw the huge red welts along his arm. "No, it can't be." He touched them and gasped as pain erupted along his arm. "It was just a dream."

Xavier moved closer and studied the welts. "What the hell did you dream, Foster?" Lessa laid her hand on his arm. He hissed quietly as she prayed for him to be healed.

When the pain lessened, he breathed a little easier. "Lessa was dead. She was just eviscerated." She reached up and cupped his cheek as he kept talking, "Then I was home. Everyone was dead, even little Saphy. They were hanging on the tree. It looked like they had been dead for a while. Then I saw my mother."

"Oh gods, you saw Lily dead?" Xavier sounded just as upset as he was. It was understandable. He had grown up with Foster and knew his family well.

"No, she wasn't dead. She said Otto was dead. But then, it wasn't her that said it."

Lessa ran her hand through his hair. "Of course not. She would never say that."

Foster shook his head. "There was a creature there, he had a mask, and he said that my blood was his now. He said that we would be his nourishment. I don't know what that means."

Xavier sat back. "That's intense."

He gave an involuntary shiver. "It felt so real, I'm almost afraid to sleep tonight."

Lessa hugged him. "It was just a dream, you'll be fine."

"I know, but it was so real."

Xavier got to his feet. "Why don't I give you some time? I'll see you downstairs later?"

Foster nodded. "Yeah, that would be great, Xavier, thanks." When the door closed behind him, Lessa pulled Foster into a kiss.

"I've never heard you like that before. I thought you were dying."

He could hear the tears in her voice and hugged her tightly. "It felt like I was." His stomach complained loudly, and she chuckled.

"Let's get some food in you, I think you had a hard night."

He nodded and kissed her cheek. "Good idea."

They got dressed and made their way downstairs. Lucius and Sunette were already there, along with Xavier, who was waiting by the bar. "Xavier, come join us," Foster called out. He nodded and joined them as they sat at the table.

Lucius smiled. "Who's your friend Foster?" But before he could answer, Sunette quickly got up from her chair and held Foster's face.

"What has happened?" She sounded so worried.

He stared into her eyes as they seemed to study him. "What do you mean?" She started casting spells around him, her eyes wide and excited the entire time.

"Sunette, what is it?" Lucius sat forward as she kept studying the fighter. She said a few words in her native tongue before she kissed his forehead. He gasped, her lips were warm on his brow, and he could smell her floral perfume.

"Dear Foster, I fear you are marked," her voice was quiet and scared.

"Marked?"

"What happened to you last night," she ran her hand through his hair, still studying him. "Did you go anywhere?"

He shook his head and looked over at Lessa. "No, I didn't do anything. We stayed in all night."

"You had that nightmare," Xavier said.

"Nightmare?" She looked at the half-elf, who nodded. "Tell me." Foster sighed and recanted his tale again. When he was done, he saw tears in the mage's eyes. Her delicate hand was covering her lips in horror. "Oh, Foster, it can't be."

"What? What is it?" He felt Lessa grab his hand, and he

squeezed it.

Sunette sighed. "Incubo."

Twig and Raven joined them at the table. "Incubo? Don't tell me someone's marked," Raven said. He could tell whatever this was, had to be bad if it made Raven sound nervous.

"Are you sure?" Xavier asked. Sunette nodded while the others looked at each other, confused.

"Oh shit." Raven looked over at Foster. Her eyes were full of worry.

"What's Incubo?" Lessa asked.

"Nightmare," Sunette said. "You have been marked my Apple Picker by a dark entity. He will plague you until your dying day, feeding off your fear and the fear of your children. We need to get rid of it immediately."

Lucius sat straight, looking between Sunette and Foster. "How the hell did it get him?"

Sunette shrugged. "It must have been drawn to him for some reason," She looked over at their boss. "But it will stop with us."

Foster sighed and shook his head. This was insane. "How do we get rid of it?"

Sunette began pacing, holding her chin in her fingers while she thought. "I've heard of an artifact, an urn that could help, but I don't know where it is."

"I do," Xavier said.

Sunette quickly turned to the half-elf. "Do you know of what I speak?"

He nodded. "Yes, I do. I also know where it is."

Foster's eyes widened. "Well, what is it? What do I have to do?"

Sunette sighed. "It's not a pleasant thing, I'm afraid. It's said that if you start a fire with the oil you find in its resting place and breathe in the fumes, the Incubo will leave your body."

"Well, that doesn't sound too hard. Where is it?" Foster asked.

"That's the hard part," Xavier said. "It's said the last

resting place of the urn is in the elven woods."

Lucius sighed and rested his hands behind his head. "That is the hard part," he agreed.

Foster sat back and thought about what that meant. "Sunette, are you sure that's what my dream was?"

She nodded, still studying him. "There is a dark aura around you, stitched into your soul." Her fingers wavered over his body like she could feel the curse.

Raven reached out and touched his arm. "Oh shit, she's right." Foster could feel something invisible trying to get away from Raven's touch. Something deep inside him that he didn't even know was there. He laid his hand on hers and met her eyes, but she just stared at his hand, refusing to meet his gaze.

"I guess I don't have a choice," he took his hand off Raven's. "I have to try." She sat back and crossed her arms, looking worried.

"Don't worry," Xavier patted his back, "I'll go with you."

Foster gave him a small smile. "Thanks, Xavier."

"You're not going anywhere without us, Apple Picker." Sunette crossed her arms on her stomach. He could see that stubborn side of hers glaring at him. He never thought he'd go somewhere as dangerous as the Elven woods, and the thought of Sunette in them with him, he couldn't let her do that.

"I can't ask you to come with me."

"No, you can't. That's why we're telling you we're going. Right Lucius?"

She turned, and they all looked at their boss as he sighed and scratched his chin. "No one is being *made* to go. If they want to, I'm not going to stop them. But it would be the most dangerous thing we've ever done. Few go into those woods and come back alive."

Everyone was quiet for a moment before Lessa spoke up. "Otto will be with us. No matter how many trees hide the stars above our heads, He will still see us."

Lucius nodded and sat back. "Okay, I guess we'll ask the others. Foster, just know if you were any less a person, I'd leave you to your nightmares, and it has nothing to do with who your family is. You've proven yourself to be a fierce fighter and friend, and I know the world would be remiss if you were disabled by this entity."

"Thank you, Lucius, I appreciate it."

———

While Lucius spoke to the rest of the group upstairs, Foster and Xavier sat at a table with their drinks. Foster always got along with Xavier when they were children, but he didn't know how the half-elf viewed him after his failed proposal to his sister.

"So, how's your family?" Foster asked, staring into his mug of warm cider.

"Good. Lily's living in the woods now." Lily was the youngest of them, named after Foster's mother as thanks for a safe delivery.

Foster chuckled. "That girl never could stay away from the wild."

"No, she couldn't. Macon sees her most, but sometimes he comes back and says even he couldn't track her."

Foster clicked her tongue. "She could make a lot of money for some Lord with skills like that."

"True, but I doubt she'd do it. She loves the forest too much." Foster saw Xavier peek at him through the corner of his eye. "Ada's in Ardenry now."

At the mention of her name, he gave a little twitch. "She always knew she'd be there," he said quietly.

Xavier sighed. "I always thought it was a mistake of her to say no to you, Foster, but it's her life."

Foster was quiet for a moment. "True."

"Ada never told us why she said no."

Foster shifted in his chair, trying not to think back on that day too hard. "She said that there was another love for me. That she wasn't supposed to be my wife."

Xavier whistled. "Well, that sounds like something she'd say. As hard as it was to hear, I'm sure everything will work out in the end." They sat quietly for a few moments before

Xavier cleared his throat. "But I see you have moved on, Lessa's gorgeous," he said appreciatively.

Foster chuckled. "She is, she's wonderful." He noticed Raven giving him glances, so he motioned for her to come over. She slid off her stool and joined them, not meeting his eyes. "Raven, Xavier."

She nodded and sat down next to Foster. "Pleasure."

"Wanna tell me why you look nervous?" He was only half kidding, she did look nervous, but he figured it was because of where they had to go.

Her eyes narrowed, and she shook her head. "I'm not nervous."

"No?" Xavier asked, his brows lifted like he didn't believe her.

She gave a little annoyed growl and rolled her eyes. "It's just...the last time I felt an Incubo in someone, it didn't end well."

"I see," Foster nodded. "How *can* you feel it?"

She shrugged her shoulders. "I don't know. I just know it can tell when something bad is around. Not like how a paladin can, but whatever it is, it doesn't like evil."

Xavier chuckled. "Well, who does?"

"Kind of how you knew there was death under Ral Hava?" She nodded. Raven clearly had more power than she knew, but those could often be the hardest things to figure out. The ones you didn't understand. "What can you tell me about this thing?"

She leaned forward, laying her head in her hands. "The creature, the Incubo, used to be human. It's said that in life, he... built the temple of The Shackled One, and to keep his secrets hidden, he had the man burned alive, along with his family. He placed their ashes in a silver urn, but the ashes turned to a kind of oil for some reason. That's the oil we have to burn. Sunette was right. It's said that if you light the oil on fire and breathe in the fumes, the Incubo will be grateful for the reunion with its human family and leave the victim and all those of his blood alone. I don't know why it works. That's just the story."

Foster laid a hand on her shoulder. "I'm glad you said

you'd come along. I'm going to need all the help I can get." He licked his lips, "What happened to the other person who had this thing in them?"

Raven sniffed and looked down at her drink. "They died in their sleep." Foster's heart began to race when he saw his group coming down the stairs.

Bereck reached him first and gave his back a hearty pat. "Don't worry, Foster. We're going to help any way we can."

"Thanks, I appreciate it." They all sat down, Lessa gave him a little kiss and held his hand.

"So, I guess we have a new job, cleansing our fighter," Lucius said. "His friend Xavier is joining us, so what do you bring to the table?" He motioned to the young man.

Xavier took a big breath and sat back. "Well, my father trained me in the elven woods, I can find my way around. I can also shoot a bow pretty well."

"He's also got a mean lute," Foster said with a little smile.

"Another bard?" Twig sat across from Raven. "You two will have to duel it out for us." He leaned close to her and ran the back of his finger down her cheek.

"Oh, no one's been able to beat me in a bard duel," she teased and gave Xavier a wink.

"Well, I don't know how useful that will be in the woods," Xavier chuckled. "But I'll help any way I can." Foster looked over at Mason. He was staring into his mug, looking apprehensive.

"Mason?"

He quickly looked up. "Hmm?"

"You don't have to come."

Mason shook his head. "No, I won't abandon you now." Foster could see the rogue shaking a little and felt horrible. The Elven woods were somewhere no one without a death wish went.

"Thank you for that."

Lessa leaned over and laid a hand on her brother's shoulder. "Otto will be us with Mason." Foster heard her whisper to him.

"I think we're all in on this, so I have an idea," Sunette spoke up. "I think it would be safest for us if we looked like we belonged."

"Belonged?" Bereck's eyebrows rose as he looked at his love.

"Yes, like Elves," she said with a smile.

"So, how are we going to pull that off?" Lucius asked. Foster thought he sounded a bit irritated.

Sunette tapped the bag her spell book was in. "A spell, it'll change our features, so we'll look like Elves. It only lasts about sixteen hours, so we'll have to stop and 're-apply,' so to speak, but it should work."

Lucius sighed and sat back. "If you insist, Mistress Mage." Yeah, he was irritated.

Everyone agreed, and Sunette nodded. "Wonderful, I just need to pop out to the shop for a few things. We should be ready to go before nightfall."

"Good, the sooner the better," Lucius turned to Xavier. "Any idea where in the woods this urn is?"

Xavier cleared his throat. "My father used to say that his village's treasure room held a silver urn that no one could open. The mages said it was evil, and it was basically left alone. It's probably the one we're searching for."

"Your father?" Lucius crossed his arms across his chest as he stared at Xavier.

"Yes, he's an Elf. He used to tell us all about the woods and what his village looked like. I could probably get us around without much trouble."

"You actually know your father?" Lucius sounded like he couldn't believe what Xavier had just said. It's true that the elf half of most pairings didn't know their offsprings. Most were of the male persuasion, and their children were created in less-than-ideal situations. It seemed Lucius was one such child. Foster felt bad he hadn't asked his boss much about his upbringing.

"Yes, Foster's mother actually married my parents. It's how we know each other." He smiled at Foster and gave his foot a little kick. "We practically grew up together."

Lucius sighed. "I see. Well, we thank you for your

knowledge of the woods."

"It's no problem, I assure you," he said, clearly unaware of how displeased Lucius seemed. The group looked between the half-elves, and when it was clear the exchange was over, Sunette and Bereck got to their feet.

"We shall be back." She laid a hand on Foster's shoulder. "Don't worry, Apple Picker," she whispered. "We'll take care of you."

He reached up and gave her hand a squeeze. "That means a lot." He turned and watched them leave the tavern. "I hope she finds what she needs."

"I don't doubt she will." Lucius got up from the table and stalked to the bar.

"What's wrong with him?" Mason asked quietly.

Xavier sniffed, finally realizing the other man's irritation. "Most don't like to hear that an elf could genuinely love their children. I've had it happen before."

"Damn." Raven got up and sat next to Lucius at the bar. "Not looking forward to being more elfy?" Her tone was half kidding, half concerned.

"Nope. Maybe I don't have to do the spell." He took a long drink of his new ale.

"Maybe. I don't know how Elves feel about Half-elves. You could see if Sunette could turn you into a Half-orc like Twig. He'll get in fine, and you'll be even more handsome." She pinched his cheek, and he sputtered, laughing.

"I think I'm handsome enough without being green, thank you." He wiped his mouth of the spilled ale. "What about you, bard? Do you get along with your parents?"

"I did." She knew he'd understand what that meant.

He nodded. "I did not. I suppose that's why I like traveling so much. It keeps me busy and away from them."

"Are you worried your father's going to be in the woods?"

Lucius shrugged. "Even if he was, he wouldn't know me from a hole in the ground. Which is a good thing. The last thing we need is someone recognizing us in that place."

"True." She turned around, leaning on the bar. "Last chance to be green."

He chuckled and gave her cheek a kiss. "I'll leave the green to Twig, thank you." He walked back to the table, and Raven hoped he was in better spirits. The last thing they needed was a boss who wasn't his best.

————

Foster spent the day sipping warm cider and catching up with Xavier. When Sunette came back, he felt his heart begin to race.

"I got everything we'll need."

He nodded and got to his feet. "I guess we should get ready then."

Sunette reached out and took his hand. "This will work, I promise." She turned, and he watched her walk up the stairs, Bereck close behind. He wondered if the paladin truly knew what a wonderful woman he had by his side.

The group left the Inn as the sun went down. "Is this wise? Shouldn't we wait till the sun is up?" Mason asked as they stopped at the edge of the woods.

"Don't worry, Mason, our disguises will allow us to see as an Elf does. We will be fine." They stepped into the woods, and when the village was no longer visible, Sunette stopped them. "All right, I have clothes for us all. Elves don't really dress like this. It'll help with the illusion," she said as she dug through her big holding bag and handed everyone some clothes. The men quickly changed while the women expertly swapped clothing without revealing a bit of skin. It was impressive. When they were done, they were all dressed in dark clothing that didn't cover them completely.

"I feel naked," Bereck complained, pulling on the bottom of his shirt that didn't quite reach his navel.

"You won't as an Elf. Now come here, my love." Bereck stood close, and she laid a leaf on his forehead. They listened as magical words spilled from her lips.

The paladin began breathing hard. "I feel dizzy."

"Just hold on, Bereck, it's almost over," Lessa said. Suddenly, the six-foot human shrank a few inches, his ears became pointy, and his eyes became foreign to them.

Sunette took the leaf off his forehead and smiled at her work. "There. How do you feel, my love?"

His hands touched his torso, then moved to his ears. "Amazing, you do good work, love."

She smiled and held up the leaf. "Okay, who's next?"

It took almost half an hour before the whole group was turned into elves, except Lucius and Twig. Lucius declined, saying his visage should be enough to get him through. Twig, being a half-orc, wouldn't have an issue with the Elves, but Foster noticed how much more attention he was paying to Raven. Her disguise even changed her hair. It was long, straight, and much darker. He was running his fingers through it, talking softly to her. He couldn't help but see the smile on her face as Twig spoke to her. If he didn't know any better, he'd think they were in love. Everyone looked around and realized they could see just fine in such low light.

Foster smiled, "I could get used to this."

Lessa smiled a new smile and hugged him. "You're so small now," she teased.

Foster laughed and twirled her around. "Not everywhere," he whispered in her ear.

She laughed loudly and playfully slapped his shoulder. "Foster, really! You speak such words to a priestess?"

"You're not a priestess right now, Lessa. Remember that," Sunette said.

"Right, that's going to take some getting used to." They hid their clothes in the bushes and started for the Elven village.

"How long will it take to get there, Xavier?" Foster asked.

"A day and a half, two days at most." Two days, Foster thought, he wondered if he could stay up that long.

The group only walked for a few hours that first night, and Foster was the first to take a watch. He didn't feel like sleeping anyway. He had been to the woods a lot as a kid, visiting Xavier's family, but never this far in. The small fire crackled, and his ears heard the normal sounds of a forest. Leaves rustling in the wind, nocturnal animals skittering on the forest floor, and owls hooting.

"Foster?" He turned and saw Sunette sitting up, looking at him. Her Elven visage suited her, she looked younger, but he could still see the wisdom she held in her eyes.

"Can't sleep?"

She slowly brought her knees under her chin. "Not really. I keep wondering about something."

"What?" She lifted her hands, and Foster's eyes widened. They were covered in blood.

"What happened, Foster?" He could hear the tears in her voice and quickly crawled over to her. "What happened, Foster!"

She started crying as he took her hands in his. "Blessed Otto," he whispered and searched her hands for wounds. The blood was still warm as his fingers moved up to her face. "I don't see anything wrong, Sunette, what hurts?"

"My heart!" She screamed and flung herself over Bereck's body.

"No, no, this is a dream. It has to be," he said to himself. Sunette laid Bereck in her lap, and he saw a huge hole in the man's chest.

"It's gone, Foster, my heart is gone!" She screamed and rocked the paladin back and forth.

"Wake up, please, gods, wake up!" He tried pinching himself but didn't feel anything.

————

Lucius was first on duty. Being in the woods unnerved him, and he didn't think he'd sleep well anyway. He was letting the sounds of the forest speak to him when Foster began thrashing around in his sleep.

"Gods." He moved over and shook Foster's shoulders. "Foster, wake up!" But the big man kept thrashing and didn't show any sign of waking. Lessa was the next to wake up, she was sleeping next to Foster, and his arm had hit her on the head.

When she turned over, she saw his hands were covered in

blood. "Blessed Otto, what happened?"

"I don't know. I don't see any wounds on him." Foster was breathing erratically, and Lessa put her fingers against his pulse.

"His heart is racing. He can't take much more." Lessa sat up and straddled Foster's legs. "Forgive me, sweetheart," she whispered and slapped his face as hard as she could. He froze for a moment, then sat up, his eyes wide with fear. "Foster!" Lessa wrapped her arms around him. She could feel his heart racing in his chest.

"Sunette!" He twisted from underneath Lessa, who was dumped rather awkwardly onto the ground. "Sunette!" The mage was awakened by her name and sat up just as Foster almost tackled her back to the ground.

"Foster, what are you doing?"

He took her hands and held them up to his face. "A dream, thank gods," he whispered.

Slowly, she sat up and was able to hold his face. "It was all a dream, Foster. Whatever it was didn't happen." He breathed in and looked over at Bereck. The man was still snoring through the commotion.

"I dreamed—"

"Shh, shh, it's okay, Foster, you don't have to say it. We know it was bad."

He took a deep breath and slowly moved off her. "I'm sorry I woke you," he said quietly and looked down at his blood-covered hands, her face now bearing the bloody prints. "Oh no, I'm sorry."

"Don't worry about it." She cast a spell, and all the blood disappeared. "All gone now."

Lessa laid her hands on his shoulders, and he leaned back against her. "I didn't want to go to sleep. I didn't think I had." Lessa ran her fingers through his hair over and over until he calmed down.

"We'll get this thing out of you, I promise," she whispered against his temple. Lessa didn't move, and soon Foster was asleep again. *Blessed Otto, please help us.* She prayed silently until the sun rose.

———————

The next day, Foster, Lessa, and Lucius were exhausted. Foster tossed and turned all night while the other two couldn't go back to sleep. Sunette offered to help with the watch the next night, but none accepted. They walked all day, and it was late afternoon when Xavier suddenly held up a hand.

"Elves," he whispered and took the lead. Everyone stiffened and hoped Xavier could get them through the first hurdle. A few minutes later, they saw them, wild and angry looking, as they walked up to the group. Their skin went from pale to tan, and some had their hair up in fancy braids.

"Where was your patrol?" The one in front asked in elvish. Luckily, Foster knew elvish, so he didn't feel so useless. Xavier, of course, did as well and answered.

"To the northwest, found a few wolves but nothing of note." One of the elves pushed their way to the front of the group and stopped in front of Xavier.

"Ralan?" Foster and Xavier's eyes widened at the mention of the elf's name. "What do you think you're doing here? Seize him!" He yelled out. The elves were quick and pulled Xavier away from the group, who stood stunned. Xavier didn't resist, but Foster could see how shocked he was at being tied up.

"Did you not realize who you had with you?" the arresting elf asked.

Foster shook his head. "No?" Xavier started speaking in some odd language that made everyone turn and stare at him in disbelief. "He joined us a day ago, is he wanted?"

Sunette suddenly laid a hand on Foster's arm. "We are glad to be of service," she said in elvish.

"You must be young then. Everyone knows to keep an eye out for this criminal. You might as well follow us back. I'm sure the chief will reward you for bringing such a dangerous criminal to justice. Even if you didn't realize it." The elf sounded annoyed, and Foster hoped he wouldn't ask too many questions as they turned and started back for the village.

Foster nodded and motioned to his friends. "Let's go."

They walked quietly for a few miles before Lucius spoke up. "Pardon me, but what has this man done that was so dangerous?" he asked in elvish. That surprised Foster, most who hated their elven heritage didn't bother learning the language.

Without turning, the one in front spoke. "You *are* young," he shook his head. "This is Ralan. He was famous for spreading propaganda about how we are the same as the others on this continent. That we could all live in peace," he said scathingly. Lucius opened his mouth, but Foster put a hand up and stopped him. Lucius rolled his eyes and moved to the back of the group.

"He should have known better," Foster said.

"The chief should have killed him when he had the chance. He won't be so lucky this time." Xavier didn't struggle, he never looked back as they walked, and Foster hoped he had a plan of some sort. He looked around and saw that Sunette and Bereck were missing. He motioned at Lucius, who pointed to his face, and Foster realized that their disguises were almost gone. A hand grabbed his, and Sunette pulled him away slowly towards some bushes.

"I can't do this in front of them. Luckily, it doesn't take as long as the first time." She put the leaf on his head again and began speaking.

"What did Xavier say earlier?"

"That we should let them take him. They'll lead us to the village, and we can get him out later."

"His disguise will be gone soon."

She shook her head and put the leaf away. "I know, but maybe their blind hatred of this Ralan will keep them from noticing too much."

"Ralan is his father. He already looks a little like him."

She sighed and shook her head. "Then we'll just have to trust that they won't look too closely." They emerged from the bushes and found one of the other elves standing over them.

"What are you doing?" Foster was frozen, he had no idea

what to say, but Sunette got in the man's face.

"I wanted a moment with my lover. Is that a problem?" Foster held in the chuckles rather well as he stood behind her and wrapped his arms around her waist.

The elf shrugged and studied them. "No problem, but are you always so undisciplined that you leave those you are meant to guard to dally in the bushes?"

"Wouldn't you be with someone like her?" Foster said and nuzzled her neck.

The elf shook his head. "You will get killed that way, I guarantee it." The elf turned and started walking back towards the group. Foster and Sunette breathed a sigh of relief, but as they stepped from the bush, the elf turned. "We've been getting reports of humans pretending to be elves walking around in our woods. Haven't run into any, have you?"

"A few, they've been dealt with," Foster said. The elf stepped so close to Foster that he could smell the dirt and herbs on the man's skin.

"Well, you wouldn't mind if you and your lover prove it, would you?" Foster stepped up even closer. He wasn't used to being so small and missed how his size could intimidate smaller people.

"Just what exactly do you expect us to do?"

"Give her a kiss," he motioned over to Sunette with a nod of his head. "That's not a problem, is it?" Before Foster could even look at Bereck or Lessa, he felt Sunette grab his hand and turn him around.

"Not at all," she said and pressed her lips on his. His hands quickly found her waist and slid them around her back. He held her close as she slipped her tongue in his mouth. The moan that came from his throat was unexpected. She tasted of spices and honey, and Foster found himself kissing her deeper than he'd ever kissed a woman. His hands moved up and buried themselves in her hair. He felt the back of his shirt bunch in her hands. Sunette suddenly broke away from his lips and stared into his eyes. He swore he could see her pulse at her neck racing.

Foster started leaning in for another kiss when she turned her attention to the elf behind them.

"Satisfied?" Foster settled for the crook of her neck. He wondered if it was these new elven senses that made her smell so good, all he wanted to do was breathe her in. She smelled of herbs and roses, and he let himself get lost in the sensation for just a moment. The Elf finally walked away, and Foster stood straight. Sunette turned and put a hand on his cheek. "Come on, let's catch up."

"Yeah." He was still a little breathless, but they hurried back to the group, their fingers laced together. When they caught up, Bereck turned and glared at Foster. He knew if they weren't surrounded by elves, the man would punch him in the face. He glanced over at Lessa, who was just walking next to her brother. She didn't seem to see what happened, but Foster knew he'd have to tell her.

———

They reached the village as the sun was starting to set. One of the elves that had tied Xavier turned to the group.

"If you'll come with us, we'll take this traitor to the Chief. I know he'll want to reward you." The group followed him up some wooden stairs, high into the trees, to a large house. Foster tried hard to keep his shock in check, he'd never seen such a thing, and it really was a marvel to behold. Houses were built into the trees themselves, and bridges went from one house to the other. It was a really smart way to live, he thought. They walked into a large, warm tree house and saw an ancient elf sitting on a throne of twisted roots at the end of the room. Foster had never seen such an old elf. He thought they didn't age after a certain amount of time, but clearly, they just aged incredibly slowly. His gray skin was wrinkly, and his fingers were bony.

"Chief, we have captured the rogue elf Ralan." The old elf slowly opened his eyes and looked over the captive young man. Xavier kept his head down, and Foster hoped this would work.

"Come here," the old elf said. Slowly and with a great deal of trouble, Xavier walked up to the chair. "Closer, closer!" He stopped barely an inch away from the chief, who reached out and grabbed his chin and forced his face back and forth, studying him. "Hmm, my eyes aren't what they used to be, but I believe you have finally captured my traitorous son." Foster's eyes widened in shock. The chief was Xavier's grandfather. Ralan never talked about his elven family, but Foster didn't remember anyone asking either. "Lock him up. I will decide what to do with him later," he said lazily as he sat back in his chair. "You all have done well and will be rewarded. A feast for the heroes on his auspicious night," he called out and hit his fist on his leg.

A younger elf next to him bowed. "It shall be done!" and ran from the room. Everyone bowed to the chief as they dragged Xavier out of the room.

"Now go, see your loved ones, and be glad you made it home." He rested his chin in his hand and closed his eyes. Slowly, the group made their way out onto the bridge that led to other houses. Down below, they could see elves scurrying around, carrying trays of food, and putting wood in a big pile for a bonfire. One of the elves who escorted them to the village came out of the house and clapped Foster on the shoulder.

"Better clean up. It's going to be one hell of a party," he said happily as the rest of his group filed away.

Foster and Mason regained their composure and gripped the bridge supports. "Okay, now what?" the young man asked.

"First, we need to find what we came for." Lucius crossed his arms. He looked incredibly uncomfortable, his eyes darting back and forth, keeping an eye on those around them.

"We can't leave Xavier alone. One of us needs to stay with him," Foster said, looking around at his friends. No one spoke up, and Foster started getting nervous. "Please."

Lucius sighed and ran his hand through his hair. "Okay, I'll stay with him."

Foster gave Lucius's arm a squeeze. "Thank you. We'll try to be quick." Their boss walked away, mumbling as he tried to catch up with the captured half-elf. Foster turned back to Sunette, "Do you think you can find it?"

She nodded. "Something so magical shouldn't be hard to find. I just need a little privacy."

Bereck quickly took her hand. "I can help with that," and started pulling her down the stairs.

The irritation in his voice was obvious to everyone. "What's wrong with him?" Mason asked.

Foster cleared his throat and started following them down. "Come on, we don't want to get separated." He heard his friends' feet behind him but made sure to give Bereck some space.

Sunette found a quiet place behind a building and began casting while the group waited around in front. They watched as Xavier was untied but put in a wooden cage in the middle of the village. He quickly sat down and hid his face so no one else could see he wasn't the man they thought he was. Lucius was sitting next to the cage, his arms crossed across his chest, and they could see the scowl on his face from across the village.

Bereck stepped around the building. "This might take a while, so I suggest you mingle." He gave Foster a mean look before disappearing behind the building again. Foster pushed himself away and started walking towards the big fire they were building.

"I sure hope they don't plan on burning Xavier," Mason said quietly.

"Me too," Raven said.

Lessa linked her arm through Fosters and stopped him. "Mason, can we have a minute?" He looked rather put out but shook his head and walked off. "Foster, look at me." He felt her fingers gently turning his head towards her. "This will work."

He nodded and wrapped his arms around her. "I know." They were about the same height as elves, so he didn't have to bend down as much to kiss her as he usually did. Her elven lips felt different, but he could tell it was her under all that magic. They stood, their arms wrapped around each other while Sunette stood in the shadows and cast her spell.

———

Lucius sat next to the cage, crossing his arms across his

chest. "I don't know how to get you out of this, Xavier," he said quietly.

He carefully lifted his head. "Don't worry, whatever my fate may be, I accept it."

"You can't mean that!" Xavier was stunned by the man's sudden anger. "You should be angry and fighting against these monsters who want to kill you for simply looking like your," he huffed an angry noise. "Father."

"They don't want to kill me because I look like my father. They want to kill me because they think I am my father. There's a difference."

"Not to me." Lucius poked himself in the chest.

Xavier sat quietly and watched him for a few minutes. "You really hate your father, don't you?" Lucius rolled his eyes and turned his head away from the cage. "You were shocked that I knew my father. You didn't think it was possible, did you? That an Elf could possibly want to stay with their human love and raise children."

"He did not love my mother!" He rounded angrily at the young half-elf. "He violated her and left her for dead. And when her father found out she was going to have me, he kicked her out. She never wanted me, and neither did the Elf that raped her." Xavier stared at him, wide-eyed. He knew most half-elves only knew their human parents, but to actually hear of it was heartbreaking.

"I'm so sorry that happened to you."

"I don't need your pity," he spat at him and turned away from him.

"You seem to be doing well, though." Lucius sat quietly, but Xavier could tell he was still incredibly angry.

"Better than anyone ever thought I would do."

"We make our own fate, Lucius. No matter where we come from, we can be great."

Slowly, he turned and met his eyes. "We can."

———

Foster and Lessa were still waiting for Sunette's spell

to finish. He was gently petting her hair as her head lay on his shoulder.

"Lessa, I need to apologize to you." She looked up, and he could tell she really had no idea what had transpired between him and Sunette.

"Why?" If Bereck was angry, he dreaded to think what Lessa would do when she found out.

"I… kissed Sunette."

"Oh. Why?" He was shocked at her reaction, he expected her to be just as angry as Bereck, but she seemed genuinely interested.

"One of the elves caught us hiding in a bush while she re-cast her spell on me. She told him that we were lovers, and we wanted a few moments alone, and he asked us to prove it. So, we kissed." He didn't want to put everything on Sunette, even though, as he thought about it, it all seemed to be her idea.

Lessa nodded and licked her lips. "I see. Well, you had to. It's not like you just took her in your arms and started kissing her for no reason." Foster couldn't believe it, she was being completely understanding, and he felt his shoulders relax as he hugged her.

"I thought you'd smack my face and leave me."

Her hands pressed into his back, and he smiled as she kneaded at his muscles. "I'm glad you told me, but I understand." She looked up into his eyes. "It's not like you love her. You had to."

He nodded. "Yeah, besides, I think Bereck will punish me enough later."

Lessa's jaw dropped. "He saw?"

"He did. I think I need to toughen up my face for when we get out of here."

She held his chin still. "He will not hit you, Foster, or I'll kick him where it counts. He should not be mad at you or Sunette for what happened. I'm sure if we explain why, he'll understand."

Foster sighed loudly. "I think it's going to take a lot of explaining." He looked up at the roaring fire in the middle of the village. The elves seemed to be sufficiently distracted now as they danced around the fire. "I hope she can find that urn soon. I think now is the ideal time." As the words left his lips, Sunette and Bereck came walking around the building, and she looked stressed. The little wrinkle above her nose was prominent.

"What is it?" Lessa asked.

"I found it, but it keeps moving."

Their eyes widened in shock. "Moving? What does that mean?" he asked.

"It means that someone has it," Bereck said. Foster's heart dropped. If someone had it, then he knew it would be infinitely harder to obtain. "We might as well join the party. Maybe we'll run into the elf that has it," Bereck suggested.

"Not likely. They're moving around the borders of the village. It doesn't look like they're going to join us," Sunette said sadly as she pulled her love towards the fire.

Foster felt Lessa's arms tighten around him. "Don't worry, Foster, we'll get it."

He looked down into her pretty blue elven eyes with their thick, dark lashes. "Thank you for your faith, Lessa."

———

Elves danced and played music around the captive half-elf until late into the night. It was wild to their eyes. Men and women dancing so close it almost looked like they were doing something that was reserved for the bedroom. No one in the group really felt like dancing, especially like that, so they just walked around and watched. Except Raven, she pulled Twig to the bonfire, and they did their best to blend in. He had his hands on her hips as she moved them in circles, her back against his front. They were smiling so big everyone could see.

The group watched as she turned and wrapped her arms around his hips and moved them both side to side.

Lessa turned to the group. "Has anyone actually seen them…kiss?" Everyone shook their heads.

"If they do, they certainly keep it under wraps," Bereck said. They watched as Twig sat on the ground with other men while they watched their partners dance. "Reminds me of the Suya dances during the Bell festival," Bereck said. "It's a love and fertility celebration." Twig reached up, and Raven held his hands. They watched as he drew her down to his lap and kissed her like he had been doing it for years. Everyone clapped and cheered at the display, and they weren't the only couples to forget about dancing either. One by one, the couples stopped dancing and started kissing.

As happy as the display was, Foster started worrying that they'd never get the urn. His eyes were constantly searching for whoever might have it, but he saw nothing. Not even Lessa's lips could distract him from the thought of going to sleep that night.

They were sitting on the ground, next to a building as the fire died in front of them. It was late into the night, and Foster was fighting his eyes. He felt if he could close them for just a minute, maybe he wouldn't dream, but the fear was too much.

"If you want to sleep, you can," Lessa whispered.

He jerked upright at her voice, "No, I can't, not until we get that urn."

"Incubo." They both gasped and turned at the voice. The Chief was standing about two feet away. Neither of them had heard him. "I know why you've come, my eyes are not so blind, and I am not so dumb to see humans through your disguises. They are good, though. I must give your mage credit."

Mason walked up behind him, holding a big silver urn, a smile on his face. "I got it, Foster. The chief here actually caught me, but I told him why we needed it. He seems to understand."

"Of course I do, that damn thing plagued my people for almost ten years. There is a cave about two miles to the south. Meet me there. There is something I must do first." Foster stood and looked over at Xavier. He seemed to be asleep in the cage. Lucius was still next to him.

The chief reached out and laid a hand on Foster's shoulder. "I am not so blind that I do not see that man is my grandson."

Foster turned to him. "I grew up with him. His father's a good man."

The ancient elf nodded. "Yes, I'm sure he is. But he is not his father and does not deserve that fate. I will bring him to the cave unharmed. You have my word for whatever it means to you. Oh, and let the newlyweds alone. They won't be needed."

Everyone stopped and looked at him, their eyes wide. "Newlyweds?" Sunette asked.

"The half-orc and his woman, they're married now. That was a marriage dance they participated in." Everyone looked at each other, jaws practically on the ground.

"That'll be a fun conversation to have with them," Bereck said.

Mason motioned with his head, a big smile on his face. "Come on, the cave is this way."

———

The entire group, except for Xavier, Lucius, and the apparent newlyweds, walked through the woods to the cave. When they found the opening, Sunette and Lessa created light, and they could see carvings made into the stone.

The priestess walked up to one of the walls and held her lighted seashell close. "I think the carvings are about the creature."

Foster saw someone carved half a mask on the wall and shuddered. "Yeah, they are." Footsteps drew their attention, and they saw Xavier, Lucius, and the Chief, who had yet to give his name, walk into the cave.

"Build a fire," the old elf said as he picked up a big stick. "Come on, don't just stand there. The longer that thing is with him, the longer it takes to get it out. Now hurry up." Sunette cast a spell, and a little fire started crackling in the cave. "Now, sit down, boy. I don't want you to hurt yourself."

"Hurt myself?" Foster slowly sat down, staring at the old elf.

"You'll see. You," he motioned at Mason. "Put it on the ground."

Mason laid the urn at his feet. "Do you know how to open it?" he asked.

The elf scoffed. "How would you open any urn, boy." He

twisted the lid, and it came off rather easily.

"Oh. We heard that no one could open it," Mason said.

"We spread that rumor. We were afraid of someone coming and using it all, leaving us with nothing, and since we had just been plagued by this creature, we didn't want to risk anything." He dipped the stick into the urn. As he lifted it, everyone could see a black sticky substance dripping slowly from the end. "Now, prepare yourself, boy." He stuck the stick in the fire, and the black tar erupted in flames. "Be strong. If you aren't, it could turn out bad."

He blew the smoke into Foster's face. "Bad? What do you mean by bad?" Foster's body suddenly went limp and fell to the ground.

"Foster!" Lessa and Sunette kneeled next to him. His breathing was deep and even, and his heart was strong. "He's asleep," the priestess said.

Sunette looked up at the elf. "What's happening to him?"

"He cannot be awake," the elf made his way to a big boulder and sat down. "He must be asleep for the creature to see his family."

Bereck sat down across the fire. "Sunette, he'll be fine. You needn't fuss." She looked over at her friends. They all looked worried except Bereck.

"Is he in any danger, Ancient One?" She looked up at the elf who was studying Foster.

He shrugged his shoulders. "Some, but I have a feeling he's strong."

"Some?" Mason's voice was small as he sat next to Bereck.

"If the creature wishes to, he will try and take over the boy's body. But I doubt that'll happen."

Lessa gasped and held Foster's hand against her cheek. "Blessed Otto, please let Foster come back to us whole and healthy," she prayed quietly.

———

Foster opened his eyes and saw his friends sitting around him. Lessa was holding his hand, and Sunette was biting her lower lip and pacing.

"Lessa?" But she didn't respond.

"She can't hear you." An unfamiliar voice made him turn, and he saw the masked man standing at the entrance to the cave, the chains floating in the air around him.

Foster got to his feet and started running at the man. "You bastard!" Running full tilt didn't help, as Foster seemed to run right through him.

"You are in my realm now. You think I couldn't keep you from harming me?" Foster turned and saw the man sitting on the ground. He reached up and took the mask off. He looked unimpressive without the double-sided mask. "Yes, I am just a man. Your mortal minds turned me into this," he motioned to his body. "I don't even know how long I've had this mask or these chains."

"Do you know why I'm here?"

The man looked up and ran his hand through his still greasy hair. "You inhaled the fumes. You want rid of me. That's the only reason others are in my realm."

"Why did you choose me?" Foster sat on a nearby rock and could hear his friends still chatting in the cave, though he couldn't make out their words.

"I choose at random. I saw you and your lover sleeping peacefully in your bed, and I thought, 'Who would have the worst nightmares?' I tried you first, and your mind was so troubled I couldn't resist." He looked over at Foster, "I spoke the truth. You carry a lot of fear in you."

Foster shrugged and turned away from him. "So do you." The man chuckled, and Foster prepared to be bombarded by fear like he was in his dream, but nothing happened.

"I never thought of it like that."

"So, how long is this going to take?"

The man shrugged. "I have no concept of time. It just happens." Foster huffed and began pacing. All he wanted to do was get rid of this creature and get back to his life. "I am no creature!"

Foster's eyes went wide. "What? I didn't-"

The man stood and walked angrily into Foster, "You think I can't hear your thoughts in my realm! I am a man trapped, and you best remember that!" The chains flew up and wrapped around him, they burned, and Foster fell screaming to the ground.

"Stop it, please!"

"It's not my fault! Those bastards killed my family for no reason! I didn't care about myself. I was willing to die in their place, but my wife! My sons and my unborn child did not deserve to share my FATE!!!" He screamed, and Foster thought he felt his heart stop for just a moment. He never imagined such fear and anger could be felt by a single person.

The chains lifted him off the ground, and he screamed as his skin caught fire. "Please stop!"

"Please? Please? My family screamed please as the warlord and his men burned them to death. They didn't listen. Do you think I will!!"

"Ricmaer?" The chains suddenly disappeared, and Foster fell with a grunt to the ground. He looked up and saw a woman with a big pregnant belly and two small boys standing by the tree line.

The man stood still, staring at them. "Mayrien," he whispered.

The woman smiled, and Foster could see tears streaming down her cheeks. "Ricmaer, it is you." She took the little boys' hands, and they ran to each other and embraced as much of each other as they could.

———

Lessa held Foster's hand and kept an eye on his breathing, "How long does it take?" she asked.

"Hmm, it depends, really," the old elf said. It wasn't the answer she was looking for, but it told her not to hold her breath.

"Bereck, what's wrong?" Lessa heard Sunette whisper to her lover.

"Now's not the time, Sunette. Let's get out of these gods forsaken woods first."

"Forsaken?" The elf got to his feet. "These woods have been our home and sanctuary for hundreds, thousands of years! If anything, your lands are forsaken."

"How dare you!" Bereck got up and stood in the elf's face. "If you elves weren't so xenophobic, perhaps—"

Foster screamed in his sleep, and everyone jumped. "Foster!" Lessa held him down, but he was shaking violently. "Gods, what is happening to him!" His back arched, and it was so stiff Lessa was afraid it might break.

"Foster!" Mason crawled over and tried helping his sister put him back down, but he wouldn't budge. His body was shaking, and everyone could see large red welts forming on his skin.

"No, not again, please, Foster, wake up!" Lessa screamed. His body fell back against the ground, and his head lolled against his shoulder, his open eyes staring at Lessa. "Foster, you're awake!" She lay on his chest and hugged him. "We were so scared for you." She listened for his strong heart that often soothed her at night but couldn't hear it. "Foster?" She sat up and recognized the look on his face. She had seen it on many dead men, and tears poured down her face as she sobbed. "No!"

Sunette quickly kneeled beside him and laid her hand on his pulse. "What's wrong?"

She looked up at her friend. "His heart," she choked before she could finish.

"It's strong," Sunette said.

Foster took in a deep, ragged breath, and Lessa gasped. "Foster!" She held his face as he coughed and tried to sit up, "Relax, just stay still." she pleaded with him.

He gave in and laid back down. "It's over," he whispered.

Lessa leaned over and hovered over his lips. "I thought you were dead," she whimpered quietly.

He reached up and gently touched her cheek. "I thought so, too."

Mason sat back, looking between Foster and the Chief. "What happened? Is it gone?"

Lessa laid on his chest, and Foster turned to the rest of the group. "It was like the legend said, he was reunited with his family, and he let me go. His name was Ricmaer Stone, a warlord killed him when he was finished building him a dungeon. Apparently, he wanted everything about it kept a secret and killed Ricmaer's family as well."

"How sad. I don't blame him for wanting revenge on the Lord, but he didn't have to cause nightmares in others," Sunette said.

"He was burned to death. It was the one way he feared to go," Foster said quietly.

Lessa nodded and kissed Foster's head. "If it's truly gone, I say we get out of these woods."

"He is. He said he'd leave me alone."

"Well then," Bereck walked over and offered Foster his hand. "Up on your feet, we got a ways to go." Foster reached up, and the strong paladin yanked him to his feet rather hard and heard him whisper in his ear, "But the next time you kiss my betrothed, I don't care what's possessing you. I'm going to knock your head off your shoulders, got it?"

Foster nodded and stepped back. "Yeah, I got it," he said quietly.

"Good." He took Sunette's hand, and the group slowly started walking out of the cave.

Foster felt Lessa's hand in his. He stopped and pulled her close. "I'm so sorry I kissed Sunette," he whispered.

Lessa leaned back and held his face. "I'm not angry with you, Foster. You don't have to be sorry. I don't care if you had to kiss a hundred girls to get better," he chuckled, and it made her smile. "I just want you well."

He gently kissed the tip of her nose. "You're so special to me, Lessa."

"As are you." He leaned down to kiss her lips when they both heard the familiar groaning of her younger brother.

"Jeez, can't you two wait until we're out of the woods?" He put his hands up to block his eyes.

Lessa snickered and quickly pecked Foster's cheek. "Okay, okay, we're coming." She pulled Foster out of the cave.

———

They ran into no one as they made their way back to the village, the chief still accompanying them. He and Xavier talked most of the time. He asked about Xavier's childhood, and he asked about his father's life before them. Everyone knew the elves weren't likely to change, but it was clear the two men were glad to know each other.

The chief pointed at Mason. "You, small one, go get your friends before her disguise wears off." He nodded and ran over to another small fire. Twig and Raven were still seated by it, kissing without a care in the world.

They quickly parted at the interruption and joined their friends. "Is it over?" Twig asked.

Foster nodded. "All good now."

"Shit, sorry I didn't help like I said I would," Raven said, embarrassment in her eyes.

"Oh, that's all right," Bereck said, a note of mischief in his voice. "We'd never begrudge newlyweds the chance to kiss."

Confusion flashed on both their faces. "Newlyweds? Who?" Raven said. Everyone pointed at them, smiles on their faces. "Nuh-huh," she put her hands up, "we were just dancing."

"That is a wedding dance," the old elf said. "You danced, you kissed, you're married. Now get going before your disguises wear off." He walked away without another word, and the group quickly decided to follow his advice.

"He's teasing, right?" Raven asked, but no one said a word.

"I don't think he knows the definition of teasing," Twig said with a smile. "Come, wife, let us away." Everyone snickered quietly as she rolled her eyes but took his hand.

The group walked back towards Blackridge without stopping. Xavier decided to go home and visit his parents and parted from the group a day out from their destination. He and Foster exchanged hugs and wished their families well.

When the half-elf was out of earshot, Lucius spoke up. "That friend of yours is something else, Foster."

He nodded. "Yeah, he is."

The first night back in Blackridge, everyone looked like themselves, and Foster headed straight for bed. He slept peacefully for an entire day as Lessa watched over him, but that first night was not so peaceful for Bereck and Sunette.

They settled into their room, and she cleared her throat. "So, my love, why did you say such things to Foster?" She didn't bother keeping the irritation out of her voice. He was a man, after all, and often the subtleties of women were lost on them.

He sat down on the bed and started taking his boots off. "I saw him kissing you in the woods."

"Yes, I assumed as much, but you didn't have to be so rude to him. You could have asked me why we did it instead of just letting your ego take over."

His eyes went wide. "We? What do you mean 'we'?"

She walked in front of him. "*I* kissed him," she said, poking herself in the chest. "One of the elves accosted us, and I had to do something to get him away. That's what I thought of."

He rubbed his face vigorously before standing. "It was your idea?"

"Yes! It meant nothing except survival, Bereck, so I'd appreciate it if you'd stop blaming Foster. I thought you two were friends."

"As did I, but I usually frown at men who kiss my betrothed!" She started pacing back and forth, yelling at him in her native tongue, which he didn't understand until it became common.

"We are not married, Bereck, and I don't appreciate you acting so possessive. You are to stop acting like I'm some sort of loose woman who goes around kissing everybody she sees! I'm starting to wonder if you are the man I thought you were."

His annoyance quickly disappeared as he reached out and held her still. "Don't say that, Sunette, I love you more than life itself."

"Do you? I thought you were a forgiving man, but right now, all I see is a jealous man who's acting like I'm his property. I belong to no one, Bereck!" She could feel tears in her eyes and turned away from him. "I belong to myself, and no one will tell me otherwise!" She sniffed and tried to hide her tears, but she knew it was futile.

He slowly laid his hands on her arms. "I'm sorry, Sunette, just seeing you with another man broke me. I want you happy," he slowly turned her to face him. "And if you'd be happy with another, I'll accept that," he said quietly.

She sighed and wrapped her arms around him. "No other man will do for me, Bereck, you know that." She felt his arms hug her tight as he laid his head on hers. "But I want you to apologize to Foster. Be the man I know you are and apologize to him."

She felt him nod against her head. "As you wish, my beautiful mage," he whispered.

———

Twig and Raven sat on the bed in their room, their hands in their laps. "Are we really married?" she asked.

"I think to the Elves we are. To everyone else, no." He shook his head.

Raven sighed. "Do you regret it?"

Twig laughed and turned to her. "Not for a minute. I've been wanting to kiss you since the first time I heard you sing. I've just been too nervous to go for it."

Raven laughed and got to her knees on the bed and held his face. "I had so much fun. I want to have more fun with you, husband." He growled, and it made her giggle as he wrapped his arms around her and flipped her onto the bed.

"Then fun we shall have, my wife."

———

When Foster finally woke up, the group was eating dinner in the common room downstairs.

Lucius smiled as he pulled out a chair and sat down. "Well, look who's up from his nap," he teased.

Foster chuckled and smiled at Lessa, who gave his cheek

a kiss. "I needed that nap, Lucius." A serving girl brought him a plate of food without asking, and he dug in.

Bereck cleared his throat. "Um, Foster?"

He looked up and wiped some gravy off his chin. "Hmm?"

"I, uh, wanted to apologize for what I said in the cave." Foster's eyes widened. He didn't really blame Bereck for being angry and didn't expect an apology.

"Oh. Well, thanks, I guess. I don't suppose I blame you, but I really didn't—"

Bereck held up a hand. "I know, you didn't have a choice." Sunette kissed Bereck's cheek while the others looked on confused.

"Well, now whatever that was is out of the way, I think we need to think of where to go next," Lucius said.

"Onto the next!" Mason cheered, and the others lifted their mugs in agreement.

CHAPTER 5
TO SERVE FULLY

The next year flew by, and Foster fell more in love with his priestess every day. It seemed like a light had been lit inside of her. None of them ever remember seeing her so happy. Her beauty and smarts made Lessa irresistible, but lately, he had noticed that she seemed restless. She would stare at the fire, and it would take a moment before she responded to anyone trying to get her attention.

She even tripped over her own feet as the group walked, and Foster caught her several times before she fell flat on her face. After a week of blank stares and tripping, the group settled into an inn. Before they snuggled into bed that first night, Foster pulled her close and kissed her forehead.

"Lessa, is something bothering you?"

She looked up into his eyes. "What do you mean?"

"You seem restless lately, not yourself."

"Hmm." She sighed and sat up, "Noticed that, huh?"

"Yes, ma'am, I did." He reached out and tucked some of her hair behind her ear, "I know you better than anyone save yourself. I should hope I would notice when you felt off." He ran his hand along her thigh. "Tell me what's wrong." She reached out and laid a hand on his cheek. The look on her face was something he had never seen before. Like she was happy but regretted what she was about to say.

"You know I love you, right Foster?" She had never said it before. Hell, he had never said it before, and it took him by surprise.

"You love me?" A smile slowly spread along his face, and he could feel his heart beating with excitement.

She nodded and smiled. "I do, but I can only think of one thing that will make me truly happy."

Foster sat up and took her hands. "What is it?" Whatever it was, he was damn well going to give it to her.

She took a deep breath. "To serve Otto fully, to commit my life to him." Slowly, the smile disappeared, and his heart began to break all over again. His beautiful priestess wanted to leave him.

"A Temple? Do you not want to marry, to have children with your beautiful hair and my eyes?" He tried to keep the desperation out of his voice, but it was hard.

Lessa chuckled and gave him a little smile. "Are you asking?" It felt like his heart leapt into his throat. The last time he asked someone to marry him, she said no. He didn't want to hear 'no' again.

"Um..."

Lessa giggled, "Calm yourself, Foster, I don't expect you to propose. In fact, I was hoping you wouldn't. I've thought about this a lot, and Otto calls to me louder than any biological or romantic need of mine."

He felt himself relax and processed what she had just said. "So, you want to...join a temple."

"Yes." He leaned forward and hugged her tight as his hands rubbed her back. This was always a possibility when dating clergy, he knew, but he never expected it from Lessa.

He took a deep breath and said words that broke his heart. "Lessa, if you feel Otto's call, then answer it." Just saying the words made the world a bit less bright and a little lonelier. "I will miss you so much, my beautiful priestess," he whispered and gave her a kiss. "But I will be comforted in the knowledge that you're happy."

Her eyes got teary as she smiled brightly. "Oh Foster! Thank you, thank you." She cried happily into his arms. *I guess she wasn't the one after all,* he thought to himself as Lessa hugged him tight.

———

The next morning, as the group was eating breakfast, Lessa cleared her throat. "Excuse me, everybody. I have an announcement." Everyone looked up at her, Mason sat back and crossed his arms.

"You're not getting married, are you?" He didn't sound particularly happy about it and glared at the big man.

"Mason!" Sunette smacked his chest, "Be polite," she hissed at him.

Lessa smiled at her brother. "No, we're not getting married."

Sunette turned to her, a little frown on her face. "You're not?"

Lessa chuckled. "No." She took a deep breath and squeezed Foster's hand, who gave her a little nod. "I've decided to join a temple if they'll have me."

"A temple?" Lucius said, "You're leaving us?" He sat straight, his hands resting on the table.

"Otto is calling me to a higher purpose. I'm going to re-do my vow and commit my life to Him."

"Lessa," Raven reached over and held her hand, "are you sure? I mean…" she pointed from her to Foster several times.

She nodded. "I've been thinking about it for a while now. I know it's what I'm meant to do."

Mason stood and hugged his sister. "I'd rather have you marry Foster."

Lessa laughed. "You should be glad. It's kind of hard to get killed in a temple."

Lucius cleared his throat and sat back. "Which temple were you thinking about joining?"

"Well, Ardenry could always use more, I bet."

Bereck turned to Foster like he couldn't believe what he was hearing. "How do you feel about her leaving?"

He turned and smiled at his priestess, even though it hurt. "It's what she wants to do, and if it makes her happy, I'm happy for her."

Bereck looked at him like he was an idiot. "You're not

going to sweep her up in your arms and tell her she can't leave. She's your life, your love, and you'll be a hermit if she leaves?"

Foster laughed and shook his head. "It's hard to compete with the call of a God, Bereck."

"I suppose you're right," he shrugged.

Sunette smiled sadly at Foster. "You're really okay with it."

He nodded. "I am."

Sunette stood and hugged Lessa. "I will miss you. You've been like the sister I never had."

"I'll miss you too, Sunette. I expect to be at your wedding. I hope you know." The women laughed and wiped away little tears.

Twig reached across the table and took her hands. "I'm happy you found your calling, but I will miss you every day."

She smiled. "I'll miss you too, Twig."

"Before you go," Raven sat up. "We still need to give Foster that manicure."

Foster quickly looked between them and considered running. Lessa laughed. "Oh, I haven't forgotten."

———

A month later, the group arrived in Ardenry and made their way to the Temple of Otto. When they walked in, Bereck, Lessa, and Foster kissed their fingers and touched them to their heads as they saw acolyte walk up.

"Can I help you?" Lessa sighed and told him her plight. When she was done, he smiled, "Follow me, Mother." Foster stood in the back and watched her walk down the aisle to her new calling.

"Well, that's that, I guess," Lucius turned to the group, a smile on his face that didn't reach his eyes. "Shall we find an inn nearby?"

Foster turned to the group. "I think I'll wait here."

"As you like, young man." Foster watched them leave and took a seat at a back pew. He thought about Lessa and what it would be like without her. He smiled sadly and thought about lazy mornings in bed. Her ferociousness in battle made him proud to fight along her side, and he knew he'd miss everything about her. He heard tapping by the door and turned. Raven was standing in the doorway, her arms crossed over her stomach, her foot tapping nervously on the marble floor. She looked like she didn't want to intrude but was curious.

"Raven, come on in." She looked over at him and tapped her foot a few more times before slowly making her way over to him. "Ever been here before?"

"Ardenry, sure. A temple of Otto, never," she said quietly as she stood next to the pew. He scooted over and patted the seat. She looked at it for a moment, then sat down.

"Why are you so nervous?"

She shook her head and shrugged. "Just waiting to catch on fire, I guess." Foster laughed and sat back. "Shh, you're being loud." She scolded him, but it only made him laugh more.

"You can laugh in a temple, Raven."

Her eyes were wide, taking in everything. "You can?" She looked like someone was going to jump out and scold them.

"Of course you can. Happy parishioners make the gods happy, especially Otto." He watched her sitting, almost curling in on herself like she was actually scared. "You have nothing to fear here. Nothing will hurt you."

"It's just…I spent a great deal of my life…Otto wouldn't be happy," she said as she started picking at her fingernails.

"As long as you aren't doing whatever that was now, I don't think he cares."

"I'm definitely not doing it now. I never will again, and I feel awful that…" He waited for her to continue, but she didn't.

"You can tell me anything, Raven, I won't think less of you." She stared at him through the corners of her eyes.

"I don't know about that," she mumbled.

Foster scooted closer to her and whispered in her ear. "I promise, whatever you say, I won't repeat it." She put her feet on the pew and hugged her legs. After a few beats, she turned her lips to his ear and whispered. Foster listened to her heartbreaking tale and hugged her when she was done. "You're braver than you think," he said, sitting back. That unusual holy feeling surrounded him again, and then he felt it sink back into her.

"I don't feel like it."

"Does Twig know?" She shook her head. "He's your husband, and he might want to know."

She scoffed. "Maybe." She sat straight, putting her feet on the floor. "You'd make a good priest, Foster."

He barked out a laugh. "Oh no, my brother Christopher is the priest, I'm happy just worshiping."

She swallowed, slowly unfurling herself on the pew. "What's he like, your brother?"

Foster sat back and spread his arms along the back of the pew. "He's two years younger than me, smarter than me," he teased. "And a real nice guy. He volunteers with the church every chance he can get. I miss him so much."

She gave him a little smile. "Sounds like a good guy."

He nodded. "We fought when I left, I still feel bad. It was the only time we'd ever fought like that, honestly. I didn't know he had it in him." Raven chuckled. "I think he'd make a great husband and father, but he just wants to join the church like Lessa."

"Hmm, shame."

Foster nodded. "It is, but it's his life." He turned to Raven, "Do you feel better?" She looked around the temple. He could tell she didn't seem scared anymore.

"I do. I don't feel the impending heat of holy fire on my neck anymore."

Foster laughed and patted her back. "Why don't you talk to your husband about all this? I think it'll help, too."

She rolled her eyes again. "He's not really my husband." And got to her feet.

"You know we're never gonna say otherwise."

"I know, I know!" She called back as she walked out of the temple.

————

It was evening before Foster saw Lessa walking towards him. She was practically glowing as he stood and hugged her.

"Did it go well?" he asked, his arms still around her.

"It did. They have a place for me."

He stepped back and lifted her chin. "I'm going to miss you, Alessa Fray, everything about you."

She smiled as a tear fell. "I'll miss you too. Thank you for keeping the nights warm for me. I'll pray for you every day."

Foster smiled. "Thank you, I know I'm going to need it." He bent down to give her one last sweet kiss.

———

An hour later, he found Lucius in a tavern a few blocks from the temple. He sat down next to him and ordered a drink.

"How are you, boy?"

He sighed, "I'm good, sir." The half-elf chuckled, and when Foster had a mug of ale, Lucius raised his.

"To Lessa, may she give 'em hell."

Foster chuckled and raised his mug. "May the life she chose bring her much joy." They clinked mugs and drank deep to their old cleric. "Where is everyone?"

"The couples are upstairs, and Mason decided to follow a pretty young bard to another tavern."

Foster chuckled. "Good luck to him."

———

Raven had pulled Twig up to their room right after dinner and decided to give Foster's advice a try. Twig seemed completely enamored of her, so she hoped her story wouldn't scare him off. She was crazy about him, too, and didn't want to see him go.

"Twig, what's your real name?" she asked, shutting the door behind her.

He chuckled and sat on the bed, taking his boots off. "Why?"

She shrugged and kicked her shoes off. "I am your wife, am I not," she teased, and he took her hands. "I feel like I should know."

He smiled up at her, nothing but love in his eyes. "I'll tell

EXALTED   121

you mine if you tell me yours."

She looked down at their hands, shocked at the request. "Mine isn't just some nickname, though. It's to keep me, keep us safe."

He pulled her close and cupped her face. "I will tell no one, and you will be safe with me," he said as he ran an affectionate finger down her cheek.

"Promise?"

He leaned up and gently kissed her lips. "Promise."

She sighed and closed her eyes. "Sana."

When she opened her eyes, she saw a soft smile on his face. "That's beautiful, it suits you."

She playfully slapped his shoulder. "Your turn."

"Godric."

Raven smiled and held his face. "That is a wonderful name." She pulled him down to the bed and whispered his name over and over.

———

Lessa had been gone a week, and the group was camping a few days away from Ardenry. Foster was on duty that night, and everyone but he and Sunette were asleep. She was reading her spellbook by lit coin, and Foster could see her eyes moving across the page. "I thought you read in the morning?"

She looked up, the loss of concentration gone from her face. "Usually, yes, but I can't sleep."

"Mind too busy?"

She nodded and closed her book. "I keep thinking about Lessa."

Foster sighed. "Me too."

She clicked her tongue, and he could see she looked sorry. "I'm sorry I'm horrible. I'm sure you're missing her more than any of us, save for Mason."

He held up his hand. "No, you're fine. I think we'll all miss her for different reasons."

"True, but one thing I know I'll miss is seeing your smiling face when she walked into a room."

Foster chuckled. "Did I smile?"

"You did. You always looked so happy as she walked over to you." Foster thought about how Lessa would always walk over to him, her arms already outstretched, waiting for him to settle in

"Well, she made me happy. But I'm glad she's following her path. If she's happy, then I am too."

Sunette set her book down. "Liar."

He sighed loudly and laid his head in his hand. "Well, maybe not *as* happy as she is."

Sunette got up and sat next to him. "I don't know what it is, but I can't stand to see you sad."

He chuckled. "I'll try and cheer up so you don't have to work so hard."

"Oh," She scoffed and playfully hit his arm, and he laughed. "Really, Foster, you're my friend, and I care about your happiness."

"Thank you, I care about your happiness too."

She looked over at Bereck, asleep in his bedroll. "Being in a group creates bonds, Foster, like family and I know you'll find your love. Wherever she is."

He gave her a little smile. "Who knows? I probably knew her back in Raventree, and I was too dumb to see it."

Sunette giggled quietly. "You're not dumb, but I am exhausted. I think I'll turn in." She crawled over to Bereck and slid into the bedroll with him. "Good night."

"Night, Sunette."

CHAPTER 6
HOLY OR NOT

"So, where are you from, Lucius?" Foster asked him as they walked. He knew where everyone else was from, but Lucius didn't talk much about his life before he started traveling.

"Tolhallow, but I don't really consider it home." Foster knew Tolhallow was on the east side of the elven woods and Blackridge was on the west side. Both towns had more half-elves than most smaller towns did.

"When did you leave?"

Lucius blew out his breath. "Oh, I'd have been thirteen, I think."

"Damn," Foster turned when he heard Raven speak up. "That's younger than when I left home."

Lucius turned halfway to her, "how old were you?"

"Fourteen."

"Hmm," he shook his head. "Sometimes leaving is best."

"Especially when you're leaving Dal En Val." Twig didn't seem to realize what he said as he kept an eye on the horizon and bumped into Lucius, who had stopped. Raven was staring at the half-orc. Foster swore she looked betrayed.

"Dal En Val?" Lucius's eyes darted to Raven. "You're from The Empire?"

She smacked Twig in the arm. "Ow, what?"

"I think she didn't want anyone to know." Lucius's eyes bored into hers, "Right?" Everyone had caught up to them and was confused at what was going on.

"No, I didn't want anyone to know. Your reaction says why." She crossed her arms and shook her head.

"Sorry, Raven, I didn't think it was a secret." Twig put a

hand on her back, but she didn't acknowledge him.

Sunette stepped up and put a hand on Raven's arm. "I am glad you got out of that awful place."

"Was it an order or by choice?" Everyone looked at Lucius. He sounded angry.

"She was fourteen, Lucius," Sunette stood up for her. "Why would it be an order?"

"To get people to trust her easier."

Raven sighed. "My parents were spies for Ardenry."

Lucius scoffed. "A likely story."

"Lucius, what is wrong?" Foster stepped up to him, "Who gives a shit where she's from?"

"Dal En Val is dangerous, so are the people who live there."

Foster shook his head. "That's ridiculous, and you know it," Lucius's eyes widened like he couldn't believe Foster was talking to him that way. "We've been traveling with Raven for years. She's amazing! No one who feels holy like her could be evil." Now, it was everyone's turn to stare at him.

Raven blinked a few times. "What?"

"Yeah, what?" Bereck looked between them.

"You haven't felt that holy feeling around her?" The paladin shook his head.

Raven scoffed and started walking again. "I'm not holy, Foster."

He quickly caught up with her. "Well, you're something, but it's not evil. I'd bet my life on it."

Lucius started walking away. "Be careful what you bet, young man."

As they traveled, everyone could feel the tension between Lucius and Raven. Neither had said a word to each other for days despite the efforts of Twig and Foster. Raven seemed more inclined to let their schemes succeed, but Lucius was unmoving, which only made Raven crawl further into herself.

One day, as they were walking, Bereck turned back and saw how sad the bard looked. Her eyes were down as she hugged herself. Normally, there was always a smile on her face and a song on her lips. But it had been days since any of her lovely songs had pierced the air. He remembered the first time he heard her sing. Her voice was truly Gods-given. Then he remembered what Foster had said about her. Why did he think she was holy? She had to be the furthest from. She was wild, had quite the mouth on her, and, as far as he knew, didn't even worship a god. He gave Sunette's arm a little tap, and she looked up.

"I'm gonna have a word with Raven." She gave him a little smile and nodded her head as he stopped walking and let Raven catch up to him. He met her stride and cleared his throat. "Can I ask you something?"

"Sure." Twig was walking beside her, but Bereck didn't think she'd care if he heard their conversation.

"What did Foster mean by you were holy?"

She snorted, and the faintest smile finally crossed her lips. "No idea. He never said that to me before."

"He never mentioned anything?" She shook her head. "Hmm."

"Why? Wondering if it's the wrong kind of holy?" He could hear the snark in her voice, and since Lucius wasn't speaking to her, he was gonna take the brunt of her attitude.

"No." He noticed Foster walking back towards them. "You're not evil."

"I could be."

It was his turn to snort. "The way you sing, the gods wouldn't give a gift like that to someone evil." They caught up to Foster, who walked next to Bereck. "Foster, what did you mean by Raven's holy?"

"Yeah, I've been meaning to ask you, Raven," the tall fighter looked down at her, "if you've noticed that at all?"

Her left eyebrow went up so high it disappeared under her hair. "You think I've noticed a holy feeling on myself?"

He shrugged. "I don't know, I guess?"

Raven laughed. "No."

Bereck turned to Foster, "When did you notice it?"

"Almost every time I touch her, I feel it."

She groaned, "Make it sound creepier, Foster."

Twig laughed. "When did you touch my wife, little man?" Raven laughed, mainly because Twig and Foster were the same height.

He rolled his eyes, and Bereck chuckled. "Not like that, gross. Don't tell me you haven't felt it, Twig. You touch her more than any of us." They all laughed, and Bereck found himself silently thanking Otto that Raven was still able to laugh.

"No, she's just my wonderful wife." He put a hand around her waist and kissed her head. Bereck thought through the years he had known her. He had never actually touched her with a bare hand. If he had to wake her, he'd nudge her with his boot. They never hugged or put an arm around each other like she did with Foster or Mason. Hell, he'd seen Lucius kiss her cheek. He looked over at her and wondered if he had been missing out on getting to know her.

Bereck held out his hand. "May I?" Raven stopped, so did he, and she stared at his hand. Sighing, she put her hand in his. Bereck almost fell over at the power he felt from her. It was most definitely holy, but different, subtle almost. "Blessed Otto." He covered her hand with his other and concentrated on the feeling. "Foster was right."

"He tends to be," she said, not looking at the paladin.

"Do you have any idea what it is?"

She shook her head, not meeting his eyes. "No idea," she slowly looked up, "but you can tell it's good, right?" Her tone was almost desperate like she needed him to know in his heart that she wasn't the bad person Lucius thought she was now.

He smiled. "Most definitely good." He patted her hand.

"Maybe you can tell Lucius to get the stick out of his ass then." She started walking again, pulling her hand from him. He took two quick strikes and caught up.

"I'll see what I can do." He silently admonished himself for not realizing how special she was before now. He might have even been able to help her hone that power. But he was too blind to get over his own prejudices about her behavior to realize that. *Otto, forgive me*, he said to himself as they continued to walk.

————

A week later, the group arrived in Port Wind. It was a peaceful town on the southern coast, not a lot of trouble with pirates or bandits. Pippa's biggest temple was here. Most wondered why this little port town dedicated itself to the Goddess of Love instead of Otto. But the water god's clerics always respected their choice. As they walked through the town, there was little evidence of the Korites or the Orcish Empire, just a few propaganda fliers that everyone ignored.

"I wonder why this place remains untouched?" Mason asked.

"It's not the only place. Raventree doesn't have any Korites or Imperial Orcs either," Foster said.

"Yes, but it's fairly obvious why," Bereck said. "I'm sure having their own Mother Lily and orc god to protect it makes a difference," he said with a smile. It was early, so there weren't many people in the streets, but the temple lay before them at the end of the road. It was small as far as temples went, but a bright, white building shined in the morning sun. Foster watched as the doors opened, and someone in a purple cloak fell to their knees before collapsing at the top of the stairs.

"Something's wrong." He started running for the temple, the group behind him. As he ran up the stairs, he saw the person was one of the clerics, and the smell of blood hit his nose.

"Miss?" He pulled her into his lap, but it was clear she was gone, her eyes staring up at the sky.

Bereck landed next to him and closed her eyes. "What happened?" Foster looked at the doors, they were closed, and her bloody handprint was smeared on them.

"I don't know, but it's not good." Everyone drew their weapons, and Bereck pulled the large wooden doors. They swung open with a whisper, and Foster felt a scream halt in his throat. There were bodies strewn everywhere, all wearing the purple cloaks of Pippa's clerics. The smell of blood tinged the air.

Sunette covered her mouth, and Lucius ran down the stairs to the first person he could reach.

"Get the constable. The clerics are dead."

The man blanched as his eyes went wide. "All of them?"

"Yes, go!" The man ran down the road, and Lucius ran back up the stairs.

"My gods," Bereck breathed out. Foster had never seen such butchery, had never thought he'd see anything like this, least of all in a temple. Pippa's clergy were peaceful. They didn't even have any paladins. They devoted their lives to the Goddess of Love and spreading that love. To be struck down in such a violent manner, it was sacrilege of the highest order. They walked inside and started checking bodies, but none of them were alive.

"Blessed Otto, I know these are not your clergy, but please let them find peace, let them find love in Pippa's embrace," Bereck prayed. Bodies were strewn everywhere, on the pews, the floor, and the dais looked like whoever did this started to pile bodies on it but then didn't give a shit.

"How could anyone do such a thing?" Sunette ran her fingers down a cleric's eyes and closed them. The door slammed shut behind them, and they turned. A rather unimpressive man was standing there, a sword strapped to his back. His hands were covered in blood.

"It wasn't hard. They had no weapons." The smile on his bland face was hideous. There was even blood on his teeth. Footsteps swarmed into the chamber, and everyone was glad they kept their weapons drawn as Korite warriors surrounded them, all covered in blood.

"Why?" Raven screamed, "They did nothing to you!" Angry tears ran down her face, and Mason put an arm around her.

"The authorities are on their way," Lucius yelled out. "I suggest you leave!"

The man laughed. It echoed off the marble around them. "The more, the better. Kill them! Take her, though," he drew the sword on his back and pointed at Sunette with it. "Kore will love her." The group braced for the rush of fighters coming towards them.

"Otto, give us strength!" Bereck yelled while Lucius laughed and disappeared before their eyes. Twig roared and started swinging his axe at whatever got close while Raven let loose a dagger that hit its target. Foster kept Sunette at his back and heard words of magic spill from behind him and watched a wall of fire erupted between him and the encroaching enemy.

"Foster, get back!" Sunette yelled. As he moved, he heard the Korites screaming in agony as the smell of burning flesh filled the air.

Bereck ran through the fire and met the Korite head-on. "You will pay for your unholy ways!" They heard him yell before their swords clashed in the air. Twig was four deep but took a man down with every swing. Mason threw a dagger, and his mark dropped to the ground.

Foster's eyes took in the scene and found a man hiding in the shadows, his hands were moving in front of him, and he was looking at their mage.

"Sunette, look out!" He shoved her aside and shot an arrow just a fraction too late and watched as light streaked from the hidden caster and hit her square in the chest. She cried out and hit the ground. Foster quickly kneeled and rolled her on her back. Her pale lavender robe was singed, and her skin was blistering. "Oh, gods."

"Get me up, Foster, I'm all right." Her face was brave, but he could hear the pain in her voice. He helped her to her feet, and she stared right at the mage. "Is that all you have!" She yelled out and started running for the caster.

"Sunette, what are you doing?" Foster ran after her and could hear she was already preparing a spell. Her hands moved fluidly in front of her, and Foster watched as the man, with an arrow in his arm, was lifted helplessly into the air. "See what happens when you mess with me!" She yelled and floated the man over to Twig. "Hey, Twig got one for you!"

The half-orc turned and smiled his orcish smile. "Bring

him over, Suney!" He laughed and sank his axe into the man as she floated him over. Foster drew his bow and started picking them off before they could surround them. He glanced at Bereck, and his eyes went wide when he saw Raven next to the paladin, taking on the man who seemed to be in charge. Her voice was dissonant, and the man shook his head at her words. She charged and stabbed him in the back. He roared in pain and rushed backwards, slamming Raven into the wall. She screamed from the impact, and then Foster noticed she stopped moving.

"Raven!" Twig yelled as his last opponent went down, and he ran for her. Foster fired an arrow and watched it sink into the man's throat as Bereck quickly plunged his sword into his chest. Blood ran down the man's chin, and he fell flat on his face and slid helplessly down the wall. With the man out of the way, Foster saw Raven on the wall, impaled through the shoulder by some kind of metal sconce. Her chin was on her chest, and blood poured down the wall.

"Blessed Otto!" Bereck yelled. Twig reached them, and together, they pulled her off the sconce and laid her on the ground.

"Lucius, where are you!" Foster yelled. The response he got was a man falling from the rafters in front of him. He landed at an odd angle, and Foster could see his spine sticking out the back of his neck.

"Are you worried about me?" He looked up and saw the half-elf standing among the beams. "Sweet of you, but you should worry about yourself!" Lucius looked over at Raven, and Foster swore he could see the color drain from his face. "Oh shit." He disappeared and reappeared next to Bereck. "How bad?" There was desperation in his voice that surprised Foster.

"I've done all I can," Bereck said. "But she needs more." Her blood was spreading on the floor. Twig was desperately trying to stem the flow of blood with his hands, but it wasn't working.

"Here." A small voice made Lucius look up. One of the clerics of Pippa was reaching for them, she was barely conscious and slowly dragging herself over. "Bring her to...me." Twig pulled with all his might and stopped next to the cleric, who laid her hands over the wound and prayed. "Blessed and most cherished Pippa, please give me the strength to heal this woman who had the courage and talent to avenge us." Twig watched as the wound started to close. "Pippa, I give you my life for hers," the cleric whispered, and Twig watched helplessly as the woman collapsed and didn't move. Raven took a deep breath and opened her eyes.

"Oh, thank the gods." Twig leaned down and kissed her head. "I thought I was going to lose you."

She groaned as Twig helped her sit up. "That really hurt."

Bereck took her hands and helped her to her feet. "Thank you for your help."

She nodded. "That's what family does."

Lucius quickly shoved Bereck aside and held her face. "Are you all right?" He hugged her tightly, and she could hear how scared he sounded. "I'm so sorry."

She hugged him back. "Apologize after we're out of this mess." He nodded and kissed her forehead as Sunette, Foster, and Mason joined them.

Mason hugged the bard. "Are you okay? That looked painful."

She wrapped her arms around him and relaxed. "It was."

Lucius wiped his rapier off on a nearby dead Korite. "I'll make sure the city guard is coming." He ran over to the door and opened it, flooding the temple with light. There was even more blood and gore now that the parties responsible were dead.

Sunette looked around and laid a hand on Bereck's arm. "We should stay, help them clean and whatever else they need."

He nodded, "I agree."

———

The group was standing around the temple, answering questions from the local sheriffs. Lucius was done answering questions when he saw Raven sitting in one of the pews. She looked tired, and her back was still covered in blood. When he saw that sconce through her shoulder, he wished he could take back every rude thing he said to her about where she was from.

He walked over to her and cleared his throat. "Raven?" She looked up at him with tired eyes. "May I?" He motioned to the pew. She nodded, and he sat down. "I wanted to apologize for how I acted when I learned where you were from."

"Oh yeah?" She turned towards him, her arms crossed. It was clear she was going to make him work for this apology, but he expected that.

"It was unbecoming of me. I normally pride myself on not caring about a person's background, but...I've never had anyone from Dal En Val in my employ before. I should have seen how close you and Foster are, how obvious it is that you love Twig. Those things alone should have immediately told me how wrong I was. You are as much a part of this family as any of us, and I apologize." He held out his hand, and she slowly laid her hand in it.

"Thank you, Lucius."

He lifted her hand and gave it a kiss. "But I'll never forgive you for chasing off the barmaids like you do."

She laughed and gave his hand a squeeze. "You don't relish the challenge?"

He smiled and gave her a wink. "Not those kinds of challenges."

"Well maybe when we're settled, I'll make it easier on you." Despite the blood loss and sadness around them, he could see a spark of mischief in her eyes.

He chuckled and got to his feet. "I'm glad you're okay." He leaned down and kissed her forehead. "The world would be bleak without you in it."

"Thanks, boss."

CHAPTER 7
BIRTHDAY WALK

Winter was in full force now. The group had settled in Port Winds after the temple was decimated to help in whatever way they could. Pippa's clerics came from all over to repopulate the temple and get it back into shape, but it was still going to take months. The group spent their time working for the city guard or helping around Pippa's temple, cleaning, or doing anything the new clerics needed. While it was a hard job, Foster felt a sense of fulfillment, helping a temple come back to life.

One night, Foster was up late, drinking a special whiskey from the bartender. It was his twentieth birthday and his second away from home. As he sipped the amber drink, he thought about his family. How on his birthday, Christopher would make ice cream from the snow outside. Every time he thought of his brother, he felt awful, and his little smile wilted a little. Saphy would dress like a little lady and complain that she hated dresses. But she'd still twirl around, watching her skirt fly in the air. He had a suspicion she liked them more than she let on.

"Foster?" He looked up and saw Sunette standing across the table from him.

"Hi, Sunette."

"Drinking the hard stuff?"

He could hear the tease in her voice and chuckled. "It's my birthday, I thought I'd treat myself."

She smiled, and Foster felt his heart speed up. "It's your birthday? Why didn't you tell anyone?" She sat down and gave him a hug. "Happy birthday, dear Foster."

He wrapped his arms around her and sighed. "Thank you."

When she sat back, she crossed her arms. "So, how old are you?"

"Twenty."

She chuckled and shook her head. "I always forget how young you are, Apple Picker. When you joined, I could have sworn you were at least twenty-five."

Foster laughed and drank the dregs of his birthday spirit. "You can't be much older than me."

"Thank you," she gave a playful bow, "I think I make twenty-three look sophisticated."

He felt the whiskey giving him courage and turned to her. "Well, your gift to me can be a walk. How about it?"

Sunette nodded her head. "For you, Foster, of course. Let me get my cloak, and I'll be right down." He couldn't help but smile as she got to her feet and walked up the stairs. He didn't think she'd say no, but the reality of them spending some time alone suddenly made him nervous. He quickly got his cloak off the bench and bundled up while he impatiently waited for her to come back down.

———

Sunette walked into her room and saw Bereck in bed. "There you are, finally coming to bed?"

He watched her grab her cloak and put it around her shoulders. "Not yet, Foster and I are going to take a little walk."

His eyes widened. "A walk? It's snowing outside."

She turned and saw snow falling softly out the window. "So, it is." She walked over to Bereck. "I imagine I'll be cold when I get in. I may need you to warm me up," she said, intending it to be intriguing, but instead, he crossed his arms.

"I don't see why you need to go outside in the first place."

She sighed and put on a pair of gloves. "Bereck, it's Foster's birthday. He was sitting downstairs alone, sipping whiskey, and he asked to go for a walk. It's the least I could do."

His annoyed eyes melted away. "Oh, well, don't stay out too long, I don't want you getting sick."

"All right, I promise." And with a little cheek kiss, she

started for the door.

"Sunette?"

She turned with her hand on the doorknob. "Yes?"

She could tell he wanted to say something, but instead, he just sighed. "I love you."

"I love you too, my paladin."

————

Foster watched Sunette come back down the stairs. The smile on her face lifted his spirits in a way he hadn't expected.

"Ready?" He held out his arm, and she slid her hand around it, her fingers curling around his muscle. Her hand felt so delicate against him.

"Yes." Foster smiled and led them outside. The snow was falling lightly and clung to her hair, making it seem even darker.

"So Foster, tell me the story of how you were born, anything exciting happen?"

He chuckled. "Other than me coming into the world?" His father always told the story about how each of them was born on their birthdays. Foster used to think it was embarrassing, but now he'd give anything to hear him tell it.

Sunette laughed. "Yes, I suppose."

He walked a few steps and patted her hand. "Tell you what, I'll tell you mine if you tell me yours."

She looked a little shocked at the request. "Mine? Why do you want to know mine?"

Foster shrugged. "I hardly know anything about you, Sunette. I know you're kind, and a talented mage and hate chicken." She chuckled. "But of your life before you started traveling, I know nothing."

She sighed. "Hmm, you first."

"Okay." He cleared his throat and repeated the story his father would tell every year. "It had snowed the night before but just barely. There was a thin coat of white stuff all over everything, and it was bitterly cold. My parents' house wasn't quite done yet, so they were still living in the castle. They woke that morning and began doing what they normally did. My father went hunting with Lord Raventree, and my mother had decided to go pray by a little tree that they had planted in front of where the new temple would be. So, she bundled up and made her way outside. As she sat and prayed, she felt someone kneel next to her. She looked up and saw it was her first husband, Henri, who had died a few years before."

Sunette's eyes went wide. "Your mother was married before?"

"She was. They met while traveling, and she said she had never met a man who was so dedicated to helping people while being a complete flirt at the same time." Sunette laughed. "They were only married about six years before he died. Two years later, she met my father and said she knew he was for her from the moment they met."

Sunette sighed, "How romantic. So, her first husband visited her?"

Foster nodded. "He did. He was surrounded by light and smiling at her. She couldn't believe it and sat frozen for a moment before he spoke. She told us he said, *'That big belly suits you, My Lovely,'* and he touched her stomach. All the cold she felt left her body as if she weren't kneeling in the snow. Then he told her, *'That baby will be blessed, My lovely. He'll be so special and so lucky that you're his mother.'* He couldn't help but notice the smile on Sunette's face as he talked. It was beautiful.

"My Lovely?" She practically giggled.

"That was what he called her. She said when he first started calling her that, she hated it, she thought he was just trying to flirt for flirting sake. But he was sincere."

She nudged him a bit. "You don't seem to mind me calling you Apple Picker."

"No," he shook his head and looked down at her. "I love it." Her eyes stared into his, "I've always loved it." He swore her eyes were sparkling in the moonlight. "Anyway," it was so hard to tear his eyes away from her. "She said Henri leaned forward and kissed her cheek. But Mom suddenly found herself in bed and was in a little bit of pain. My father was holding her hand,

and she said he looked nervous. The midwife was in the room, and she realized that nothing was making sense. When she told them she saw Henri as she prayed by the tree, they all looked at her funny. Then, everyone in the room said she didn't go outside. That Dad had left her sleeping in bed when he left that morning, and when the midwife had come to check on her, she was laying on the floor and had to put her in bed."

Sunette gasped. "Oh my, did she have a vision?" He looked down and could see she was absolutely enthralled by his story. Her big blue eyes were staring at him, and he lost his train of thought for a moment.

"That's what they think." He stared at Sunette's flawless face, the cold making her blush in the right places. "Um, where was I?"

Sunette giggled, "They told your mother she didn't go outside."

"Oh, right! So, when Mom realized that she was going to have me that day, she held my father's face and said, *'We're going to have a baby today.'* My father loved that part, he'd always hold her face how she held his while he said those words. He told us how there were a lot of strong women around that day. The midwife, his mother, even Lady Raventree, and he knew my mother was well cared for."

"Certainly, sounds like she was."

"Later that night, he and my grandfather were pacing back and forth in the hall. He stared out of the window and saw it had started snowing again. He prayed to Otto that everything was all right, and then he said he just *knew* I was here. That I was born, and everything was perfect. The midwife's apprentice poked her head out and said he could come in, and he raced inside." Sunette chuckled at that. "He saw the midwife cleaning me, but when he started walking over to see if I was a boy or a girl, she blocked his way and said, *'Go see to your wife first.'*"

Sunette laughed, "I think I like her."

Foster smiled. "We all do. She's good at her job. Anyway, my father said he sat next to my mother, and she smiled. He could tell she was tired, but there was something in her eyes that held pure joy. When I started crying, the midwife brought me over and handed me to my mother, and she said, *'We have a son, my husband.'* My father just smiled and stared at me. He said I was the most perfect thing he'd ever seen and knew that Otto would bless all our lives."

Sunette smiled and leaned against him. "That's a lovely story, Foster."

"Thanks. My father tells the story of how each of us was born on our birthday, so I've heard it a lot. What about you? What happened on the day you were born?"

Sunette sighed and shook her head. "It's not as happy as yours, Foster."

"I imagine most people's aren't, but I want to know what happened the day you graced the world with your presence." He could see her biting her lower lip as her breath made little clouds in the air.

She sighed, and Foster wondered why her story upset her so much. "Okay, I'll tell you. My family was traveling when my mother felt the pains, but they didn't stop."

Foster noticed how haunted she looked as she told her story. "Why didn't they stop?"

She took a deep breath. "We were running from some men. My mother had me in the back of a fast-moving cart with my grandnana's help. When I was born, my brother said I was cute, but he hoped I'd stop crying."

He noticed a little smile on her face. "How old was he?"

"He was, um, five, I think." He smiled as he thought about seeing Saphy for the first time. He was almost five and thought she was a tiny little doll. Sunette sighed, "The next morning, the running stopped, and the rest of my family met me, all except my papa. He didn't make it through the night." Her voice was quiet, and he could hear that she still mourned him.

"Oh, Sunette, I'm so sorry." He hugged her shoulders and was glad she didn't push him away.

"That's pretty much my childhood. One by one, my family

died around me. I was five when Massus brought me across the sea. He told me everything about my family, he wanted me to remember something about them, and I hung on every word he said."

"Sunette, I had no idea." He pulled her into a hug and felt her arms squeeze him.

"It's alright, Foster."

After a few moments, he laid his head on hers. "Who was Massus?"

She sniffed. "One of my family's bodyguards. We were all that made it to Ardenry. He raised me until I was sixteen when I started studying magic in the city. He died a year later of old age. He held my hand and told me to keep moving. To live long and love and that he was immensely proud of me, and he felt privileged that he got to raise me as his own."

Foster slowly ran his hands over her long hair. "He sounds like a good man," his voice was barely louder than the falling snow.

She nodded, and her hair tickled his cheek. "He was. I loved my father even though I never met him. But Massus was my father, too, and I loved him just as much. It wasn't long after that I met Lucius and Bereck. My life felt complete, and we were always moving, so I knew Massus would approve."

Foster felt the snow in Sunette's hair melt against his skin as he ran his hand over it. "Are you happy with your life?"

"Yes, I am. I want to settle down with Bereck, but it also scares me. One place all the time? They could find me, hurt Bereck and our children. In a way, I'm thankful he still has such wanderlust."

Foster's eyes widened in shock, and he looked down at her. "These men are still looking for you?"

She rubbed her cheek against his cloak. "I would assume so."

"Well, why are they after you?" She looked up. Her nose and cheeks were red from the cold, and her eyes looked so sad that he couldn't help but reach up and cover one of her cheeks. It was so cold it was a shock to his warm hand. "Maybe we should go in. I think Bereck's arms need to warm you."

She nodded. "I'm sorry if your walk wasn't as pleasant as you hoped." He shook his head and kissed her other cheek.

He could still feel her skin under his lips as he spoke. "I loved my walk, Sunette, thank you." For some reason, he had no reservations about kissing her, but what seemed to surprise him was that she didn't object to his behavior.

"You're welcome," she whispered. They stared into each other's eyes for a moment. Foster felt his self-control wavering as his lips suddenly ached to feel hers, but she wasn't his to kiss.

"Sunette, I…" His heart was pounding in his chest.

"Yes?" Her voice was quiet, and he gently ran his fingers down her cheek. He could barely feel her skin, his fingers were so cold. He knew he shouldn't be getting so familiar with her, but something told him it was okay.

"You're the most beautiful woman I've ever seen," he confessed quietly.

She reached up, and he felt her fingertips on his cheek. "Foster," she whispered. "The things you say." He noticed she was looking between his lips and his eyes. "It's your birthday, I think…you deserve a kiss." His heart felt like it was about to burst out of his chest as her fingertips gently brushed his lips, so he kissed them.

"I've dreamed of that kiss we shared in the woods, Sunette. It was—" She pressed her lips on his. Her lips were cold but soft. She lingered a moment, and then the freezing air was once again between them.

"I've dreamed of it too," she whispered, staring into his eyes. "We should probably go back inside before we freeze."

He nodded. "Thank you for my walk, Sunette, I'll treasure this night."

"As will I." She linked her arm with his, and they walked back to the inn. Without another word, he walked her up to her room, and she went inside. Foster walked into his room and leaned against the door, glad he wasn't sharing it with anyone.

He ran his hand through his hair and sighed.

"She's not yours to love, stop it," he mumbled but couldn't stop thinking about his birthday kiss.

CHAPTER 8
STIFLED EMOTIONS

It had been about eight months since they lost their cleric to Ardenry, and they were at an inn resting from their latest job. Bereck sat still and glassy-eyed at the table while everyone around him drank and talked.

Suddenly, he sneezed loudly and moaned. "Oh, gods, I feel terrible," he said pathetically.

Sunette felt his head and clicked her tongue. "You have a fever, darling. Come, let me put you to bed."

"Okay." They stood and slowly walked up the stairs.

Mason scooted farther away from where the paladin was sitting. "Hope he doesn't get us sick."

"Naw, she got him away early," Twig said with a wave of his hand. "He should sleep it off for a few days. We'll be fine."

Sunette came down a few minutes later. "Poor man fell asleep as soon as his head hit the pillow," she said, sitting back down.

"Maybe you should bunk with someone else while he's sick," Lucius suggested.

"Oh, that's all right, Lucius, I'll be fine." She returned to her dinner, clearly not interested in listening to their boss.

"No, really, we don't need two people sick."

She looked up, and Foster could tell she was turning confrontational. "Lucius, I don't think—"

But the half-elf held up a hand. "Well, I do. Pick who you will. You may stay with Bereck during the day and care for him, but I'll not have you in the same room getting sick as you sleep. Now, if you don't like it, then maybe you and your betrothed should leave." Foster was shocked. He'd never heard Lucius speak to anybody like that. Sunette scoffed and started talking heatedly in her native tongue and pointing angrily at him before she stood. She knocked the chair over before walking up the stairs, her feet stomping with every step. When it was clear she wasn't going to hear, Mason burst out in laughter.

"You're lucky she didn't turn you into a duck, Lucius," Raven said, which made Mason laugh even louder.

"What was that about?" It had been a long time since Foster had seen Sunette so angry.

"Sunette forgets that I'm in charge, not her," Lucius said, sipping his ale.

"You've never talked to her like that before."

He shrugged. "It's been a long time, I admit."

"You're not going to drag her out by her hair if she tries to sleep in his room, are you?"

Lucius shook his head. "No, she'll listen to me."

Foster looked up the stairs. "If you say so."

———

Sunette didn't come down for the rest of the night. Foster figured she would spend as much time with Bereck as she could before she went to bed. He was in his room, about to turn in for the night, when he heard a knock at the door.

"Foster? It's Sunette. Are you awake?"

His heart leapt into his throat. "Yeah, come on in." She opened the door, and he could tell she felt like she was intruding.

"Would you mind if I stayed in here? There's no way I can sleep with Mason, and I'm still mad at Lucius, and there are no other rooms available." Her face still looked a little pouty as she talked about their boss, and it made him chuckle.

"Don't want to bunk with Raven and Twig?" he teased.

She scoffed. "Please, I don't even know how *she* can sleep next to him."

He nodded. "Sure, it's no problem."

Sunette sighed and shrugged out of her robe. "Thank you." It was the first time Foster saw her silky slip. When they slept outside while traveling, she always wore her robes, and he'd never shared a room with her before. The slip was long, touching her ankles, and the material softly hugged her hips. He knew she had a nice body but never really paid attention before. As she bent down to get into bed, her slip gave him a glance at the top of her breasts. It only lasted a second, but he still tried not to look as she slipped under the covers and folded the pillow under her neck.

"No problem. I don't promise not to snore, but hopefully, it won't be as loud as Twig."

He looked over and saw she was all covered up and smiling. "No one can be that loud."

"How's Bereck?" Sunette stretched her arm out towards him and yawned. Foster couldn't help but see how flawless her skin looked in the candlelight.

"Sick as a cat, he gets this way sometimes."

Foster chuckled, "Dog."

"What?"

He sat up and leaned on his elbow. "Sick as a dog is the expression."

"Oh," she scoffed. "Bereck never corrects me, so I'm sure I have a few of them wrong. Good night, Apple Picker."

"Good night." She closed her eyes, and Foster watched as her breathing became steady and deep. Just like in Ral Hava, he could see her dark hair shining in the light. He reached over and blew out the candle before more inappropriate thoughts flew into his mind.

———

Sunette stayed with Bereck all day, taking care of him and only coming down for food. Foster tried hard not to look at her. Every time he did, all he could picture was her body in her slip. The next night, she walked into their room exhausted and sat on the bed. "Long day?"

She nodded. "Oh my yes, it's worse than I thought. Bereck has the flu. It's been years since he's been so sick."

"Did you take care of him then?"

She nodded and slipped out of her robe. "Yes, it was about

a week after he professed his feelings to me," she smiled at the memory. "We had been sharing a bed, but not intimately. He woke with a raging fever and said it wasn't proper for me to bathe him. But he was so weak he couldn't stop me."

"Stubborn man."

She chuckled, "Yes, he was. The day his fever broke, he held my hand and said, *'Thank you for not listening to me.'*" She crawled into bed and slipped under the covers.

"He probably wouldn't mind a bath now," Foster teased.

She laughed and threw her pillow at him. "You young men, that's all you think about is sex," she teasingly scolded him.

Foster laughed and picked up her pillow. "Well, how can we not? We're constantly surrounded by beautiful women." He threw her pillow back, and she caught it, but he noticed she was staring at him. "What?"

"You've said that before," her face was soft and attentive. "That I was beautiful."

His smiling face dropped, and he felt his stomach flip from nerves. "Oh yeah, um —"

She laid her hand on his chest. "It's okay." He really didn't have the right to think she was beautiful, let alone tell her. She wasn't his to admire, but what happened between them last winter in Port Winds was almost always on his mind.

Foster sighed, and the words tumbled out of his mouth. "I can't help it. I know you're not mine to admire." He couldn't believe he had just said that, but he felt better when he realized she wasn't going to slap him. She was smiling.

"It's all right, Apple Picker. Sometimes, we admire what we can't have. I know I have." She laid down and turned away from him, "Good night."

"Good night." *Did she just say what I think she* said he wondered, could she have been admiring him all along? His heart started racing as he lay down and stared at the ceiling. *No, no, she's with Bereck, they're to be married, and I need to quit this foolishness,* he angrily told himself and closed his eyes. But sleep came slowly since his mind was on the beautiful mage in the bed next to him.

———

A week later, Bereck's fever finally broke, and Sunette breathed a sigh of relief that he would recover. When Lucius said she could go back to sleeping in the same room, she bounded up the stairs to tell her love.

"Bereck!" She quickly walked in as he finished tucking his shirt in his pants, "Lucius says I can stay with you now." Sunette shut the door and quickly wrapped her arms around his waist. "I missed you," she whispered as she got to her tiptoes and kissed his cheek.

Bereck leaned in and sighed. "Finally, I'll have to thank him for looking after you."

"Who, Lucius?" Sunette stepped back, "I didn't stay with him."

"Oh," he leaned down and put his boots on. "Don't tell me you actually got some sleep with Mason?"

He smiled, and Sunette crossed her arms under her breasts. "No, I stayed with Foster. You know I can barely sleep around him as it is. Why would I voluntarily sleep in his room?"

Bereck pushed his foot rather quickly into his boot and stared at her. "You stayed in Foster's room?"

"Well, where else was I going to stay? I was mad at Lucius, and there weren't any other rooms to be had. I wasn't going to interrupt Ravin and Twig, either. I didn't want to be a fourth wheel."

Bereck cleared his throat and got to his feet. "I don't like how he looks at you."

Her eyes widened in shock. "How he looks at me? Does he look at me in a particularly rude or disparaging manner?"

Bereck shook his head. "You know what I mean, Sunette, he—"

She put up a hand. "Don't Bereck, don't say it."

He walked close and pulled her hand down. "Foster likes you. I don't know why you don't see that."

"Of course he likes me, I like him too, and if I didn't, I'd give him a harder time!"

"Damn it, Sunette, he loves you!"

She pulled her hand away from him and started pacing around the room. "Are you threatened by him, Bereck? Do you feel my love for you isn't enough or weak? Do you think I am a little girl who can't keep her heart in one place because I'm not! You know I hate it when you get possessive of me. I don't know how many times I've told you that I don't belong to you!"

———

Foster walked out of his room, his stomach grumbling for breakfast, when he heard shouting coming from Bereck's room.

"I know you don't belong to me, but I don't like it when others ogle my betrothed! It's disrespectful!"

"It is not! Grabbing my ass and stealing a kiss that's disrespectful! Foster is a nice guy, Bereck. What kind of paladin has such jealousy issues, I ask?" Foster felt horrible. They were fighting because of him. But he was a smart man, so he'd stay out of it and let them deal with it on their own.

"A paladin who sees his love being swayed by another, that's who! Tell me you don't want him, Sunette. I've seen the way you look at each other, and it kills me!" Foster didn't realize he looked at her in any particular way, hell, he didn't realize she looked at *him* in any particular way. But when he heard loud footsteps coming toward the door, he quickly ran back into his room and shut the door. He did not want to get in the middle of this. Not a second later, the door to Bereck's room slammed shut, and footsteps receded down the stairs.

Foster steeled himself for an uncomfortable breakfast and opened his door. "Bereck jeez!" The paladin was standing in the hall, and his hand was raised like he was about to knock on the door. "You scared the hell out of me. How are you feeling?"

He lowered his hand and stared at Foster. "Thank you for looking out for Sunette while I was laid up."

Foster didn't think he sounded grateful but just nodded. "No problem." He hoped that was it, but Bereck just stood in the hallway staring at him. "You look a lot better. Sunette said you had the flu. Those are the worst."

"Yes, they are." Bereck stared at him for a moment before quickly turning around and walking down the hall. Foster sighed heavily and shook the nerves from his body. He may have been a big guy, but Bereck was so much more experienced. He knew he wouldn't get away injury-free if the paladin insisted on fighting.

CHAPTER 9
MISTAKE

As the group left their summer inn, they traveled west, looking for some work. Everyone noticed the change in Sunette and Bereck. Sunette would hardly speak to the paladin, who was constantly trying to woo her back in his good graces. Foster wasn't sure if they were together or not but decided to keep his distance.

One night, Foster was sleeping when voices woke him. He opened his eyes and saw the couple standing a few yards from the camp. Sunette was hugging herself and looking at the ground while Bereck spoke. "—stand being apart from you, Sunette. Seeing you hurt because of my own insecurities kills me, and I feel horrible. I don't know what I can do to make up for what I've done." He reached out and took her hands. "Tell me what to do, and I'll do it. I can't imagine my life without you, my beautiful mage." Foster watched as he kneeled in front of her, still holding her hands. "I love you more than I ever knew I could. I'll never stop."

Sunette sniffed, "Bereck, I miss you. I can't help it. My heart has seen only you for so long." Foster could hear the tears in her voice as she spoke. It was hard to hear and not be able to do something about it. "I can't deny what you said, Bereck, but I need you to trust that I love you. If I didn't, I wouldn't be so hurt. I would never leave you, do you understand?"

He nodded. "I do," he leaned forward and kissed her hands. "I'm so sorry I let my insecurities get the better of me. Is there any chance you could forgive me?"

She quickly wrapped her arms around his neck. "Bereck, I'll always forgive you." Her voice was muffled as she buried her face in his shoulder. Foster watched as they embraced like they hadn't in weeks, and he couldn't help but think it looked wrong. *It should be me,* he thought and closed his eyes.

———

A few weeks later, the group came across a large military outpost four days outside of Meeker's Hold. It looked like everyone there was preparing for a big battle. Lucius led them to one of the guards and introduced himself.

"Hello there, my name is Lucius Silverblade. Are you expecting trouble?"

The man nodded. "We've had small battalions of undead attack us every night the last three nights. We're preparing for another one."

"We'd be happy to offer our services to your General." He looked back at his group.

Bereck stepped forward. "We would be honored to help rid you of such a menace."

"Your help would be welcome. Please follow me." It was a grand outpost, but it had definitely seen signs of battle. Scorch marks on the wall and piles of undead burning throughout. The group followed him into a large room on the first floor and saw five men talking around a table covered in maps. "General Haltom, this is Lucius and his people. They have offered to help."

An older man wearing fancy plate mail looked up from the maps and nodded. "Thank you for volunteering." He walked up and shook hands with Lucius.

"You're most welcome, General. Anything we can do will be our pleasure."

He walked back to the table. "What do you know of our situation?" Lucius followed him while the group stayed back and observed.

"Some trouble with undead," was all Lucius said. General Haltom explained at midnight every night for the past three nights, hordes of undead had attacked his keep, and he had no idea why. He sent his family away two nights ago and asked for help from Meeker's Hold but hadn't received word either way yet.

"I'm grateful for any help you can give."

"We're fighter-heavy, but Sunette is a mage and a pretty good one, if I may say so." He motioned back at her, and she bowed, flashing them a friendly smile.

Lord Haltom nodded. "Magic's what we've been missing. It'll be a tremendous help. Nick, if you would show them to some rooms, I'll have some food sent up."

"Thank you very much, General, it's appreciated." Lucius turned, and they all followed the man named Nick up to the third floor.

"These three rooms are all connected by a common room. I think you'll be most comfortable here."

"It's perfect, young man. Thank you." Lucius ushered everyone in, and Foster made sure to bunk with their boss.

That night, they ate dinner in Lucius's room while they came up with a plan. Twig and his big axe would be outside with the Lord's men, as would Raven. Lucius and Mason would hide in the shadows around the fort. Bereck would be just inside the gate in case they got in. Since Foster was the only archer, his job was to protect Sunette as she flung spells from the battlements. They figured that would be the best place for her since she needed to see the enemy without getting into an actual fight.

The food was good despite the coming battle, and they tried to relax over dessert and some wine when Bereck stood up and cleared his throat.

"Pardon me, everyone, I have an announcement." Everyone quieted and looked at him. Foster noted how Sunette had a confused look on her face. "As you all know, Sunette and I have been betrothed for some time now."

"Little too long," Lucius teased.

Bereck chuckled. "I quite agree, that's why after we finish with our current job," he turned and looked down at her. "I'm going to take Sunette home, where we'll finally marry."

She gasped, "Really?" A smile spread along her face that made Foster's heart involuntarily speed with excitement.

Bereck nodded and took her hands as she got to her feet.

"I've made you wait far too long, Sunette."

She laughed. "Oh, Bereck, I love you." She rose on her tiptoes as he wrapped his arms around her and kissed her deeply. When they parted, Foster saw a happy, peaceful look on both their faces. But he couldn't help but feel a little pit growing in his stomach.

Raven clapped and cheered. "About time."

"Congratulations, you two. I'm sure you'll be happy," he managed to say.

"Thanks, Foster," Bereck said, still staring at Sunette.

Lucius laughed. "You two better spend the rest of the night in your room."

"Lucius, really," Sunette scolded him, but Bereck picked her up and walked out of the room to everyone but Foster laughing.

When the door shut, Mason chucked a piece of bread that hit him in the head. "What's wrong, big guy?"

"Nothing," he picked up the bread and threw it back at Mason's head. "Missing Lessa." It was a lie, but he knew everyone would believe it.

"Cheer up, Foster. I'm sure after the battle, a lusty servant girl will fall into your arms," Lucius said.

"I think you're mistaking me for you, Lucius."

He laughed, "May we all be so lucky."

"Speaking of rooms." Raven got to her feet and pulled Twig away from the group as Mason laughed.

———

They rested for a few hours until they heard an alarm bell ringing. Foster sat up and quickly strapped on his armor and belted his sword around his waist. He grabbed his bow by the door and ran to his post. As he ran through the courtyard, he saw Bereck preparing, swinging his sword around and stretching.

The paladin turned as he ran past. "Take care of her, Foster."

"I will," he said as he ran up the stairs. When he reached the battlements, he saw Sunette staring at the field beyond. He walked up behind her and surveyed the land before them. There were hundreds of undead chanting and banging on the ground.

"There's so many Foster. General Haltom said there weren't nearly as many the previous nights." He looked over at the mage, she looked scared, and Foster laid his hand on her shoulder.

"As long as we have faith, we'll prevail."

She sighed loudly and shook her head. "I don't think even your mother would have so much faith." He didn't know what to say to comfort her. He was just as scared.

"Ready yourselves," General Haltom yelled out. "Sorceress, the second you see them move, you give it to them!"

"Yes, Sir." Foster closed his eyes and listened. There was a faint squeal under all the growls and grunts. He opened his eyes and searched the darkness.

Finally, he saw them. "They've got ballistas!" He yelled out and pointed. Haltom cursed loudly and ran to tell the others. The sound of hundreds of undead walking filled the air, and Sunette took a deep breath. Words of magic spilled from her mouth as she raised her hands. The men watched as a large wall of fire erupted in front of the encroaching army. They heard the screams of the horde as the fire engulfed them, but it wasn't enough to counter all of them. They watched the General's men engage the undead, but they were soon overrun, and they heard the gate crash open.

"Gods, Bereck is down there!" Sunette yelled as she summoned a tornado to rip apart the back ranks of the army.

"He'll be fine. He's made for this, perhaps more than any of us." Foster had seen the paladin banish and turn undead to dust for years. They were no match for him. The faint sound of steel on steel filled the air, and Sunette cast as many spells as she could at the groups outside, but they kept coming. They watched as little groups of them would fall to the ground, no doubt Twig and Raven's doing.

Foster heard running footsteps and turned as three rotted, undead bodies made their way up the stairs. "Watch out, Sunette, they're coming!" He yelled a warning before sinking arrows into two of them. The third was too close, so he drew his sword and engaged it. It was strong but slow, and Foster had no trouble handling it and separated its rotted head from its shoulders. He turned and saw another was trying to sneak in the shadows and was heading straight for the mage. "Sunette, look out!" She ducked as he yelled, and Foster watched the undead's sword slice through the air just where her head once was. He ran to her and skewered it on his sword. He was about to kick it off when he heard the first ballista round hit the stone wall. Sunette screamed and ducked behind the wall. She dared a quick look over the battlement and cast another spell. Foster didn't have time to see the effect it had before she yelled out.

"Foster duck!" They both flattened themselves on the ground as another ballista knocked some stones loose and covered them in dust. He looked up and saw Sunette was reaching for him, so he quickly crawled over as another projectile rocked the platform. Foster took her hand and could see how tired she looked. "I don't have much left."

"Just stay down. I won't let them get you," he said as five more shambling undead walked into view.

Foster tried to get up, but Sunette held fast. "No, you'll get hit!" Her hand flew in the undead's direction. He heard her say odd words before all the undead were encased in a thick dome of ice. "Maybe the ballista will get them," she said hopefully. Running footsteps got their attention, and they turned as Bereck appeared on the other side of the platform.

"Sunette!"

"Bereck, get down!" She yelled but was drowned out by a booming noise behind them. They turned and saw a large hand gripping the battlements. Sunette screamed as a huge undead ogre crawled over the wall.

"Foul beast!" Bereck yelled and engaged the lumbering undead. It was strong and swung a large club at the paladin's head. But Bereck tumbled out of the way, and the ground shook as the club cracked the stone beneath their feet. More running feet and the roars of undead got Foster's attention, and he turned as more humanoid undead ran up from the other side.

"Stay down, Sunette!" He yelled as he got to his feet and met the undead head-on. These were different from the others, they were fast and seemed to know how to fight, but Foster was quicker, and in three strokes, his combatants were missing arms or legs, rendering them useless. A loud roar pierced the air and made Foster's bones shake. He turned and saw Bereck pulling his sword out of the ogre's neck before it fell dead against the battlements. Stone cracking filled the air, and both men dashed to Sunette as the wall behind her broke away. She screamed and reached out for anything as the stone beneath her began crumbling away.

"Sunette!" Foster screamed and slid on his stomach and caught her arm as she fell through the air. "I got you!"

"Foster!" The sound of her voice was almost enough to break him. She was so terrified. With his other hand, he reached over and was able to get both hands on her.

Bereck reached down and put an arm under her. "Don't worry, sweetheart," he said, lifting her up, "I—" a sudden jerk dragged both Foster and Sunette back up onto the battlement as another loud crack filled the air. When the dust cleared, Sunette was in a heap on Foster's lap. She had a large gash across her forehead, and her face was covered in deep scrapes.

"Sunette, are you okay?"

He picked her up, and she moaned. "What was that?" Her eyes opened, and a sound he never wanted to hear escaped her lips. "Bereck!" He didn't know such agony and heartache could be made by a human voice, and when he looked up, he felt ill. Bereck was pierced through the chest by one of the giant javelins from the ballista. He was pinned to the wall, six inches off the ground, and his chin was on his chest. Sunette got to her feet and started pulling on the projectile. "No! You can't die Bereck!" Foster got up and could see blood pouring from the paladin's unmoving body.

"Oh gods," he whispered. Sunette's crying was becoming hysterical as she tried to pry the large spike from her love's body.

"Sunette, stop. He's gone." Foster ran over and captured her arms as she screamed in agony.

"No, he can't be!" She fell to her knees.

"We have to move. We're exposed here." He could feel tears daring to fall. He didn't know what hurt worse, Sunette in pain or that his friend was gone. He could hear her hyperventilating a moment before she collapsed in his arms. Foster sat on the ground and held his hand over the cut on her forehead. "You're going to be alright," he whispered as his tears fell on her cheeks. Running footsteps got his attention, and he saw Lucius appear. He was out of breath and had a nasty cut on his chest, but he looked okay.

"Did you see," but he didn't finish speaking as his eyes landed on Bereck. Lucius slowly walked over to them and then collapsed to his knees. "Gods, we shouldn't have come here." Foster heard him whisper. "We shouldn't have come."

General Haltom came running up behind him, "The necromancer was on the field. He's dead. We should be..." but he stopped talking when he saw the scene. A few of the other guards were able to pull the large spike out of Bereck and lay him on the ground while Foster held Sunette tight and looked at her peaceful face. A healer ran up and healed the wounds on her face.

"Please wake up, Sunette. I love you. Please wake up," he whispered in her ear. Suddenly, she took in a deep, ragged breath and coughed. Foster held her face until she was able to catch her breath. "Can you hear me?" After what seemed an eternity, she opened her eyes, and tears were already falling from them.

"It's not true," she whispered.

He laid his forehead on the side of her head, "I'm so sorry honey, I'm so sorry." She cried, her arms wrapping around Foster. Everyone who could hear knew her heart was broken. General Haltom laid a hand on Lucius' shoulder. "I'm so sorry, Lucius."

"Don't apologize to me. Apologize to Sunette. They were to be married."

The General was quiet for a few more moments. "You can stay as long as you like. You'll want for nothing."

"Except our friend."

———

Foster carried Sunette back to her room as she sobbed. He put her in bed, where she continued to cry. Foster never left her side and let her squeeze him until he was near suffocating. An hour passed before a priest walked in. "Let me put her to sleep. I fear it's the only way she'll rest." Foster nodded and started sliding off the bed and gave her cheek a kiss.

"I'll be right here." The priest touched her temple, and Foster watched her eyes slowly close, and when her breathing was deep and steady, he relaxed a bit. "Thank you, Father." He gave Foster a nod and left the room as he tucked her in. He couldn't dream of what she was going through. The thought made him feel cold.

Lucius came in and walked over to them. "How is she?" His eyes were red, and Foster could see tear tracks on his face.

Foster reached out and took her hand. "The priest put her to sleep. She hasn't stopped crying." He held her hand to his lips and said a little prayer to Otto in hopes that Bereck's soul was where it should be.

Lucius leaned over and kissed her cheek. "Let's let her rest for now. Come get something to eat. You must be hungry."

Truthfully, he was starving, but he didn't want to go. "I don't want to leave her."

The half-elf laid a hand on Foster's shoulder. "We need to be strong for her. That means taking care of yourself so you can take care of her. You will be no good to her if you're not healthy. Now come, Haltom's servants have prepared some food for us."

Foster could hear the wisdom in his words. "You speak as if you know from experience."

Lucius nodded, "I've been traveling a long time. Come, eat with those who are still here." Slowly, Foster stood and followed Lucius as he led him to the rest of their group.

There was a fire going in the hearth in the main hall, Mason was sitting next to it in a chair. Raven had her arms around Twig on a couch as if he'd float away at any moment.

Foster hadn't realized he didn't know if the others made it or not, and he felt guilty. He walked over to Raven and gave her a hug. "Glad you made it."

"Barely," she whispered.

Mason turned to the couple on the couch. "Raven, what was that light?"

Her eyebrows furled. "You saw that?" He nodded. "Just a powerful healing spell, Twig was badly hurt." Twig kissed her head, and she snuggled closer to him. A servant walked in and gave them all mugs of ale, but no one drank. Twig was staring at the fire, his hand absentmindedly running up and down Raven's arm. Her face was red from either seeing Twig so hurt or Bereck's loss. Mason had his elbows resting on his knees, and Foster could see his bottom lip trembling.

"How's Sunette?" he whispered.

"She's asleep for now." Mason covered his face and held back sobs. Lucius walked over to the young rogue and laid a hand on his shoulder.

"It's okay to cry, Mason, Bereck's loss is a great one." He wiped away his own tears. For a moment, the little rogue looked like he might take Lucius up on that offer, but he quickly sat up and wiped his face.

"Bereck was the best of us. It shouldn't have happened. Besides, we have to be strong for Sunette."

Lucius took a seat next to Raven on the couch. "We are allowed to grieve as well, Mason. Don't forget that. Sunette is strong. She'll pull herself up after a while." He laid a hand on Raven's leg, and she reached out and held it. Foster saw there were several haunches of meat by the fire and couldn't stop himself from digging in. Fighting like that always made him ravenous, but he stopped and held up his mug.

"To Bereck."

They all raised their mugs together. "To Bereck."

———

Sunette stayed in Foster's arms for days, crying, refusing to eat, and only sleeping when the cleric put her to sleep. Raven helped her wash the blood off and changed into clean clothes. Five days later, General Haltom gave Bereck a grand funeral fit for a hero. Sunette could only watch from her window.

"Are you sure you don't want to go down?" Foster stood behind her. They could see the pyre and Bereck's body wrapped in white, surrounded by the group and the General's men.

"I don't know if I could take it," her voice was quiet, her throat raw from crying.

Foster laid a hand on her arm. "You're stronger than you know."

"I don't feel strong."

"You don't have to right now, but I know you are." They watched the funeral from the window. A priest of Otto stood by the pyre, speaking, but they couldn't hear him. Eventually, the priest lit the kindling around Bereck's body, and the General's men started to leave, but the group stayed. Sunette turned from the window without a word. Foster followed her as she walked outside to the pyre. The group was sitting on the ground, consoling each other, when Lucius looked up.

"Sunette." Everybody stood and hugged her. "I was hoping you'd come down."

"I wasn't sure I could."

Lucius squeezed her hand. "Let's give our paladin the funeral he deserves." Sunette nodded, and they walked closer to the fire. Lucius sighed, still holding one of Sunette's hands. "I remember when Bereck answered my call for people. I was in Meeker's Hold, and my last group had just split. I wondered if maybe I should head to Salthole and wait for Stella. Then this big human walked in, sword on his back and a smile on his face. That's how this group started, just the two of us." He squeezed Sunette's hand. "We went to Ardenry next, and one day, we happened across a little illegal mage fight." Sunette closed her eyes, and her shoulders shook as she tried not to chuckle. "We watched this spitfire of a woman fling spells at a young man who was desperately trying to block them." Lucius laid his forehead on hers, "He was sorely outmatched." She let a teary chuckle leak out. "That's how two became three, the start of the best damned group I ever had."

She hugged him, burying her face in his neck. "It feels like it's been ages," her voice was thick with tears.

"Oh, it has." They all laughed and hugged the two of them.

"Who else wants to say something about our paladin?" Lucius looked around at everybody.

Raven took a breath and held Sunette's hand. "I'm terrible at this type of thing," her bottom lip quivered a bit. "Bereck was a good man. He loved Sunette, Otto, and helping people. That much was evident. One thing, I don't know if you know, is that he had a decent singing voice." Everyone but Sunette looked surprised at that. "One time when we were in Salthole, I was coming back from trying to earn a few coins at 'The Giggling Orc,' and I saw Bereck sitting outside our inn, a crying, dirty child in his lap. Bereck was rocking them and singing, trying to comfort them. I was quite impressed with his voice, and I wondered why he didn't sing more. I watched as the child stopped crying and hugged him. The barkeeper came out and handed Bereck a bag of something which he gave to the child. They smiled so big and ran off home, I assume. Bereck watched them until they disappeared around a corner. I walked over and teased him about his voice, saying if he ever needed a duet partner, I was available. He laughed and said my voice is as close to perfection as one could get, and he wouldn't dare sully it with his." She took a breath, and a tear slid down her cheek. "I wish I made him sing with me."

Mason took her hand and gave it a squeeze. "I remember when Lessa and I joined, I could tell Bereck just thought I was a loud-mouthed kid."

"You were," Lucius cut in.

Mason smiled. "True. But I think Bereck realized that I was in for the long haul when we were traveling in the woods outside of Buckland. He was on watch, but I couldn't sleep for some reason, so I sat up with him. He was honing his sword by the fire like he always did. I told him it was loud and it might cover up footsteps or something. He shook his head, not taking his eyes off his sword, 'There are leaves all over the ground. If anything comes up, we'll hear it,' he said. But I was still scared." He smiled and took Sunette's hand from Lucius. "I remember my ear twitching, and I took my dagger out. Something made a noise, but Bereck insisted we were fine. Then I saw them, two glowing eyes staring at us from the trees behind Bereck. Before I could even get the words out, the wolf had lunged at him. I jumped at Bereck, and thankfully, he rolled out of the way, and I slammed into the wolf. Gods, it hurt," he chuckled. "But my dagger struck true, and it died right there, inches from where Bereck was once sitting. He helped me up, gave me a little healing, and stared at the wolf. He said, 'I'm sorry I didn't listen to you, I thought you were just a foolish boy wanting to play hero, but clearly, you aren't."

"I remember that," Sunette spoke up. "He told me how he misjudged you and that I should think about calling you by your name instead of 'you.'" Everyone laughed, "I think it took me a few more weeks."

He hugged her tightly. "That's okay. You can call me whatever you want."

Sunette wiped her eyes and walked closer to the pyre. It was just embers now. "My sweet, brave paladin, you taught me how to love, how to see the beauty in everything. You will always be in my heart. I will miss your kisses and waking up in your arms." She started crying, "I hope that you are with Otto now. You deserve to be by his side. Goodbye, my love." She kissed her fingertips and laid them on her forehead. Foster walked up next to her and did the same. One by one, they stood next to their mage and touched their kissed fingers on their foreheads. Sunette sniffed and stood straight. "I'm hungry."

Foster laid a hand on her back. She hadn't eaten for days, it seemed. "There's plenty of food inside."

She nodded and took his hand before walking inside. "I didn't wither away." He heard her whisper as they walked into the keep.

"No, you didn't." He gave her hand a squeeze and felt her squeeze back. They stayed at the fort for a week while Sunette got her strength back. The General gave each of them plenty of supplies and three hundred gold pieces worth of gems as thanks. Sunette had Bereck's ashes in a little box the priest gave her. She requested they go back to Salthole so she could spread his ashes on Otto's turf, and they all agreed.

CHAPTER 10
ANSWERED QUESTIONS

It would take them another month to get back to Salthole, and the group took their time. While Foster was on duty, he'd watch over Sunette. Sleeping seemed to be the only time she seemed at peace. Daytime brought waves of grief, hell, they all felt it, but she was the only one whose cries filled the air. He started thinking back to last winter when she told him that her family was gone because they had been hunted down. She never answered him when he asked if they were still looking for her. If it had been that long since she'd seen them, perhaps they had finally lost sight of her. But he wanted to make sure. He didn't want to lose anyone else, especially her.

The next night, the group settled by a little stream, and everyone put their bare feet in, grateful for the cool respite on their skin. Foster sat next to Sunette and sighed as his feet plopped into the water. "Much better."

She smiled. "I do miss swimming. It's been ages."

"Same." He cleared his throat, "Can I ask a personal question?"

"Of course." She looked up and met his eyes. He could tell this was a good moment. The grief was ebbing for her. Her eyes were bright, and there was a little smile on her face.

"Last winter, you said that your family was running from men, that they killed your family. Do you know if they're still looking for you?"

She sighed and looked back down at the water. "I have no idea. I was so young when we left the continent, and Massus only told me so much about them."

"Why were they after your family?"

She pulled her hair over her right shoulder and ran her fingers through it. "Somehow, these men got it in their head that our blood was the key to finding the Cup of Kuraim."

His eyes narrowed in confusion. "The hell is that?"

She shrugged. "A chalice of some kind, I imagine. I never found evidence of its existence. They believed whoever had the cup would have untold power, but it was hidden, and a certain family line held the key to finding it. Only one person in the family was the key, and they didn't know who it was. So, their brilliant idea was to pick us off one by one and see if that person was the key. Of course, none of us were. We had no idea what they were talking about. You'd think if our family were so important that we were the guardians of a dangerous artifact that we would know!" She kicked her feet in the water. "When it first started, Massus said that my grandparents went to our local constabulary and said these men are killing our family. But this family, they were rich and could cover up anything and pay off anyone. The northern continent failed us, so we ran. We were never in one place for long because eventually they'd catch up."

Foster suddenly remembered something about her story. "Gods, your brother was just a kid then, huh?"

"He was ten when he died. It was just us and Massus by then, and he had bartered passage for us to this continent. We were almost gone when they caught up to us. I remember him hugging me and telling me to go with Massus, and I did. I didn't realize until we were on the boat without him what he had done."

He reached out and laid a hand on her shoulder. "What was his name?"

"Vittore, he had brown hair and brown eyes, a little freckle on his left cheek. That's all I remember about what he looked like." He couldn't imagine what she had gone through. Foster couldn't dare to think of his brother dying. The thought chilled his blood.

"How do you know he's dead?"

She shook her head. "I don't, not really. I've been too afraid to send him a message. I don't see how he could have survived.

Massus believed he died," she looked back up at him, finality in her eyes. "So, I did."

"Do you know the name of these people who were chasing you?"

She shook her head. "No, if I did, I forgot. I don't remember Massus ever saying it. He didn't want their names associated with me in any way, just in case."

"I suppose I understand. If you were running, why didn't you change your name?"

She gave a dark chuckle. "Massus said I should be proud to be a Chelri. We were brave and talented, and fuck anyone who comes messing with us. I think moving to the continent gave him enough hope that they wouldn't follow. I often wondered myself why we never changed our names. When I was eleven, I started picking names for myself in case he changed his mind. I was going to be Viviana Massi."

Foster chuckled, "Nice name."

A little smirk played on her lips as she looked back at the water. "I thought so."

Foster hoped he wasn't overstepping any boundaries, but he had to know. "If there were a way to find out if your brother was gone, would you want to know?"

She kicked her feet in the water a few times. "Maybe." She looked up at him, "What do you have in mind, Apple Picker?"

He nervously licked his lips and leaned closer. "When we're in Salthole, we find someone who can speak to the dead. We can ask him what he remembers about these people, and we can keep an eye out."

Sunette stared at him for a moment. "We can do that?" she whispered. He nodded.

"Hmm," she chewed on the inside of her lip. "If it means knowing more about these people, I say we try."

Foster nodded, "Leave it to me."

She took a shuddering breath and held her hands up to her lips. "I will."

———

The group got to Salthole a little more than a month later, and the waves of grief hitting Sunette were easing like she knew they would. It was still hard when they hit, but her friends were a great help. Raven would sit with her and brush her hair or sing something soothing. Mason always tried to make her laugh, but it was his failure to do so that made her laugh instead. Foster was the ever-present rock, always by her side. She had never been more grateful for him. After they dropped their belongings in an inn, they walked to the docks, Sunette carrying the box with Bereck's ashes.

No one said a word as they made their way to an empty dock and stood around her. Footsteps made them turn, and they watched a man with a sharp goatee walking over to them.

"I hate to interrupt, but it looks like you have recently lost a loved one, yes?" He had dark hair that was slicked back and looked maybe thirty, if that.

"Yes," Sunette spoke up. "He was a Paladin of Otto. I wanted to spread his ashes in the ocean to be closer to his God."

The man put a hand on his chest, and his expression softened. "A Paladin of Otto, I am so sorry for your loss. My name is Captain Nightingale, and my ship, the Double D, is right over there. If you'd like, we could go out to deeper water?"

Sunette turned to Lucius, who whispered in her ear. "I've heard of him. Stella mentioned him a few times. He's trustworthy."

She looked back at Nightingale. "Why did you come over? Hoping to make some coin?"

He smiled, "Honestly, yes, but when you said he was a servant of Otto, I knew I must help put this man to rest where he deserves. Not where crabs and mud dwellers make their home, but in the depths of the sea, where Otto's heart resides." She looked back at her friends. Their faces all said the same thing. It was up to her.

"All right."

He gave her a little bow, "Follow me." They followed the man to his ship, it looked seaworthy, and they all walked up the plank. It seemed the moment the crew saw Sunette with the box, they knew what they were doing. Some took off their hats and nodded, while others moved quickly, getting the boat untethered, and soon, they were off. They sailed for half an hour, Salthole shrinking behind them. The boat stopped, and Nightingale walked up to them. "Here you go, Madame, a proper send-off."

"Thank you." She walked to the side of the boat, Foster and Raven flanking her. Twig next to Raven and Mason next to him, Lucius next to Foster. "Bereck, you dedicated your life to Otto to protect the innocent and destroy evil where you found it. You deserve to lay where Otto's power is greatest, where your soul will rest in his loving arms." She opened the box. Nightingale was good. Where she was standing, the wind blew his ashes away from the boat onto the ocean. "Rest, my love, you deserve it." She lowered the box and closed her eyes as tears ran down her cheeks. Foster laid a hand on her shoulder, and Raven put her hand on the other one. "We can head back," she said.

"As you like." Nightingale turned and motioned for the crew to head back to Salthole.

"Thank you," Sunette said to those around her.

"Anything for you." Lucius hugged her, and she laid her head on his shoulder. "I feel I must apologize to you, mistress mage," he whispered. "If I wasn't so keen on volunteering our services in a clearly desperate situation, I feel you'd still have your Paladin."

He felt her shake her head. "I do not blame you, Lucius. Bereck died doing what his god asked of him, and I know he doesn't blame you either. We started traveling with you because we wanted to do good in the world, and ridding the world of the undead was a part of that."

"Still, my heart is heavier than usual at the loss of our paladin because I know he loved you with his entire soul, and you him." He stood straight and kissed her forehead. "If there's anything I can do for you, tell me."

"I will." As the boat pulled back into port, they thanked Nightingale once again and walked back to their inn. They got drinks and, one last time, toasted the paladin they'd all miss.

———

The next day, Foster went to the Roasted Orc. He knew the more unsavory denizens tended to hang out here, so he thought he'd start there for someone who could talk to the dead. He sat at the bar and ordered a drink.

"Can I ask you something?" He asked the bartender as he slid him a mug.

The man cleared his throat, and he leaned on the bar. "Yeah."

"You know anyone, not in a temple, that can speak to the dead? I wanna keep the priests out of this."

He nodded, "Don't blame ya, there's a woman, Ebba. She lives a few blocks away." He grabbed a napkin and a pencil. "Here's the house number. Little tip: don't go while the sun's up. Makes her cranky." He handed Foster the napkin.

"Appreciate it." He put the napkin in his pocket and finished his drink before making his way back to the Inn. He found Sunette in their room, reading her spell book. She looked up as he closed the door. "I found someone."

She took a deep breath and put her book down. "Who?"

He sat in front of her. "Woman named Ebba, I was told not to go when the sun's out."

Sunette looked shocked and chuckled. "What, she a vampire or something?"

He smiled. "No, I think she's just a night owl."

She looked relieved. "That's much better."

He reached out and laid a hand on hers. "This is your decision. If you don't want to do it, we won't."

She laid her hand over his, keeping her eyes down. "I know. But I think I want to. You were right. We need to know if these people are still after me."

Foster nodded. "Just let me know when you want to go, and we'll go."

"Tonight, before I lose my nerve."

He reached up and ran his thumb against her cheek. "You

got it."

———

The sun had been down for a few hours. Foster and Sunette walked over to the rougher part of town and found Ebba's house easily enough. There was a light on in the window. The closer they got, they saw it was a weird candle with a red flame. It didn't seem to flicker like a normal flame.

"I've never seen a candle flame like that before." Sunette stared at it.

"Me either. Hopefully, it means she's open for business." They walked up the steps, and Foster knocked on the door.

A woman with dark, graying hair stood in the doorway. "Help you?"

"We're looking for Ebba," Foster said to her.

"That's me." She looked impatient and crossed her arms over her stomach.

"We heard you can speak to the dead," Sunette spoke up.

"Need to talk to someone?"

"Yes, if you could." Ebba moved aside, and the two of them walked inside. The incense was heavy, and Foster knew it had to be covering up a worse smell. They followed Ebba into a room off the hallway, it was filled with bookshelves and trinkets that he couldn't identify for the life of him. Ebba motioned for them to sit at a round table, and she took the single chair across from them.

"How long have they been gone?" She started pulling things onto the table, a mortar and pestle, some herbs, and salt.

"Almost twenty years." Sunette swallowed at that.

"That's nothing." She sounded confident, at least. "Name?"

"Vittore Chelri, he's my brother."

Ebba gave a little chuckle. "Fancy." Everything looked to be set up on the table. "Twenty gold, you get five questions. They'll not see you, only me, but you will see and hear them." She held out her hand, and Foster put a little pouch in her hand, and she put it away without counting it. They watched her put salt and herbs into the mortar and grind them up. She took a pinch and threw it into the fire of the candle that was in the middle of the table. "Vittore Chelri, someone wishes to speak with you. Will you answer?" They watched the smoke rise into the air and swirl in an orb shape.

Sunette gasped as the smoke made the shape of a young boy's head. "Vittore," she whispered as the head looked around.

"Vittore Chelri?" Ebba asked the smoke.

"To've?"

Ebba looked over at Sunette, an eyebrow raised. "Oh, I didn't learn common until we came to the continent. He won't understand you."

She cleared her throat. "Well, translate for me and tell me what to say. We'll get through this." She sat back. "How do I say your sister is here and has some questions." Foster watched Sunette tell her syllable by syllable how to say what she needed to say. Ebba repeated it pretty well, and Vittore turned to her.

He answered the question, and Sunette smiled. "He said, my little sister? How is she? I miss her. How old is she?" She laughed, and tears sparkled in her eyes. "I had forgotten what he sounded like." She sniffed and turned to Ebba and gave her another phrase to say. Ebba reiterated, and they listened to his reply. "He said their name was 'Coscarelli,'" she repeated. She turned to Foster, "I don't know that name."

He shook his head. "Me either." Sunette turned to Ebba and said another phrase, which she repeated. As Vittore spoke, Foster could see a smile on his face.

"He said that I became the last after he," she swallowed, "threw himself off the cliff. He's sad he isn't with me but is so happy that I am grown up and safe."

Foster put an arm around her, and she laid her head on his shoulder. "Do we need to know anything else?" She sat up and gave Ebba another phrase. Her brother answered it seemed like a lot. Sunette nodded but didn't repeat what he said. She gave Ebba one more phrase, and she repeated.

Her brother smiled. "Si laith ven err." Foster's ear twitched in recognition. He had heard Sunette say similar words before to

Bereck.

The head disappeared, and Sunette looked over at Foster. "We can go now." She turned to Ebba. "Thank you for your help."

"I gotta say that was a first. Never conjured someone who didn't speak common before." They all stood and walked to the door. "Come back if you have more questions," Ebba said as they walked out of the house. She closed the door behind them, and Foster took her arm.

"So, we have a name that neither of us know. You know the fate of your brother," he looked down at her. "How do you feel?"

They walked a little before she answered. "More comforted than I thought I would be." She looked up and met his eyes. "But I'm grateful I know his fate. Thank you for suggesting this."

He nodded. "I'm not losing anyone else, and I think we've concluded that these men have given up the chase."

"Seems that way."

"If you don't mind, what was the last thing you asked him?"

She smiled, not meeting his eyes. "I told him I had a good life, and I hoped he was at peace because he was a wonderful big brother." Foster smiled and patted her hand.

CHAPTER 11
HEALING AND HEARTBREAK

Four months later, the group was in Shade's Peak after clearing out a den of kobolds. It didn't go quite as planned, but the den was clear, and they were alive with more gold in their pockets, so overall, it was a success.

"I can't believe you missed that snare, Mason." Raven shook her head while rubbing her ankle. "I have never been more embarrassed in my life."

The little thief laughed. "I'm sorry, I'm only human, and it was dark. Maybe Twig could scout more if you have a problem with me."

Twig grunted. "Fuck that." He finished his ale and stood, "I'll be back later."

"Oh," Raven looked a little put out, "you don't want to dance?" The group on stage was good, so the air was thick with music.

"Naw, besides, you need to rest your ankle." He wasn't wrong. When Raven stepped into the snare, everyone heard her ankle pop out of place, and without a healer or paladin, her meager healing skills weren't enough to get her totally back on her feet just yet.

"Fine," she grumbled and watched Twig leave the tavern, something like concern on her face. Foster finished his dinner and listened to the music. The group was good, it had been a while since they heard decent music and turned to Sunette. She was staring at her plate, picking at the carrots. She didn't seem to be paying attention to the music or conversation. As he looked at her, there was only one thing he could think about, and that was dancing with his arms around her. So, he decided to give it a shot. "Sunette?"

She looked up, finally putting a carrot in her mouth. "Foster."

He chuckled and leaned forward, "Will you dance with me?"

Shock showed on her face as she swallowed. "Pardon?"

He held out his hand for her. "Dance with me, you'll have fun."

She shook her head and sat back, crossing her arms over her stomach. "I can't."

"Of course you can. I've seen you dance lots of times." Foster could see the others at the table were watching, waiting to see what she'd do, and he hoped the audience wouldn't annoy her.

She scoffed, "No, I mean, I just...can't let myself have fun."

He sat back, shocked at her words. "What, why not?"

Sunette sighed, "I can't imagine having fun while Bereck's gone." She shook her head and looked away from him. "It's not fair."

"Oh." Foster took a breath, "Sunette, I don't mean to sound like a jackass, but do you really think Bereck would want you to stop having fun?"

"Bereck's gone," she looked down. "It doesn't matter what he would think." Foster knew that she should mourn her love, and it would take time. But he could see the loving, bright woman he knew start to disappear into herself.

"You should dance with him," Raven said. "It'll be good for you." The mage looked up at her, Sunette's eyes filled with sadness. "Foster's great at cheering people up."

She looked back down without a word. "Sunette," he scooted closer and laid his hand on her shoulder. "You are alive, we are alive, and we deserve to enjoy life. We're allowed to dance and laugh and tell jokes. What kind of life is worth living if there's no joy in it? And you bring so much joy to my life, Sunette, I want to bring you joy as well." He noticed Raven from the corner of his eyes, biting her lip like she was trying not to ruin the moment somehow.

Sunette sighed and ran her hands through her hair. "How in the world do I bring you joy?" She sounded like she didn't believe him.

He chuckled. "Just by being next to me, you bring me joy," he scooted closer. "Seeing your face every day, watching you read your spell book. Hell, the sound of your voice brings me joy." Her eyes slowly rose from the table to his, her face softened, and she swallowed hard. He held out his hand again, "So, will you dance with me and let me bring you some joy?"

She stared into his eyes for a moment. "All right, Apple Picker, you win this one," she said and slid her hand into his.

He smiled, "If I win only one argument with you my whole life, let it be this one."

She scoffed and stood with him. "It will be the only one, I assure you." Foster laughed, and it made her smile. "Come on, dance with me before I lose my nerve." He noticed Raven giving him a thumbs-up as he led her to the dance floor.

The song was fast-paced, and soon, they were both smiling and laughing. As they danced, he watched how her hair bounced around. Her laugh was still infectious and beautiful. The pain of losing her love hadn't dulled it. The pair danced the night away until Sunette finally spoke up. "I'm exhausted, Foster," she said, laughing.

"Bedtime it is." He danced her back to the table, her laugh making his heart speed up. "Sunette and I are going to turn in," he told the group as he finally let her go.

"All right, good night," Lucius said. "Oh, Mistress Mage?"

Sunette rolled her eyes at him. "Yes?"

"It's lovely to see you smiling again."

She lowered her eyes before looking up at Foster. "Thank you, Lucius." She reached out and took Foster's hand, and led him up the stairs to their room.

Foster sat on the bed and pulled his shirt and boots off. When he turned to toss his shirt by his pack, Sunette was still standing by the door, staring at him.

"Something wrong?"

She shook her head. "No, pardon I didn't mean to stare." She turned and hung her robe on the door before slipping into the bed next to him. "Thank you," she whispered as her arms wrapped around his torso.

"You're most welcome." He laid his head on hers and listened to her breathing become steady and deep.

———

Sleep found Sunette quickly that night, and she dreamed of dancing alone to beautiful music. Her eyes were closed, and she felt hands hold her and move her to the music. She opened her eyes and saw Bereck smiling at her.

"Hello, my love," he said.

Her smile went from ear to ear. "Bereck!" She stopped and wrapped her arms tightly around him.

"How are you, Sunette?" He said, his lips against her forehead.

She sniffed and wiped tears from her cheeks as she looked up at him. "I miss you so much."

He smiled a sad smile. "I miss you too. I wanted to tell you that I enjoyed seeing you dance tonight. You looked happy."

She nodded with a little smile at the thought of the young fighter. "Foster's good at making me happy."

"I noticed that." He bent down and kissed her cheek. "The last thing I said to him was to keep you safe. It seems he is still doing it. I want you to be happy, Sunette, and if Foster makes you happy, don't shy away. He loves you so much."

She leaned back, her hand on his chest. "What are you talking about?"

He gently cupped her face, "I want you to live life to the fullest, love and dance, and have fun. I'm saying, please don't shy away from anything that makes you happy."

She laid her hands over his. "You made me happy, Bereck."

"And you made me happy, but I can't make you happy anymore."

She sniffed and looked up into his eyes. "I love you,

Bereck."

He kissed her forehead. "And I you but promise me you'll love and be happy, Sunette." He leaned down, and she felt his familiar lips on hers.

———

Sunette opened her eyes and saw the sun was up. She also found herself lying on Foster's broad chest, her arm wrapped around his waist. She slowly sat up, trying not to wake him, and smiled at her dream. Bereck wanted her to be happy, she vaguely remembered him saying something about Foster as well, but she couldn't remember.

As Bereck's face floated through her mind, she felt a hand on her back. "Did you sleep well?" Foster asked sleepily.

She turned and couldn't help but smile. "I dreamed of Bereck."

He sat up and blinked himself awake. "Really? How was it?"

Sunette sighed. "He said he wanted me to be happy."

Foster gave her a little smile. "As do I."

She reached out and laid her hand on his cheek. "Thank you for all your support, Foster. It seems wondrous things happen when I'm with you."

A faint pink blush crept into his cheeks, and it warmed her heart. "You're welcome."

———

They walked downstairs for breakfast and saw Raven sitting with Mason, their heads together, whispering about something.

"Morning, you two," Foster said as they joined them.

Raven sat back, her arms crossed over her stomach. "Morning," Mason said.

"Everything all right?" Sunette reached across the table to Raven, who sighed and took her hand.

"Can't find Twig," she said.

The newcomers looked at each other. "What do you mean?"

Raven shrugged. "He didn't come in last night, when he left at dinner was the last I saw him."

"I went looking, but I couldn't find him." Mason patted her leg.

"I'm sure he's fine. He can take care of himself." Sunette squeezed her hand but could tell Raven was still worried. The door jingled, and everyone looked up as the half-orc in question came walking in but didn't acknowledge them.

"Twig!" Raven jumped up from the table, and he turned in time to catch her as she jumped into his arms. "I was so worried. Where were you?" As he turned, everyone saw he had a black eye, and his lip was cut.

"Damn man, what happened?" Mason's voice got Raven's attention, and she gasped when she saw his face.

"Twig, what the hell?" She tried to drag him to the table, but he resisted.

"Just a fight. I'm tired. I'm going to go up and catch a few hours of sleep," he put Raven back on her feet and walked up the stairs.

"He didn't give you a kiss," Mason said like he couldn't believe what he just saw.

Raven sighed, "You heard him. He's tired." She walked out of the inn, hugging herself.

"I think something is wrong." Sunette laid her head in her hand.

"He's tired," Foster shrugged. "I get it."

She shook her head. "No, there's something else."

———

As happy as Foster was that Sunette was finally starting to heal, things with Twig and Raven seemed to be deteriorating. As the weeks passed, they still shared a room when they stayed at an inn, but they never danced anymore. They never sat in the corner and talked all night like they used to. He'd eat, then leave. Sometimes, Raven would go after him, but she'd come back with red eyes and lock herself in her room. There were few things that could change a man that suddenly, but he'd never believe that

Twig didn't love the bard anymore. Something else had to be wrong.

CHAPTER 12
KILLING ISN'T ALWAYS THE ANSWER

Foster and Lucius were walking down the crowded streets of Meeker's Hold. It was the first time the group had made it here, and it was Foster's first visit. He wanted to find a tailor to fix his cloak, and Lucius said he knew just the woman.

"She's usually booked up, but I think she'll squeeze you in," the half-elf said.

"What makes you say that?"

Lucius shrugged, "She just seemed rather grateful the last time I was here." Foster snickered and had an idea what he meant. The woman's shop was next to the temple of Alar, and Foster couldn't help but notice there were a lot of notices pinned on the temple's board. They walked into the seamstress shop, and a woman walked in from the back. She did indeed look busy. Her hair was pinned behind her head but looked as if it could come free with a gentle shake, and her face was flushed.

"Lucius Silverblade, never thought I'd see you again." She leaned on the counter, a smirk on her face.

"Lorilee, you are the best seamstress I know. Of course, you'd see me again." He leaned on the counter in front of her and flipped the string of her apron back behind her.

"What do you need?"

"Not me," he motioned back to Foster, who stepped up. Lorilee's eyes went wide as she looked up. "My friend here just needs a quick mending."

"Hi, I'm Foster." He held out his hand, and the woman shook it. He put his cloak on the counter and showed her the rip. "Got caught on a tree, so it's kind of jagged."

She spread it flat on the counter. "Oh, this is nothing. Wait right here." She disappeared in the back again.

Lucius gave his arm a tap. "See, told you."

"I'll never doubt you again." They waited while she quickly sewed up the awful rip, and Foster gave her a gold for payment, which she happily took.

"Come back anytime, Silverblade, I have a feeling your people rip a lot of clothes."

He laughed and gave her cheek a kiss. "Will do." They walked back outside, and Foster stopped at the board by Alar's temple. "Anything catch your eye?"

"Hmm," he lifted a paper, and a word made him gasp. 'Litch.' He pulled that paper off and read it.

He showed it to Lucius, who rubbed his chin. "Are you sure?"

"Yes. We'll be more prepared this time."

Lucius sighed. "We don't have a paladin or a cleric," he said without meeting Foster's eyes.

"Maybe we can see if anyone from the church wants to come with us?"

He folded the paper and put it in his pocket. "If we do, we're asking a follower of Behest."

"Fine with me." Foster wouldn't turn down any of the battle god's followers for this job. "Let's see if the others think it's a good idea." Lucius nodded, and they made their way back to the inn.

They found Mason trying to teach Sunette a card game at the bar, but it wasn't going well.

"This makes no sense, Mason!" She slapped down her cards.

He laughed. "It does if you pay attention. Clubs are worth four, hearts are three, spades two, and diamonds are one. Take the number of the card and add the suit number to get twenty-five,"

She scoffed. "I think you made this game up."

He gave her cheeks a playful pinch. "All games are made up."

Lucius walked up and patted her back as she slapped the thief's hand away. "He isn't wrong, Mistress Mage. Have you two seen Twig and Raven? We have something to propose to the group."

"Last I saw, Raven was sitting over there," Sunette pointed to a corner, but it was empty. "Maybe they're in their room."

Mason gathered the cards and leapt from his chair. "I'll go see." He ran up the stairs, and the others moved to a table.

"What is the proposal?" Sunette asked. Lucius pulled out the paper and handed it to her. "Oh." She looked over at Foster. "You are okay with this? I heard the last litch was rather nightmare-inducing."

He nodded. "We won't be caught off guard this time." Mason came running back downstairs and slid into a chair next to Foster. He looked distressed.

"They're in their room, but they're fighting." He looked over at Lucius, "They wouldn't answer the door, but I could hear them yelling."

"Hmm," the half-elf looked up the stairs. "Bad yelling, right?" Mason nodded. "I'll be right back." And he walked up the stairs, disappearing down the hallway.

Foster looked down at the little man. "They were fighting?"

He ran his hand through his hair, the nerves plain on his face. "Yeah, it sounded bad."

Foster sat back and crossed his arms. "They never fight."

"They don't," Sunette looked up after Lucius. "I wonder what happened." The three of them were coming down the stairs now. Lucius had a look on his face that said he had to pull rank, but on who they weren't sure. Raven sat on the other side of Foster and laced her fingers on the table.

He leaned down and whispered, "You okay?" She just nodded without looking at him. He looked over at Twig, who sat next to Lucius. The look on the half-orc's face gave nothing away, but from what he could tell about Raven, she hadn't been the one to initiate the fight.

"So, Foster found a job outside the temple of Alar. It asks

for help in ridding the world of a litch." They all looked at him. "The last one we encountered was bad, and this time we have no holy people." Foster noted he said it gentler than the rest of his words. "If we go, I say we head to Behest's temple and ask for a volunteer. I don't want to go without holy help."

Everyone nodded. "Sounds good to me," Twig said. "One less litch in the world is a good thing."

Raven nodded, and Mason spoke up, "Where is it?"

"Outside of Silver Springs." That was a small hamlet about five days to the north of Meeker's Hold.

"I say we go for it." Sunette crossed her arms over her chest. "Less evil in the world is a good thing, and I agree we'll need someone holy."

Lucius gave her a wink. "I'll head to the temple. Anyone want to come with?"

"I'll go." Everyone turned to Sunette. They assumed she'd be the last to want to go.

"Done." They both stood, and Lucius put a hand on her back as she walked through the door.

"That was unexpected." Foster watched them walk down the street. "Maybe it means she's feeling better."

"I hope so." Raven raised a hand, and the server nodded, filling a mug for her.

Mason smiled and glanced at Foster. "She's definitely feeling better."

———

Lucius walked next to Sunette, making their way to the temple of Behest. It was more like a fighting ring on the inside. It was open air, with a dirt-packed floor, and the yells of warriors were their prayers to the battle god. They walked up the steps, and a priest in green robes walked over to them.

"Welcome. Are you looking for a blessing?"

"Looking for a Paladin, actually," Lucius said, shaking the man's hand. "We're going up against a Litch, and we have no holy people in our group."

"I see. Well, we have several that might like to go." He

motioned towards a few people who were training in the ring. They stopped fighting and walked over to them, sweaty and breathing hard. "These people are going after a Litch and need help. Who would volunteer?"

Right away, a man walked over and bowed. "I will go." He was as tall as Foster, with short-cropped blonde hair and blue eyes. He was sweaty from fighting and had a large hammer in his hand.

"Ah, Bold, perfect, this is," the priest turned back to them. "Sorry, I didn't catch your names."

"Excuse me, Lucius Silverblade, and Sunette Chelri."

The priest nodded. "Lucius and Sunette, this is Bold. He's one of our strongest paladins."

He gave them both little bows. "It'll be an honor to take this evil out of this world with you." Lucius and Sunette held out their hands, and he shook them.

"Welcome, we're staying at The Dazzling Otter," Lucius said. "Why don't you clean up, meet us there for dinner, and we'll head out in the morning?"

"I will see you there." He gave them a smile and walked off.

"Well, that was easy." Sunette turned and started walking back down the road. Lucius caught up with her, and she felt his hand on her back.

"How are you doing?"

She knew what he meant. "Fine, why?"

"Making sure. You seem like you're healing."

She shrugged. "I don't have a choice but to heal. Foster seems insistent upon it."

Lucius laughed. "We all insist."

She sighed and turned to him. "Not that I don't appreciate the help, but I think you're all focusing on the wrong person."

His eyebrow raised at that. "Oh? Who should we be focusing on?"

"Twig."

"Hmm," He took his hand back, "What makes you say

that?"

She spoke as she walked. "Something is off with him. He doesn't feel the same." Lucius wasn't going to argue with her. He had seen the change but assumed his heart was waning when it came to the pretty bard.

"You think it's more than just a wandering heart?"

"Much more. He would never fall out of love with Raven."

Lucius sighed. "I'm inclined to agree."

———

That night, the group had gathered for dinner, and Lucius saw the paladin walk in. He had on a black shirt and pants, the hammer strapped to his back. Lucius raised his hand, and Bold walked over and sat between him and Sunette.

"Everyone, this is Bold. He's a Paladin of Behest. He's going to join us while we take out this Litch. Bold, this is Foster, Mason, Raven, and Twig."

"Nice to meet you all."

Everyone but Twig acknowledged the man. "Have you ever been up against a Litch?" Foster asked.

"No, not yet. That's partly why I volunteered. Have you?"

A few of them nodded. "Once a few years ago," Lucius said. "Unsure how we got out of there, but we did."

"What happened?" The server set down plates of food for them, and Bold dug in, waiting for an answer. Foster looked at everyone. He was the only one there that was conscious for most of it.

"Like Lucius said, we're not sure. It was about to run me through when Lessa, our old cleric, said there was a bright light, and the Litch started screaming. When it was gone, it was a pile of ash on the ground. I remember my arm hurting, I thought I had gotten stabbed, but I hadn't."

"Hmm, sounds like holy power overcoming another," Bold said. "You aren't a priest, right?"

Foster shook his head. "No, my mother is," he touched the mark on his arm. "My father and I share a birthmark, though. That's what hurt on my arm. He said it meant we were favored but couldn't elaborate on it."

Bold took a bite of his bread. "Can I see it?" Foster nodded and rolled up his sleeve and showed the paladin the white crescent moon shape on his shoulder. He leaned forward, and Foster swore the man had a hint of recognition in his face. "You and your father have this but don't know what it is?"

"Yeah."

Bold pointed at it with his fork. "That's the Mark of the Exalted," he bent down and lifted his pant leg. Foster saw the same mark on his calf. "Means you are descended from one of the original heroes that first defeated Kuraim, whoever the hell he was."

Everyone looked at Foster, their eyes wide. "How do you know that?"

Bold shrugged and took a drink. "Guess my family actually remembered the story."

"But not who Kuraim was?" He crossed his arms. Bold shook his head, and Foster noticed how still Sunette was. "You okay?"

"Bold, do you really know nothing about this Kuraim?" He could hear the caution in her voice.

"Hmm," he swallowed whatever he was chewing. "Evil god in all accounts. I don't know what he did, but it was bad enough that the other gods tried to banish him. It was only with the help of our ancestors that they were able to achieve that goal, hence the marks they were given as thanks. You won't find anything about him in any book, just stories told through the ages. And even those are rare."

"An evil god?"

Foster leaned down to her ear. "What's wrong?"

"Remember what my family was supposed to be guardians of?"

He thought for a moment, and then the name rang through his mind. "Oh shit."

"What?" Lucius saw them conspiring and leaned forward.

"Why would a family be guardians of an artifact such as

that? Were they evil too?" she wondered.

Foster shook his head and laid a hand on her shoulder. "No, I bet they were pious and believed they could hide the cup well."

"Would you two mind explaining why our mage looks like she's seen a ghost?" Lucius sat back and crossed his arms.

Foster rubbed her arm, and she nodded. "My family is believed to be the guardians of an artifact called The Cup of Kuraim, and it's the reason my entire family is dead." Everyone looked sympathetically at her, but Bold dropped his fork.

"Are you shitting me?"

"It's not like I know where it is. My family didn't even know about it! They were hunted over something we didn't even have."

"You don't know where it is?" Sunette's eyes darkened, and lightning flickered at her fingertips as she looked at the paladin.

"No."

He put his hands up. "I don't want it. I'm just amazed that someone from the family is still around. Everyone knew back then that whoever guarded it would be hunted. Maybe they thought if they forgot about it, others would too."

She crossed her arms and sat back. "Well, they didn't."

"That's why your family's gone?" Lucius asked gently.

"Yes. But it seems they either think I'm dead as well or unreachable since we haven't seen or heard a trace of them since we came to this continent."

"They better be gone, anyone comes for you they'll have to deal with us," Lucius said.

Bold sat back and wiped his mouth. He looked between Foster and Sunette. "So, this Litch has nothing to do with the cup or our marks, and this just happens to be an insane coincidence?"

"Seems that way," Raven drained her mug. "Your name is really Bold?"

His eyes turned to the bard, and Foster noticed how they seemed to study her. "Theobold Arkwright, Bold is a name my brother gave me when I was young." He leaned on the table, "Your name really Raven?" Her eyes widened at how deep his voice was when he asked that.

Twig slammed down his mug. "Yes, it is, she's also my wife."

Raven rolled her eyes as Bold looked back at her. "Really?"

"Sort of," she said, clearly still irritated at him.

"Sort of?" Bold laughed, "This will be an interesting job." He drained his mug, "So, where is this, Litch?"

"Outside of Silver Springs." Foster handed him the paper from the board, and he read it.

"Hmm, didn't know there was a Litch so close to us." He handed it back, "We'll get rid of it."

"We leave in the morning." Lucius sat back, and Raven got to her feet.

"I'm going to earn a few coin before I turn in. Twig, want to come?"

"Naw, I'm gonna look for a card game." He got up and left the tavern. Raven couldn't stop the annoyed growl she let out as she watched him leave.

"What do you do to earn coin?" Bold asked.

"I'm a bard." She glared at the door.

"The best bard." Foster toasted her, and Raven gave him a small smile.

"I'll go." Bold got to his feet. "It's been ages since I've heard any decent music."

She crossed her arms over her chest. "If you like." And started out of the tavern.

"Don't stay out too late. We leave early," Lucius called after her.

"Yes, Da!" She yelled back and left, Bold chuckling behind her.

Lucius turned back to Foster and Sunette. "Well, this is turning out to be more interesting than we thought."

"I don't really like how things from my past are starting to show up." She turned to Foster, "You had no idea about your mark?"

"None. Maybe Bold can bring a few things to light while he's with us."

————

Raven walked to a tavern down the road called The Glamourous Lord and went to the barkeep while Bold took a seat by the stage and ordered a drink. Raven walked up on stage, and a few people clapped.

"Evening, I'm Raven Bladespell. Hopefully, you like my songs so much you empty your pockets!" A few people laughed while she cast a spell, and a few incorporeal instruments appeared behind her and started playing. Bold had never seen such a display and didn't bother hiding his shock. Raven gave him a little wink and then started singing. Clearly, this group was made up of special people, and Bold wondered if they knew just how special they were.

When she was done singing and gathering the coins people threw on the stage for her, she joined Bold at his table.

"What'd you think?" She sat back, her arms crossed across her chest.

Her face said she already knew what he was going to say. "Holy shit, I have never seen anything like that before." He leaned toward her, resting his arms on the table. "Have you always been able to do that?"

"Yeah."

"Why aren't you rich?"

She laughed loudly, it had been a while since she laughed like that. "Traveling really puts a damper on that. I don't like to stay in one place too long anyway."

"Well, I hope you do one day." He sat back and crossed his arms. "So, you're married to the half-orc?"

She cleared her throat. "He has a name, and...sort of."

He raised an eyebrow in confusion like most did when they said that. "How can you be sort of married?"

She shrugged and thanked the waitress, who gave her a drink. "It's a long story, but to the elves, we're married. To everyone else, we're not."

"So, you're not," he leaned closer.

She took a long drink, never breaking eye contact. "No."

———

The next morning, everyone met downstairs. Lucius had stocked up on more rations for them the night before, and Sunette had learned a new spell that would let them stay in a shelter instead of camping outside. Everyone was glad for that. As the group walked towards Silver Springs, Twig took his new place at the front, but Raven stayed back, and Bold walked at her side. No one blamed her for spending time with the paladin, who gave her attention like Twig once did. At least he seemed like a decent guy.

The first night Sunette cast her spell, everyone cheered when the cabin popped up.

"It's lovely!" Raven walked around the building. It looked like a cozy cabin that belonged in the woods. "How many rooms?"

Sunette opened the door. "There's one for each of us."

"Silence at last," Twig grumbled and walked inside. Sunette scoffed, her hands going to her hips as she shook her head.

"Come on in, I guess." She walked in after the grumpy half-orc, and everyone followed after. It was homey, there was a fire going in the fireplace, and it smelled like food was cooking over it in the cauldron. There were chairs enough for everyone, and there were seven bedrooms spread out between two floors. The door to one slammed shut as Lucius walked in last.

"Well done, Mistress Mage. This is much better than sleeping under the stars."

"I don't know. I rather like sleeping under the stars, but it'll keep bears away for sure." Foster laughed and put his stuff in the first room on the left on the first floor. Raven ran up the stairs and picked a room, as did Bold. Lucius sat by the fire and stirred whatever was in the cauldron while Sunette picked the room next to Foster. Mason was going through every drawer he could find and opening every door.

"This place has everything!" He yelled from the second story.

"Just about, young man," Lucius said to himself.

———

Foster was lying in his bed, the window was open, letting in a nice breeze, when he heard a knock on his door.

"Come in." Sunette stepped inside. "Hey, something wrong?"

She looked tired, her eyes half-shut, and closed the door behind her. "I'm tired, but I can't sleep."

"Mind busy?" He scooted over, and she sat on the bed, her back facing him, and rested her arms on her legs.

"Yeah."

Foster sat up and laid a hand on her back. He felt her lean into it. "Tell me."

She shook her head, "I don't really want to talk about it. I want to get my mind off it." She turned to him, "Tell me a story."

He chuckled as she scooted next to him and lay down. "What kind of story?"

"Something with a happy ending." She cast a spell, and above them, the stars shone down on them.

"Wow." He lay next to her and held her hand. "How about I tell you how my mother met Lord Raventree."

———

Raven was lying on her stomach, a book open on the bed in front of her. Bold was next to her, his hands behind his head. The sheet was covering her backside and his front. That was it. Neither had bothered to get dressed after their little tryst.

"This place really does have everything." She hadn't seen this book outside of a library in ages.

"She's talented, your mage."

"We're lucky to have her." Raven hoped this book would be available every time she made the cabin pop up. She forgot how much she liked it.

"Can I ask you something?" Raven nodded, still reading. He chuckled, "What's that holiness emanating from you?"

She sighed and closed the book as she looked over at him. "You too?"

His eyebrows went up. "Others feel it?"

"Foster and our old paladin Bereck. But I don't know what it is. I don't feel it." He turned and laid a hand on her bare back. "What does it feel like?" His hand moved up to her neck. He splayed his fingers as he ran his hand down to the small of her back.

"It feels like power, pure power," he leaned over and kissed her bare shoulder. "And love."

"Does it now?" she teased.

"To me, anyway." He wrapped an arm around her, "So, where is your old paladin?"

She sniffed, "He died."

"Oh shit, I'm sorry." He laid his head on hers, and Raven slowly exhaled. She still had nightmares of that fight. Legions of undead between her and Twig, or her and Mason, everyone dead in the keep, Foster, Lucius, Sunette. She knew it wasn't true, but the dreams still woke her with a scream in her throat.

She reached up and put a hand on his cheek. "He and Sunette were going to marry."

He sighed sadly and shook his head. "I thought there was a sadness in her eyes, how long ago?"

"Oh, four or five months now. He was a paladin of Otto, and a good man. He didn't deserve that." She leaned over, and he kissed her. She hadn't planned on sleeping with Bold, but the way Twig had been treating her, she wanted to feel something good from someone who at least cared a little bit. And when he smiled at her in the tavern that first night, she couldn't resist.

"Was it after your friend died that your half-orc started acting differently?"

"Yes, and?"

He shook his head. "Maybe that's what's wrong with him? Maybe he feels guilty that he couldn't save your friend and is taking it bad."

She shook her head. "I wish, but no. We weren't anywhere

near him when he died, so there's no way we could have done anything. He just…doesn't feel like the man who accidentally got married to me."

Bold laughed. "He really doesn't seem to care, I agree. But I'm also sorry."

She gave him another kiss. "What kind of paladin sleeps with another man's wife anyway?" She teased and rolled him on his back as she straddled his hips.

"The kind of paladin who never made a vow not to do so." Raven laughed loudly as Bold tickled her sides.

———

The next morning, everyone ate breakfast the cabin seemed to provide. It was heartier than rations, for sure, with biscuits and sausage. Twig didn't seem to care that Raven and Bold came out of the same room. For that, Lucius was grateful. As the group walked toward Silver Springs, Lucius caught up with Twig.

"How goes it?"

"Fine," he grunted.

"Yeah, good. How are you and Raven?"

He shrugged. "She seems fine."

Lucius rolled his eyes. He was just going to have to say it. "You still love her?"

"She's not my wife, we've just been fucking for years." Lucius fought hard not to react to that. He didn't think he'd ever heard Twig sound so nonchalant about his relationship with the bard. Especially since he loved to call her his wife.

"That's not what you said the other day."

He looked down at Lucius. "When?"

"You don't remember?" Twig shook his head and looked forward. "The hell is wrong with you, Twig? You're gonna lose her if you keep acting like this."

He shrugged. "That's up to her." Lucius stopped and let the orc walk ahead. There was something really wrong with him.

———

Raven and Mason were at the back of the group, singing a dirty song at the top of their lungs.

Bold laughed and turned to Foster. "So why aren't Raven and Mason together? They seem like two peas in a pod?"

Foster smiled at the song. "If you saw how she and Twig were when we first joined, you'd understand. They always seemed like two halves of a whole to me. Now?" He sighed heavily, "I don't know what's going on with him."

"Hmm, well, sometimes feelings fade."

"Yeah, but I never thought it would with him."

They walked in silence for a few minutes. "Raven told me about your paladin, I'm sorry."

Foster nodded. "It was rough." He shook the flash of Bereck run through with the ballista out of his mind. "Still is sometimes."

Bold shook his head. "Shame when a good paladin dies. Some of us believe we're so untouchable that nothing can hurt us. Or that it doesn't matter if we die. We'll be rewarded in the afterlife. But we forget about those we leave behind, how they hurt."

"True. So, what do you do in the temple?"

"I train the newcomers. When I heard Lucius was asking for volunteers, I thought it'd be a good opportunity to learn more skills to bring back to the acolytes."

"So, you're going back to the temple when we're done?" Foster glanced back at Raven, who was laughing with Mason. They seemed to be trying to outdo each other while coming up with new names for the male appendage.

"Yes, my place is there. I know that."

"Hmm, hopefully, Raven won't get attached." He teased and elbowed the paladin.

Bold laughed. "No, we know what this is."

"And what is it?"

Bold patted him on the back. "We're just having fun. Haven't you ever had fun with anyone before?"

"Not like that."

———

The group walked while the sun was up and stayed in the

cabin when the sun went down. Twig never joined them when they gathered in the common room. No one tried to change his mind. One night, Raven sang 'Fading Echoes' and danced with her large, winged shade. Foster sat next to Sunette as the bard sang and danced. She reached over and held his hand. As she turned to him, he leaned down to her lips.

"I think I finally understand this song," she whispered. He reached up and cupped her cheek. "I wish I didn't."

"Do you want to go look up at the stars?" She gave him a little smile and nodded, so he helped her up, and they disappeared back to his room.

The song ended, and Raven flopped in a chair by the fire. "How come you don't sing that more often?" Mason asked, "It's so pretty."

"Hmm, it makes people sad. They stop tipping."

Lucius chuckled. "Ever the opportunist." She gave him a wink.

"How'd you come up with that shade?" Bold put his feet on the ottoman, and she put her feet over his legs.

"Dreamed him up, sort of. I had a dream about a tall man, he was sad because he couldn't be with his mate because he died, and he missed her more than anything. I swear I could feel his heartache. It was an intense dream. I woke up absolutely sobbing. It was a lot. But he didn't have wings. He had a long black tail. I thought wings would be more appealing to the masses."

"Your song is a tribute to that man's heartache?" Mason stared at her. He looked like she had three heads.

"Unsure you can make a tribute to someone who wasn't real, but it's about how he made me feel, talking about missing his mate."

"Have you ever seen him in your dreams since?" Bold gently tapped her foot with his.

She nodded and looked at the fire. "A few times, just one of those dreams, you know."

"Yeah." Lucius reached over and laid a hand on her leg. "I think they happen more on the road." She smirked and nodded.

———

It took the group the usual five days to get to Silver Springs. The note on the board said to talk to a man named Hycis Woodburn. He was the one who put up the bounty on the Litch. It didn't take long to find him, Silver Springs was small, and the first person they asked knew who he was and told them he lived on the edge of town in a green house. They found it easy enough, and Lucius knocked on the door. They didn't wait long before a tall half-elf answered the door.

"Hello, we're looking for Hycis Woodburn?"

"That's me."

"Wonderful, my name is Lucius Silverblade. These are my people. We heard you were looking to have a Litch dispatched." He held out the paper from Meeker's Hold.

His eyebrows raised. "Oh good, I had given up on anyone trying. Come in." He moved aside, and the group walked in. "Please have a seat," he walked into a nearby room with several couches. "Hungry? Thirsty?"

"We're fine, thanks," Lucius said, and they all sat. "I guess we'd like to know what you know about this Litch? Why, besides the obvious, do you want it gone?"

Hycis nodded. "Her name is Sable. She's been a Litch maybe five years now."

"That's not old at all." Raven looked at the group, "She'll still look human." She turned to Hycis, "She was human, I assume?"

"Yes, human. She holds up in a cave about five miles to the north."

Lucius nodded. "Is she causing trouble?"

Hycis cleared his throat. "She has enthralled my brother, Oswald, and he insists on trying to save her. She won't get her claws out of his heart, so I figure the best way to deal with the situation is to get rid of her. She is an abomination. It's not like it's murder. She's already dead. I just can't do it myself. I'm proficient in business, not weapons. Get rid of her, and I'll pay your group one hundred gold."

"Sounds fair." Lucius nodded, and the group looked at each other.

"I didn't think a Litch was capable of affection." Sunette looked over at Raven, who shrugged.

"Some stay married after the transition, so I guess?"

"Either way, Hycis is right. One less Litch in the world is a good thing," Bold got to his feet. "Shall we?"

"Is your brother here?" Lucius asked, "Would it be possible to speak with him before we go?"

"He'll be in the tavern, big guy, can't miss him."

Lucius nodded and shook his hand. "We'll let you know what happens."

"Appreciate it." He showed them out of the house, and they walked back into the middle of town and found the tavern. Hycis was right. His brother was easy to spot. The big man was sitting in the corner, nursing an ale by himself. He looked human, so Lucius assumed they were half-brothers.

"Let me go speak with him. You all get a drink." Lucius gave Sunette's arm a little squeeze and walked over to the big man, who looked up as the half-elf walked over. "Oswald?"

"Yeah?"

"Your brother Hycis hired us," he took a seat across from him. "I hear your heart is taken by a rather sinister woman."

He scoffed and rolled his eyes. "Of course, he'd say that. Did he hire you to kill her?"

"He did." Lucius noticed he was wearing a necklace, but whatever was on the chain was under his shirt and seemed to be glowing red.

"He never understood her. The only reason she turned into a Litch was because she was ill."

His eyes narrowed. "I thought—"

"I bet you did, but no, it's not like that. She didn't want to die. I didn't want her to die, so she changed. I wanted to change too, but making a phylactery is expensive, and my brother hid mine, and I need it to complete the ritual."

Lucius's eyes went wide. He couldn't believe what he was

hearing. "You want to—"

"I want to spend eternity with the woman I love. No matter the way."

Lucius sat back. "I see." He motioned to the trinket under his shirt. "That's not yours?"

Oswald shook his head. "No, it's hers. I took it the day she created it."

"So why aren't you with her now?"

He cleared his throat. "When she turned, at first, she was glad because she wasn't sick anymore, but then, the weight of what she was hit her. She wanted to take it back. To die."

"And you don't want her to die."

"I do not. So, we're in a kind of a three-way stalemate. If I go to her, she'll want to destroy her phylactery. If I try and hide it, I know my brother will find it and destroy it anyway."

"How do you know he hasn't destroyed yours yet?"

"He said if I stayed away from her, he'd keep it safe. If I went to her, he'd destroy it. It took two years to gather enough coin to make that thing. I don't want him to destroy it."

"I understand. Does she—"

"No, she harms no one. Neither of us would. We just want to be together. It was the only way we could think of without becoming a vampire."

Lucius knocked on the table once. "Understood. Let me speak to my group."

"Yeah, you do that." Lucius got up and joined everyone else at a table by the window.

"So, this just got a lot more complicated." He explained what Oswald said, and everyone but Bold shook their heads.

"She must have been so sick to turn into such a creature for relief," Sunette said.

"He must really love her to be willing to be one too." Mason took a drink, and Lucius noticed how his eyes roamed over Raven for a moment before he looked back at the table. The bard simply avoided looking at Twig, who had just finished his drink and ordered another.

"So, we have a choice," Lucius laced his fingers on the table. "We kill her like we were hired to do. We know where her phylactery is, and he doesn't look like much of a challenge despite his large stature. Or we look for his phylactery and let him try and convince her to 'live.'"

Bold's eyebrows went high. "What?"

"She isn't evil, she doesn't cause problems, she was desperate to live. We don't have to kill her." Lucius knew it was going to be hard to convince the paladin, who had sworn to rid the world of evil.

He stared at the rest of the group. "You want to help the Litch, not kill it?"

"It's an option, yes."

Sunette took a deep breath. "I'd like to help her."

Foster rubbed her arm and nodded. "Me too."

Mason nodded. "I want to help. I bet I could find his phylactery in that guy's house, no problem."

"So now we're breaking and entering?" Bold crossed his arms.

"No, just me," Mason said with a smile.

He sighed and sat back. "Never in all my life did I think I would find people who sympathized with a Litch."

"It's unusual, I know," Raven said. "But I grew up around them, and I never thought I'd see a person willingly become one just to stay with a love. I think she's worth helping."

"Twig?" Lucius turned to the half-orc, "What say you?"

He shrugged. "I'm leaning towards the paladin, but I'll go with whatever we decide."

Lucius turned to Mason. "How long do you think it'd take for you to get the thing?"

He shrugged, "Hopefully less than thirty minutes, if Oswald can get his brother out of the house, I could be quicker."

"Okay, make your way over. I'll get Oswald to get his brother out of the house." Mason stood and left the tavern while Lucius walked back over to Oswald.

"I can't believe we're doing this." Bold ran his hands over

his short hair.

"Welcome to adventuring paladin, where plans don't mean shit." Foster raised his mug. They watched Oswald run from the tavern. Clearly, he liked the idea.

Five minutes later, they watched the brothers come into the tavern and order dinner. The group did their best not to pay attention. It didn't take long before Mason came back and slid in next to Lucius.

"I assume this is it?" He was wearing it around his neck, and like Oswald's, it was hidden in his shirt. Sunette leaned forward and cast a spell.

"Yes, that's it."

"Good," he sighed, "I've never actually seen one, but the glowing red gem seemed to stand out."

"So now what?" Bold crossed his arms, staring at the jewel hidden under Mason's shirt.

"We wait for the brothers to part, then Oswald takes us to her." Lucius sat back and crossed his arms. "Then he tries to convince her not to waste the time she has now."

Bold sighed, clearly still unsure of this plan, while everyone nodded. "You know," the paladin said. "I'm wondering if you're letting your recent loss affect your decisions with this job."

Sunette's eyes narrowed angrily at him. "Bereck's loss has nothing to do with this," she hissed at him. "And if this woman has done nothing wrong, there is no reason we shouldn't help her." He put his hands up before crossing them again. Lucius watched Sunette, she had been doing better the last month, and he hoped this job wouldn't set her back.

The group kept an eye on the brothers, and after two hours, Hycis left, and Oswald walked over to them.

"Did you get it?"

"We got it." Mason touched his chest.

"Let's go." They all got up and followed the man out of town towards the cave where his love had taken refuge.

———

The full moon gave them plenty of light as they reached

the cave. "Oh yeah, she's in there," Bold said.

"Let me go in first," Oswald said. "Give me five minutes."

"No, we all go in." Bold started for his sword, but Lucius put a hand over his.

"We all go in. We don't need weapons, not right now." Bold sighed, clearly annoyed, but let go of his sword. Sunette took out a wand, and the tip of it lit up, and they started inside.

"Sable!" Oswald yelled when they got a good twenty feet inside. "I'm here!" They turned a corner and saw a fire about ten feet away. There was a pile of blankets next to it, but that was it. "Sable!" They saw a pale face peek from under the blankets, and Oswald ran over. "Sable, it's okay." The pale face was joined by pale shoulders and arms as she moved the blanket.

"Oswald?" He hugged her, and Sunette cast another spell, and the cave filled with light. There wasn't much in the cave, just the fire and pile of blankets where she lay down. "What are you doing here?" She was young, still in her twenties, and had long brown hair. "If Hycis catches you, he's going to—"

"These people are going to help us," he interrupted her. She looked around his shoulder, and her eyes narrowed as they landed on Bold.

"He won't."

"Don't worry about him," Oswald helped her to her feet. She did indeed still look human, but with the pale skin and sunken eyes, it was hard to think she wasn't dying of something. "I have my phylactery, and I also have yours." He touched his chest, "We can be together now."

"Oswald, I told you. I made a mistake. I should have died." Her voice was quiet and pained.

He held her face. "No, no, we can be together forever, love, together it will be okay."

"If she wants to die, who are we to stand in her way?" Bold took a step away from the group. "Honestly, if a Litch wanted to end their life, I would gladly help, make it as painless as possible." He spoke gently, but Lucius pointed at him.

"Paladin, not another word. Let them work it out." Bold

sighed and crossed his arms as he turned his back on the group.

"Can I have it?" She held out her hand, but Oswald didn't hand it over.

"Not if you want to kill yourself. Please, Sable, you're not ill anymore. We're together. We can get away from this town. Hell, we can go to another continent where no one knows us. We can start over."

"But," he leaned forward and kissed her. "Oswald, I can't ask this of you."

"You're not. I'm doing it because I love you, and I want to be with you. I am lucky that we can spend forever together."

"Oswald, no god will hear you. There is no comfort in prayer, and your family will disown you. I can't tell you how much I miss the comfort Alar used to give me. But he has forsaken me, and I'll never feel his love again. I don't want that for you."

"I don't care if no god will give me comfort. You are my comfort. And my brother is an ass and the only family I have left. He'll be fine without me. You are my comfort and family now." Tears streamed down her face as he spoke, and Foster felt an arm on his back and looked down. Sunette was next to him and had her arm around him. He leaned down and kissed her head, letting his lips linger for a few moments.

"Are you okay?" he whispered. She nodded, and he felt her hand grip his side, her fingers shaking.

"Oswald," Sable laid her pale hand on his cheek. "Are you sure?"

"Absolutely," he smiled. "We can do this together."

Lucius walked over to them. "Can we trust you two to do the right thing here?"

Sable nodded and gave Oswald a small smile. "Yeah, we'll go to Garythane," she kissed him. "We'll finish your transition there. I bet it'll be easier."

Oswald smiled and hugged her tightly. "It's been so long since I've seen hope in your eyes, my love." Mason walked over and handed her the phylactery he had around his neck.

"Thank you." She put it around her neck and looked up at

her love. "I have your soul, and you have mine."

"Forever."

Lucius cleared his throat. "I guess we'll leave you for now. Good luck." Bold sighed, clearly irritated that there were going to be more litches in the world, but he didn't raise his blade. Lucius patted his arm, "Least they'll be on another continent." He growled a response and walked back to the front of the cave.

"Guess we didn't need holy help after all." Mason gave Oswald a pat on the back and held his arm out for Raven, who took it and followed Bold out of the cave.

"Be good to one another, please." Sunette took Foster's hand and pulled him from the cave. She stopped when the moonlight engulfed them. "They're luckier than most."

"They're delusional," Bold said. "No love is worth turning into a monster."

"Spoken like a man who's never been in love," she spat at him, and with Foster's hand still in hers, she began walking back towards the town.

He gave her hand a squeeze. "I'm sorry."

She looked up at him. "For what?"

"This job was my idea. I don't think we should have gotten involved."

She shook her head. "No, we did. Anything to help a couple in love. Even if it means damning their souls, they'll get to be together the way they can."

"Don't you think damning one's soul is a bit much for love?"

"I do. *I* wouldn't do it, but that's their love story, and now it will have a happy ending. Their happy ending." Bold stopped and took out his sword.

"What is it?" Lucius ran past the others and saw Hycis standing before them with five other armored men.

"I hired you to kill her, not steal from me and damn my brother to the hells." He pointed at the group, and the men charged with a yell. Lucius went invisible like he usually did, and Twig pulled his ax and charged with a yell.

"Get behind me." Foster stood in front of Sunette and pulled out his bow, glad the moon was full. Behind him, he could hear Raven singing something, and the charging men stopped and dropped their swords.

"You should take your men and leave," Lucius called out. "This won't end well for you." Everyone stopped and waited, but Twig rushed past them all and sank his axe into one of the men's necks. He fell to the ground, and the other men woke from their stupor and picked up their weapons.

"Damn it, Twig, what the hell!" Raven yelled out and threw a dagger. It stuck in one of the men's legs. He ignored her and went to the next man. Bold swung his hammer, and it knocked one of their swords away. Then, he quickly sank his weapon into the man's side, who crumpled like paper to the ground.

Lucius appeared behind Hycis and put a dagger to the man's throat. "Call them off," he said quietly. The man stiffened against the blade and put his hands up. "Call them off now."

"Stop!" Hycis yelled out, "Stop!" His men stopped, as did Bold, but Twig was still pressing one of the men.

"Twig enough!" But he didn't listen to Lucius, so Bold dropped his hammer and ran, smashing into the half-orc and knocking him off his feet. Hycis's man was able to run back to his comrades.

"What the fuck!" Twig tried to get to his feet, but Bold held him down.

"You should have stopped with the rest of us," he hissed at the half-orc and got to his feet. Twig growled and slowly got up, staring at the paladin.

"Now," Lucius spoke low and clear, hoping Hycis would get the point. "You all go back to town. Sable isn't in there, and neither is your brother, so I suggest you leave."

But the half-elf just stared at him. "I didn't want my brother to be one of those creatures, can't you understand? I'd do anything for him."

Lucius put his dagger away. "Then let him live his life the way he wants, with the woman he wants." They watched the hired men limp away. When they were out of sight, Lucius motioned for his group to follow. They walked until they got past Silver Springs, not talking until Sunette conjured the cabin for them. It was late, and everyone went to bed, hoping they did the right thing.

———

That first full night in the cabin, Raven and Bold were sitting by the fire in the common room when Sunette and Foster walked over.

"Bold, can we have a word?" Sunette took a seat across from Raven, and Foster sat on the arm of the chair next to her.

He sat back. "Of course." Raven gave her a look, but she shook her head.

"No, you can stay, Raven. Now that the job is over, I was hoping to talk with you about your mark and this Kuraim person."

"Ah, wondered if either of you were going to ask more." He reached over and laid a hand on Raven's arm.

Foster cleared his throat, "Do you know how many people were gifted that mark in the beginning?"

"There were five of them, their names were lost, but their legacy lives on." He spread his arms wide, and Raven snickered. "For helping the gods defeat Kuraim, they were granted a mark that said they were favored. That was so long ago several of those gods aren't even around anymore. Thankfully, their power resides in a few of our current gods, so our favor is still granted."

"So, you know about this cup?" Foster laid a hand on Sunette's back as she spoke.

Bold shrugged his shoulders. "I know there was an artifact with that name. I don't know what powers it had, but there were rumors. Drink from the cup and share His power, that sort of nonsense. I imagine it's magical, so if it was real, it'd still be powerful. As for your family, the cup was given to one of the heroes to guard. The story goes that they put a spell on their family and subsequent generations, saying that their lives would be tied to the cup. But I don't know in what way, I'm sorry. You said your family was killed because of it?"

She nodded. "Yes, the men after us believed that one of our number held the key to finding the cup. Kill them, then they would learn the location of the cup. That's all I know."

Bold breathed out slowly. "I wish I knew more. I assume they couldn't destroy it. Why would anyone keep something like that around?"

"What if they did?" They all turned to Raven. "What if they did destroy it, but *that* knowledge was lost? And these asssholes still think it's around?"

Bold chuckled. "What a waste if that was true. Wish there was a way to find out."

"Not exactly my forte," Sunette sat back. "So, you, me, and Foster had ancestors who adventured together?" She looked up and smiled at the fighter, who laid a hand on her shoulder.

Bold smiled at the display. "Seems that way. I'm glad we're not going up against a crazy god."

Foster chuckled. "Same."

"But the day is young," Sunette sighed and got to her feet. "Thank you for your time."

"No problem." Sunette stood and walked back to her room. Bold turned to Raven, "Shall we retire?" She nodded and took his hand and let him help her to her feet. "Your friends are more special than they realized it seemed."

She chuckled. "Aren't we all?"

———

Five days later, the group said goodbye and thanked Bold for coming with them. He made sure to say goodbye to Raven before the cabin disappeared. They lay in bed, she was on her stomach, and he ran his hand up and down her bare back. "I will dream of you, Raven Bladespell," he whispered, his lips on her shoulder. "This has been the best two weeks I've had in a long time."

"What about me will you dream of?" she giggled.

He smiled. "Your soft skin against mine," he kissed her shoulder. "The feel of your body sheathed around mine," he growled, and she laughed.

"Careful, or we'll be caught naked outside while the cabin disappears around us."

"It'd be worth it. Next time you're in Meeker's Hold, look me up."

"I might just do that."

CHAPTER 13
THE TRUTH IS PAINFUL

Eight months after Bereck died, the group was in Arrensport. Twig continued leaving Raven behind without a word, and she gave up trying to get him to tell her where he was going. Mason asked her once if she wanted to bunk with him instead, but she said she didn't want to cause a fuss or make it difficult if he ever got a pretty girl to join him. Foster could see there was something heavy weighing on her, but she still wouldn't confide in him.

He decided he'd had enough and followed him one night when he left. He told Sunette he'd be up after a while and left a few seconds after Twig. He followed the half-orc through the winding streets to a large house on the seedier side of town. It looked abandoned, with broken windows and peeling paint. Foster stood in an alley across the street and watched Twig pay a guy in the alley some gold and was let into the basement. Foster walked across the street and did the same. He paid the man five gold and followed Twig down the stairs.

When the door shut behind him, he was at the top of a dark stairway. There was candlelight somewhere ahead, and he could smell blood, a lot of it. He quietly walked down, and when the basement came into view, it took all his willpower not to react to what he saw before him. The room was filled with cages holding everything from kobolds to goblins and halflings, all in varying states of life. There were tables with body parts lying forgotten on them, and the floor was shining with blood.

Sharp tools, from daggers to picks, were hanging on a wall, and they were covered in gore. It looked like a torture room, and Twig paid money to be there. Everyone in the room had their backs to him, and he quickly made his way back up the stairs, hoping no one saw him.

Thankfully, the guy at the door didn't care that Foster didn't get his money's worth and didn't bother him as he left. Foster reached the street and ran the rest of the way to the inn, his mind flying with thoughts of what could have happened to their friend, but only one thing came to mind.

He burst into the inn and saw Raven sitting with Mason at the bar. "Raven!" He ran over, both staring wide-eyed at him. He grabbed her hands and pulled her up the stairs. "Come with me."

She let him drag her upstairs. "Okay, what's going on?" She opened her door, and Foster stalked in, rubbing his face.

"Something is wrong with Twig." He faced her, his hand still on his chin.

"And?" She tapped her foot, her arms hugging her torso.

"No, I mean really wrong." He walked closer to her, his hands gripping her shoulders. "I followed him tonight."

Her eyes went wide. "You did? Where did he go?" She sat on the bed and started picking at her thumbnail.

Foster huffed loudly. "It was a torture chamber under this big house on Gray St. He paid five gold to go in. I followed. The basement was filled with cages. There were goblins and kobolds and halflings in them. They all looked tortured or dead. People paid money to go down there and torture these beings, and Twig was one of them."

She slowly looked down at the ground. "You saw him do this?" Her voice was quiet, like she didn't want to say the words.

"Honestly, when I saw what was going on, I left. I didn't see him do it." He flopped next to her. "What on earth is going on with him? We've all seen the change. It's like..." he didn't want to say it.

"Like what?" She looked up at him and could hear how defensive she was, but it was to be expected.

"Did something happen the day Bereck died?" It was the only time they'd fought when they couldn't see each other. The only time he could think of when something might have happened.

"No." She looked back down at the floor.

"Raven, please."

She stood up and started pacing. "There's nothing to talk about, Foster!" She took a deep breath, but he could see her eyes shining with tears. "Just go hang out with your *girlfriend*. Leave me alone." He ignored the jab and reached for her, but she shirked away. Clearly, this needed a more direct approach.

"Raven, did he die?"

"Go!" She yelled and pointed at the door. "Leave me!" He knew that tone, that defensive stance. She did something but couldn't bring herself to say it.

"I'll be around if you need me." He started for the door.

"I won't." Those words stopped him. They'd always been there for each other. The fact that she didn't want his help stung. He shut the door and laid his forehead on the doorframe. *You will.*

————

Two hours after Raven had yelled at Foster, the door to the room opened and she watched Twig walk in and go straight to the water basin and wash his face off.

"You all right?" She could see the water turning red from blood.

"Yeah." He sat on the bed and started taking his boots off.

"Did you kill someone?" She knew there was no point in denying it anymore. He had changed. It was her fault, and now she was going to have to deal with the worst mistake of her life.

His boots hit the floor, and he looked over at her. "What?"

"I know you went down to that kill club." His eyes went dark. "You aren't yourself anymore."

"I'm more myself than ever, *wife*." He spat the last word like it was a curse. "Maybe if you understood me, you'd see that."

"I understood you when you were my husband, not this monster." She got off the bed and started for the door. There was no more denying it, and she hoped Foster was still up. She only got a few steps away when he grabbed her and jerked her back to him. Sharp pain in her wrist made her unsteady, and he suddenly backhanded her so hard she fell to the ground. Stars were floating in her vision, and her cheek hurt something fierce. She tried to get up, but he pushed her back down, straddled her hips, and wrapped his hands around her neck.

"Who's really the monster here, my love," he hissed. "Me, or the one who made me what I am." She felt her face going tingly as he cut off her air. Her hands flailed against him, and she felt the dagger at his side. She pulled it free and stabbed him in the thigh. He yelled, taking his hands off her throat, and she quickly sucked in air as she twisted from underneath him and unsheathed her dagger. He pulled the dagger out of his leg, still on his knees and breathing hard through gritted teeth and tusks. "I didn't know you wanted to play that rough," he growled. He was gone. She knew this. The half-orc she once loved was gone and had been gone a long time.

"I'm sorry." She threw her dagger, and it struck true, sinking hilt deep through his eye. His arms dropped, the dagger in his hand skittered away, and he fell with a hard thump to the floor. Blood spread from his body, and he didn't move. Raven felt her heart break all over again as she crawled through the blood and cradled his head. She let out a cry that echoed her breaking heart as tears flowed down her face.

The door burst open, and Foster stood above them. "Gods." He kneeled on the floor and pulled her against him as she cried, shaking and hyperventilating at the same time.

"I'm so sorry," she cried. "I'm so sorry. Forgive me, gods, I'm sorry! I love you!" She screamed, and footsteps ran into the room.

"Oh shit, Raven, are you okay?" It was Mason, and he did the same as Foster and wrapped himself around her while she cried.

"I didn't mean for this."

"Shh, shh, Raven, don't say a word." Foster brushed the hair off her face. "Don't say a thing. Mason, go get the sheriff. Someone killed Twig." He looked between Foster and the crying woman in his arms. He could tell Mason didn't want to go, but he finally ran from the room after giving Raven a kiss on the head.

"I didn't mean for this to happen. They don't always come back wrong!"

He leaned down and held her face in his hands, and looked in her eyes. "Here's what we're going to say, do you hear me?" She managed to nod through the mournful noises that came from her. "You walked in, saw someone standing over Twig, they hit you, and jumped out the window. You don't remember seeing a face, just that Twig was dead when you got here, understand?"

She took a few breaths, still unsteady. "Why?" He let go of her, it was harder than he thought it would be and opened the window.

"If you tell them you killed him, they'll want to know why, and you can't tell them cause you resurrected him, and he came back wrong. They'll arrest you, and we can't let that happen." He kneeled in Twig's blood and wrapped his arms around her again. "So, we have to make sure they think someone else killed him."

"I'm so sorry, Foster!" She cried and wrapped her arms around him. He could feel her squeezing as hard as she could. Her entire body was shaking. "I didn't want it to be true."

"Foster?" Sunette walked in and gasped, saying something in her native language as she, too, wrapped her arms around Raven. She ran her hand over Raven's hair, speaking softly in that lyrical language as tears fell from her own eyes.

"Good gods." Lucius walked in, "What the hell happened?"

"Someone killed Twig," Foster said, without looking up.

———

Hours later, the authorities were gone, and clergy from Alar's temple carried Twig's body away.

Raven was lying on the bed, her arms wrapped around Foster. Both had new clothes that weren't covered in their friend's blood.

"I've never felt so guilty," she said, her throat raw from crying, "The gods will never forgive me."

He ran his hand over her short hair. "They will, that's what they're good at."

She sniffed. "I'm sorry I yelled at you. I just didn't want to believe it."

He turned and laid his cheek on her forehead. "It's all right, I understand." He did, too. If he had a spell to bring back a loved one, he didn't know if he would be able to resist or not, despite the dangers.

"Do the others know?"

Foster sighed. "I don't know. I wouldn't put it past Lucius, but the others? I'm not sure."

She was quiet for a moment, and he wondered if she had fallen asleep before she asked. "Do you hate me?"

He sat up, shocked. "What? No, of course not. I could never hate you. You're like another sister to me! I know why you did what you did. It wasn't from a place of malice. It was from a place of love. Lesser people have raised the dead for worse."

She sniffed. "Good. I don't know what I'd do if you hated me."

There was a knock on the door, and Mason walked in. "Hey Raven, I put your stuff in my room if you want to move?" She sat up, wiping her eyes as they glanced at the now dried puddle of her husband's blood.

"Yeah, thanks, Mason, I appreciate it."

"Don't mention it. Any one of us would do the same." She walked over, and he put an arm around her shoulders. "If I snore too loud, just kick me, I heard it helps." She let out a little chuckle, and Foster knew she'd be okay. He walked back to his and Sunette's room and found her sitting on the bed, her hands laced on her lap.

"How is she?" She looked over, her eyes red.

"She'll be okay, Mason's got her." He sat next to her and put a hand on her back. "What an awful night."

"Poor girl, poor Twig." Sunette leaned into Foster, and he put his arm around her.

"How are you?"

He looked down, and her eyes locked with his. "Sad for Raven, sad for Twig, sad for us losing another friend." She reached up, and her fingers touched his cheek. She looked like she wanted to say something else but couldn't.

"Me too." He reached up and pressed her hand against his cheek. He noticed her eyes looking at his lips, and he let go of her hand and held her chin. His thumb ran gently along her bottom lip, and she sighed, her eyes closing at the sensation. He felt her hand move from his cheek to his neck, pulling him down to her.

She opened her eyes and met his. "I remember something Bereck told me in that dream I had all those months ago," she whispered.

She was so close he could feel her breath on his skin as she spoke. "You do?" The urge to kiss her was overpowering his sense of judgement. He didn't think he could hold back anymore.

"He said you loved me."

"I do," he whispered without hesitation, and she took his lower lip between hers. His arms wrapped around her, and his hand ran up her back to her neck. "I've loved you for so long, and I'm sorry if it's too soon for you," he said against her lips. The words came so easily it surprised him. "You're the most amazing woman I've ever met. You're so beautiful, artists should paint you so people can see what I see every day and so smart, so much smarter than I am," she laughed and kissed his cheek. "I've dreamed of spending my life with you."

She ran her lips across his. "I don't want to go another day without you knowing I love you too," she kissed him again. "Longer than I should have. But life is too short not to take what you want, and gods help me, I want you." He kissed her deeply, slipping his tongue into her mouth. She licked and sucked at him. He could hear her breath coming quicker. Her arms pressed him against her as he pulled her into his lap, her knees settled on either side of his legs. He felt her pull his shirt over his head, and she kissed his neck as her fingers reached down between them and unlaced his pants.

Her lips were soft and burned a line of passion from his neck back to his lips. She sat back and shed her robe, her slip already bunched at her hips. "Take me, Foster, I beg you." She breathed out before she captured his lips again and moved against the hard bulge under his pants. He moaned at the feel of her against him and knew he'd do anything she wanted.

"You never have to beg, my beautiful mage." He got to his feet, her legs wrapping around his waist. Her hand went between them, and he couldn't stop the groan that came from him as her hand stroked the hardness she found. Her palm pressed along that hard length as her fingers wrapped around the base of him. The shock of pleasure he felt almost made his knees go out from under him.

He pressed her against the wall, and she guided him into her. They both moaned as he pushed himself into her, inch by inch, until they were one. He had never felt anything so good in his life as this woman, and he could barely contain himself as he moved within her. With every thrust, the door shook, but they didn't care as their cries filled the air. His lips found hers, and he felt her hands in his hair, pressing him to her mouth, her moans rumbled through him. He moved one hand between them and rubbed around that bundle of nerves between her legs in time with his movements.

She broke the kiss, "Oh gods, Foster!" Her arms flew back against the wall, searching for something to hold onto, but there was nothing. She started saying something in her native language, haltingly a moment before she cried out, and he felt her tighten around him. The feel of her silky, warm skin pumping around him was his undoing as he spilled inside her with his own cry. The shock of desire he felt was like nothing he'd ever felt before, and he sank deep into her one last time, her muscles still tightening around him as she whispered his name over and over. He thought he'd die of pleasure right then and there. When their hearts calmed, she looked down at him, her eyes were soft, and there was a peace he hadn't seen in them before. "You are mine, and I am yours."

He smiled. "I am yours, and you are mine." Still holding her up, he made his way over to the bed and laid down on top of her.

She smiled, her hands going to his cheeks. "Let's do that for the rest of our lives, Apple Picker."

He nodded. "Probably need a studier wall." She laughed and pulled him down to her lips.

The next morning, the group was sitting at a table downstairs. Mason rubbed Raven's back while she just stared at her food. She looked exhausted, but they knew it wasn't from Mason's snoring.

"I know a job for us." Foster was running his fingers over Sunette's hand as if he'd been doing it his whole life. "Doesn't pay anything, but some people need help." Lucius' eyes quickly moved from the little gesture on their mage's hand back up to Foster.

"Whatcha got?"

"There's a house on Gray St., the basement is full of poor creatures and people being tortured. I say we go in and clean house."

"I second," Raven said without looking up. Lucius looked at Mason and Sunette. They nodded like they knew exactly what they were doing.

Lucius nodded. "When?"

"Tonight," Foster said. "I have a feeling there will be a lot of people who need to be punished there after the sun goes down."

Lucius raised his glass. "Tonight, it is."

The group would leave in stages. Mason and Lucius were first. Their job was to get rid of the guard outside the door. Once inside, Raven would start singing a song that would hopefully paralyze whoever heard it. Sunette and Foster were last, she would get those the song didn't affect, and Foster would kill anyone who got too close. They had a plan. Now, they just had to see if it would work.

The sun had been down an hour when Mason and Lucius left the inn. The little thief walked past the alley while Lucius turned into it.

"Evening," he said as he walked up to the dirty-looking human by the door.

"Five gold," the man grunted. Lucius studied the door. It looked like it just had a simple lock, and he assumed the man had the key. He nodded and made a show of pulling out his coin pouch. He saw movement behind the man and started loudly counting out the coins.

"One, two," the man grunted as Mason's dagger twisted in his back. "Three." Lucius quickly drew his rapier and stabbed the man in the throat for good measure. "Look for a key." Mason's nimble fingers quickly found a key in one of his pockets and unlocked the door.

Raven walked around the corner and over to them. "Ready?" Lucius put a hand on her back, and she nodded as she descended the stairs. She took a deep breath, and halfway down the dark stairwell, she started singing a haunting tune. Her spell made it sound like two others were singing with her, one a third higher, another half a step above that.

> "As I walked along the shore to gather the cockles
> and stones, not far into the water, I saw the most
> handsome man of all."

She stepped into the room and saw four men, their backs to her, but they didn't move. The smell of blood hit her nose, and she had to concentrate not to be sick. She heard footsteps behind her and knew Foster and Sunette were on their way down.

> "He waved to me. His captivating smile was more
> than I could handle as I walked into the sea."

Foster appeared to her right, Sunette on her left as a man ran from behind a pillar towards them, a sword drawn. Sunette cast a spell, and he froze, falling flat onto his face as the other ghostly voices weaved minor chords around them. Another man appeared to Foster's left but died quickly with a sword to his gut.

While the rest of her group quickly tried to free the ones who were still alive in the cages, Raven walked over to the group of four. Still frozen from her song. She walked in front of them and held her hand up to their faces.

"His hand was gentle as he pulled me down below,
now we're one down here forever, in the dark and
raging sea."

Blood began dripping from their eyes. She wanted them to die, and she wanted to punish them for all the evil acts they did because it might just help with the debt she felt in her soul where her husband was concerned.

"Raven." She heard Foster's voice somewhere next to her. "We got them, you don't have to kill them."

"Don't I? I took one good man from this world. I should take four evil ones out in exchange." Her hand was shaking as their blood started dripping on the floor.

"You can let go. It's all right." It was Mason. He laid a hand on her outstretched arm but didn't try to push it down. "Sunette went to get the sheriffs. They'll see how guilty they are." She looked over at him, his eyes big as saucers. "I know you want to hurt them, but you don't have to." The grief over Twig started washing over her again, and she lowered her arm. Her chest felt tight, and she put her other hand over her heart.

"Are there any survivors?" she asked, her lower lip quivering.

"Yes, a few." Lucius walked up and wrapped his arms around her. "I'm sorry I didn't say something sooner. I should have. I let you both down, and for that, I am exceptionally sorry." She grabbed at his jacket and sobbed her grief into his chest.

Thankfully, she was able to halt her crying as the basement flooded with the sheriff's men. They helped the few survivors out and quickly arrested the four frozen men, who were more than happy to get away from Raven.

"Get that siren bitch away from me!" One of them yelled

when the spell finally wore off, and he was being carried away.

"How'd you find this place?" The one in charge asked Lucius.

"Our friend Twig was looking into it. We think they're the ones who killed him, so we came here looking for answers and found this." Raven was impressed at how easily he lied. She almost believed it herself.

The officer nodded. "I'm sorry about your friend, but at least we got rid of this awful place." He held out his hand and shook hands with them all. "We owe you."

"Think nothing of it." He turned to the group, and with a look, they followed him out of the basement, back to the inn.

Halfway there, Raven stopped. "I think I want to go to the temple."

"I'll go with you." Mason put a hand on her shoulder, and she nodded.

Sunette gave her a hug. "Be safe." Raven hugged her back and turned to the temple, Mason's arm around her waist.

It took a while to get there. Arrensport was almost as big as Ardenry, and they were staying on the opposite side of the city. She didn't talk as they walked, neither did Mason. He just kept a comforting arm around her.

When they finally got to the temple, they found the nearest priest and asked to see the half-orc that was brought the night before. He gave them his condolences and showed them to the room where bodies were prepared. Twig was lying on a slab of marble, naked but for a cloth over his midsection. His ruined eye was covered with a patch, and the blood had been wiped from his body. Raven walked over and laid a hand on his. His skin was cold, and his fingers were stiff.

"He just looks like he's asleep," she whispered.

Mason stood next to her and sniffed. "Hey, big guy," he laid a hand on his arm. "I don't think I ever told you how amazing I thought you were. You were this big, strong half-orc who protected us, and I think I took that for granted. I knew if you were there, we'd be safe. I'm gonna miss you," he said quietly and wiped his eyes. Raven looked over at him, tears rolling down both of their cheeks. "Talk to him." She blinked her eyes a few times and looked back at Twig, willing her lips to form words.

"I'm so sorry. I wish I could take it all back, but I love you, and I didn't want to be without you. I'm selfish." She licked away the tears that rolled across her lips. "I remember the first time I saw you, walking in with Lucius, looking dangerous and protective. Then, when I took a break, you came over and talked to me, and you were so sweet. I wanted to leave with you immediately," a little chuckle leaked out. "I will always cherish our late-night talks, and how I always felt loved with you. I hope one day you can forgive me." She leaned down and kissed his cold cheek.

A priestess walked over and gave her a little smile. "How would you like the body prepared?" she asked gently.

"Cremated, if you can." She laid her hand on his unmoving chest, surprised she could still speak.

"We can. You can come collect him tomorrow, or we can bring him to you if you prefer?"

She looked over at Mason, his eyes red. "Up to you."

Raven sniffed. "Can you bring him to me? We're at The Four Winds, room five."

"We'll bring him tomorrow evening. What is his name?"

She took a few breaths before she could find her voice. "Godric." She noticed Mason's eyes shift to her as she said it.

The priestess smiled. "A worthy name."

She nodded. "It really is."

Raven and Mason walked back to the inn. The others were still sitting at a table despite the late hour. They sat with them and picked up the ales that were waiting for them.

"They're going to bring his ashes tomorrow," she said and took a drink. "Thank you for getting rid of that kill den." She managed to look up at her friends, "I..." The grief was once again washing over her like a wave, and it stole her words as she covered her mouth to quiet her sobs.

Mason quickly laid an arm around her, the other holding her hand. "It's what we do," he said.

———

A week later, the group was on top of a hill, sitting under a large oak tree. Raven had the box of Twig's ashes on her lap. Mason was next to her, like he had been since Twig died, and Lucius was leaning back against the tree. Sunette was lying against Foster's chest between his legs, her hand on his knee and his hand on her waist.

"This seems like a nice place," Foster said. "Peaceful. Kinda familiar, though." He laid a kiss on Sunette's head, and she smiled. Lucius tried hard not to make a big deal at the exchange. He knew Foster and Sunette were together, but they hadn't said anything to anyone. It felt as if they'd been together all along.

"It is," Raven said quietly and opened the box, and got to her feet. The wind blowing through the tree was the only sound as she lifted it in the air. They all watched as the ashes swirled out of the box and flew away in the air. "Be at peace, Godric. I love you," she whispered and watched the ashes disappear.

CHAPTER 14
"THERE IS ANOTHER FOR YOU."

Four months later, the group reached Salthole. It was a dry, windy day, and they were happy to see the 'Blue Wind' in port. Lucius greeted Stella much the same as before, to the hoots and hollers of her crew as they kissed deeply. When she came up for air, Stella told them they didn't have as much cargo, so they could split up below if they liked. Te'a ran over to Foster and gave him a hug. She had grown a lot, but it was clear she had more to do as she hadn't quite grown into her nose yet.

"I can't wait to show you what I've learned, Foster. I'm much better with a sword now."

He smiled. "Well, good. I can't wait to test you." Te'a giggled and followed her mom into town.

Foster smiled down at Sunette. "Thank goodness," the mage was clearly glad they could find some privacy while on board. "I was not looking forward to hearing Mason's snoring." She smiled and pulled him down the stairs. They found an empty room at the back of the boat and unburdened themselves of their things. Foster made a little nest of blankets, and they both flopped down.

"Oh, a room to ourselves!" Sunette exclaimed happily.

Foster chuckled. "We should hang a blanket up over the door."

"Good idea." She waved her hand, and a conjured blanket appeared and gave them some privacy.

He turned and gave her a little kiss. "Do you realize it's been four years since we met?"

She turned to him. "It has, hasn't it, doesn't really seem like it." She stayed facing him and studied his face. Foster really was a handsome man. He had a strong jawline, and he'd filled out over the years. His muscular shoulders were broad, and his thighs, gods, his thighs. She loved running her hands over the dips and curves of his muscles there. His blonde hair had white streaks in it from the sun, and it hung around his neck, curling a little at the end. Sometimes, she'd twirl it in her fingers while they lay in bed talking. His green eyes seemed to sparkle when they looked at her.

Sunette smiled at him, and he chuckled. "What?"

She shook her head. "Nothing. Shall we relax a bit?"

"Sure." Sunette gave him a kiss and pulled her big spell book from her pack, and started studying some new spells.

———

Foster loved watching her read her spells. He scooted close so he could see her face behind the book. Her eyes moved slowly around the pages, and every once in a while, she'd move her hands in graceful ways. He knew she'd been studying for a while when her face got serious. About halfway through, she always looked irked at her book. He smiled and just watched her. She never made any noise save for the turning of her pages.

———

An hour later, Sunette shut her book and looked over at Foster. His eyes were closed, and he was breathing deep and even. He always slept with his mouth slightly open. He looked so peaceful and cute when he did that. She quietly put her book away and lay next to him. Reaching over, she gently moved a lock of hair off his forehead.

"Foster?" she whispered.

"Hmm?"

"You asleep?"

"Mm-hmm," he said slowly. He reached out and wrapped his arms around her, bringing her close. She waited for him to settle in and relaxed in his arms, laying her hands on his chest. The sound of his heart soothed her more than anything in the world, and Sunette closed her eyes and let sleep take her.

———

Neither one knew how long they had been asleep when a yell woke them. "Foster!" It was Raven, yelling down the hallway like a sister, calling her brother, loud and annoying. Lucius must have sent her to get them. "Sunette!" She was knocking all over the doorframe like she was trying to find a hidden wall, and they laughed. "Dinner!" she sang out.

Foster stretched, and Sunette rolled over. "We're coming!"

She sat up and ran her hands through her messy hair as Foster got to his feet. "That was a good nap."

Sunette chuckled. "Apparently, we needed it." Foster held out his hand, she took it, and he helped her to her feet.

He raised her hand to his lips and gave her hand a kiss. "Hungry?"

"Starving," she said with a smile. They walked over to the galley and saw their friends sitting at one of the back tables. They made their way through loud and raucous pirates and sat down. "Interesting knock, Raven," she teased the bard.

She held up her hands. "I don't wanna hear what you guys are doing in there. I gotta be loud."

Sunette scoffed and rolled her eyes. "Bards." Raven and Mason laughed at her reaction.

"So, how long are we going to be at sea?" Foster started putting food on Sunette's plate, a biscuit, some stew meat, and beans.

"Few weeks, I think," Lucius said. "Stella mentioned trading with someone soon. Maybe they'll have some good stuff." They always spent that first dinner together, and after that, Lucius spent most of his time with Stella. Sunette passed Foster an ale, and he kissed her cheek.

"Never traded on the sea before. Nothing like cutting out the intermediary."

Lucius gave him a little salute. "She's heading towards Fairwinds," he took a bite of his biscuit. "We could get off there or see where she's going after that."

"Sounds like a plan." Foster took a drink of his ale, "So, Lucius, are we going to replenish our ranks at all?" He had been wondering about that for a while now. Not that five weren't plenty of people, but he was used to more.

Lucius tapped his fingers on the table. "You know, I don't think I will."

"No?" Sunette looked up, surprised at that.

"Five is a good number," Lucius sat back, his hands wrapping around his ale. "Maybe we should try being a bit smaller for a while."

"If you want." Mason shrugged his shoulders. "Less ways to divvy up treasure."

Lucius laughed. "True."

When they were finished with their meal, the ship's bard, Izan, started playing his lute on deck, and Mason dragged Raven up to the stairs to dance.

"Come on, we gotta get a dance in before you steal his spotlight." Raven laughed and let him lead her away.

The others followed and watched them dance, their smiles bright and happy. "You know, if I didn't know any better, I'd say Mason was in love with our dear bard." Sunette looked at Lucius and Foster.

"Yes?" Lucius turned to her, "Was that a question?" he chuckled.

"What?" Foster clearly didn't see what she did. "No."

She scoffed. "Look at them." She motioned to their dancing friends. "They're closer than ever, and, well, they look like they're in love."

"They're just friends," Foster watched them and saw how he smiled at Raven and how she touched his face as she laughed. "I mean, aren't they?"

Sunette waved her hand and wrapped her arms around Foster. "Forget I said anything. We shouldn't be gossiping about them anyway."

"Hmm, turnabout is fair play and all," Lucius said with a teasing smile.

She turned to him, an eyebrow up. "What does that mean?"

He shrugged. "It's not like they didn't gossip about you

two."

Sunette's eyes went wide. "Seriously?"

Lucius laughed. "Oh yeah. I should start charging for matchmaking services."

Sunette rolled her eyes. "Gods." Foster laughed and kissed her cheek. They kept watching their friends dance for a while, before Foster walked over and tapped Mason on the shoulder.

"May I?" He held out his hand, and Raven took it, Mason giving her a silly bow.

"Have fun," he said with a wink and walked over to Lucius and Sunette. The music slowed down, and Foster moved her skillfully around the deck.

"Can I ask you a question?" Foster hoped she wouldn't get mad at him.

"Sure, you may even ask me another." She teased, and he scoffed at the bad joke.

"Mason seems good for you."

Her eyes furled. "That wasn't a question."

"No, I suppose not. I guess I just hope you don't kick me in the balls when I ask if you two are more than friends?" He winced a little, still dancing, waiting for a kick, but none came.

Raven shook her head. "No, just friends."

"If he did love you, what would you do?"

She sighed, "Nothing, probably." She was quiet for a beat, "I feel like I don't deserve love."

He couldn't believe she had said that. "What? That's ridiculous. Of course, you do."

"Yeah, yeah, I know."

———

Mason leaned against the side of the boat next to Sunette. "Good bard, he wasn't on the ship last time we were here, was he?"

"No," Lucius said. "Stella picked him up a few months ago. So, are you in love with Raven?"

Mason sputtered at the sudden question. "Damn, Lucius, just say what you mean already." Sunette chuckled and watched them.

Lucius crossed his arms over his chest. "I mean, the way you look at her, I can't help but wonder."

Mason sighed. "She still needs to heal after what happened. You don't see her at her worst because she refuses to show it to any of you." Sunette and Lucius looked at each other, both worried, and Sunette leaned toward him.

"What do you mean?"

"When we're traveling and sleeping in the cabin or outside, she'll sleep through the night. No nightmares or anything like that. But when we stop and stay at an inn," he thought about his words. "Sleeping is hard for her."

"It is?" Lucius glanced over at Raven, laughing with Foster. He had no idea she was having such a tough time.

Mason nodded. "I've lost count of the nights where she'd wake from a nightmare, drenched in sweat and unable to go back to sleep. So many nights, I had to hold her as she cried in her sleep, saying how sorry she was. Sometimes, she feels so guilty she won't even come to bed. She just sits by the window, staring down at whatever city we're in, so I'd sit with her and talk. Just seeing if I could wear her out." He glanced back at her for a moment. "She feels so guilty about what she did, but she won't talk about it with anyone. So, I'm just going to stay by her side until she feels like herself again."

"I had no idea you were both suffering so." Sunette laid a hand on his arm.

He patted her hand. "I'm not suffering, don't worry about me."

Lucius looked at the young man and walked to the other side of him. "You didn't really answer my question."

Mason shook his head and looked back at Raven. "I've been crazy about her for years, but she was with Twig, so I let it be."

"I had no idea you were so patient, Mason." Sunette reached for his hand, and he gave it to her.

"Growing up with my sister and mom, you'd have to be,"

he said with a chuckle.

———

Everyone danced the night away, and the moon was high in the sky when Sunette pulled Foster down to their little room. She took her robe off and turned as Foster pulled his shirt over his head.

She admired his muscles for a moment, biting her lower lip. "How quiet can you be, Apple Picker?"

"Huh?" She smiled and let her slip slide down her body and pool at her feet.

"How quiet can you be?" She watched his eyes roam over every inch of her body. He kicked his boots off and walked over to her.

"As silent as a temple mouse," he whispered and unlaced his pants. "Unless it's the opposite you want?"

She laughed and pushed his pants down, and he stepped out of them. "No, the last thing I want is pirates hearing and teasing us." His hand slid around to her back, then moved lower and cupped her backside. Tingles spread along her body as his hand gently ran over her skin.

"Me either." She smiled a wicked sort of smile. "What are you thinking?" She raised her hand and slowly snuffed out the lamp in the room, plunging it into darkness. "You wicked little thing," he teased, and she laid her hand on his chest.

"Maybe a little," she whispered and pulled him down to her lips. "I want your tongue," she took his hand and moved it down her body, and slipped one of his fingers between her legs. "Here," she breathed out. He moaned and kissed her deeply as he picked her up and laid her on the blanket. She could barely see him. The light in the hallway let in a tiny bit of light. But she was able to feel him kiss his way down her body. He gently bit a nipple, drawing a small gasp from her mouth.

"Shh," he whispered quietly. "We don't want anyone knowing what we're doing, do we?" His voice was low, and if she wasn't already wet, his voice was enough to do it.

"No," she whispered as he kissed down her stomach.

"Open your legs for me." Her stomach tightened as she did just that, and she felt his hair tickling the inside of her thighs.

"Yes, Foster, yes." She felt him lick straight up her middle and stop on that bundle of nerves between her legs. Her hands flew to her mouth to contain her moans as his tongue swirled around exactly where she wanted him to. Waves of pleasure flowed through her, and her hips began moving in time with his tongue. He moaned, just a quick, quiet noise, but she felt it rumble through her, and she gasped. His hands grasped her hips as he began to suck, and that wonderful pressure was building inside her. She wanted to feel more, so she grasped one of his hands and ran it up her torso. Foster was a smart man, and it didn't take long before he covered one of her breasts with that hand.

His thumb ran over her nipple, and a soft moan escaped her lips as she covered his hand, feeling what his hand was doing. He gently pinched that pebbled skin, and without warning, that pressure between her legs erupted, and she couldn't stop the noise that came out. She felt him moan against her, which didn't help her relax at all, and after one last lick, he kissed the inside of her thigh and up her body.

"I don't know if that noise means you just can't help yourself," he teased and kissed her breast. "Or I'm just that good."

Sunette laughed. "You caught me off guard."

"Did I?" She leaned up and moved him onto his back, and straddled his hips.

"You cheated," she purred and reached between them. He was hard and groaned as her hand wrapped around him. "Let's see how you do." She lowered herself onto him, and his eyes closed. She sat back and let him sink deep inside her. His breath shuddered out a moment before she began rolling her hips. His hands gripped her hips, and she felt him rise up in time with her.

He had never done that before, and she reached down and held his hands. "Fuck," he whispered, and she laughed. The more she moved, the easier it was to get him to rub that spot inside that made her shiver. Every move was perfection as pleasure was building with every pass of him against her.

She sighed, "Oh, Foster." Her hips moved faster, and she felt him twitch underneath her. He moaned, keeping his lips closed, but the faster she moved, the faster his breathing became. He whispered her name over and over until he thrust his hips up and didn't move. His hand slammed over his mouth. That move hit that spot inside her, and the warmth that spilled inside her undid her. Her own pleasure throbbed around him. She leaned down and pressed her face against his chest, her moan vibrating against his skin. She laid still, catching her breath, and could feel how fast his heart was beating. His hands landed on her back, and he ran them up and down her smooth skin.

"You know," his chest rumbled as he spoke. "I think you on top is my favorite position."

Sunette laughed and looked up at him, still lying on his chest, him still inside her. "Is it?"

"Mm, even with so little light, I get to look at my beautiful love as she gives herself pleasure," he leaned down and kissed her forehead. "You have no idea how incredibly sexy you look." He quickly flipped her onto her back as she gave an amused squeal. His hand ran up her torso, and his thumb made little circles on the underside of her breast. "The way your breasts bounce as you move, how you look at me with me inside you," He ran his lips along hers, and she nipped at him. "I love everything about you, Sunette."

Her heart began racing. "I love everything about you, too, Apple Picker."

He kissed the skin between her breasts. "Your heart is racing, my beautiful mage."

She ran her hands through his long, wavy hair. "It beats for you."

He leaned down and kissed her softly. "The most wonderful woman in the world loves me. The gods must be smiling down on us," he said against her lips. "I didn't think such a love was possible."

She felt her eyes get teary and tried to keep her lip from quivering. "Foster, the things you say, really." She pulled him close and laid his head on her chest. She loved Foster with all her heart, she knew it, but she had never been more scared in her life.

———

A few days later, Lucius rolled over in Stella's bed and saw her sitting at her vanity. Her white shirt was open, her sun-kissed chest on full display.

"Hello," he crooned. He relished these mornings when they woke together. They happened so infrequently that he remembered each one with clarity. The one where the thunder of a vicious storm woke them and kept the crew up for the next twenty-four hours, wondering if they would make it out alive. Or his favorite, when he woke and was finally able to admire his newborn daughter as she lay on Stella's bare chest, her breath smelling like breast milk. He'd swear Te'a was the most beautiful baby he'd ever seen.

Stella was smiling at him in the mirror. "Morning." Her eyes sparkled with something mischievous, and he felt his body react.

He smiled back, matching her playful stare. "Cel said we were going to lash to Nightingale's ship today."

She nodded and ran a brush through her hair. "Mm-hmm, he said he was on one of the islands off the coast of Garythane, and he'll have some good things to trade and buy." She turned and winked, "Plus, I think a party is what we need."

"Agreed. We met Nightingale a while back. He took us out to let Sunette lay Bereck's ashes to rest."

Stella sighed and put her brush down. "He does that a lot. I'm sorry about your paladin. He was a good man."

Lucius nodded. "He was, he is missed." Crawling out from under the covers, Lucius walked over to her, naked. "It's been a while since I've spun you around."

She turned and wrapped her arms around him. "It has." She kissed his stomach and felt it jump under her lips and giggled. "Still ticklish, I see."

He laughed. "Only for you, my beautiful pirate." Her hands grabbed his ass as she kissed down his body to his cock that hardened from the attention. "I thought you were getting ready for the day." His voice was breathier than he intended.

She laughed. "This is part of it." Her hands squeezed his backside, and he moaned as her lips slipped over him. He preferred lying down while she did this, but he wasn't going to complain. Her lips moved down the length of him while her tongue pressed against the underside of him as she moved him in and out of her mouth. Her mouth was always perfection on him. Her lips were soft, and her teeth would barely scrape against his skin, just this side of pain. And her tongue, gods, her tongue felt amazing on him, the perfect amount of pressure. He buried a hand in her thick, silky hair, and the other reached down and brushed her nipple. She moaned around him, and he shook from the sensation. He pinched her nipple, and she pressed him closer, as her hand wrapped around the base of him and stroked as she moved him in and out of her mouth.

"Oh fuck," he moaned, and his hips moved against her mouth, and felt her suck on his head as he moved. Her hand squeezed the base of him, and he moved faster, his head flung back as his breath quickened at her touch. "Gods, I can't decide," he looked down at her, his cock moving in and out of her beautiful mouth. It almost made him finish right there. "Do I want to fuck you, or do I want you to finish me off with your mouth." She laughed around him, and he closed his eyes at the sensation.

The fact she didn't release him, told him what she wanted. Her hand moved faster, and that sucking, gods, that sucking, he didn't hold back as he thrust himself into her mouth one last time and moaned as he spilled inside her mouth. She swallowed down every bit of him, and as he looked down at her, it was a miracle he didn't get hard all over again. He watched as she slowly licked and sucked before she slipped him out of her mouth.

"I suppose it's time to get ready." She had a wicked little grin on her face.

He shook his head and got to his knees between hers. "Not just yet, my lovely pirate." He kissed her thigh as a hand ran up her torso, lightly caressing her breast. She breathed out appreciatively and leaned back against the vanity, spreading her legs for him. He kissed her knee, her thigh, and her inner thigh as his left hand ran up her torso and cupped her breast. She sighed and leaned back farther as his tongue found that bundle of nerves between her legs. She moaned as his tongue ran over that spot.

"Gods, I've missed you doing that." He slipped a finger inside her, and he felt a hand in his hair, holding him still as she gasped. He loved the way she felt inside, no matter if it was his finger, cock, or tongue. He loved the silky, warm feel of her around him. His finger found that spot inside, and she bucked against the vanity with a moan. As his tongue moved faster in a circle, he felt his own body reacting and moaned at the pleasurable pressure growing between his own legs. The things on the vanity started jiggling around, little perfume bottles almost fell over, and her brush rocked back and forth. "Fuck me, Lucius, please." While he didn't like stopping before he felt her orgasm, she did say please. He gave her one last long lick and pulled her to the floor. She turned and laid her cheek on the soft velvet of her bench as he rose up to his knees and slowly pushed himself inside her.

Stella sighed as he pushed himself as far as he could go. "Gods, I've missed you," he moaned.

She turned around, a little smile on her face. "It is nice that you're really here. I don't have to pretend my hand is yours."

His jaw dropped as he fucked her against the bench. "You naughty little wench." He leaned down against her back. "I'll have to think about that when we're apart." She laughed and pressed against him, which made him move faster. He reached around and continued that onslaught between her legs, which made her gasp and tighten around him. Why he ever let this woman go was beyond him. He pumped into her as she rocked back. He could tell he wasn't going to last much longer. Her breath hitch, and a second later, he felt her muscles pumping around him. She tilted her head back and moaned her pleasure into the air. That noise undid him, and he spilled into her, crying out at how fucking amazing it felt.

They stayed still a moment, breathing hard, until Stella

laughed and turned to him. "Well, if that isn't the best good morning ever." He chuckled and kissed her cheek, wondering how many of these wonderful mornings they would have.

———

Foster and Sunette were on deck when 'The Blue Wind' pulled next to a familiar boat. They watched as Te'a and the crew lashed the two ships together with rope and a few planks that were set across them.

Sunette pointed at the ship. "That's Nightingale's ship," she said as the other captain walked onto the deck of their ship. He looked the same, his facial hair as sharp as ever.

Te'a walked over and shook his hand. "Young Shadow, how is your crew?" Foster chuckled at his tone, almost serious if not for the smile on his face.

"Doing good, Nightingale. Moms with Lucius, they'll be out soon." Her hand waved dismissively towards the main quarters.

"Good," he clapped his hands once. "We got a few things we'd like to trade." His eyes landed on Sunette, and he smiled. "I remember you." He walked over and took her hands, "How are you?" His tone was one that knew she had mourned a great love.

"I'm well, thank you for asking."

He didn't let go of her hands. "I don't think I caught your name last time."

"I'm Sunette," she motioned over to Foster. "This is Foster, and the rest of our group are around here somewhere."

"It's lovely to see you again," he finally let go of her hands. "I have several fruits on my ship that I bet you'd love."

She chuckled. "Maybe." Nightingale started telling where his men could put the boxes while Foster leaned down to her ear.

"He was flirting hard with you," he teased.

She giggled and turned into his arms. "Jealous?"

"No, I know you only have eyes for me." He kissed her, his arms wrapping around her. Stella's crew brought their own boxes up, and they started trading their goods. There were silks and jewelry, spices, and fruit. The fruit was the first to get traded as it was a coveted item when you lived on a boat. Te'a put jewelry on and twirled around but didn't take anything. Lucius and Stella finally emerged from her stateroom and admired everything Nightingale had brought. Sunette noticed that Lucius bought a bracelet from him and gave it to Stella, who quickly put it on and kissed his cheek. In all the years she'd been with Lucius, he'd never bought anything like that for anyone but his pirate love.

————

That night, a bard from Nightingale's ship came onto theirs and started playing. Everyone started dancing and trying the special fruit that he found on that faraway island he went to. Sunette watched as Foster twirled Te'a around, big smiles on both their faces. She imagined he was missing his little sister. He once told her Te'a seemed to be around the same age as Saphira, maybe a little younger.

"Bite?" She looked over and saw Nightingale offering her a piece of the fruit. It was pink and had tiny seeds.

"Thank you." She took the fruit and ate it. It was sweet and juicy, and the little seeds burst in her mouth. "That's good."

"Isn't it? It doesn't grow anywhere else but the Western Key, don't know why." He popped a piece in his own mouth.

"Maybe it doesn't want to live anywhere but home."

He chuckled. "Perhaps. You're from Emperia, aren't you?"

She nodded and smiled at Foster, who gave her a wink. "I am. Not many know the name."

Nightingale shrugged. "I've been everywhere. I've heard every accent. How long since you've been home?"

"Gosh, twenty years? I fear I'll never go back."

"I'm sorry."

She shrugged and turned to him. "It's all right. I've been gone for so long that it doesn't really feel like home anymore. Too much heartbreak anyway." He held out another piece of fruit, and she popped it in her mouth. "What about you? Where is home?"

"Crystal Rivers." Her eyes narrowed, "It's in the middle of

the northern continent, tiny little hamlet. You can see why I left."

She chuckled. "I can."

Foster walked over to her, a big smile on his face, and held his hand out. "Dance?"

"Of course."

"Save one for me," Nightingale called out as Foster pulled her to the dancing area. She gave him a little wink before she was twirling with Foster. The music was amazing, and dancing with Foster while the moon was shining down on them was as close to feeling at peace as she had in years. She looked up at her love. He was smiling down at her, love in his eyes.

She leaned up and kissed him. "I love you, Foster, *Mi Epier*," she whispered.

He gave her cheek a kiss. "What does that mean?"

"My love," she kissed him. "My heart," she kissed him again. "My beloved."

His smile got wider. "You honor me."

"You deserve it. But I must confess to being scared."

Concern spread across his face. "Why?" He laid a hand on her cheek, and they sat off to the side. He held her hands, and she confessed what she had been holding in for months.

"Everyone I have ever loved has died, and I wouldn't be able to handle it-"

"Sunette," he leaned forward and kissed her, stopping her from saying the words she dreaded. "I'm not going anywhere."

She swallowed hard and shook her head. "But the lives we lead, they're dangerous, and things happen."

He wrapped a hand behind her neck and rubbed at her muscles. "True, so there's always a chance that you could succumb as well. I still have nightmares about that first mission we had, where we almost lost you. That thought is terrifying. But I trust you, and I trust all of us not to let that happen. I will defend you to the best of my ability." She nodded and held back tears. "You are my soulmate, Sunette, I have no doubt in my mind about that."

She smiled and wrapped her arms around him. "You are

mine as well, *Mi Epier."*

———

"Silent flute," Raven said, popping a piece of the fruit in her mouth. She and Mason had been sitting on the floor in their room for the last hour. He had snuck a box of the fancy fruit away from the pirates, and they had been eating it without a care in the world. They could hear the music and dancing above their heads, but neither wanted to dance.

Mason laughed. "Hmm, shaft of delight."

Raven roared with laughter. "Only a man would say his penis is a delight."

He nudged her. "My partners think it's delightful."

"What about shaft of invisibility?" She laughed, and he tackled her to the floor, tickling her sides. Her laughing squeal filled the room as she tried fighting back, but he was willey.

"I'll show you invisible." They laughed as they tried tickling and pinching each other until she laid on her back, and Mason laid on top of her. Their laughter slowly ebbed away as they calmed down. "Have you been sleeping okay?" His thumb ran gently on her cheek.

She nodded. "Yes. It's different than being at an inn, I kinda like the rocking motion." Ever since Twig died, sleeping inside had been difficult. She didn't understand why, but her nightmares seemed to find her more easily inside these days. Mason had stayed up with her, held her while she cried, and talked to her when her mind wouldn't shut up about the awful thing she had done. Since they'd been on the boat, she'd had no nightmares, and her mind was calm enough that they both had slept through the last few nights.

"Good." Mason smiled. "I wanted to make sure I wasn't ignoring you."

"No, you weren't." She wrapped her arms around him. "Thank you for helping me. You don't have to do it."

His eyebrows went up. "Of course I do! You're my best friend, Raven, I care about your happiness, and I don't want you to suffer." He laid his head on her chest, "I know you really loved

Twig, and I'm sorry he's gone." Raven sniffed, and he looked up. Her eyes were closed, and tears were leaking from her eyes. "What's wrong?"

She sniffed again. "It was my fault," she whispered. "It's my fault he died." She opened her eyes and saw Mason listening. "I lied to you."

"About what?" He wiped some tears away.

"That light you saw on the battlefield, that you asked me about, it wasn't just a healing spell. It was a resurrection spell. Twig died on that battlefield, just like Bereck. But I couldn't...I didn't want to live without him. I stole it from my parents when I ran," Mason kissed her, and she felt her stomach tighten at the kiss.

"You don't have to apologize or explain," he whispered. "What happened was awful, but I want to see you whole again, no matter what happened." She had no words. For the first time in years, she had no words, so she just nodded. He laid his head on her chest again, and she laid a hand on his head.

"You don't hate me for bringing him back, causing that mess?" she whispered.

"I could never hate you, Raven. I love you." The words spilled so effortlessly from his mouth.

"I love you too." She squeezed him, not surprised the words flowed flawlessly from her own as well. He was right, she was his best friend, and he would help her heal.

———

Lucius twirled Stella around to the music, her dark hair flying behind her. He wondered if the time for him to join her on her ship was closing in. He was finding it harder and harder to leave her ship the last few times they had boarded. He loved Stella, he knew that now, but he didn't want to crowd her. She was so free, and he knew she coveted that freedom.

"What would you say if I were to stay on your ship?" He dared to ask.

Her eyebrows went up, but that didn't surprise him. "I wouldn't ask that of you. I know you love traveling with your group." Not exactly the answer he expected.

"You wouldn't have to ask it of me, not really."

Her head tilted a little. "I wouldn't?" He shook his head. "Do you want to?"

He couldn't tell if her tone was excited or cautious. "Soon, I think, yes." He leaned forward and whispered in her ear. "I'd like to be a family with you and Te'a when you're ready." He stood straight and saw the surprise on her face. With every passing year, the want of a family had crept up on him. His group was a family, sure, but it was different with Stella and Te'a. He wanted to be a better father than his own. He wanted Te'a to be happier than he was growing up, and he wanted to be there for her.

"You would?" He nodded. "She doesn't know."

"I know." When Te'a was two months old, Stella sailed her boat north, and out of stupidity, he decided not to go. He didn't blame her for not telling Te'a who her father was. It could confuse a kid when their dad wasn't around. "But that can be changed." The music stopped, and he bowed to her and moved over to Te'a. She looked so much like him sometimes, especially when he caught her sword fighting with Foster. They both tended to squint while dueling, a bad habit of course. "A dance?" He held out his hand, and she giggled.

"Of course." While they weren't particularly close, they got along well. She took his hand, and he started twirling her around the deck.

"So, I hear you have learned a new language, impressive. What is that four now?"

"Yep, how many do you know?"

He smiled. "Just two. I'm afraid I don't have the ear for languages like you do."

She shrugged. "It's not that hard. After you learn one, you can hear the differences and similarities in the others."

"Can you?"

Her smile warmed his heart. "Oh yes, especially between Dwarvish and Halfling. You'd be surprised at how similar they are."

He chuckled. "You're so smart. I wonder where you get it."

"It's all me."

"That it is." He smiled down at her. "Te'a, what would you think if I stayed on the boat with your mom?"

"Hmm," She looked away from him as she thought. "It'd probably keep her from bitching about how much she misses you." Lucius laughed loudly at the curse and how apparently Stella missed him just as much as he missed her.

"She bitches about it huh?"

"Oh yeah, all the time." She rolled her eyes. Clearly, she'd had enough of hearing her mother yearn for him. "But I think she thinks you wouldn't do it. She said you love your freedom too much. That's why she hasn't asked."

He smiled softly as he looked down at his daughter. "True." The music stopped, and he bowed. "Thank you for the dance."

"You're welcome!" She bounded off to a crate of the fruit that Nightingale had brought. Cel walked up to him and shook his hand. He had been with Stella for years, her battle priest and healer. Lucius was grateful to him for taking care of Stella and her crew.

"Glad the Captain picked your group up. She's been missing you something fierce."

He raised an eyebrow at that. "Oh?"

"Yeah, she gets this way around Te'a's birthday." Lucius' heart leapt into his throat. Te'a's birthday was tomorrow.

"Ah, I feel that mothers often do. Excuse me." He walked over to the stuff Nightingale had brought to trade. He had seen Te'a spin around earlier, draped in jewelry, but she didn't take anything. He looked over and saw Sunette and Foster talking, and he quickly walked over. "Mistress Mage," he leaned on a crate next to her.

"Yes, Lucius?" She turned, half amused.

"Might you have a book you could part with? I'd replace it when I could."

"What kind of book?" She crossed her arms, her books were her pride and joy for sure.

He leaned closer. "Tomorrow is Te'a's birthday."

Sunette smiled. "I see, well why don't we go look?"

"Perfect, Foster, keep Te'a distracted." The fighter laughed and joined Te'a as she ate the fruit. Sunette hopped down from the crate, and the two of them went down to her and Foster's little room. Lucius walked quietly like he usually did and froze as he glanced into Mason and Raven's room and saw the thief had his lips pressed against hers. He turned and gave Sunette a 'be quiet' with his finger to his lips. She nodded, and they both snuck past, not disturbing them.

Sunette opened her magical bag and began pulling out books. "What kind of book? She doesn't seem very magically inclined."

"No, I was thinking maybe something exciting, like an adventure story?"

She nodded, her arm reaching deep into the bag. "Ah, here we are." She pulled out a book that was maybe an inch thick. "This is a good one." She handed it to Lucius, who smiled.

"Perfect." He gave her cheek a kiss and ran back up the stairs. He found Te'a and Foster throwing candied beans into each other's mouths. Well, trying to, they mostly bounced off their faces. Te'a was laughing so hard that she missed everyone. Lucius walked over and snatched one of the beans mid-air, and handed it to her.

"The birds will love your boat tomorrow."

"Yeah, they will," she said, laughing as she popped the bean into her mouth.

"I have a birthday gift for you."

She gasped and turned to him. "What is it?"

"Close your eyes." She did so, holding her hands out, a big smile on her face and he prayed she'd like it. He placed the book in her hands, and she opened them. She turned the book over and gasped. "Do you like it?" He had never been so nervous to ask that question. His heart was practically in his throat.

"I have been begging Mom to get this every time we're in port!" She leapt into Lucius' arms and hugged him tight around the neck. "Thank you, thank you, thank you!"

He hugged her back just as tight. "You're most welcome."

She slipped from him and ran over to Stella. "Mom! Look what I got for my birthday!" She shoved the book into her hands, and Stella smiled. Te'a pointed over at Lucius, and Stella looked up at him. He gave them a little bow, and she gave him a wink. Te'a took the book back and sat under a torch, and started reading.

"Looks like the book was a good idea," Sunette said behind him.

"Indeed."

CHAPTER 15
LOST LOVES

The next year flew by for Foster and Sunette. They stayed with the group and couldn't help but notice the jobs that Lucius took weren't as dangerous as the ones when he first joined. Clearing out kobold holes and guard jobs around Blackridge mainly. One late summer day, the group found itself in Ardenry. After they settled into an inn, Foster snuck out to a jeweler. He sold the old ring he bought for Ada and got a new ring for Sunette. When he walked back into the inn, he saw Lucius already working his magic with the serving girl. Foster sat down, and the half-elf finally tore his eyes away from the pretty girl.

"Ah, Foster, have a drink." The girl passed him a mug and then got off Lucius's lap to get more.

Foster took a drink and chuckled. "You waste no time."

"No, I do not." He took a big swig, and Foster could see his eyes following the young woman as she walked around the tavern. "Ah, I do love Ardenry."

"As do I." Foster pulled out the ring he got for his mage and held it out towards Lucius, who did a double take at it. "Is that what I think it is?"

Foster smiled. "It is."

Lucius held out his hand, and Foster shook it. "Then all my heartfelt congratulations to you."

"Thank you, sir."

"Any idea how you're going to do it?"

He shook his head. "Can't decide if I should do it with everyone here or in private."

Lucius held his chin. "Bereck did it in front of the group. Maybe something more private this time?"

Foster nodded. "Good idea." He took a breath. "If she says yes, I want to take her home to Raventree. No more traveling, no more dangerous jobs. I want to take her home to start our lives together."

He swore he saw Lucius breathe a sigh of relief. "Good plan. I will miss you two, but I'll be happy knowing you're safe at home."

"Thank you for everything over the years, sir."

He chuckled. "Thank you, Foster."

———

After Raven and Mason visited with Lessa, they decided to stock up on some essentials while they were in town. As they walked, Raven noticed Mason kept looking at her. He had taken such loving care of her since Twig died. She'd always be grateful to him. But even after that kiss they shared on the 'Blue Wind,' she still couldn't bring herself to love him. Though it was getting harder to dismiss the happy tingles she'd get when she woke up with his arms around her. Or when they'd dance, and his arms would press her closer, and her heart raced. It was just dancing, not the fact that she was so close to him that her lips could kiss his neck.

When they were done shopping, Raven heard music coming from one of the town squares.

"Let's go listen." She grabbed his hand, and they made their way to a stage by one of her favorite fountains. It was of a young girl carrying a basket of flowers, who seemed to be enjoying a spring wind. She thought the girl in the fountain was the happiest person ever. No death, violence, or starvation, just beautiful flowers and a lovely spring zephyr. A troupe was playing on a stage near it, and everyone around them was dancing.

"They're good," Mason said appreciatively. She pulled him over to the fountain, and they sat and listened to them play. "I guess you're one to play more than listen, huh?"

"Sometimes," she nodded and turned towards him, folding her leg under her knee. "But just listening can really soothe my soul."

He reached out and rubbed her arm. "Does your soul need soothing?"

"Whose doesn't," she chuckled. "But I'm fine. I feel better than I have in a long time."

He smiled. "Good."

"You're a big reason for that, Mason, you know that, right? Without your help, I think I would have sunk into myself, and it would have been hard to crawl out of that pit." She still felt guilty for what happened to Twig, but it didn't feel like she had been buried by it in a while. Talking with Mason helped. He wasn't a healer, trained in the ways of helping those through trauma, but he was there for her. He knew Twig, so that connection helped her. He was always able to pull her out of those pits by talking about Twig and their happier memories.

She was surprised he had remembered so many, some she had forgotten. Like, when they were washing off in a river one day, she and Twig were the only ones in the water when suddenly they were surrounded by huge fish. Lucius called out and said they were in the middle of their spawning territory, and Twig had joked that they better get out before he got pregnant. That had made her laugh, and she was finally able to fall asleep that night.

The music eased her heart, and she looked up. Mason's eyes met hers. They were a pretty light gray. She'd been admiring them a lot lately. She looked down and cleared her throat. "So, thank you for that."

"You don't have to thank me." He reached out and took her hand. She squeezed it. "I care about you, and I would do anything to make sure you healed."

She nodded, staring at their hands. "I care about you, too." She looked up and noticed he was leaning towards her. His fingers brushed her cheek, and she sat still as he kissed her. Just a gentle brush of lips before he sat back. "What...why did you do that?

He ran his thumb along her cheek. "Did you not want me

to?"

She did so much. "I...don't feel like I deserve it. After what I did."

He held her face, and she couldn't remember a time when he looked so calm. "You do. You made a mistake, Raven. That doesn't mean you need to punish yourself for the rest of your life. You are amazing, beautiful, and funny, and I have loved you for so long. Let me love you, Raven. Let me show you how much—"

"Shut up." She pulled him to her lips and kissed him deeply. His arms wrapped around her. She slipped her tongue into his mouth, and heard him moan. They sat like that for a long time, kissing without a care in the world, while the music played around them. While she still didn't feel like she deserved Mason, she couldn't deny herself anymore.

––––––

An hour later, everyone was gathered for dinner. Foster couldn't help but stare at Sunette. She was talking to Raven about a shop down the road that had beautiful jewelry.

"I saw the loveliest silver hair wreath, with little green jewels. I think it would go well with your hair."

Raven laid her head in her hand. "Maybe. I don't really wear jewelry besides my earrings. Most of it seems like such an unneeded extravagance."

Lucius cleared his throat. "I believe that's the point, dear Bard."

Sunette laughed and turned to Foster. "What are you looking at, *Mi Epier?*"

"Sorry, I don't mean to stare."

"That's all right, you're allowed to stare." She turned to Mason, "How is Lessa? I was going to see her tomorrow."

He hurriedly swallowed his food. "She's great, much more powerful. I was surprised. She's really excited to see you." The group ate, and the couples danced while Lucius put his best moves on a pretty serving woman.

Foster and Sunette said good night to their friends and headed upstairs. When the door closed, Sunette captured Foster's lips and started taking his shirt off. He chuckled the entire time.

When their bodily needs were met, they lay on the bed, breathless and sweaty. "Oh Foster, *Mi Epier,*" she chuckled quietly.

"You're amazing," he said. He got out of bed and fumbled through the clothes until he found his shirt with the ring in it.

"My, my, what a view." He realized his bare butt was flashing her and chuckled as he wiggled it a little for her. Sunette laughed loudly as he strode over and kneeled next to the bed.

She calmed down and lay on her side, smiling peacefully at him. "I love you so much, Sunette."

"I love you too, Foster."

He reached up and held her hand. "I can't imagine my life without you. You're beautiful, smart, and sassy, just how I want our children to be. I want to take you home to Raventree and start the most wonderful, blessed life with you." He held up the ring, silver with a dark blue gem with little stars in it. There was no doubt in his mind that she'd say yes. "Sunette, will you marry me?"

Tears sparkled in her eyes, but she was smiling brightly. "Oh, *Mi Epier,* of course, I'll marry you!" She laughed as she threw her arms around his neck and hugged him tight. When she finally leaned back, he wiped away her happy tears and put the ring on her finger. "Oh, it's beautiful."

"A beautiful ring for a beautiful woman." He gently kissed her lips before she gasped.

"We must celebrate. How about some champagne," she said excitedly.

He smiled. "Champagne I shall get," he stood and pulled his pants on. "I shall return," he walked up and whispered in her ear. "And it will taste wonderful as I lick it off your naked body."

She giggled. "Oh, promise?"

He kissed her lips and ran to the door. "Don't move. I'll be right back." He caught a glimpse of Sunette's naked body and felt his body start to react, *gotta hurry* he thought as he ran down the stairs, his feet thumping loudly on the steps.

The tavern was busy now, but he was able to hear Lucius over the commotion. "Foster!" He turned and saw Lucius had a question on his face. "Well?"

"She said yes!" He yelled out and held his arms up in triumph.

"Whoo!" Lucius whooped and banged on the table. Foster got a bottle of the finest champagne and two glasses before running back up to the room.

He was able to open the door and pushed it open with his backside. "As promised, my love," he said as he turned. He looked at the bed, expecting to see Sunette's naked body, but there was nothing there. He set the champagne down. "Sunette?" He walked quietly around the room. He bent down and looked under the bed, nothing. Foster was really confused. *Maybe she snuck out to get me something*, he thought.

He searched through her bags but didn't find any money missing. He did, however, find a rather nice dagger he had never seen before. He unsheathed it and saw it was engraved, "Mi Epier, may it strike true" was engraved on it. Obviously, it was meant for him. He searched the room but was too flustered to really take it all in. None of her clothes were missing. In fact, the room looked exactly the same, except she wasn't in it. He ran from the room and started banging on Mason and Raven's door.

"Mason! Raven!"

When it opened, he saw the rogue was wrapped in his bed sheet. "Worst timing ever." He clearly did not appreciate the interruption. Raven walked up behind him, wearing one of Mason's shirts, her hair messy.

"Something's happened to Sunette. She's gone!"

Their eyes widened. "What do you mean she's gone?" Raven stepped up between Mason and the doorframe.

"She just disappeared, nothing of hers is missing, everything is where she left it. I think something bad happened." Mason ran back into his room and quickly pulled on some pants while Raven and Foster ran back to his room.

"When did you last see her?" Her eyes searched the room.

"Literally five minutes ago. I left to get some champagne, and when I came back, she was gone." Mason stood in the doorway, taking it in before he started searching.

After a few minutes, he mumbled. "Foul play."

"What?"

They both turned to him and saw he was kneeling by the bed. "Look here." When Foster looked closely, he saw a drop of blood.

"Gods, what happened?" He started panicking and ran down the stairs and out into the street. He could see the window, but nothing looked out of place there either. Lucius came running out after him.

"Foster, what's wrong?"

"Someone's taken her, she's gone."

The half-elf tensed, "What?"

"I went back to the room with the champagne, and she was gone. Mason found blood by the bed."

"Shit." They ran inside and back up to the room. Mason was still searching for anything.

"Find anything?"

He looked up and shook his head. "Other than the blood, nothing."

"Damn it!" Foster kicked the bed and grabbed his hair. He was at a loss. He didn't know what to do.

"Let me try something." Raven stood in the middle of the room, still just wearing Mason's shirt, and closed her eyes. She took a deep breath and held out her hands. Strange music filled the air, and her voice weaved around the notes, filling the room. Suddenly, Foster saw shadows in the room, one was on the bed, and it looked like Sunette.

"Otto." He breathed out and watched two other shadows appear in the room. They were cloaked, so there was no way to see their outlines. Sunette started to get off the bed, but the shadows enveloped her, and they disappeared. Raven fell to her knees, breathing heavily, and Mason quickly held her up.

"Anything?" she asked breathlessly.

"Some," Lucius walked over to the window. "It looked like some people teleported in and took her."

She finally caught her breath. "Sorry, it's not clearer."

Mason rubbed her shoulders. "Hey, don't worry about it, that was amazing."

"Okay, someone obviously took her, now where do we start?" Foster took a few breaths, trying to stay calm.

Raven stayed on the ground, her hand on Mason's. "We start as if we were the ones who wanted her. Why her?"

Foster sighed. "She's a powerful mage. But if that were the reason, they would have taken her book as well." He pointed at the thick leather-bound book next to the bed.

Raven pointed at him. "Exactly, so that's not the reason."

"If she were rich, her family could pay a ransom," Mason suggested.

Foster shook his head. "She had no family," then he remembered what she had told him on his birthday years ago. Why he had taken her to Ebba in Salthole and thought he might pass out and he sat on the bed. "Oh, gods, they found her."

"Who found her?" Lucius walked up and laid a hand on Foster's shoulder.

"Those men who killed her family, Coscarelli is their name." He looked up into Lucius's eyes and knew he looked terrified. "They found her, I know it."

Mason sat back and sighed. "They must have been really powerful to overcome her."

"Okay," Lucius started. "We have an idea. Now we have to find her."

"Where on earth do we start? We can just go willy-nilly searching. It could cost her her life," Mason asked.

"True," Foster clenched his hands to keep them from shaking. "But I don't know Ardenry enough to know where to find someone who could help."

Mason gasped. "I bet Lessa would know!"

Foster felt hope welling up and got to his feet. "Right! Mason, come with me. You two do something you think is productive," he said as they ran from the room.

———

When they reached the temple, Mason ran to the nearest priest he could see. "I need to see Lessa again. It's an emergency!" He nodded and ran into the back of the temple.

Foster kneeled at the seashell-covered dais and prayed. "Please be with her, Otto, I love her so much. She's to be my wife. I can't lose her. Please be with her, Otto." He prayed until he heard a door open and feet running over.

"Mason, what is it?" Lessa hugged her brother and saw Foster getting to his feet. "Foster!" She smiled and hugged him as well. He had never seen her so happy and full of life. Being a priestess really did suit her.

"Lessa, we need your help."

She stepped back and nodded her head. "Whatever you need."

"Sunette's missing. Someone took her."

Lessa gasped, "Oh no, what happened?" They stood in the temple and told their story, what they knew anyway.

"You can see why we're at a loss as to how to go about finding her."

"I do." She paced a few times, "There's a woman in town I met about a year ago. She's a seer, and people rave about her. You could start there. Maybe she can scry on Sunette."

Foster sighed. "It's better than nothing, I suppose. Thank you, Lessa. I'm sorry our visit couldn't be happier."

"Me too." She reached out and gave his arm a squeeze.

"What's the woman's name?" Mason asked.

"Adalaide, she lives on Curr Street. There's a sign out front. You can't miss it."

Foster nodded and gave her cheek a kiss. "Thank you, Lessa," and dashed towards the city.

"Foster, wait!" Mason yelled after him and stopped, "You might want to put a shirt on if you're going to see a complete stranger." He looked down and realized he'd been running around Ardenry shirtless.

"Damn, I didn't realize." He turned and stared for the inn.

Mason caught up with him. "Don't worry, we'll find her Foster."

"I know."

———

They ran back to the room. Lucius and Raven, now in her own clothes, jumped to their feet.

"Well?" Lucius asked.

"Lessa said there was a woman," Foster pulled on a shirt. "A seer that might be able to find her."

"Well, what are we waiting for?" Raven started for the door. "Let's go."

They all made their way out of the room and followed Foster. "Curr Street is what she said. The woman's name is Adalaide."

"I hope she'll see us," Raven sighed. "It's awful late." It took the group about ten minutes to get to Curr Street and another five to find the right house. A big wooden sign with stars and swirls got their attention, and they ran to the door.

Foster began banging on it. "Hello, Adalaide. I need to see you!" He didn't stop banging until the door opened. A human man was standing inside wearing dark leather armor. He was as tall as Foster, which was a feat in and of itself, and he looked really irritated.

"We're closed right now. You'll have to come back in the morning."

He tried to shut the door, but Foster stuck his big, booted foot in the way. "I'm sorry, but I really need to see her."

"Yeah, you and everyone else. In the morning!" He tried kicking Foster's foot away, but it was too big, "If you don't move, you'll force my hand." The man reached for a sword on his back but didn't pull it out yet.

"I don't care, Adalaide!" Foster yelled into the house, "Adalaide, I need to see you. It's an emergency, please!"

The man let go of the door and finally drew the sword. "Leave now, or I'll make you."

But Foster paid the man no mind and kept yelling for the seer. "Adalaide, please!" The man raised his sword. Raven was ready to throw a dagger when they all heard a woman's voice.

"Foster?"

"Boy, she's good," Mason whispered. The man lowered the sword, and they all saw a small female half-elf walk into the doorway.

Foster's eyes widened. "Ada."

"Foster, it is you." There was a little smile on her lips before she looked worried, "What's wrong?"

"You two know each other?" The big man asked.

Foster stepped up and took Ada's hands. "Please, Ada, my betrothed is missing. Someone took her right out of our room. We were told you could help."

Ada's eyes widened. "Gods no, come in, come in." She moved out of the way for them to pass while the man with the sword started to object.

"Ada, should you really be doing this right now?"

"Please don't fuss, Dryn. I'm fine, I need to do this." As Foster brushed past her, he felt how far her stomach was away from her body and looked down.

"Ada, you're—"

He pointed at her stomach, and she gave him a little smile. "Come on in, Foster. We can catch up after I look for your love."

The man behind Ada sheathed his sword. "If you'll follow me." He didn't sound happy about it, but Foster was glad he put up his sword. They followed him through a beaded doorway and sat around a large oak table. They all laid their elbows on the table except Raven, who sat back and started chewing on her thumbnail. Ada quickly sat across from them, pulling a piece of paper and a charcoal pencil closer.

"What is her name?"

"Sunette Chelri." She wrote it down and lit it on fire before throwing it into a silver bowl. Flames licked the inside of the bowl before quickly burning out. "Do you have anything personal of hers?"

Foster's eyes widened. "Oh, um—"

"Here, try this." Mason held out the inscribed dagger and turned to Foster. "Thought you might want it later." Ada took it from the rogue and laid a hand on it before she began whispering over the bowl.

After a few minutes, Foster spoke up. "Do you see anything?"

She shook her head. "She's being shrouded, but that's somewhat good news."

"Somewhat?"

"Means she's alive." Foster let out a breath he didn't know he was holding. "I can find her, but it'll take all night. Nothing they can do can keep me out. What exactly do you want me to find out?" She asked the group.

"Where she is? Who has her," he looked over at Lucius. "What else?"

"Maybe why?"

Ada nodded her head. "All right, that I can do. The rest of you can go, Foster, if you would stay?"

Lucius sighed. "All right then, Miss Ada-laide?" He said awkwardly, not knowing which name to call her by.

She smiled. "Ada's fine."

"Ada, we'll see you in the morning. How much do we owe you?"

She held up a hand. "Don't worry, this I'll do for free."

"It's much appreciated, Miss Ada." Lucius gave her a little bow, and the others followed him out, leaving Foster alone with Ada and the man with the sword, whose name was apparently Dryn.

"I can't believe you're here. I never thought I'd see you again," Ada said before he could.

"I wish it were under better circumstances."

"As do I." Dryn walked over and offered her his hands to stand. "Thank you, darling." She pulled herself up, and her belly was plainly obvious now.

"My goodness, Ada," Foster said quietly. He had

envisioned having a family with her one day, envisioned how she might look carrying his child. Once it hurt. But now he was happy for her, as happy as he could be with Sunette missing anyway.

She chuckled as Dryn laid a hand on her stomach. "Big, isn't she? Going to be a boy, I tell ya," he said proudly.

Foster looked between the two. "You and him?" Foster pointed at the man who, not half an hour ago, pulled a sword on him.

"Yes. Foster, this is Dryn. He's my husband and guardian. He watches over me while I search."

"Seems he does a little more than watch," he said, getting to his feet.

Ada laughed. "I suppose he does."

Foster moved over and offered Dryn his hand. "I'm sorry for trying to barge in earlier."

Dryn took it and gave it a hearty shake. "That's all right. I'd probably be the same way if my wife were suddenly gone." Ada started for a nearby bedroom, and they both followed. Dryn helped Ada into the bed and kissed her forehead. "I'll bring you some tea."

"Thank you." He walked out, and Foster stood at the end of the bed. He couldn't help but feel rather shy around her.

"Will the tea help you relax?"

"Sort of. It's a special brew that lets me," she stopped and seemed to search for a word. "Travel in the planes. Mortals cannot hide from me while I look for them that way." She had a wicked little smile as she spoke. It made him chuckle.

"I didn't know you were so powerful." He wasn't surprised, though.

"Neither did I." She groaned and laid a hand on her stomach.

He sat next to her and tried not to touch her. "Are you okay?"

"Oh, I'm fine, just kicking up a storm. Would you like to feel?"

He smiled a little. "Sure." He reached out and laid his hand on her big belly, and the baby gave a furious kick, making them both chuckle. "How much longer do you have?"

"Six weeks." She sounded tired already.

"I don't think it'll be that long."

She laughed. "Gods, I hope not."

Dryn walked back in and handed Ada a mug of tea. "Did he kick you?" He asked Foster.

"About took my thumb off," they chuckled. "So, do you know it's a boy?"

Dryn shrugged. "Well, no, but look at her! It's gotta be a boy in there."

Ada chuckled and drank the entire mug. "Thank you, honey."

He bent down and gave her a sweet kiss on her lips. "You're welcome, my lovely," he whispered and took the mug back to the kitchen.

Ada turned to Foster and took his hand. "Tell me about your love."

He tried to relax while her face came to his mind. "She's beautiful, long dark hair and beautiful, kind, blue eyes. She's got quite a temper." He told Ada of their first meeting, and she laughed.

"That's a wonderful story." Ada fought against a yawn.

Foster nodded and continued. "She's a mage, powerful. The last of her family, actually."

"The last of her family? What happened?"

Foster sighed and shook his head. "Before she was born, these men got it in their heads that her family were the guardians of some magical artifact. They had no idea what they were talking about, of course. And to find this artifact, someone in her family had to die, it made no sense. One by one, her family died around her. I'm afraid they are the ones who have her."

Ada's eyes were tired, but she was clearly astonished at the story. "Where is she from?"

"Emperia."

"Mm, you have a mysterious woman indeed, Foster. Have faith, I will find her." Her voice got quiet, and she closed her eyes. He listened to the sound of her steady breathing while he got up and sat in one of the chairs next to the bed.

Dryn came back in and handed Foster a mug of coffee. "You look like you need it."

He took it and drank deep. "Thanks." He watched Dryn sit on the bed next to Ada. He ran his thumb lightly on her cheek. Foster could tell he loved her, from his soft eyes as he looked upon his wife to how he doted on her. "How did you and Ada meet?"

"My group was using her services, looking for something. The leader asked me to hang around and make sure no one took her while we were procuring her services. I annoyed the crap out of her, I know," he said with a smile. "When my group was done, I came back and offered my services as her personal guard. Surprisingly, she accepted."

"How long have you been married?"

"Two years. How long have you been with your woman?"

"Well, we've been in the same group for almost six years, but the last two years we've been together, it's been the best years of my life."

Dryn smiled. "Don't worry, Ada will find her for you. Nothing has been able to hide from her."

———

Foster watched Ada sleep through the night. She looked almost comatose. Every once in a while, her belly would jump, and Dryn would chuckle and kiss it before telling the baby to let their mummy sleep. Ten hours after she fell asleep, Ada breathed deeply and opened her eyes. Dryn leaned forward. "Are you all right?"

"Hmm-mm," she turned her head and held out her hand. "Foster?"

He quickly got up and took her hand. "Did you find her?"

She nodded. "I did. She's as beautiful as you say."

"She's alive?"

"Yes."

Foster felt relieved. "Where is she?" Dryn kissed her cheek and left the room in a hurry.

"You were right. It's the same men who chased her when she was young. They took her to Old Cyranar."

His eyes went wide as he breathed out. "Gods, that's a long way away." Old Cyranar was a cursed city several weeks north of Raventree, on the western side of the continent. It's said a thousand years ago, the gods destroyed it in a bid to eradicate The Shackled One. They only succeeded in destroying the city, and now it was home to creatures and evil beings who combed the city, looking for artifacts that might bring them power. His mother told them about her time there. She was turned to stone for a few hours and died moments after Sobrei was freed. Foster never wanted to go there.

"I listened a bit, and it seems Sunette was partly correct about these men. They do, in fact, believe her family are the guardians of an artifact, but it wasn't that one person was the key to finding it. Everyone was. They said they had to kill the entire line, and when you did, you became the guardian and would know all its secrets."

"That's the most ridiculous thing I've ever heard! You'd think if it were true, she'd know about this stupid chalice."

She shrugged. "It's hard to argue with insane men, but it's what they believe. To have access to the artifact would give them great power, and I don't think they would use it for much good. What was it called, did she know?"

"She said the Cup of Kuraim."

Confusion flashed on her face. "What the hell is Kuraim?"

Foster shook his head. "No idea." He watched her, seemingly making a mental note to search for information on this thing.

Dryn came back carrying a tray of food. "I brought you some food, Love."

She sat up, and he put the tray over her legs and put some jam on a biscuit. "Get me a map, and I'll be able to point where in Cyranar she is."

Foster nodded. "Okay, I can do that."

"I heard them say they had to wait for the full moon to sacrifice her, so we've got almost an entire month."

"They won't get antsy? She made it seem like those men just killed her family whenever they wanted." He felt his heart lift at the news, time was something they desperately needed, and now it seemed like they had plenty.

"No, the moon was important because she's the last. The others were killed just to get to the end. Now that it's here, they must do a ritual in order to truly become the new guardians."

He nodded and sighed. "All right, thank you so much."

"Be back in the morning. You need to rest before you go."

He picked up her hand and gave it a kiss. "Thank you again, we'll be back," he said and dashed from the house.

———

"Glad you could find her," Dryn said as his hand slowly pet her leg.

"They'll need help, Dryn." She sipped the juice he brought her.

He nodded. "I agree."

She took a bite of her biscuit, the jam squeezing out through the two halves. "I want you to go with them."

His eyes widened in shock. "Excuse me?"

She looked over at him. "I want you to go with them."

"No. Absolutely not, Ada, you need me here." He rubbed her belly.

"I'll be fine. I'll get Krell to teleport you there. You shouldn't be gone for more than a week. It'll be plenty of time."

He stood. "Ada, damn it!" He crossed his arms and walked over to the window.

"Dryn!" He didn't turn around. She only sounded like that when he knew she was desperate for someone to listen. He heard it a lot while he was guarding her. "Foster and Sunette's children are special. It's important they get all the help they can."

"Not more special than ours," he turned. "How can you

expect me to leave you like this?" He motioned at her.

"I won't be alone, I'll get Trisa to stay with me. She'll be an immense help."

"Ada, I just—"

"Dryn, listen to me, please!" He could hear her getting upset and knew he was close to crossing a line. "It's hard enough knowing what's going to happen when no one believes or listens to me. You know I can't stand it when you don't heed my words."

Dryn sat down and took her hand. "I'm sorry, love, but you do understand why I don't want to leave you, don't you?"

She looked into his eyes, a little calmer. "Yes, I do."

He ran his fingers through his hair. "Fine. I'll go," he said quietly. She touched his shoulder, and he looked up at her. She was smiling, as beautiful as ever.

"Thank you, Dryn."

He touched her hand with his cheek. "You're welcome, love."

CHAPTER 16
UNPLANNED SAVIOR

The next morning, the group went back to Ada's, and Dryn led them to the comfy room in back. Ada was sitting in bed, and there were also two new people in the room. One was a tall man in mage robes. He had wavy blonde hair and looked rather young. The other was a woman with shoulder-length brown hair and a friendly smile.

"Okay, here's what's going to happen." Ada clapped once and motioned to the young man. "Krell here can teleport you to Cyranar. Along with Dryn, the seven of you will be attacking the men who have Sunette. There's one magic user. He's in charge. The rest are fighters. I only saw eight people there, two outside and six inside, so you should be able to get rid of them for good. The door to Sunette's room is trapped, so be careful."

"She's in a room?" Foster asked. He expected them to chain her in a dungeon in the crumbling city.

"Yes. They want her healthy and alive for the sacrifice, so they're taking care of her."

"Wait, did you say Dryn was coming?" Lucius pointed at the tall man, who looked annoyed.

"Yep, I'm going," his voice matched his face for annoyance.

"But," Lucius pointed at Ada, and Dryn held up his hand.

"We've already had this argument. That's what Tris is for," he said, pointing to the young woman next to the bed.

The half-elf shrugged. "All right then."

"Another reason I'm asking him to go is because I have a connection with him." She laid a hand on his arm. "I can keep an eye on Sunette and relay to Dryn if anything changes. You shouldn't be surprised."

Lucius nodded and looked at the group. "That would come in handy."

He sighed in acceptance. "Yes, it will."

"Well, we're ready, not sure about you two," Lucius asked Dryn and the tall mage.

"We're ready." The mage smiled. His voice was unexpectedly deep.

"Let's say goodbye to Lessa first," Mason said. "Maybe she'll want to come along."

Lucius nodded. "Good idea, I bet we'll need a healer," he walked from the room, followed by Raven and Mason.

Foster bent down and hugged Ada. "Thank you for everything, Ada."

"You're most welcome. Now go and get your wife." He chuckled and walked from the room.

Krell leaned way down and hugged her. "Thanks for the job, little girl."

"Little girl, my butt. I'm older than you."

He laughed. "But you're so small." He clapped Dryn on the shoulder and left him alone with Tris and Ada.

Dryn sat on the bed and hugged his wife. "I will miss you."

She sighed, "And I you, husband."

He gave her a passionate kiss, then laid a sweet one on her belly. "You stay in until I get home, okay?" Her belly jumped in response.

"Yeah, that'll happen," Tris teased.

"I love you, Ada."

"I love you Dryn. Stay safe."

"I will." He stood and turned to Trisa. "You take care of her, you hear me?" He pointed at her.

"The best I can, I promise." He gave her a quick hug, and with one last blown kiss, he joined the others waiting in the front of the house.

"All right, let's see this Lessa, before I lose my nerve and face my wife's wrath for not going." Lucius chuckled, and the group followed him out of the house.

———

Ten minutes later, they walked into the temple and saw Lessa at the altar. "If you pray to Otto, now's the time for a blessing," Lucius said as he walked towards the red-haired priestess.

When she turned, her eyes went wide. "Oh, Lucius!" She jumped up into his arms, and he swung her around.

"Hello, you gorgeous priestess."

He set her back on her feet, and she looked over at Foster. "Have you seen Adalaide yet?"

Foster nodded. "Yes, we know where Sunette is. We're going to get her."

Lessa seemed to relax a bit. "Good, I want to go too."

"Wonderful!" Lucius said.

"Just let me pack really quick!" And she ran off towards the back. They only waited about five minutes before she came running back, "I'm ready!"

"Did they say you could go?" Foster asked.

She began walking towards the door, and everyone followed. "Best thing about clergy, Foster, they always forgive."

Mason laughed, "All right."

"We're going to Old Cyranar, so prepare yourself," Lucius said.

She gasped. "Oh my, how did she get there?"

"Same way we are, I suspect." Lucius pointed at Krell, who bowed.

"One more?" The mage asked as they stopped in front of him.

"That won't hinder you, will it?" Foster asked.

He smiled and waved him off. "Not at all. Shall we go?"

Mason pulled out a map and pointed. "Ada said she was in an underground house structure here." And pointed to a mountaintop on the Northwest side of Cyranar.

"Not a problem, everyone hold hands." Odd magical words spilled from his mouth, and everyone felt a magical pull in one direction. Foster's feet felt like they weren't standing on solid ground anymore. Suddenly, it felt like they ran headfirst into a wall, and Foster felt he was being flung like a rag doll in all directions before he landed hard on the ground. He opened his eyes but saw nothing except flashes of light before there was nothing.

———

"Foster? Foster, wake up!" He heard a voice and felt a hand on his face. He groaned as he realized how badly he was hurt. His head was pounding, and his left leg felt stiff and swollen. He opened his eyes and saw Lessa leaning over him. "Oh, thank Otto. How do you feel?"

"I never want to teleport again," he moaned.

Lessa sighed. He could tell she looked troubled. "I don't think it was meant to happen that way."

He sat up and gasped. "Ahh, my leg!" He grabbed it and saw his knee was dislocated. Lessa laid a hand on it and prayed. Soon, it felt pain-free and better than ever. "Thank you, Lessa." He looked around and saw Lucius and Raven sitting up, tending to Mason and Dryn, who were still unconscious. "Where's the mage?" Lessa swallowed and pointed behind him. He turned slowly and gasped. It looked as if he had been smashed into the tree. There was nothing left but red bits. "Good Gods, what happened?" He stood and examined the large red stain.

Lessa shook her head. "I don't know." Foster walked over to Dryn, Lucius was trying to stem the blood from a bad cut on the man's head, and his arm was badly broken.

"Lessa, help Dryn. Maybe he can tell us what happened."

"I'll tell you what happened," Raven said, her cheek bleeding from a bad cut. "Whoever has Sunette made it so no one could teleport in. We were thrown off course." Lessa knelt by Dryn and popped the bones back in place before healing them.

A few moments later, he moaned. "What the hell was that?"

Foster helped him sit up. "Seems Krell ran into an issue we hadn't thought about."

"What issue?" He turned and saw the tree but didn't

understand what I was. "Where is he?"

Lessa laid a hand on his arm. "I'm so sorry, Dryn."

His eyes darted around them for a moment. "Why?"

She slowly pointed back to the tree. "That…seems to be Krell," she said slowly. His eyes widened, and he stood up and ran to the tree, staring dumbfounded at the red stain.

"I don't understand." His voice was quiet, "He's never missed a mark."

"Lessa," Raven called her over to Mason, and she crawled to her brother. His left foot was twisted funny as was his right knee. His elbow appeared to be dislocated as well. Dryn stood staring at the tree while Lessa slowly worked on her brother.

Foster walked behind the tall man and laid a hand on his back. "I'm sorry about your friend."

"He was one of the most powerful mages I ever knew. I don't understand."

Foster heard Mason scream. "Ahh, bloody hell!"

"Give me your arm, Mason." Lessa chastised her brother. Raven held him down, and Lessa finished healing him.

"Better?" Raven laid a hand on his cheek, and he nodded.

"What happened?" He sat up and put an arm around Raven, and she helped him up.

Foster turned to everyone. "I think Raven is right. We were thrown off course."

Mason looked around. "This doesn't look like Cyranar."

"No, it doesn't." Dryn sounded ominous as he looked around.

Foster felt panic rise up in him. "Please don't tell me we're lost." They had time, but not an infinite amount, and the thought of being lost made his heart jump into his throat. Raven helped Mason put his pack on, and he gave her cheek a little kiss. She reached up to the nearest tree and held a branch close. "Hmm, well, it could have been worse. It's a Shiphax tree. They're only around Salthole."

"Salthole!" Foster rubbed his face vigorously in frustration. Lessa laid a hand on his back, but it wasn't as comforting as it once was. Salthole was at least three weeks south of where they needed to be.

"Let's hurry into town," Lucius said. "Maybe we can find another way to Cyranar. Going around those mountains would take too long." Everyone agreed and began walking towards the small port town.

———

Half a day later, they reached the tree line and could see Salthole in the distance. As they walked, Foster noticed Dryn was sniffing, and his eyes were red.

"Dryn?" He looked up at Foster for a moment before turning his gaze back to the road.

"I can hear Ada crying. I can feel her pain over Krell's loss."

His heart fell a little. "That must be hard, knowing she's in pain and not being able to comfort her."

Dryn nodded. "Not the way I want to comfort her anyway," he said quietly.

———

It was night when they finally reached Salthole. Lucius suggested they search for a boat to take them north. Hopefully, from there, they could find somewhere to get horses and ride to the fallen city. Foster knew it might still take too long, but they had no other choice at the moment. Since teleporting didn't seem to be an option, they had to do the only other thing they could think of.

As they searched for a good boat, Lucius started laughing. "Well, by the gods, I do believe Otto is with us." The group looked at what made Lucius so happy and saw 'Slick Stella' walking toward them.

"Lucius, what on earth are you doing here?" The smile on her face would make many a man crawl to her for just a touch of her hand.

Lucius ran over and wrapped his arms around her. "Stella, my wench, I don't believe I've ever been so happy to see you." He twirled her around while her hearty laugh filled the air, and

Lucius sat her on her feet. "But all happiness aside, we really do need passage north." He began to tell her what happened to Sunette, and the group could see her happy face turn serious.

Stella nodded when he was done. "My ship and crew are at your service. We can leave in the morning. The tides can be rough going north this time of year, but we'll be fine." They helped her crew pack for a hopefully short trip, and in the morning, they set sail. Every night, Foster stared at the ever-growing moon, his anxiety growing worse by the day.

One night, Dryn joined him at the rail. "Got a message from Ada."

He quickly turned. "What news?" Foster's heart skipped a beat when he saw Dryn's careful face.

"Ada thinks there may be cause for concern." He didn't look at him as he said it.

He sighed and rubbed his face. "Gods, why?"

"She's looked up Sunette every day the last week. Yesterday, she seemed to feel ill, and today, she couldn't keep any food down."

Foster laid his head in his hands. "Gods, they're poisoning her, so she's weak and can't fight back."

Dryn was quiet for a moment. "It's possible. Ada said every time they came in, she would try to fight them. The room has an anti-magic field in it, so Sunette can't use her magic. But she throws heavy books and anything else not nailed down at them." A smile he didn't feel like showing appeared on Foster's face. He knew his hellcat of a mage wouldn't go down without a fight. "They could be trying to keep her docile."

"We have even less time than before." He looked over at Dryn and saw a worried look on his face. "How fares Ada?"

Dryn looked up from his daydream. "Hm? Oh, she's fine, she tells me. Still sad over Krell, but no news of the babe."

"I'm truly sorry you aren't with her now."

"Me too." He pushed off the rail and walked below deck. Foster turned away from the moon's gaze and saw Raven and Mason across the ship. His arm was around her, and he noticed she gave him a brief kiss. Almost like they hoped if someone was watching, they'd miss it. So, Foster decided not to tease them and to keep their little secret.

———

Almost two weeks later, they pulled into a small town on the coast. It was the last town that far north, according to Stella. The group ran from the ship, quickly gathering supplies and horses for them all, which included Stella, her first mate Ty, and the ship's healer Cel. Lucius wasn't so keen on her coming, but she said he needed all the help they could get, and nothing was stopping her from joining. Her words made Lucius press her to him and give her the most romantic, fiery kiss they'd ever seen him give her.

"That's my pirate wench," he said, squeezing her backside.

They ran the horses ragged, but they were still three days away from Cyranar as the full moon rose.

Foster yelled at the heavens. "No! Don't take her from me, please!" When the horses could go no further, Foster leapt off his horse and prayed on his knees, screaming to the heavens. "Please, Otto, this can't be how my love dies. This can't be how it all ends. Please help us!"

"Foster, Foster!" Dryn ran over and tried to shake some sense into him.

He sat back and motioned to the bright moon. "The full moon rises. It was our clock. We're too late." Tears ran down his face. Lessa hugged her brother and wept while Raven sank to her knees, her head lowered.

Lucius sank his sword into the ground angrily. "We won't let these bastards get away with this!" Foster felt his heart break. He was numb and didn't know what to do.

"Would you all just listen to me!" Everyone stopped and looked at Dryn. "I got a message from Ada. Sunette is still alive."

Slowly, Foster realized Dryn had a huge smile on his face. "She's alive?" He wiped his face and got to his feet.

"Yes," He put his hands on Foster's shoulders, "Ada said it will stay that way for some time."

"Oh, thank you, Blessed Otto," Lessa said as she wiped her cheeks. Mason let go of his sister and sighed heavily as Raven stood and wrapped her arms around him.

"Not that I'm not fucking ecstatic about that," Foster said, "But why the change?" Dryn's smile was as bright as the full moon above their heads.

"Ada stayed asleep for two days listening. You know Sunette's family were guardians for an artifact. To kill every living member of that line meant the secret of where and how to use it would be revealed to whoever sacrificed them. Being the assholes they are, they had trouble trying to decide if an unborn child would have to go through the ritual or just the mother, so they've decided to wait until the child is born." Foster stared at him, trying to make sense of the words he had just heard.

Lessa gasped. "You don't mean—"

"They believe that Sunette is with child," Dryn said, laughing, patting Foster on the arm.

Foster blinked like Dryn had spoken a language unknown to him. "What?" He heard Lucius laughing before the half-elf wrapped his arms around him, giving him a bear hug.

"Oh my gods," Raven breathed out. "They weren't poisoning her, she has morning sickness." She turned to Lessa, and the three of them hugged. Dryn chuckled at the sight of Lucius trying to shake some sense into Foster, but he was just too big compared to the half-elf.

"Ada heard the men say she's with child." Dryn laid a hand on Foster's shoulder. "If that's true, your unborn child has saved her, given us more time."

Foster fell back to the ground and stared at the moon. "Thank you, Otto, for this little miracle."

They schemed and talked strategy the last three days, taking a much easier pace than before. When Cyranar was in sight, they loosely tied up the mounts and began on foot. Ada gave Dryn a safe path through the city, which Foster was grateful for. The last thing they needed was to be waylaid by cultists or some creature that could turn you to stone. When they reached the tunnel that Ada pointed them to, Mason went ahead, looking for traps and bad guys who got separated from the pack. Lessa and Cel blessed them for a successful raid, and they headed inside.

As they crept in, they passed a dead man with his throat slit, some of Mason's handy work no doubt. They turned the corner and saw a long, dark stairwell. Lessa took a coin out, and it lit up like the sun, lighting their way.

They walked down a stone hallway until they reached a fork in the road. "Which way?" Foster asked.

Mason came running silently back from the left. "No one's that way," he said and ran down the right.

"All right then," Lucius said and followed.

"Do we find Sunette first to disable everyone here?" Lessa whispered.

"Probably disable first. They want her alive, they won't hurt her," Foster said. They rounded another corner and saw Mason messing with a lock on the big wooden door.

"Sounds like three on the other side," he whispered. Lessa touched the door and cast a silent spell just in case the door was as creaky as it looked. Everyone unsheathed their weapons and watched as Mason opened the door just enough so he could sneak inside. "Count to ten," the little thief said, "then bust in." Foster nodded, pulling his sword free.

Everyone quietly snuck inside ten seconds after Mason, who disappeared. Foster, however, was not so quiet. He kicked the door open the rest of the way and saw three men, just like Mason said. One was old, sitting by the fire across the room, and the others were standing as guards, their hands on their sword hilts.

"Where's my wife!" Foster yelled, his voice booming around the room like a vengeful god. His friends, except Mason, appeared around him, ready for anything.

"Well, that's quite a little army you've brought." The old man sneered at Foster. His accent was thicker than Sunette's.

"Tell me where she is!" Foster was breathing hard. He had never been so angry in his life. He didn't care if they just gave up and led Sunette out to them. He was going to make sure every last one of these men died before the day was out.

"No." The old man waved a hand, and his guards stepped up and engaged Foster. They were quick, but nothing could keep him away now. "My entire line is almost gone, having chased that family. And now that we have the last of them. We will have what we deserve!" Their swords clanged against each other, one went high, the other low. Foster couldn't get both, so he rolled backwards, and Ty and Lucius engaged the guards in his place. Foster rolled up onto his knees and saw the old man still sitting and watching the fight. "I'll have her life as well as the child in her belly, and all the knowledge of the chalice will be mine."

"You won't touch them!" Foster ran at the man who stayed seated, looking calm. He raised his sword and brought it down quickly on the man's head. But inches from his goal, the sword bounced off something invisible, and the man laughed.

"You really think I'd let you get that close without some protection." Foster reached out and felt an invisible wall between them. It went from one wall of the room to the other, isolating the old man. His laughter grew and grew as Foster realized there was no way to get to him. Foster hit it angrily and turned to see the other guards dead on the ground.

Lucius ran up and hit the barrier. "You fucking coward! Some mage you are, hiding behind your—" his words were cut off as a bolt of lightning came from nowhere and hit the half-elf. He yelled out in pain and fell to the ground before Stella could reach him.

"Lucius!" She picked his head up and laid it in her lap.

"You were saying spawn?" The old man got to his feet, "I have looked for that little girl for over twenty years. I'm not about to let her slip through my fingers again."

"Wanna bet?" Foster said as he hit the barrier again. "You fucked with the wrong family, you son-of-a-bitch."

"The only thing her family is good for is finding that

chalice."

Foster stepped closer to the barrier. "My name is Foster Voltain, I am the son of Mother Lily Voltain, and when I get my hands on you, old man, you're going to wish you stayed in the north. Because Sunette *is* my family." Foster swore when he said his mother's name. The color drained out of the old man's face.

"Voltain? She carries a Voltain child?" Foster swore he looked scared for a moment before his body went rigid, and he gasped. Mason popped up from behind him, and Foster saw the tip of a dagger protruding from the old man's chest. Foster reached out and didn't feel the barrier. Seems he was in too much pain to concentrate on it. Mason pulled his dagger out as Foster stepped up onto the dais and lowered his face to the old man.

"*My* wife and *my* child will sleep soundly, knowing you and your entire line are dead." He raised his sword and separated the man from his head in one smooth motion. The body crumpled to the floor with a loud smack. "Thank you, Mason."

"No problem." The little man said as he kicked the man's head across the room. Lessa ran over to Lucius and gave him a little of her healing magic, and he was able to get to his feet.

"Gods, that was unpleasant," he said, still leaning on Stella.

"A'pa!" They all looked up to see a large man walk through the far door. He was wearing red armor, and the sword on his back was large. His eyes stared at the headless body of the old man. "You will pay for what you've done to my father!" He pulled the sword from his back and charged the group. Stella got Lucius out of the way, and Lessa jumped to the side.

The healer, Cel, yelled and met the new man head-on. The war priest fought ferociously against the red man, and soon, Foster and Ty joined him. The three young men clanged swords and used the man's impossible armor to their advantage, hoping to tire him out. Suddenly, he kicked at Ty, and the pirate went sprawling into a bookcase. It creaked, and he couldn't get out of the way before it all came tumbling down on top of him.

The man feinted high, and Cel went to block but got a

sword in his gut. "Behest, help us," he croaked out before he went limp.

The man in red laughed, "Just you and me, *boy*," he said and started swinging his sword faster and deadlier than before. All Foster could do was block, hit after hit. He felt his fingers going numb from the near-constant vibrations from the attack. *Otto, help me,* Foster thought as the man pressed him harder and harder. He felt his arms cramping up from the effort. He'd never fought like this before and always hoped not to. He got a lucky blow to the man's leg, and he stumbled. "It's' no use, boy, I'm stronger, and you know it."

"Strength doesn't matter, you bastard. I have something to fight for!" He heard Raven start singing, and the cramps in his arms went away. He felt like he hadn't been fighting for his life for the last five minutes. He swung hard and fast, the man stumbled again, and Foster kicked him backwards. The man fell to the ground, his sword skittered a good five feet away, and Foster could hear him breathing hard.

He walked up and prepared for the final blow, but the man put up his hands. "No, please, mercy," he said. Foster looked at him and threw off the man's helmet. He was in his mid-thirties, with dark hair and black eyes. "Mercy," he repeated.

"I have no mercy to give a person like you," and ran his sword through the man's throat. The room was filled with the sounds of his wet choking until Foster twisted the sword, and with a crack, he went silent. He felt a hand on him and jumped around.

It was Lessa, and he quickly calmed down. "Are you okay?"

He thought for a moment. "Almost." He saw Ty digging himself out of the books and Stella pouring a potion into Cel's throat.

He sputtered a moment before finishing the potion. "Thank you, Capt."

"Hey, I owe you several hundred from all the times you've helped me." Everyone got to their feet and headed through the only other door.

"Ada said her door was trapped, so be careful," Dryn said. They ran down some more stairs and saw two more men down the hallway who looked like they were guarding a door.

"Bet that's it!" Mason said rather loudly in a cheerful voice.

The guards jumped and looked over at the group. "Stop right there!" One yelled while both ran at them. Dryn stepped up and ducked under one blade while stabbing the other. He spun and sunk his sword deep into the other man's side. It happened so fast the others could barely believe their eyes.

"Blessed Otto Dryn, how did you do that?" Lessa exclaimed while Mason ran to the door.

"What? You mean you can't?" He smiled and winked at her as he walked behind Mason. Clearly, Ada was well protected.

"It's got a magical and mundane trap," Mason said as he took his tools out. "Everybody step back. I don't want you getting hurt 'cause if I mess this up, it's gonna be bad." They all took a step off to the side and watched Mason work. After a few minutes, the door shimmered, "Okay, one down." He took out a set of more complicated tools and worked on a plate on the floor in front of the door. They heard a loud click, and Mason stood up, facing the door. "Okay, all —" his words were cut off as a huge spike shot from the wall behind him. It was so fast he couldn't get out of the way, and it pinned him to the door through his spine.

"Mason!" Lessa and Raven screamed and ran to him. Lucius pulled the spike out, and the young rogue limply fell into his sister's arms. They laid him on the floor as blood welled up on the front of his shirt and spilled from his mouth.

His eyes were wide, and his breathing was ragged as he looked up at Foster. "But I..." he choked and went limp in Lessa's arms. She was trying to heal him the best she could, but Foster could tell something wasn't working right as she got increasingly frustrated. Raven started singing to supplement the cleric's spells, but her voice was shaking with every word. No one had ever heard her like that before. Cel started praying, too, but it didn't take long before he looked just as frustrated.

"Damn it, this should work!" he growled.

Foster felt a hand on his shoulder and jumped a little. "Go to her," he heard Lucius say. He stood and turned. Mason's blood was dripping slowly down the door.

"Gods, Otto, be with him," he whispered and opened the door.

———

Foster walked into the room. Before him lay fancy furnishings, rugs, and bookshelves. It was warm, and he could hear a fire crackling somewhere to his right. He looked around and saw Sunette huddled in the middle of a large bed. "Sunette!" He ran over and crawled on the bed to her. "Sunette, wake up!" He laid his hand on her head and gently ran his fingers through her hair. She opened her eyes and turned to him. There were bags under her eyes, and she held her hands over her stomach.

"Just stop, please. I can't take it anymore." She sounded so weary, as if she would break apart with the next word.

"Sunette, it's me, Foster." He reached out and tried to touch her cheek, but she winced away.

"Just stop, it's cruel," she started crying and laid back on the bed.

"What did they do to you?" He slid next to her and wrapped his arms around her.

"No!" She sat up and wrenched his arms from around her. "Stop, get away!" She fought against him, but he twisted around her and held her against his chest. "You're not Foster. You're never him, never him!" She sobbed and kept fighting like the caged animal she was, pushing him away and trying to slap whatever she could reach.

"It's me, I promise, Sunette, it's me. We're all here to get you." He tried to sound calm, but she managed to slap him. His cheek stung something fierce, but he ignored it. "Gods, what did they do to you?"

"No, you're not!" She finally managed to wiggle her way free of his arms, "You just want to torture me like always." She slid out of the bed, wearing a wrinkly silk nightgown. "You're cruel. I hope you die." She walked over to a plate of food and knocked it over.

Foster slowly got off the bed and stood behind her. "Sunette, it's me. I can prove it."

"No, you can't," she whispered, not turning around.

His hands dared to touch her shoulders. "The night you were taken, I asked you to marry me."

She turned and kicked a roll at him that bounced off his shin. "You said that before," she hissed at him. "Try again!"

"Lucius told me later you had planned to ask me yourself," he pulled out the dagger. "You were going to give me this dagger as a gift."

He held it out, and she looked at it, her face softened. "I was," she whispered. She picked it up, and her breathing became shaky as she read the inscription. "Foster?"

She looked up, and he smiled. "It's me, I swear."

Lucius walked into the room. He was covered in Mason's blood. "Foster, Sunette?"

She turned and gasped, "Lucius?"

"Hello, Mistress Mage." His smile was jittery, like he wanted to smile but just couldn't manage a believable one.

Sunette turned back to Foster. "It is you!" She jumped into his arms and sobbed. "I never thought I'd see you again, *Mi Epier*!"

He held her tight and felt tears leak out of his eyes. "I love you, I love you. I was so scared I'd lose you."

She sobbed into his chest. "Is he dead? Please tell me they're all dead!"

He kissed the top of her head. "Yes, they're dead, love, dead and gone." Suddenly, she pulled from Foster's arms and emptied her stomach in a nearby bucket. He bent over and held her hair back as she sat gasping on the floor.

"I think they poisoned me, Foster." There was a rag nearby that she grabbed and wiped her mouth. "I can't eat anything, and I get sick all day. They probably got tired of me throwing books at them."

Foster helped her sit up and laid a hand on her belly. "They were under the impression that you were with child."

She froze and slowly met his eyes. "What?"

"That's why they kept you alive. They wanted to sacrifice both of you, just in case." He saw a thought come across her face, and she touched his hand.

"I lost track of time. How long have I been here?"

"A little over a month." She slowly smiled and began speaking softly in her native tongue as she laid her hands over his.

Foster laughed. "What?"

"I must have been pregnant when they took me, but I didn't know." She hugged him, and he kissed her cheek. "What a miracle."

He hugged her tight, knowing they'd never be parted again. "Come, love, let's go home."

They walked past Lucius, and he squeezed her shoulder. "Glad you're okay."

She smiled and kissed his hand. "Thank you for coming."

"You've all done the same for me over the years. I'd never leave you behind." When Foster opened the door, he only saw Raven and Lessa bent over Mason.

"Where did everyone go?"

"To see if they could find anything that could help," Raven said, her voice thick with tears. Lessa was still trying desperately to save Mason, but the wound kept re-opening.

"I don't know why it's doing that!" she yelled through angry tears.

Sunette stepped around Foster and gasped, "Mason!" She quickly kneeled next to Lessa and took the young man's hand. "What happened?"

"A trap," Lessa said.

"No, no, no, Mason, you can't do this. You can't die." She held his face, but his head just flopped limply between her hands. "No, please."

They heard running footsteps and Stella's voice yelling.

"We didn't find any potions or scrolls, but we found this." She and her crew, as well as Dryn, skidded to a halt. The captain handed Lessa a wand.

Sunette gasped, "Stella?"

She looked over when she heard her name. "Sunette, thank the gods you're okay," she said and gave her a hug while Lessa studied the wand.

Cel set a large chest down. "This should fill our pockets," he said as Lessa handed Sunette the wand.

"Can you tell what it is?" she asked, wiping the tears from her face.

She took it and nodded. "Thank Otto, a teleport wand, everyone hold hands!"

"Take us to the temple of Otto in Ardenry," Lessa said. Sunette nodded and thought of the temple as she waved the wand. The next moment, they opened their eyes and saw they had arrived just outside the temple.

Cel picked Mason up, and they all ran inside. "I need help!" Lessa screamed, her voice echoing around the temple. A paladin ran over and took Mason from Cel, and started running down the aisle. "Follow me!" Lessa and Raven ran through to the back of the church with a contingent of priests and disappeared. The others collapsed to the floor, afraid for their friend, who they could no longer see.

"By the gods, we did it," Lucius said, breathing hard. He got up and kissed Stella. "Thank you for your help. We'll forever be in your debt."

Stella chuckled, "I'd rather have you forever in my bed."

Lucius smiled. "You got it, Captain." And he kissed her more passionately than one should in a temple.

Cel sighed as he and Ty picked up the chest. "Let's go find a room, Capt. I don't want to be lugging this around much longer."

Lucius nodded. "We'll go get a nice big suite. Someone should stay here for the rest of them." He pointed to where they all ran.

Dryn got to his feet. "I'm really sorry about your friend, but I got to get back to Ada. Foster, Sunette, when you're settled and rested, you should come by. I know Ada would love to meet Sunette."

Her eyes widened. "Ada?" She looked up at Foster, "Your Ada?"

He nodded. "Well, his Ada. We'll come by soon." And the fighter ran from the temple, eager to get home.

Foster turned to his newly freed love. "Do you want to rest or stay here?"

"I've been resting, I want to stay."

Stella took off the coat she was wearing and put it around Sunette's shoulders. "Didn't think you'd want to wander around in only a nightgown."

She pulled her arms through the sleeves. "Thank you. Honestly, I had forgotten."

Foster gave Stella a nod in thanks. "We'll let you know if something happens." Lucius patted his shoulder as Ty and Cel carried the large chest from the temple. The reunited couple put their arms around each other and sat in some of the cushioned pews.

"I hope Mason will be okay," Sunette whispered and laid her head on his shoulder. "That was a really bad wound."

"He's a tough guy. He'll pull through, I know it." Foster reached down and laid a hand over her belly.

"You are okay with this? A child?" Her hand laid over his as she gently rubbed his skin with her thumb.

He looked down and kissed her brow. "Of course I am. I do wish when I heard the news, I had time to appreciate it and wonder about them. But we can do that now, together."

"How did you hear?"

"Ada. Seems she has a way of looking in on people that some haven't thought of. She heard them talking about how they thought you were pregnant. She told Dryn, and he told me."

"And you told me, "She shook her head. "I can't believe I didn't think of that."

"You were in a stressful situation. It probably would have been the last thing on your mind."

She laid her head on his chest. "I knew you'd try to find me, but I had no idea if you could. I've never been so scared in my life." She lifted his hand and kissed his palm. "So, what do you want?" She looked up at him, a small smile on her face. "A boy or a girl?"

"Hmm, I don't know, either would be nice. A darling little girl I could spoil, or a happy little boy. I just know that whoever they are, they will be loved like no child has been loved before."

A tear ran down her cheek. "Indeed." Sunette sniffed and turned her head into Foster's shoulder, and he listened as she fell asleep in his arms. *Thank you for this miracle, Otto,* he prayed silently. *Please be with Mason, I beg you.*

———

An hour later, he watched an acolyte walk up to them. "Sir? Are you one of the ones that came back with Mother Alessa?"

"Yes, we are, what news?"

"She's asking for you if you would follow me?"

He nodded and kissed Sunette's forehead. "Sunette? Lessa's calling for us."

She breathed in deeply and opened her eyes. "Okay." They followed the acolyte down deep below the temple. It was cold, and when she finally opened a door at the end of a long hallway, they could hear crying. Tears instantly blinded him. But he managed to find Lessa and Raven in a room, sitting next to a raised platform. Mason's body lying motionless on it.

Raven was sitting across from Lessa, her head in her hands, her shoulders shaking as heart-wrenching sobs spilled from her mouth. Lessa had her cheek on the platform, holding her brother's hand as she cried. Sunette quickly wrapped her arms around Lessa, who turned and hugged the mage. Foster stood by Mason's head, his lips were blue, and a cloth laid over the horrid wound in his chest. He felt ill at the sight. He'd never seen Mason so still and quiet. It was heartbreaking.

"I'm so sorry." He could barely speak through the tears,

letting them fall with abandon. "I'm so sorry." He laid his hand on Mason's forehead. He was cold, and Foster laid his head on his hand. "Be...at peace...little brother." He could barely say the words as grief washed over him. He turned and hugged Raven, her arms wrapped around him and squeezed him tight as she could as they sobbed into each other's arms.

———

The next day, the group gathered around a pyre in the garden outside of Otto's temple. Mason's body was wrapped with white cloth and surrounded by kindling. Raven stood as close to the pyre as she dared, her arms hugging herself so tight her fingers were white. Lessa stayed back with the others. One of the paladins, a tall, bearded man, had his hand on her shoulder. It looked like that was the only thing keeping her on her feet. Stella had her arm around Lucius. Both their eyes were red, and Sunette had her arms around Foster, both crying.

One of the High Priests walked up to Lessa and laid a hand on her unoccupied shoulder. She gave him a nod, and he faced the group.

"Losing a friend is never easy, especially when they're so young. Mason Fray lived life to the fullest. He loved his friends and enjoyed dancing, drinks with friends, and song. They filled his heart with happiness. He is with Otto now, knowing only comfort and love, and while that isn't much comfort for you now, in time, the grief will be replaced by all the loving memories you have of him. Does anyone wish to say anything?"

Lucius cleared his throat. "I think I'd like to say a few words," his voice was thick with tears. Stella kissed his cheek and let him walk next to the pyre. "Mason was a great guy. He lived a full life for someone so young. Admittedly, when Lessa approached me about joining my group, I only wanted her. I could tell her brother was more trouble than he was worth. But I took them both anyway, and I've never regretted it. He was always happy. He loved each of us with his entire heart, and we him. I told him quite often that his smart mouth was going to get him in trouble, but it never did. He was one of the luckiest men

I've ever known, and I feel blessed that someone like him will be watching over us."

Lucius turned and gave Lessa a big hug. "Thank you, Lucius."

Tears streamed down his face. "Think nothing of it." He kissed her head, and he walked back to Stella.

Foster cleared his throat and wiped his eyes. "Mason was unlike any brother I ever had. He was excitable, a constant flirt, and sneaky as hell. The day I met him and his sister, she threw mashed potatoes at his head." Everyone managed to chuckle at the memory. "I watched his skills grow, though *he* seemed to stop growing when he was twelve," Lessa chuckled, and the paladin rubbed her shoulder. "So, I hope Otto will take care of him. Your memory will live on, I promise. I love you, Mason." Lessa walked over and hugged him. He could feel her shaking in his arms.

As the High Priest set the kindling alight, everyone moved back except Raven. Lessa stood back by the paladin, his hand going back to her shoulder. As the fire began licking the wrap on his body, Raven started singing 'Fading Echoes.' Everyone instantly knew it, and the tears flowed faster. Normally, when she sang it, she conjured a shade that she would dance with, but this time, she conjured two shades above the pyre who danced. They looked like her and Mason, dancing and kissing.

> "In the depths of darkness, where my love resides, now resides pain, my heart bound with loss. A love song once played now echoes in my mind, but the melody has faded, leaving emptiness behind. Oh, Love, my once guiding star, now you left me alone, so broken and far. In the shadows of silence, my heart shall weep for the love that was lost, and the memories I'll keep."

Raven's shade disappeared, and one resembling Sunette joined him, and they continued the dance. Sunette gasped at the display.

"The lyrics we wrote, filled with hope and light, now shrouded in sadness, dimming out of sight. The promises we whispered, like fragile dreams, now shattered like glass, tearing at my seams. Oh, Love, my once guiding star, now you left me alone, so broken and far. In the shadows of silence, my heart shall weep for the love that was lost and the memories I'll keep."

Sunette's shade moved away, and it was replaced with a shade that looked like Lessa. Brother and sister dancing and laughing. Lessa's sobs pierced the air again as she turned into the paladin's arms. Foster didn't know how Raven kept a strong voice when everyone there was sobbing.

"I search for solace in melodies of the past, yet they only remind me of love that didn't last. The harmonies I once cherished now stab like a knife as the lyrics of our story dissolve into strife. But still, I hold onto these fading echoes, hoping they'll bring you back, where love flows. Yet deep down, I know it's just a bittersweet refrain, a melody of longing, a symphony of pain."

The Lessa shade walked away, and Mason's shade walked over to four new shades. Foster gasped, his tears fell faster as he saw the shades were of himself, Lucius, Bereck, and Twig, shaking hands and hugging Mason. There wasn't a dry eye around the pyre as the song weaved around the sound of their sobs.

"Oh, Love, my once guiding star, now you left me alone, so broken and far. In the shadows of silence, my heart shall weep for the love that was lost, and the memories I'll keep. Fading echoes linger in my soul's abyss, a reminder of a love I'll eternally miss. Maybe someday the music will find its way, through the tears and sorrow, to a brighter day."

Raven sang while the fire consumed their friend, their brother, and when it was all over, she fell to her knees and cried.

———

That night, they were sitting in Lessa's room in the temple, not one smile among them.

Lessa sniffed and turned to Raven. "You know, he told me that he loved you." Raven let out a little sobbing laugh at her words. "Of course, he was drunk when he said it." Lessa chuckled and shook her head, "But that was when he was usually, he most trustworthy. He could not tell a lie when he had alcohol in his system."

Raven sniffed and wiped her eyes. "He never left my side after Twig died. He was a constant comfort to me, and I'll never forget that." She chuckled a little, "Sleeping next to Twig got me used to the snoring, but the talking! Mason never shut up at night. It was like we were having a slumber party, like a couple of little girls instead of heroes." Lucius finally laughed, Stella was covering her mouth, trying to hide her smile. "I loved it." A few tears rolled down her face. "I'll miss it."

"This is how Mason would want us to remember him," Foster said, his hand on Sunette's back. "Laughing and enjoying life."

"It's just not fair, though. He was my little brother," Lessa said quietly, her head hanging.

Sunette leaned over and laid a hand on hers. "He was everybody's little brother."

CHAPTER 17
THE START OF A BLESSED LIFE

A few days later, Foster and Sunette felt they could hold themselves together to visit Ada and Dryn. They knocked on the door, and like before, Dryn answered, but this time with a big smile instead of a sword.

"Foster, Sunette, welcome, come in!" He ushered them inside and shut the door.

Foster shook his hand when he offered it. "Thank you." The smell of incense greeted them like before, and Dryn talked as he led them through the house.

"Ada's in bed, but I know she'll be happy to see you."

"We don't want to be a bother," Sunette said, looking between the men.

"Oh, trust me, you're no bother." Foster thought he was awfully happy for some reason, and then he remembered he didn't know about Mason. Not that he was as attached to him as the rest of them were. But it was still sad, and the group was still in deep mourning. Foster hoped he'd be able to keep it together while visiting.

They followed Dryn into a room on the first floor, and Foster gasped, "Ada!"

She was sitting in bed, holding a little pink baby in her arms. "Foster, I'm so glad you're here."

Sunette sighed at the sight, "Oh my, what a beautiful baby." She sat on the bed across from Ada. Foster stood behind her, his hands on her shoulders.

Ada smiled at the little bundle in her arms. "She is, isn't she?"

Foster chuckled and looked up at Dryn. "Some boy, huh?"

He laughed and sat next to his wife. "I don't mind being wrong about this one."

Ada looked back up at Sunette. "It's so nice to finally meet Foster's love," she said with a smile.

Sunette managed a brave one. "It's nice to meet you too, Ada, I'm glad to see you've found such happiness."

Ada looked up at her husband and smiled brightly. "Me too." Dryn bent over and gently kissed her lips.

"What did you name her?" Foster asked.

"We named her River," Dryn said, his fingers gently touching the baby's wispy, white hair. "After my sister."

"That's a beautiful name."

Ada sighed and turned back to Sunette. "How are you feeling? I trust much better than you were."

She took a deep breath. "Honestly, I'm really sad."

Ada's eyes furled. "Sad? Why?"

Foster gave Sunette's shoulder a squeeze. "Our friend Mason didn't make it," she said quietly.

Dryn looked up, his face a mask of shock. "What? He didn't?" Foster and Sunette shook their heads. Dryn sighed and laid a hand on Ada's knee. "I'm sorry, he was a good man."

"He was." Foster nodded, holding back tears.

"Well, other than the current sad situation, how are you?" Ada asked.

Sunette gave her a little smile. "I feel so blessed I can't even begin to say."

Ada reached out for her hand, and Sunette took it. "You are blessed, Sunette. You and Foster are going to have a blessed life together. Starting with your amazing children."

Foster laid a hand on her stomach. "Whoever's in here is certainly amazing to be able to save their mother before they're even born," he said with a smile.

Ada chuckled and jiggled her baby gently. "You and yours are welcome here anytime."

"And you are always welcome in our home," Sunette said.

————

When the couple got back to the inn, they saw Lucius sitting at a table with Stella, their heads together, talking softly. They walked up to the table, and the half-elf sat back. "There you are, I've got some good news for you."

"Oh?" They sat forward and held their hands on the table.

"We counted the money in the chest. There's a hefty bag of seven hundred and twenty gold for each of you, along with four precious stones."

Sunette gasped. "Really?"

"That should be enough for your first year," Lucius said with a wink.

"First year? Try ten!" Sunette chuckled.

Stella cleared her throat and sat back a little. "So what's the plan? We got Te'a a message, and she's bringing the ship to Ardenry," she said with a proud smile. While it wasn't on the coast, there were rivers big enough that trade ships could make it to the capital.

Foster turned and gave Sunette's cheek a kiss. "Well, I think first we'd like to marry."

Stella nodded. "Where would you like to get married? Here? Fairwinds, Salthole? My ship is at your disposal. I will take you wherever you desire."

"Oh, Stella, that's so kind of you." Tears sparkled in Sunette's eyes as she smiled.

She shrugged her shoulders. "Think nothing of it. Let me know, and we'll get underway as soon as you say."

Lucius turned to her and smiled. "Very kind of you, Capt." He gave her a gentle, sweet kiss and sighed.

"I should do more kind things if I get kisses like that," she chuckled.

"You know, I just realized something," Foster said. "This is the longest I've ever seen you two together. You usually hole up in the cabin the entire trip."

They both laughed. "We tried to make the most of what time we had," Stella said.

"But not anymore," Lucius held her hand and kissed her

cheek. "We can slow down and really enjoy each other, my saucy wench." He kissed her again, and Foster could swear he saw love in Lucius' eyes.

"I'd like to wait until Lessa feels up to going," Sunette looked over at Foster. "I want her to be there."

Foster kissed the soft, dark hair on her head. "I know, I want her to be there too."

———

As the couple started for the stairs, they saw Raven sitting at the bar, an untouched drink in front of her. Her head was down and her shoulders so low there was no mistaking that countenance. Foster took a seat next to her, Sunette the other, so they flanked her.

She put a hand on Raven's back. "Did you sleep last night?"

Raven shrugged. "A little, I think." Her voice was quiet and tired, her face still splotchy and red from crying. It was a miracle she was downstairs and not locked in her room.

"Have you eaten anything today?" He asked. It was almost two in the afternoon. She shook her head. Foster motioned to the bartender for some food, and he nodded and disappeared into the kitchen.

"I feel...untethered," she finally said.

Sunette clicked her tongue. "I am not surprised. You two were attached at the hip for years." The bartender set a plate of cheese and cold meat on the bar, and Foster pushed it towards her, but she ignored it.

Foster laid a hand on her shoulder. "When we were traveling to get to Sunette, I saw the secret kisses you two would try to hide. You were more than just friends, weren't you?"

Her breath shuddered as she breathed in and looked back at the bar. "We didn't want to take any attention off what we had to do." She lifted her hand and picked up a piece of cheese but just tapped it on the plate.

"I'm sorry you felt you had to hide," Sunette said. "But I know you made those last months of his the happiest of his life."

She didn't say anything but finally took a bite of the cheese in her hand. Foster looked over at Sunette, a silent request in his eyes. Ever the soul mate, she understood and nodded.

"Raven, come home with us."

She looked up, her eyes wide. "What?"

"Come home to Raventree with us." Sunette rubbed her back.

"You're like a sister to me," Foster said, giving her a hug. "You deserve some rest, and we would love it if you came home with us."

"This one could use another Auntie." Sunette put a hand on her stomach.

"Are you sure?" She looked between them.

"Hells yeah, I'm sure. Plus, they will love your voice. You'll make a killing singing at the taverns," he gave her a wink.

She stared at them for a moment. "I'd love to." She hugged Sunette, "Thank you."

"Think nothing of it. You're family. We belong together."

"Yeah, we do." Foster laid a hand on her head and prayed to Otto that she would find some comfort soon.

When Lessa finally felt up to traveling away from Ardenry, Sunette was showing, obviously, with child at this point. 'The Blue Wind' pulled into the port in Fairwinds in mid-February after a slow journey. The first morning in town, Foster and Sunette made their way to Otto's temple. It was warm and welcoming inside, and they quickly shed their furs.

"Foster!" They turned and saw Father Leif walking over, his arms extended in friendship.

"Father Leif, hello!"

"My goodness, you've grown!" They hugged, and the priest looked over at Sunette. "And who might this beauty on your arm be?"

"Leif, may I present Sunette Chelri, my betrothed."

He smiled brightly. "Oh, how wonderful." He hugged Sunette and looked at her belly, "Well, my, it seems you're growing your family rather quickly."

They laughed. "Actually, it was just in time." They sat down and told Leif the entire story.

He sat still for a moment and sighed. "Otto really has blessed your family, Foster."

He chuckled. "Yes, he has, so does that mean you consent to marry us?"

"Of course! Nothing would give me more joy than to marry the next generation of Voltains." His hands went up in celebration. "When would you like the ceremony to take place?"

"Well…" He looked at Sunette, and she bit her lip in thought.

Leif held up a hand. "If I may suggest? The spring festival is only two months away. If you can wait that long, that is?"

Foster scratched his chin. "Spring festival in Fairwinds," he turned to Sunette, "what do you think?"

She smiled and kissed his cheek. "Sounds lovely, actually."

"So, the spring?" Leif had a hopeful smile on his face, and Sunette chuckled.

"Yes! The spring festival it is."

"Wonderful! You'll have the wedding you deserve, not a haphazardly put together one," he said.

"I don't care about that. I just want to marry the man I love." Sunette kissed Foster's cheek, and he smiled brightly.

———

The next two months went by fast. Stella said her crew was still theirs so they all pitched in with building a little arch that the couple could stand under during the ceremony.

Raven took great care in helping Sunette figure out what to wear, how to do her hair, and the flowers. Sunette thought it was the distraction the bard was most grateful for. The day of the spring festival arrived, and everyone was busy making sure there were enough chairs for the ceremony and food for the huge party afterwards.

Raven figured out how to curl Sunette's hair and put half of it up, putting baby's breath around her head like a crown. She helped Sunette into her light pink dress. The sleeves were flowy, and beaded flowers decorated the bodice. The cut of it accentuated her belly, and she stood in front of the mirror, smiling.

"Thank you for all your help, Raven."

"You're welcome. Anything to make this day go off without a hitch." Raven was dressed in a lavender dress, the skirt went to her knees, and it had matching beaded flowers along the trim. She handed Sunette a pair of earrings with delicate pink gems dangling from them.

"They're darling. Where did you get them?" She held them in her hands and enjoyed the sparkle they had.

"Foster told me to give them to you today," she said with a smile.

She gasped, "He didn't. That man."

Raven laughed, "It was hard keeping them from you. I wanted to show you the moment he gave them to me."

Sunette put them on and admired them for a moment. "That reminds me, I have a gift for you." Sunette smiled and moved to the desk in the room.

"A gift? You didn't have to do that." Sunette took a white box out of one of the drawers.

"I most certainly did." She handed her the box, and Raven took it with a sigh. She opened the box and gasped. "I thought it would go good with your dress today." Raven picked up a little necklace with lavender gems around it.

"It's beautiful." She hugged Sunette. "Thank you." She put the box down and put the necklace around her neck. They looked into the mirror and smiled.

"Perfect."

There was a knock at the door, and they heard Lucius on the other side. "Everybody decent?"

"Yes, come in," Raven called out. The door opened, and Lucius walked in wearing a fancy white shirt and a new black duster with silver buttons.

He looked at them and put a hand on his heart. "Oh, such beauty, such grace. How will I ever leave this room again?" He teased and walked over to Sunette as they smiled but still rolled their eyes at him. "Are you ready, Mistress Mage?"

"I am."

He held out a hand, and she took it. "I'll see you down the aisle." Raven walked from the room with a wink.

"Thank you for the honor of walking you down the aisle, Sunette." He kissed her cheek.

"Thank you for hiring me all those years ago."

He smiled. "It was my absolute pleasure."

————

The wedding was in a park behind the temple, the trees were blooming with white flowers, and the park was filled with a rainbow of pansies. It was a small ceremony, a few family friends that Foster knew and Stella's crew, but they wouldn't have it any other way. Sunette could see Foster standing under the arch the crew of the 'Blue Wind' had built. It was covered in pink and orange flowers, and she could see little lights flickering in it. She assumed Raven did that part. Foster was smiling, his hands clasped in front of him. He was wearing a silver tunic and black leather pants, and her heart began to race.

"Ready?" Lucius asked.

She looked up at him and smiled. "Ready." With a nod, they made their way down the aisle as soft, romantic music in the air. Her eyes stayed focused on Foster, her love. The smile never faltered on his face. Lucius walked her up to him and gave her cheek a kiss then took his place behind the groom. Foster took her hands and gave them a squeeze.

"I can't believe we're here," he whispered and laid a hand on her belly. The baby kicked, and they chuckled.

Father Leif stepped up and looked at them before turning to the crowd. "Welcome, friends and family. Today, we gather to witness Foster Voltain and Sunette Chelri join their lives together in the name of Otto. Foster and Sunette have known each other for years. They started as friends, and now they commit their lives to one another, their hearts having found each other. They have written their own vows, Foster, please tell Otto of your love for Sunette." He motioned to him, and Foster licked his lips.

"Sunette, I had a hard time coming up with vows that wouldn't take hours to say." She chuckled. "I loved you when I shouldn't have, I'll admit that now. But I never believed this day was possible. That you, the most beautiful, wild, talented mage, would be my wife. This day, we are joined, heart and soul, by Otto, and I will thank him every day for you. You are the most beautiful woman I know, inside and out, and I cannot wait to meet our child. I will spend the rest of my life proving to you how much I love you. I can't wait to begin our lives together."

Sunette wiped away a tear. "Sunette, will you please tell Otto of your love for Foster."

She nodded and laid Foster's hand on her stomach, and as usual, the baby kicked.

"Foster, when I first met you, you made me so mad." Everyone chuckled. "But you quickly showed me your true self. How kind, brave, and selfless you are. I, too, loved you when I shouldn't have. I don't know why. Maybe you stared into my eyes one too many times. Maybe you told me I was beautiful while we walked in the snow, and it made my heart see you in a new light. Whatever the reason, I am grateful for your love, and I cannot wait to spend my life with you, my apple pickler." Leif picked up the large seashell, and Foster chuckled as it was already filled with the blessed water. Leif gave him a little wink.

"Foster, do you take Sunette as your wife? Do you promise to protect, provide, and love her all the rest of your days?"

"I do." He put the shell to Foster's lips, and he drank the blessed water.

"Sunette," Leif turned to her, "Do you take Foster as your husband? Do you promise to protect, provide, and love him all the rest of your days?"

"I do." She drank the blessed water, and the baby kicked so hard that her belly moved. "Gods, child." Foster chuckled and held her stomach while Leif put the seashell back on its pedestal.

"Foster and Sunette have declared their love for one another, and Otto has blessed them. It is my pleasure to introduce

Foster and Sunette Voltain. Foster, you know what to do," he said with a wink.

Foster smiled and held her face. "I love you."

"I love you." They kissed, and cheers erupted through the crowd, Raven and Lucius being the loudest.

———

A week later, the newlyweds, Raven and, of course, Lucius, boarded 'The Blue Wind' and headed towards Salthole once again. The trip took much longer than expected because of early summer storms, and Sunette's belly grew large on board. One day, Stella told them they'd be in Salthole in two days' time, and Sunette relaxed a little. The storms were wearing on her. The thunder kept her up, and the rocking was a bit too much for her to sleep. That night, she walked along the deck during the full moon. A warm wind blew through her hair. It smelled of the sea and something she hadn't smelled in a long time, roses and peppermint. She turned to see where that smell had come from but groaned as the child kicked furiously. The child had been doing that so much lately that it was hard to sleep, and she found walking around the boat helped. She stood by the rail, holding her belly and looking at the moon. When she heard footsteps, she turned and saw a figure walking towards her.

"Who's there?" she called out. A woman walked into the moonlight, and Sunette gasped, "Ma'ma?" The woman was tall with long dark hair and Sunette's blue eyes.

She was smiling. "Hello, my little darling."

Sunette took a step towards her. "Ma'ma? I don't understand?"

The woman walked up to her and laid a hand on her cheek. "I wanted to say how proud of you I am."

Tears sparkled in her eyes. "I miss you so much, Ma'ma." She stepped up and hugged the woman who hugged her back.

Roses and peppermint filled the air as she held her mother. "I miss you too, *Ma Fi*. You've been through so much. You deserve all the happiness that is coming to you."

"I'm scared, Ma'ma."

"Of what?"

Sunette looked up at her mother. "Having the baby." She was the only person she'd ever admit it to.

Her mother chuckled and tucked some of Sunette's hair behind her ear. "It is normal to be scared, *Ma Fi*, but you are strong, and the second you hold your son in your arms, you'll feel much better."

Sunette chuckled. "You think it's a boy?"

She kissed Sunette on the cheek. "I love you so much, *Ma Fi*."

"I love you too, Ma'ma." Sunette blinked and realized she was in bed next to her beloved husband. "Ma'ma," she whispered. She felt a pain low in her belly and wetness between her legs. "Foster, Foster!"

She reached over and shook his big shoulders, but all he did was turn and moan. "Yes?"

"The baby's coming, *Mi Epier*." His hand slowly found her cheek and gave her a playful pinch. Sunette noticed his eyes were still closed.

"That's great, my beauty," he said sleepily and started snoring lightly.

She scoffed and pushed his shoulder. "You know, I always thought that when a wife tells her husband their baby's coming, they shot out of bed and start running around like a turkey with its head cut off."

His eyes shot open at that. "What?"

She stared incredulously at him. "The baby is coming, Foster."

He gasped and jumped up. *That's better*, she thought. "What do I do?"

She chuckled, "Get Lessa, please, maybe put some pants on first." She groaned as the first of her pain took her.

He nodded and shoved his long legs into the nearest pair of pants. "Okay, I'll be right back." He ran from their little room but quickly came back and kissed her. "You're having our baby," he whispered excitedly.

She laughed. "I am indeed." He smiled, gave her cheek another kiss, and she listened to his footsteps recede up the stairs.

"Ma'ma, was it really you?" Sunette wondered as the pain subsided.

———

She walked around the little room for about ten minutes before Lessa, Stella, Raven, and Te'a came in.

"We're all the girls you got right now, so I figured we could help," Stella said.

"Thank you all so much." The women worked fast, first moving Sunette into the captain's quarters with her things. Lucius was still pulling a shirt on as they walked inside.

"I hear you're having a baby." He walked over and kissed her forehead, "You have some strong women to help you. I'll go keep Foster company."

"Thank you, Lucius."

CHAPTER 18
BORN ON OTTO'S TURF

Sunette didn't know what time it was. She only knew that she had been in pain for hours. She was exhausted, but the baby was relentless and wanted out.

"Lessa, I want Foster!" She screamed during a moment of pain. Currently, she was on her knees, her arms around Stella's shoulders. The captain was holding her up and gently swaying with her. She told Sunette that it really helped her with Te'a, so she was willing to try anything.

"Sunette, you know he won't come in," the priestess said gently.

"Just try, please? I want him here!"

"I'll get him." Raven dropped the cool rag she had been dabbing on Sunette's forehead and left the room. Sunette felt better already, knowing he was on his way.

——————

Raven found Foster sitting in the mess hall with Lucius and more of Stella's men. If she didn't know who the expecting father was, she'd have trouble guessing. Foster was sitting at the table. His leg was jiggling up and down so fast that the candle on the table was wavering. Lucius was pacing back and forth, biting his thumbnail, and she smiled.

"Well, isn't this a sight," she teased them.

Foster stood rather quickly and knocked the candle over. "Is the baby here?"

She laughed. "No calm down," she walked over and righted the candle. "Sunette has asked for you."

He looked confused as he looked back at Lucius, who just shrugged. "Why?"

She shrugged. "Don't know, she just started screaming that she wanted you." Men generally weren't allowed to enter the room while their women gave birth, but he remembered that she came from another land. Maybe they did things differently there?

"All right, I'm coming."

Raven smiled. "I'm taking bets on how long before he passes out." The other men laughed, and she turned to leave.

"Ha ha, guys," he said, following her.

———————

He walked into the captain's quarters and saw Sunette kneeling in the bed with Stella. Her hair was plastered to her face, and she looked tired. "Sunette?"

She opened her eyes and smiled. "*Mi Epier* come here." Stella chuckled and moved, letting Foster take her place.

"Just hold her up."

He nodded and put his arms around her and pressed his forehead on hers. "How are you?" Raven picked up the cool rag and ran it over the back of her neck.

"Tired." He saw pain across her face and held her up as her legs shook. His mother's words floated through his mind, *a mother needs to breathe, above all, breathe while they give birth.*

"Breathe, my love, breathe in," she breathed in. "Out," she breathed out. "Again." The pain passed, and he held her up as she relaxed.

"Thank you for coming," she whispered.

"Anytime, my love." He looked up at Lessa. "How's it going?"

She was behind Sunette, rubbing her back. "Just fine, they're both doing beautifully." She smiled, and he felt reassured. Lessa had delivered a lot of babies, so he knew his wife was well cared for.

He wiped the hair from her face and kissed her cheek. "You're doing so well, my love."

Her breathing steadied, and she looked up at him and smiled. "I'm never letting you do this to me again." Everyone laughed, and he kissed her cheek.

"I fear you've forgotten what Ada said."

Sunette leaned back a bit. "What did she say?"

Foster licked his lips, "she said, 'children.'"

"Ah, fuck she did say that, didn't she?" Before he could laugh, Sunette gasped. "Lessa," she said a few words in her native tongue, "so much pressure, Lessa!"

The priestess smiled. "That's good. It means it's time to meet your baby."

Sunette sighed, her head resting in the crook of Foster's neck. "Finally."

"All right, with the next pain, I want you to push. Foster, don't let her spread her legs out. It'll make it harder for the baby to come out, keep her just where she is." Foster nodded, and when Sunette gasped, he knew she felt the pain Lessa told her to wait for. Foster felt as Sunette held him tight and started to push, groaning as her arms shook around him.

"You're so strong, my love," he whispered and held her up.

"Perfect, Sunette, this shouldn't take long at all," Lessa said. Sunette took a big breath and pushed with all her might, and screamed. "There's the head!" Lessa called out.

"Lessa, it feels like fire!" She cried, and Foster kissed her forehead.

"I know, I'm sorry, but the worst is over. One more push and your baby will be here, I promise."

"One more," she breathed, and Foster felt her hold tight as she pushed. A relieved sigh filled the air as Lessa caught the baby and moved to the side. Sunette sighed loudly, half crying, half laughing as Foster helped her lay down on the mattress as the baby's cry began to pierce the air. It was loud and strong, and they knew the child was perfect. "What is it?" Sunette asked before her eyes even looked upon the babe.

Lessa held up the squalling infant, a bright smile on her face. "It's a boy."

Sunette laughed, tears falling from her eyes. "Thank you,

Ma'ma."

Foster laid his head next to Sunette's and stroked her cheek. "He's perfect, my love. You did so well. I'm so proud of you."

She turned her teary eyes to him. "I love you, *Mi Epier*."

"Oh, he's so cute!" Te'a exclaimed as Lessa and Raven cleaned the baby. Foster couldn't help but notice the happy tears in Raven's eyes. They handed the wailing child to Sunette, and after a few gentle jiggles and kisses, he quieted and looked around. He had a head of blonde hair and Foster's green eyes.

"I thought babies had blue eyes?" Foster asked.

"They do." Lessa leaned over and saw the baby's eyes. "Well, that's odd."

Sunette chuckled. "My special little boy."

"Foster, why don't you tell the boys? We still have a few things we need to do," Lessa suggested.

"Okay." He kissed the baby's head and then Sunette. "I'll be right back." He ran from the room to the sounds of feminine laughter.

———

Foster burst into the mess hall, and Lucius jumped up from the table where he had fallen asleep. "I have a son!" he exclaimed, arms up in triumph.

Lucius whooped, and Stella's men clapped. "Congratulations, young man." Lucius walked up and hugged Foster. "I'm glad you have a happy ending. You and Sunette both."

"Thank you, sir."

Lucius chuckled, "Six years, you still call me sir."

"Habit, I guess," he said with a shrug.

"Can I see her?" He asked hopefully.

"Yes, yes, follow me."

———

Foster knocked and peeked his head in. "Can Lucius come in?"

"Yes, let him in, it's all right," Sunette called out.

He opened the door, and Lucius followed him in. "Well, look at that." Lucius bent over and kissed Sunette's cheek, and looked at the baby. He gently ran his thumb on his little fuzzy cheek. The baby twitched, and Lucius chuckled. "Foster, I can hardly believe such a beautiful thing is half you," he teased.

Foster laughed, "Oh, he's all Sunette."

"Congratulations, Mistress Mage, you have a lovely son," he whispered.

She could almost hear the relief in his voice. "Thank you, Lucius."

Lucius stood and wrapped an arm around Stella. "Does it make you want another?" he whispered in her ear.

"Gods no, Te'a was enough," she chuckled, and he hugged her.

"We should really tell her soon." Stella stood straight and gently nodded her head to him as Te'a walked up to Sunette.

"So, what are you going to name him?"

"Hmm," Sunette thought for a moment, but Foster walked up, and Sunette handed the baby to him.

"I know his name," he said as he held his son for the first time.

"You do?" she teased. "Please enlighten us." He let his eyes roam over his son, trying to memorize every bit of him, from his wrinkly little hands to his tiny toes.

"His name is William, after my father. I know no other man greater than him," he said with pride in his eyes.

"William Arturo Voltain," Sunette said.

He turned to her. "Arturo?"

"My father's name."

Foster smiled and turned back to the baby. "Welcome to the world, William Arturo."

———

They reached Salthole the next day, and after a week of rest, Sunette felt up to the journey to Raventree. They bought a wagon and horses and said goodbye to Lucius with hugs and tears. He paid them what he owed them for their time with him and said if they ever needed a ride anywhere to let them know.

Foster and Raven took turns driving the cart while Sunette and little William stayed in the back. It was a slow trip, and when William was five weeks old, Foster saw Raventree in the distance.

"We're home!" He called out.

Sunette kissed William's cheek. "We're home, little one," she whispered. He squirmed and fussed but was quickly quieted with comforting jiggles.

Raven stood in the back of the cart. "That's it, huh?" The castle was looming in the distance, a six-foot gray wall of stone surrounded the town, and they could see people coming and going.

"Yep. How do you feel?" He turned with a big smile.

She shrugged. "Oh, fine."

He chuckled. "Nervous?"

She gave him a look that said, 'What do you think?' "I imagine I'm about to meet your mother. That's nerve-wracking even *without* being your wife."

Foster laughed and patted her shoulder. "Don't worry, you'll do fine. I'm nervous, too." They traveled through the gates to many hellos from people. Foster pulled the wagon up to his childhood home and helped Sunette and William out of the cart while Raven jumped down with grace.

"Are you excited, *Mi Epier*?" Sunette asked as they walked to the front door.

"Nervous, actually."

"I'm sure all is forgiven. They'll be so happy to see you home." He sighed and knocked on the door.

"Coming!" He heard his father's voice and smiled. The door opened, and William, Foster's father, gasped. "Foster!" He pulled his son into a crushing hug. "You're home, thank Otto, I missed you so much."

"I missed you too, Dad." He patted his back.

William stepped back and held his son's face. "You look all grown up, I can't believe it," he chuckled.

Foster stepped back. "Let me introduce my wife, Sunette."

William turned to the women, his smile even bigger as he stepped in front of Sunette.

"You have no idea how glad I am to meet you."

She laughed and uncovered the baby in her arms. "I'm glad to meet you, too. This is William, your grandson."

He gasped and petted his little head. "Foster, why didn't you tell us? Oh! Excuse me, come in, come in!" He said, laughing, ushering them inside.

Sunette walked in first, Raven was behind her, and William smiled when he saw her.

"Who's this?" He held out his hand, and Raven shook it.

"Dad, this is our friend Raven Bladespell. We've traveled together since day one. She wants to settle here in Raventree." He could tell she was a little more relaxed to be introduced to his father.

"It's nice to meet you, sir."

"You as well, you call me William now." She smiled and gave him a nod. They all walked in and saw Sunette had taken a seat by the fire, the bundle still in her arms. Foster's father walked over to them and gently ran his fingers over the baby's head.

"Would you like to hold him, William?" Sunette asked.

"Absolutely, and call me Dad," he said with a wink.

"Yes, Dad," she chuckled, and he picked up his namesake.

"He's beautiful," he said, sitting down and rocking the baby a little. Foster heard footsteps from the back and watched his grandfather Etienne walk into the room. He looked a lot older than the last time he had seen him, but his back was still straight, and his eyes were clear.

"Foster!" He held out his arms, a big smile on his face.

"Grandpa!" He ran up and hugged him. "I missed you so much."

"I missed you too."

He patted his grandfather on the back. "I have people for you to meet."

"I love meeting new people." Foster led him to Sunette, who stayed seated. "Sunette, this is my grandfather Etienne. This is my wife, Sunette."

"Wife, well." He leaned down and hugged her, "Welcome to the family, young lady."

"Thank you, sir."

He pulled back a little. "You sound like you're from Emperia."

She smiled, "Foster told me you knew of Emperia. Most don't."

"I know every continent you can get to by boat." Sunette's nodded, pleased that he knew of her homeland.

"Well, I am, sir."

Foster put a hand on Etienne's back. "This is Raven Bladespell. She traveled with us and wants to settle down here in Raventree." Etienne turned, and Raven held out her hand to him. She had a big smile on her face.

"Etienne Vale, as I live and breathe."

He laughed and shook her hand. "You can't have heard of me. You're too young."

"Oh, stories of your pirate days are some of my favorites."

"Well, I'm glad to have entertained with what I'm sure are horrible exaggerations."

Foster stared at them. "Grandpa, you were a pirate?" He couldn't believe such a thing.

Etienne waved a hand. "It was so long ago. I was barely a pirate."

"Remember the story I used to tell about the pirate who gave up his exciting life for love?" Raven said, looking at Foster and Sunette, who both nodded. She pointed at Etienne, and their eyes went wide.

"No." Foster turned to his grandfather, who was laughing.

"That was one of my favorite stories, so romantic." Sunette laid her head in her hand.

The baby started crying, and William stood up as Etienne turned and gasped. "Who's this?" He smiled as he walked over to the crying babe.

"This is William, your great-grandson," Sunette said.

Etienne laughed. "Oh, listen to him. He's healthy." He ran his thumb on his little cheek.

"And wants his Mama." William handed the baby back to Sunette.

"I should feed him now."

Foster helped her up. "I'll show you to a room."

"Son, why don't you take our room? You won't have to climb any stairs with him." Foster nodded and led her to a door by the stairs. Inside was a rocking chair and a big bed that Sunette settled down on.

"I think we'll take a nap as well," she said.

"Good idea, it was a long trip." He kissed her forehead.

———————

Etienne sighed. "He's much better than when he left, isn't he?" Etienne hugged his son-in-law, "Congratulations, old man." William laughed and hugged him back.

When Foster came back, he was all smiles. "Aren't they great?" He hadn't felt this much peace in years. The smile on his face seemed permanent.

"Your wife is beautiful, and your son is strong. Otto has blessed you, son."

"I thank him every day. So where is everyone?" He took a seat at the table, and Raven sat across from him.

"Your mother is at the temple, as is Christopher." William started pouring them some drinks.

A little smile spread on his face. "Christopher's a priest?"

William nodded. "Took his vows last month."

He sighed sadly and crossed his arms over his chest. "I feel so bad about how I left it with him."

William set down the glasses with some dark alcohol. "He does too, son, believe me." Etienne sat next to Raven and clinked his glass on hers.

"What about Saphy? Don't tell me she's married and living in Ardenry." He knew his little sister would be destined for greatness but thought she was a bit young to be married yet.

Thankfully, his father just laughed. "No, no, she's traveling like you. Thought it would be good to earn money using her skills."

"What skills? Scaring people to death?" He chuckled, and William laughed.

"Tease her if you will, but you know she's a talented rogue."

Foster stretched and yawned. "Gods, it'll be good not sleeping in a cart tonight."

"You said it." Raven finished her drink.

"Do you want to rest before your mother gets home?" William patted Foster on the shoulder.

"I think I do." He stood and started for the room. "Raven, a nap?"

"Gods, yes." She stood and walked past him into the room where Sunette was with William.

As he reached the room, his father called after him. "Foster?"

He turned, and his father and grandfather were both smiling at him. "Yes?"

"I'm proud of you son."

He smiled. "Thanks, Dad." He walked into his parents' room and saw Sunette was on her side, asleep, as was the baby. Next to her, Raven was fast asleep as well. She always slept in a little ball, and he wondered how anyone could do that. He smiled and pulled the chair next to the bed and propped up his feet on the edge of it, and fell asleep admiring his beautiful wife and son.

CHAPTER 19
FORGIVENESS

Foster felt a hand on his shoulder. "Son?" he heard a woman whisper. He opened his eyes and saw his mother leaning next to him.

"Mom." He sat up and hugged her.

"Oh, Foster, I'm so happy you're home." Her hug was filled with love, motherly and holy, and he smiled, finally feeling like he was home. Foster glanced at Sunette and William, still asleep on the bed. Lily sat on the arm of the chair and looked at the sleeping pair. "You have a beautiful family, son."

"Thank you. I love them so much."

She kissed his head and fussed with his hair. "I know you do." Lily glanced over Sunette. "I take it that's Raven?" she asked, an amused smile on her face.

He chuckled. "Yeah, she's been through a lot, and we asked her to come home with us. I think she needs some peace."

Lily nodded. "Any friend of yours is most welcome." Sunette yawned and opened her eyes. She smiled at her son before looking up.

The sight of Mother Lily startled her. "Oh, excuse me." She sat up and straightened her robe before picking up her baby.

Lily raised her hand. "You're fine, dear. I understand all too well the need for a nap when you have a newborn." She sat on the bed next to her, "I'm Lily, it's wonderful to meet you." She leaned over and hugged Sunette. "You can call me Mom if you'd like."

Sunette nodded. "I'd like that, thank you."

Lily looked down at little William as she smiled brightly. "My first grandbaby, what's his name?"

"William Arturo."

Lily gasped and looked over at her son. "You named him after your father?"

Foster nodded. "And Sunette's."

"Little William." She leaned over and kissed the baby's head.

"Would you like to hold him?" Sunette began handing the baby over, knowing she'd never say no.

"I'll never turn down baby snuggles." She chuckled as Sunette placed the baby in her arms. He squirmed and whined a little before Lily expertly jiggled him just the way he liked. "Has he been blessed yet?"

"No, we wanted you to do it," Foster said.

"My pleasure, son."

Raven stretched like a happy cat and turned towards the noise. "William need anything?" She asked sleepily, but her eyes went wide, and she sat up like a bolt. Her eyes wide, staring at his mother, he swore for a split second she looked scared but quickly composed herself.

"Excuse me, I thought...you were someone else." She ran her fingers through her short hair. Foster could see she was indeed nervous around his mother.

"It's a pleasure to meet you, Raven," Lily said with a smile, rocking the baby.

Raven nodded a little and quickly got off the bed. "And you, Mother. I'll go get our stuff out of the cart." She started for the door.

"No need. William already got it all. You just relax. It was a long journey." Raven slowly sat back on the bed, her hands in her lap as she stared at the baby in Lily's arms. Foster leaned over and whispered to his mother.

"She was nervous about meeting you. Her past is something that troubles her."

Lily nodded. "I'm glad someone who traveled with them decided to stay. You'll love Raventree, dear."

"Thank you." Foster noticed how she wouldn't meet his

mother's eyes, maybe one day.

———

Later that night, the family was gathered around the table for dinner when Christopher walked in and hung his robe behind the door.

"Hello." Everyone turned and saw he had stopped. His eyes were locked on Foster. His little brother looked all grown up now. No hint of childhood was left on his face. His once rounded cheeks were gone, and his skinny shoulders were now broad. His little brother was a man. "You know Raventree is small enough that you think someone would have told me you were home."

"Sorry, son, we've been busy," Lily said, a smile on her face.

Foster stood. "Christopher, I'm—"

He held up his hand. "Stop. Foster, what happened is in the past. I'm just glad you're home safe." He walked up and hugged his older brother.

"So good to see you, Christopher, I missed you." As he hugged his brother, all the guilt Foster had been carrying melted away. Everything he was worried about was in the past. He had his little brother back.

"I missed you too."

He squeezed him just a little more. "I'm sorry."

Christopher patted his back. "I'm sorry too," he whispered.

Foster stepped back and patted Christopher's shoulder. "Let me introduce you to my family."

He laughed. "I am your family goof." Foster chuckled and turned his brother around to Sunette holding William. Christopher gasped. "Foster!" He quickly walked over, his hand extended. "Hello, I'm Christopher. It's nice to meet you."

She took it gently. "It's wonderful to meet you, I'm Sunette. This is William, your nephew."

Christopher kneeled next to her and held the baby's hand. "Blessed Otto. Foster, I had no idea. He's beautiful." He gave the baby a kiss on the head and stood, his hand out towards his brother. Foster took it, and the brothers shook hands for the first time in six years. The back door opened, and Raven came walking in carrying some wood.

"Here we go. This ought to last until next week." Foster watched as Christopher turned and watched her put the wood in the cradle next to the fireplace. Raven stood straight but stopped when she saw Christopher.

"Hello," he said, a little smile on his lips, still shaking Foster's hand.

"Hello." It looked like Raven was studying him.

Foster gave his brother gentle pats on his face to wake him up. "Christopher, this is Raven. She traveled with us and wants to settle in Raventree."

"Raven, it's nice to meet you, I'm Christopher." He walked over, his hand outstretched.

"I know," she chuckled. "I mean, hi, I've heard a lot about you."

"Oh yeah? Hopefully, good things."

"Wonderful things, really." She nodded, and they sat at the table next to each other.

"So, what's your specialty? Are you a fighter like Foster?"

"No, well, I can fight, but swords are heavy. I'm a bard, but I can fight with daggers. We were recruited the same day, me and Foster."

"So, you've been with him the entire time?" Lily asked.

Raven nodded. "Yeah, he told me a lot about his family, and I'm so glad he and Sunette suggested I come home with them. I didn't really have anyone after the group disbanded, and I didn't feel like wandering anymore." Foster could see a tinge of sadness in her eyes and hoped her time in his hometown would remedy that.

"You should sing after dinner, Raven," Sunette said. "I'm sure they would love to hear your voice."

Christopher smiled at her. "Yes, please. I'd love to hear you sing." Foster looked over at his parents. His father was smiling, clearly amused at his son's behavior, but his mom looked worried. He got his mom's attention, *did he*? He mouthed to her. She nodded, clearly worried that her son had now made the wrong decision about his role in the church.

———

A week later, family and close friends gathered at the temple as little William was blessed and introduced into the Church of Otto. Sunette held him as Foster stood next to her at the shell-covered dais, his arm around his wife. Christopher and Raven stood next to each other across from them, his hand was on her shoulder, and Foster could see a little smile on the bard's lips. The baby was wearing a little blue outfit, as was customary for infants being blessed.

Lily walked up behind the dais and smiled at her family. "Welcome, friends and family. Today, we bless little William Arturo Voltain into our family and introduce him to Otto. William was conceived in love and, because he was created so, saved his mother's life. Already, we can tell how special this little boy is. Foster and Sunette's love was born from friendship and trials, and they love each other fiercely. This is a good foundation for their son." She held out her arms, and the proud parents stepped up and handed Lily the baby. "Christopher and Raven, Foster and Sunette have named you godparents. Are you willing to take on the responsibility of teaching young William about life, Otto, and support him in whatever way he needs?"

"We are," they said at the same time.

"May Otto bless your life, William Arturo. May you grow in his love and favor." She dipped her hand in the water and sprinkled it on his forehead. He let out a little squeal, and his parents chuckled. Lily kissed the baby's forehead. "I love you, my little grandson." She whispered and said a silent prayer to Otto, thanking him for the many blessings he bestowed upon their family.

EPILOGUE

It was late for Salthole, almost four am, but Ebba was awake as always. She was restocking her herbs when she heard a knock at the door. It wasn't odd that someone would visit her that late. Everyone in town knew she was up until the sun rose. She got to her feet and brushed off her hands as she opened the door. It was quiet outside. The man on the porch didn't make a noise and didn't look up as she answered.

"Help you?"

"You Ebba?" His voice was soft, his face hidden by the wide-brimmed hat he wore. He had a long, dark duster on, and he was picking at his nails.

"Yeah, and?"

"I heard you're the person to talk to if you want to speak with a dead person."

She crossed her arms over her stomach. "That'd be me, twenty gold, and you get five questions." He pulled out a little pouch and jingled it so she could hear the coin inside. "Come on in." She moved aside, and he walked in. She could see he was a half-elf, and he smelled like the sea. She showed him to the table off the hallway, and he sat down, leaning back in his chair and putting an ankle on his knee. The hat was still pulled low, so she couldn't see his face well. He threw the pouch on the table, and she pulled her herbs and salts together. "Who you looking for?"

"Vedasto Coscarelli." The name was familiar, but she had a job to do, so she lit the herbs and salts on fire and watched the smoke rise. She'd worry about who that was later.

"Vedasto Coscarelli, someone wishes to speak with you. Will you come forth?" The smoke formed the head of an older male.

"Who wishes to speak with me?"

Ebba looked over at the man, who shook his head. "I do." It was what she always said when the person wanting answers didn't want to let the deceased know who had questions.

"Are you the last of your line?" The man asked.

Ebba repeated the question. Vedasto huffed angrily. "My son was the last, but he was killed as well. The Coscarelli line is broken."

"Good." The man said and got to his feet. "That's all I wanted to know." He drew out his rapier and, without a thought, stabbed Ebba in the neck up to the hilt. She froze, unable to breathe, blood spilling down her front. He leaned down to her ear. "I know it was you who sent Vedasto a message about Sunette and where to find her." Even though the sword couldn't go in any further, he pressed harder. She choked as she remembered how she knew that name. Vedasto had paid her handsomely for that bit of information, but now she was regretting it. "If it weren't for you, our friend would still be alive. So, a death for a death." He pulled the rapier out of her throat and slashed it across her neck for good measure. She fell onto the table, blood pooling quickly around her head. The man wiped the blade with her sleeve and walked out the back door, using the alleys to get back to the docks.

———

He hauled himself back onto the ship. Salthole lay quietly a few miles behind him. Taking off his gloves, he started for the captain's quarters.

"Dad?" Hearing her say that was still startling and made his heart pound.

He turned and saw Te'a standing by the railing. "What are you doing up?" he asked gently.

"Couldn't sleep. Where were you?" Ever since they told Te'a he was her father, she'd been shy around him, and he knew he'd have to re-earn her trust.

He walked over and hugged her. He was glad she hugged him back. "Just making things right."

He heard her sniff and knew she could smell the blood.

"Are you hurt?" She looked up, and he could see concern on her face.

"It's not mine." He gave her chin a gentle pinch. "Be at ease, Little Heart."

He felt her relax a bit. "Good, well you better sneak back in before Mom sees you gone."

He smiled and ran a hand over her hair. "I will, you try and get some more sleep." She nodded and walked back down the stairs to her hammock. Lucius snuck back into Stella's quarters and managed to undress without waking her. He slipped under the covers next to her, and she turned.

"All done?"

"All done."

Karen Thrower was born in Tulsa, OK, and still resides there with her husband, daughter, and cat. She graduated from The University of Tulsa with a BA in Deaf Education in 2005. She is a member of Oklahoma Science Fiction Writers and has served in several capacities, such as President, VP, and is currently Facebook Wizard. She has been published in various genres since 2018 and was included in the bestselling anthology 'Secret Stairs: A Tribute to Urban Legend' in 2019.